THE ISLAND OF KVORGA

THE BLESSED OF THE DRAGON

Book Two

Patrik Martinet

CONTENTS

ACKNOWLEDGMENTS

I would like to thank my wife, Carrie, for supporting me as I have pursued my various hobbies. Thank you also for your keen literary eye. Most importantly, thank you for cultivating the love of reading in our children.

Thank you, Rob. For some reason you agreed to read the early drafts of chapters as I wrote them. I feel as though I should apologize for letting you do that. I hope that you find the story much improved.

Thank you, Elayne Morgan, for your amazing editing skills. Thank you, Jake, of J Caleb Design, for once again making an amazing cover. And thank you, Zach Bodenner, for bringing Dradonia to life with your wonderful map.

A list of acknowledgements wouldn't be complete without also thanking all those who have helped me one way or another along the way. To each of you, I say thank you.

THE NORTHERN REALM
THE WESTERN REALM
THE SOUTHERN REALM
THE SOUTHERN REALM (CONT.)
THE ISLAND OF KVORGA
SOUTHERN FINGERS
The Abandoned Provinces
A Scale of 250 Dradonian Leagues
0
125
250
Eaga
Arivia
KYINTH
Reelog
Atta
Mattha
Elisa
Turnig
Eupha
Arinin
Irig
Nesh
Ronin
Eber
Loi
Onta
Marian
Ronig
Ceena
Kvorg
Aerons
Aliza
Tieger
Mindon
Ansha
Croff
Olivara
Lonely Oak
Harachin
Orla
Portstown
Reega
Hantlo
Slonan
Hunva
Yarin
Wrenda
Eaga
Ginbon
Venan
Calvi
Harwa
Eika
Baytown
Virlar
Sein
Onassa
Quen
Penwa
Southern Tip
The Northern, Western, and Southern Realms of DRADONIA
©Patrik Martinet, 2019

THE ISLAND OF KVORGA

BEFORE

245 United Era

Drakonias stood on the palace balcony, high above the sprawling city below, his hands clasped behind his back. Stoic. Regal.

In the pre-dawn light, he gazed down upon the slumbering city. He'd long been fond of the quietness of this early hour. The night's peacefulness lingered, not yet vanquished by the bustle of governing such a vast realm. But as much as he enjoyed this early hour, that wasn't the reason he ritually rose so early every day.

The emperor shifted his gaze from the sleeping city below to the horizon above. The transition from night to day was underway. The predawn light that signaled the coming of the sun pushed the darkness farther and farther from the horizon. Blackness gradually gave way to varying shades of purples and dark blues, and they, in turn, became the oranges and reds of dawn. The dimmest of the stars that peppered the night sky were fading in the growing light. Only the body and tail of the Great Dragon constellation, diving into the western horizon, still shone brightly.

This ritual of rising early to await the coming of the sun had begun many years ago as a sort of homage to the source of his power. Homage was not something he had felt the need to pay in a very long time—after all, one paid homage to show respect for someone of higher authority, and he was the emperor, so there *was* no higher authority. However, he knew that he would not be standing here, high above his realm, were it not for the sun.

His father would have told him that he was misguided—that it was not the sun to whom he should pay his homage. Rather, he should be honoring Draego, the Great Dragon. Whether or not Draego had given them their gift was anyone's guess. What he did know, however, was that the sun was what kept him in power. Where his gift came from didn't matter.

His daily ritual began when the sky was still black—when the Great Dragon constellation still shared the night sky with the other stars—and ended when the sun had fully risen. He'd been doing it so long he'd memorized the sun's pattern as it changed with the seasons. He knew the exact moment to expect it each and every day.

Lately, though, the serenity he had originally found in performing the ritual was eluding him. Instead, the process had become an exercise of patience. Something about it had recently begun to itch at him. Something about it was not quite right. It was… off.

When he had first noticed the feeling, he'd shrugged it off as an anomaly. However, the itch wouldn't go away. With each passing day, it became stronger.

With hands clasped behind his back—in part to prevent himself from fidgeting—he impatiently waited for the ritual to conclude. He wanted it to be over so he could return to the woman in his bed and put it out of his mind until the morrow.

At last, the sun began to crest the horizon. Drakonias watched intently as it slowly inched its way higher and higher into the sky. As expected, the itch in the back of his mind returned. *What is it? What are you trying to tell me?* He directed his thoughts at the sun as if the sun could converse with him, but it never did. Since the day it had begun, the meaning of the itch eluded him. Daily, it frustrated him.

The sunrise was just like every other sunrise he had watched—the thousands and thousands of them. Were it not for the presence of the itch, this particular sunrise would have seemed no different from any of those that had preceded it. But for months, the irregularity had been playing at the fringes of his consciousness.

Drakonias shifted his stance. Something felt different. Unlike the previous days, when he'd left the balcony frustrated at not being able to solve the puzzle, now the itch began to grow. His eyes narrowed in concentration as it began to claw and gnaw with ever-increasing intensity, slowly boring its way into his consciousness. As the sun continued to creep higher, the itch that had been plaguing him began coalescing into realization.

Drakonias' eyes went wide as a flood of images rushed into his mind—images of every sunrise he had witnessed for the last two hundred years.

Drakonias fell to his knees under the crushing burden. He felt as though the full weight of the palace atop which he perched had suddenly crashed down upon him.

He realized, after all this time, what he had done.

CHAPTER 1

410 United Era

While the vast northern plains were still shrouded in the vestiges of night, the snow-covered peaks to the north began to shine. That light slowly crept down the mountains, revealing their grotesque, rocky, shadow-hidden sides. As the light worked its way down, the barren slopes eventually gave way to an abundance of life. To the south, just before it reached the valley floor, the light revealed leagues of cliffs. Their starkness was offset by the cascading water of the Mindon Falls, sparkling like a river of diamonds. Smoke from a growing fire billowed behind the falls.

When the sun finally crested the horizon and its light stretched across the grassy plains, the backs of the two weary travelers quickly began to warm. Yolken and Jax drew that warmth in, feeling it melt away their weariness. They took off running, sprinting through open fields at unnatural speed. They raced each other—Jax trying to prove his one hundred seventeen years of life hadn't slowed him any, and Yolken not wanting to be beaten by, as Jax had taunted, an old man. The fun eventually ended—even those benefiting from the endurance-enhancing effects of Synthesis couldn't sprint forever—and they settled into a more sustainable pace.

Yolken's cloak flew out behind him as he ran. His mind raced as fast as his feet, shifting from thought to thought. He thought mostly about Kaylan. Ever since the night of the festival in Lonely Oak—even with everything that had happened—it had been hard to think of anything else. But he also thought a lot about Javen, and what it was going to take to free him from the Regency.

He had grown up believing the Regency were the Blessed of the Dragon. They *were* the Blessed of the Dragon. He'd stopped short of worshipping them like many of the residents of Lonely Oak did and had foregone the weekly visits to the Dragon Shrine that many made, but he respected them. They ruled Dradonia; all of it. The gift that the emperor, chancellors, and regents possessed set them apart from the rest of the world. Their rule was absolute, and uncontested because nobody could possibly hope to overpower them. And he was one Synthesizer—largely untrained—whose bloodline was nowhere near as pure as the Blessed's. But he couldn't abandon Javen to them—not after everything he'd learned. It was possible that everything Jax and Deborah had told him were the actual lies, but Kaylan believed them, so he would too. And if he was going to do anything to help his brother, he knew he needed their help.

His mind shifted to his forthcoming meeting with the Council. Jax had said very little about the Order of the Dragon and the Order's leaders, the Council. All he'd really said was that Yolken would need their help. He knew almost nothing about the Order, and even less about the Council. But he did know that his father had been an integral part of the Order.

Yolken itched to stop Jax and ask him to tell him more about the Order and the Council, but didn't want to slow their pace. Now that they were going somewhere, he felt as though he was making progress—even if only a little bit—in his effort to rescue Javen. Hopefully, Jax didn't expect him to go to the Council unprepared.

As they drew closer to Croff, the epicenter of trade in the Northern Realm, they avoided the growing number of farms. Eventually, it became unpractical and unsafe to continue, so Jax finally stopped. They stood on a small cart path leading south toward a distant farm.

"We'll follow this to the highway," Jax said as he set off walking. "And keep the sword out of sight."

A grin grew on Yolken's face when he saw Jax unscrew the cap of his water flask and use Yolken's trick of gathering water out of the air to fill it. Yolken's flask was running low as well, so he did the same.

"This close to the city, Synthesizing is much riskier," Jax said, "so keep your Energy flows close to the ground. The higher you reach with your flows, the easier it'll be for a Watcher to see you."

Yolken heeded Jax's warning, keeping his flows of Energy close to the ground as he reached for water. It made the process slower, but it wasn't as though he was in a hurry. When his flask was full, he began channeling the Energy he was absorbing into the Harachin sword. He charged the sword slowly, remembering from his lessons that absorbing Energy from the sun distorts Energy's natural flow. That, too, would be visible to Watchers. As he charged the sword, he realized how hot he was getting now that they weren't running anymore. When he finished filling the sword, he unclasped his cloak from around his neck and took it off.

"What are you doing?" Jax said.

"It's too hot." Yolken laid the cloak on the ground, then unbuckled the sword from his belt. He wrapped the cloak around the sword, tying it into a neat bundle with the cloak's cords. Then he threaded the sword belt through the cords, slung the belt over his shoulder, and put the pack in place on his back. "You should do the same."

Jax, who was wearing his tattered leather coat, ignored him and started down the path again.

After about half a league, they reached the highway. It was nestled alongside the Croff River.

"If we went that way," Jax said, gesturing off to the right, "the highway would follow the river all the way to Mindon, where the Croff River joins the Mindon River. It's a beautiful city."

When they joined the highway, Yolken marveled at the steady stream of merchant wagons moving in the opposite direction. In just a matter of minutes, they passed as many wagons as visited Lonely Oak in any given week. And they kept streaming by.

Yolken couldn't see the city yet, even when he peeked around the large wagon in front of him, hauling bales of barley. That didn't stop his excitement from growing, however. And as the farms surrounding them grew closer together, the road became more crowded. He knew that they were getting very close. All thoughts of the Order and the Council evaporated from his mind, replaced by Kaylan. They had only been apart for a couple of weeks, but it felt like an eternity. He resisted the urge to run around and between the traffic. He was past ready to hold and kiss her again.

"I can tell you're getting antsy," Jax said, "but when in the open we must remain hidden. That is how the Order operates. That is how we survive."

"We'd be there so much faster if we could just run," Yolken said.

"But two men running when everyone else is walking would draw attention."

"I know," Yolken said. The fact didn't stop him from *wanting* to run, though.

Two young girls popped out from behind a barley bale in the wagon in front of him and started waving at him. When he waved back, they giggled and ducked out of sight. As soon as they peeked back around the bale—one over the top and one on the side—he waved again. They shrieked and disappeared just as fast as they had appeared. The next time they peeked he pretended he didn't see them, and they waved frantically to get his attention. When he eventually acknowledged them, they again shrieked, giggled, and ducked behind the bale. This went on for a while, proving to be the perfect distraction. Given the contents of the wagon, he guessed that they were sisters riding into the city with their pa to sell their crop. For all he knew, he could have bought grain grown by this farmer; a lot of the grain he had used for brewing came from Croff.

"Only a few more leagues," Jax said.

They passed three more small villages nestled against the road. After the third one, Yolken stepped off the side of the road to get a look around the wagon. Sprawling buildings in the distance greeted him.

They had arrived at Croff.

The dusty road broadened as the buildings drew closer. Yolken and Jax passed through an arched gate, which Yolken found oddly out of place because there wasn't an accompanying wall. At the gate, the dirt road became cobbled. The buildings at first resembled the one- to two-story brick buildings of Lonely Oak, but before they had walked very far into the sprawling city, the buildings had grown to several stories tall. Packed tightly together, they towered over the road, making Yolken feel small.

As they made their way into the city, they passed crossroad after crossroad. Lonely Oak only had one road; the rest of the town had been erected haphazardly around that road and the buildings that lined it. But Croff was definitely no Lonely Oak. It was the seat of the Croff province, of which Lonely Oak was a part. It was also where Dalia, the provincial regent, lived. He wondered if he would see her mansion. It was somewhere in the city, he knew, visible behind its protective walls.

Jax walked deeper into the sea of buildings, then turned from the wide, cobbled road onto a crossroad paved with brick. The girls in the cart ahead of them waved frantically. Yolken waved back and blew them a kiss. Both girls screeched and collapsed onto bales. Yolken smiled as he followed Jax. He wondered if they would spend the rest of the morning arguing about which of them was going to marry him. At least he didn't have to let them down by telling them that his heart was already set on someone else.

The thought of Kaylan quickened Yolken's pulse. He had been thinking about her all morning, but now that they were in the same city, his anticipation grew. He continued following Jax as they made their way through the city, growing more excited with every step. And with every turn, he wondered how much farther they had to go.

The deeper they moved into the city, the busier the streets became. Yolken had to work to not get separated from Jax. At the same time, he wanted to take in his surroundings, and he looked around as much as he could without taking his eyes off Jax for too long. The buildings were tall and, in most places, there wasn't room to pass between them. Many of them were completely connected. The different building materials were the only indication that they weren't one large, long building.

Most of the people who crowded the streets didn't seem any different from those in Lonely Oak. They ranged from the poor and decrepit to the finely dressed. As they walked, though, Yolken began noticing people wearing styles he didn't recognize. They also passed a few soldiers wearing gray armor. Yolken looked at them with a new understanding. A large, rough-textured, oval piece covered their torsos, and the rest of the armor—arms, shoulders, backs, and leggings—were smaller oval-shaped plates. All of the plates, large and small, were dragon scales. Growing up he had always wondered about the armor worn by soldiers, guards, and the Blessed, never thinking it might actually be made from dragons slaughtered during Drakonias' war. The idea that dragons were actually real, not just fabled creatures derived from the Great Dragon, still amazed him. Dragon scales protected dragons from Energy, so Yolken now understood why everyone associated with the Regency wore the armor.

Jax made another turn and they walked down a narrow street lined on both sides by skinny, two-story buildings. Each building had steps leading up to a small landing with a door. Except for variations in color, the buildings looked identical. Jax eventually climbed the steps of a brown building on the right, and Yolken followed him up. Jax attempted to open the door, but it was locked, so he knocked.

The door opened a crack and familiar green eyes peeked through. The door closed momentarily then flew open. Jax turned sideways when Kaylan burst out, letting her around him. She crashed into Yolken's arms and he hugged her tightly, burying his face in her hair. He inhaled, breathing deeply of lilac.

"I've missed you so much!" Kaylan said into Yolken's chest.

When she eventually looked at him, Yolken cupped her cheeks with his hands and kissed her.

Jax smirked at them, then stepped into the building.

When their kiss ended, Kaylan took Yolken by the hand and followed Jax through the open door.

Deborah was standing just inside. "Greetings! We weren't expecting you so soon."

"A Watcher found us," Jax said crossly.

"Oh? That's a shame." Deborah's tone was wry. "I know how much you prided yourself on that little retreat of yours."

"I wouldn't bring that up," Yolken said with a grin. Drenan's son had tracked them to the ravine where the safehouse was, forcing them to flee. Jax had been cross because of how much effort it took to build and supply—which involved a very unhappy mule—only to be discovered so quickly. "He's still sore about it."

"Please sit." Deborah gestured to the couch and chairs. "I'm sure you're tired. Give me just a moment and I'll make tea and get you something to eat."

Yolken followed Kaylan, who still led him by the hand, to the couch along the wall. He dropped his rolled-up cloak on the floor and sat wearily beside her. He wrapped one arm around her shoulders and held her hand with the other. She leaned her head against his shoulder.

Jax followed Deborah to the kitchen at the back end of the narrow house. Yolken heard him ask, "Were my plans well received?"

"Mostly," Deborah said. "There are a few that will need some convincing but…"

As they moved through the long narrow house, Deborah's voice trailed off until Yolken couldn't hear her any longer. He was sure there would be plenty of time for them to discuss things, so he turned his attention to the only thing that mattered at the moment.

He let go of Kaylan's hand and gently cupped her chin. He turned her face up toward his and kissed her again. "I've missed you so much."

"Me too," Kaylan said. "I couldn't believe it when I opened the door and saw Jax standing there. We weren't expecting you for at least another month. In fact, we were just getting ready to go to the market when you knocked."

"It's been a crazy few days for sure," Yolken said. He didn't really want to discuss the details, have to verbalize his fight with Drenan's son at the Mindon Falls or what happened to him, so he said, "This city is amazing, isn't it?"

"Growing up in Lonely Oak, I never really thought about how big Croff actually is. I mean, I never thought of it as more than a dot on a map. Mammy says over a hundred thousand people live here!"

"A hundred thousand?" Yolken said. "Incredible."

"And Mammy says Croff is nothing compared to Tieger or Kyinth."

"That's hard to believe. It didn't take long before I got turned around. I don't think I'd be able to find my way back out of the city if my life depended on it."

"It's pretty easy to find your way once you get used to it. Mammy says the center of the city is full of twists and turns, but out here in the newer parts, the streets are laid out where it's pretty easy to find your way around. I hope I get the chance to show you around some."

"Me too, but I'm hoping Jax will take me to the Council as soon as possible."

"Well, if we *do* get the chance, you'll love it. It's so different here."

Deborah carried a tray of tea into the room, set it down on the small table in the middle of the room, then returned to the kitchen.

"You want any?" Yolken asked Kaylan.

"No, thanks. I had some just before you arrived."

Yolken leaned forward to reach the teapot. He poured himself a cup then sat back. He took a sip, anticipating the welcome relief the tea would provide from his tiredness. Deborah and Jax returned to the room, each carrying a plate with a bowl and a hunk of bread. Jax sat down and dug into his. Deborah waited for Yolken to set his tea down before handing him the plate she was holding. He inhaled the aroma of the bread, which was cool, but still fresh. Then he dipped it into the bowl of thick soup.

"So," Deborah said after Jax and Yolken finished eating, "tell us what happened."

"First, we need proper beverages," Jax said. He stood and made his way back toward the kitchen.

"Are you implying that my tea isn't good enough?" Deborah

called after him.

Jax returned with a large jug and four round glasses. He set the glasses down on the table, then filled one with the contents of the jug and handed it to Yolken.

Ale was *exactly* what he needed, so Yolken happily accepted the glass. His eyes lit up when he took a drink. "Are you serious? You have *my* ale? *Here?*"

Jax smiled. "One must prepare for all possibilities."

"You couldn't possibly have known we would end up here," Yolken protested, picking up one of the round glasses.

"No," Jax said, "but I spend a lot of time in Croff. Might as well have decent ale while I'm here."

"Seems like a lot of effort to me," Yolken said.

"You have a gift, Yolken."

"Speaking of the Regency…" Deborah interjected.

"Right," Jax said, taking one of the glasses and sitting in a padded chair. "Seven days ago, a Watcher found us in the ravine. Well, found *me*. Yolken was working in the shed."

Jax spent the next hour catching Deborah and Kaylan up on the events that had transpired at the cabin.

When Jax arrived at Yolken's confrontation with the Watcher, Yolken said, "Can we not talk about that?" He was trying to think about the fight, which ended with the Watcher's death, as little as possible. Kaylan comforted him with a hug.

"I'm sorry you had to experience that, dear," Deborah said. "Things are progressing well, then?"

"They are," Jax said. "I just wish we'd had more time to prepare before going before the Council. However, I think Yolken's progress should be sufficient to convince them to accept our plan."

"I still don't get it," Yolken said.

"What?"

"Why should my abilities determine whether or not the Council helps me?"

"It might be hard to understand, I know, but the Order has a very specific purpose, and freeing prisoners is not one of them. The Regency does horrible things—we know that—but the Order simply does not have the ability to prevent it from happening, or to do anything about it when it does."

"So you're saying the Order will help me only because I might be of use to them?"

"You and Javen both," Jax said. "I know it sounds harsh, but that's the fact of the matter."

"I don't like it."

"I understand how this sounds to you, Yolken," Deborah said. "However, if you want to help your brother, this is truly the only way. There's no one other than the Order who can stand up against the Regency. Unfortunately, the Order operates according to specific rules, and sometimes those rules prevent us from doing what's right, or what we might want to do. This is not because we're bad people, or indifferent—rather, the Order operates the way it does *because* we care."

The conversation lulled and in the quiet that ensued, Yolken slowly wrapped his mind around the reality of the situation. He sipped his ale and Kaylan gently rubbed his arm and back. "What do I need to do to convince them to help?"

"They will only authorize help if they think you and Javen are of value to the Order," Jax said. "So you must convince them that you are."

"And if I don't?"

"If you don't, then you'll likely never see your brother again."

CHAPTER 2

Hadie curled up in a ball on the bed she had shared with Javen and wept uncontrollably. Her crying dampened the sounds of the fishing town outside the carriage. She loved him. And the moment she had realized it, he'd been taken away. Worse, there was absolutely nothing she could do about it.

Drenan's forceful ogling of her made her feel dirty and sick to her stomach. His words echoed in her head: *"If I ever see you again, I promise that I will do more than simply look at you."* She pulled her thin silk robe tightly around herself and tried not to think about how she had hung suspended in the air, unable to move. She readjusted it for fear that part of her might still be visible.

"Ma'am," a tender voice said, "it's time to go."

Hadie opened her eyes and looked over her shoulder. Rennie stood at the foot of the bed, her body visible through her servant's garb.

"I've brought your clothes," Rennie said. She placed Hadie's folded clothes on the bed. "The teamsters need to move the carriages and stable the horses for the night."

Hadie sat up and wiped her tears with the palms of her hands. She started to slip the silk robe off but stopped, feeling uncharacteristically modest. "Do you mind?" When Rennie turned around, she finished disrobing, then donned the folded shirt. The thicker material was instantly uncomfortable in the hot, wet air. She was sweating before she even had her pants on. "All right," she said. Rennie turned back around. "I'm afraid the effort you made to clean them for me will be quickly undone."

Hadie looked down at the coins Drenan had thrown onto the bed. She scooped them up, then took Rennie by the hand and placed them in her palm. "Thank you for all you've done for us," she said.

"I can't, ma'am," Rennie said, jerking her hand back and letting the coins fall to the floor. "I have no need of money." She bowed and hastily moved toward the door. Before exiting she turned back and said, "Hadie?"

Hadie looked up, surprised to hear her name. "Yes?"

"I found out what happened."

"What?"

"One of the whores… no. I should go. I'll get in trouble if I say—"

"Rennie," Hadie said, hurrying over to the woman. She placed her hand on Rennie's shoulder and said, "You don't have to worry about me saying *anything* to Drenan."

Rennie nodded. "One of the whores leaving his carriage told me."

"What did she say?"

"She was terrified."

"Terrified? Why?"

"Because he told her what he did to the lass."

Hadie waited patiently for Rennie to continue. Finally, she prompted her, "Please, Rennie, tell me what happened."

"He was having trouble, so—"

"He?"

"Javen. Javen was having trouble…"

Hadie nodded in understanding. Javen had been frustrated because he hadn't been able to use his gift. His lessons had been with Dorlan, but when Dorlan got too busy for Javen's lesson, he sent Javen to Drenan. The very thought of having lessons with Drenan, the man who only days earlier had killed his aunt, had made Javen sick to his stomach.

"…so he cut her throat. I'm sorry, ma'am, I can't remember her name."

"Astora," Hadie said. Then she covered her mouth with her hand. The thought of Javen having to witness, for the second time, Drenan murdering someone he cared about made her feel nauseated. She felt nothing but contempt for the regent.

Rennie nodded again. "He cut Astora's throat to make Javen heal her, but he couldn't. And then he attacked him."

"Drenan attacked Javen?"

"No. Javen attacked Drenan. Drenan wanted Dorlan to hang him, but Dorlan wouldn't."

"But what happened to Javen?"

"I'm sorry, ma'am, I don't know," Rennie said. "Hadie?"

"Yes?" Hadie said, looking at Rennie.

"I'm sorry."

Hadie nodded. "Come with me, Rennie. We'll go somewhere where he can't hurt either of us."

"I can't, ma'am." Rennie looked down at her feet.

"You can't stay." Hadie placed her hand on Rennie's shoulder again. "He's dangerous."

"He'll kill me." Rennie locked eyes with Hadie, then opened the door. "I'm sorry," she said before hastily leaving.

"Rennie!" Hadie called after her, but she was gone. Hadie stared blankly at the door, her mind numb. Then she screamed in anguish—for Astora and for Javen.

She looked at the coins on the ground and reluctantly picked them up. Everything she owned had been left behind in Lonely Oak when an armored soldier burst into her room and snatched her away. As much as she hated to take the coins, she had nothing and would need to replace her belongings. Gripping the coins tightly in her hand, she left the bedroom where she had spent the majority of the last three days tending to Javen, who had lain unconscious after doing the Dragon knows what.

The sun was disappearing below the blue waters of the Kvorgan Sea when she stepped out of the carriage. Its reddish color reflected off the water. Some called the phenomenon 'the blood river,' because it resembled a river of blood flowing from the sun to the shore. She'd always thought it was beautiful. Growing up, her mother used to tell her that her own beauty diminished that of the setting sun. But she didn't feel the joy she'd once felt when she watched the sun set behind the sea. Instead, she felt more like the weatherworn and ramshackle buildings that cluttered the docks below.

Hadie closed her eyes. Even though it stank of dead fish, she took a deep breath of the wet air. It had only been a couple of months since she'd left the south, vowing to herself that she would never return. The continuously deteriorating conditions, devastating cyclones, droughts, and fires had left much of the south uninhabitable, and the Regency—the Blessed of the Dragon—weren't doing anything about it. She had been shielded from most of the trouble plaguing the realm for the last several years because she was fortunate enough to live in Hantlo. Her parents were wealthy—her father a Silk—and there were always plenty of Blessed to clean up when a cyclone swept through. But she'd decided that she didn't want to be around when they lost control—and she was convinced that they *would* lose control eventually. It was inevitable. So, she had packed only a few changes of clothes and what belongings could fit into her bag and left, joining the steady stream of southerners heading north.

But now, breathing in Portstown's unpleasant aroma, she was back.

"Greetings, lass," Lyoll said, appearing from around the front end of the carriage. He walked over to stand beside her and frowned. "What's the matter?"

Hadie wiped her eyes again and said, "Drenan took Javen away."

"I wondered as much when I saw the soldier carrying him naked as the day his mother gave birth. Where'd they take him?"

"I don't know. Doesn't matter anyhow."

"What do you mean?"

"Drenan threatened to hurt me if he ever saw me again."

"And Master Javen had no say in this?"

"How could he? He's been unconscious since the day he used his gift."

"'Tis a real shame," Lyoll said. "I've really enjoyed your company." After a moment of awkward silence, he added, "What now?"

Hadie shrugged her shoulders.

"Care to share one last meal?"

"I'm not hungry," Hadie said.

"Sometimes a stomach full of food does wonders to help heal a broken heart, lass. Especially if you combine it with drink. And I know just the place. See those steps over there?" Lyoll pointed down the road. "Third ones down?"

"Yeah."

"Meet me there in half an hour. I need to tend to the horses and carriages, then we'll feast on a meal worthy of the Blessed."

"Fine. So long as there aren't actually any scales there," Hadie said, using a term she hadn't used in a long time. Her father had taught her to respect the Blessed and whipped her until she couldn't sit when he'd caught her using it as a lass.

"Hah! You needn't worry about running into any of 'em down there," Lyoll said. "Don't go down to the docks 'til I arrive. Looks like a few ships have recently come in, so there's bound to be salts looking to spread some legs."

"I won't," Hadie said.

Lyoll returned to his work and Hadie walked around the back end of the carriage to survey the buildings lining the street.

She needed to find somewhere to stay for the night. A few buildings down was a small inn called the Land Maiden. She'd stayed there when she had come through Portstown before so, without wasting time looking for anything else, she made up her mind.

Hadie stepped through the front door of the tall, skinny building wedged between a pub and a cobbler. The ground floor was small and square and had a spiral, wrought-iron staircase at the back wall. Hadie naturally gravitated toward quaint inns like this one, as opposed to more boisterous ones such as the Oak, in Lonely Oak. She liked this one because each floor had only two rooms—one that faced the street, and one in the back—and they were protected by a thick door with three different locks. It wasn't the cheapest bed in town, but the extra money was worth it for the added security. The price also scared away most of the drunk sailors who roamed the streets at night looking to spend their hard-earned wages on women and drink rather than on lodging. She walked over to the long counter on the side that ran the length of the room.

The short, bald innkeeper emerged from a door at the end of the counter. "Need a room?"

"Yes, please," Hadie said.

"Quarter drake."

Hadie retrieved a drake from her pocket and set it on the table.

The innkeeper scooped up the gold coin and said, "Be right back."

"Keep it," Hadie said, "in case I decide to stay more than one night."

The innkeeper handed her a key and said, "Fifth floor, front side."

Without any belongings, she had no need to climb the spiral stairs to her room before meeting Lyoll, so she left and made her way down the road to the set of stairs Lyoll had indicated.

The number eleven was branded into the wood.

Heeding Lyoll's warning, she waited at the top of the long, weatherworn steps until he arrived. The road was busy with people going about their business. She received the occasional lewd comment from rough-looking, sun-darkened men as she waited, but that was the extent of it. With so many witnesses, most wouldn't risk being thrown into a cell and spoiling their first night back on land. So long as they weren't coming from Drenan, she could handle the comments and leering eyes. The docks, however, were another story. There the watchful eyes were much less caring, and there were plenty of places to have one's way with an unwilling partner.

While she waited for Lyoll, she did her best to distract herself from thinking about Javen by looking down at the docks that stretched up and down the length of the road. There were at least two dozen, most of which were lined with various types of ships and boathouses with rusted roofs. The majority of the boats were grimy fishing vessels with small masts and trawling nets affixed to rods sticking up haphazardly, but there were a few larger ships—with tall masts, the kind she knew were meant to sail across the sea—moored at the ends of some of the docks. The largest of them flew a green flag with a large clump of purple grapes in the middle—the official emblem of the Onta province.

"Greetings, lass," Lyoll said over her shoulder. "You find your appetite yet? Cause I'm famished."

Hadie shrugged but followed Lyoll down the worn stairs to the sloped walkway.

"Where's Ganip?" she said.

"Ah, well…" Lyoll said over his shoulder.

Lyoll didn't have to say it, but Hadie knew. Ganip was young and they had been on the road for a while…

The walkway led down to the floating dock. They passed several fishing boats that reeked of their day's catch. The end of the long floating walkway came to a T, and Lyoll turned left.

They passed several boathouses and ended up at a larger building at the end of the dock. There were large glassless windows on both sides of the door, each with a heavy canvas cover tightly rolled up at the top. Hadie looked through the windows and saw people sitting at tables, eating. *A floating pub*, she thought.

Lyoll stepped over the gap between the dock and pub, and onto a small landing. He opened the door and held it for Hadie. As she hopped onto the landing, Lyoll said, "The best fish in town."

The building lacked interior walls. A thick man wearing a greasy apron worked at a stove at the center of the building. The stove had a large metal vent over it which trapped the smoke. A square bar surrounded the stove and tables filled the rest of the room. A barkeep greeted them when they walked up to the bar.

"What'll it be?"

"Ale and fish," Lyoll said.

The barkeep retrieved two steins that hung from pegs in the ceiling. When he set the full steins before them, Hadie pulled a gold drake from her pocket. Lyoll covered her hand with his and quickly placed a few copper coins on the bar instead.

Hadie took a stein and, when it arrived, a plate of food. They searched the pub for an empty table but, not finding one inside, eventually went to the back of the building, which was entirely open to the sea. Like the windows at the front and along the sides, there was a heavy canvas rolled up tightly by the ceiling to cover the opening when need be. An uncovered deck continued out past the end of the building, also jammed with tables. Lyoll found an open one in the back corner.

When Hadie sat across from Lyoll, he leaned over the table and whispered, "This isn't the sort of place to go around flashing gold. Things like that rarely go unnoticed. Unless you want to find a knife in your ribs, you'd do well to exchange it for smaller coin."

"I don't know what I was thinking," Hadie said. She knew

better than that. She looked down at her basket filled with battered fish and sliced potatoes fried in grease. As good as it looked, she didn't feel especially hungry. Instead, she lifted the stein and drank deeply of whatever it contained. While Lyoll devoured his own food, she downed what turned out to be decent-tasting ale—nothing compared to what Javen's brother made, but still quite good.

"You need to eat if you don't want that drink going straight to your head, lass."

"I'm not hungry."

With a concerned look on his face, Lyoll placed a copper coin on the table and said, "Here."

"Thanks," Hadie said as she scooped up the coin. She walked back into the pub and got two more steins. She began to feel the drink's effect; having drank herself sick several times, she begrudgingly heeded Lyoll's advice and forced herself to eat.

Lyoll licked his fingers when his basket was empty and nodded approvingly when Hadie started into hers. "You'd be hard pressed to find better fish than right here, lass. Freshest in Portstown, it is; straight from the boat."

"If it's so good," Hadie said, staring blankly over at the water still visible in the fading light, "then why are you so sure there wouldn't be Blessed here?"

"Look around ya; no Blessed would set foot in this area. Not out of fear for their safety, but out of pride. Imagine the Blessed mingling with the likes of smelly salts!"

"Didn't I see Devin's ship moored here, though?"

"Yes, but did you notice the dock it was moored to was separate from all the rest of 'em?"

"No."

"Separate from the riffraff."

They sat in silence while Hadie ate and Lyoll downed the contents of his second stein.

"Another?" Lyoll said when Hadie finished.

Hadie nodded, so Lyoll went to the bar and retrieved another round.

"Why do you do it?" Hadie said when he returned.

"Do what?"

"Work for them."

"The money's good."

"They pay you?" she said, thinking about Rennie refusing the drakes.

"Aye. We teamsters aren't the same as the servant caste. I do what I do not because that's what I was born into, or even out of any loyalty to them—I do it for the money."

"Do you like it? Traveling all the time?"

"Aye. I get to see the world!" Lyoll said, raising his stein. His smile turned to a frown when Hadie didn't respond to his enthusiasm. Instead, he awkwardly took a drink. "What now, then?"

Hadie didn't offer an immediate reply. She didn't know the answer herself. Instead, she looked silently across the water at the darkening horizon. "When I made the decision to leave Hantlo, I swore I would never return to the south. Yet, less than three months after leaving, I find myself in the south again. Do I return home, disgraced, to my parents? Or do I turn around and head north again? My reasons for leaving certainly haven't changed."

"Why *did* you leave?" Lyoll said.

"I don't want to be around when the Regency loses control."

"Then why would you return? Turn north. Start fresh again. If the money wasn't so good driving horses for the Regency, I'd head north as well."

"Aren't you afraid to be around when the south inevitably collapses?" Hadie said.

"I can look after myself."

Hadie thought about the wisdom in what Lyoll said. With the way things were in the south, going north again really would be the wisest decision. However, what she really wanted to know was where they were taking Javen. *They're most likely taking him to Hantlo,* she thought. Drenan's threat was real, but so was her love for Javen. She knew she couldn't abandon him so easily. As much as she hated the thought, she realized the only path for her was to return home. "I can't give up on Javen," she said.

"There are other lads, you know. As pretty as you are, I'm sure you won't be having trouble finding another," Lyoll said. "So long as Javen remains in the hands of the Regency, attempting to reunite with him will be foolish."

"I love him."

"Ah." Lyoll drank from his stein and said, "It's still unwise, lass."

"Haven't you ever loved anyone, Lyoll?"

"Aye, I have."

"Then you know that I can't simply walk away from Javen. If I can find him, maybe I can convince him to break with the scales."

Lyoll frowned across the table at her. "'Tis foolish, you know."

"I know," she said. Maybe it was. But she couldn't give up on Javen. She'd never loved anyone before.

"Then when you get to Hantlo, go see Sonja."

"The whore?"

"Madam."

"Same difference."

"They aren't, actually. The madam—"

"I know the difference, Lyoll," Hadie said. "Why should I go see her?"

"Everyone knows that the way into a man's mind is through his trousers. Whores frequent the palace every day, so if you want to get information on what's happening to Javen, Sonja will know."

"Thanks," Hadie said.

"If you have more than just that one drake, hang onto as much of it as you can. Information is never cheap—especially in the capital of the realm."

Hadie appreciated Lyoll's help: for the advice, for paying for their meal, and for enough drink that she would not have long to grieve her loss once she climbed into bed. He offered her his arm to steady herself as they made their way back up the dock, then escorted her back to the Land Maiden, and waited gallantly outside her room until she slid the bolts into place.

As Hadie lay on the prickly mattress and awaited the escape of sleep, she tried not to think about the road ahead of her—there would be plenty of time for that. Instead, she turned her mind to the fact that she would not wake up next to Javen. The thought brought tears to her eyes. She curled up into a ball on her bed and cried herself to sleep.

CHAPTER 3

Sethlan studied Dorlan, the Chancellor of the Southern Realm, as he refilled his wine glass for the fifth time. Over the years, he'd mastered the art of recognizing his master's every mannerism, and tonight, Dorlan was irritated. The biggest tell was how he held the wine glass by the base and twisted the finger and thumb of his other hand around the stem. His second biggest tell was how he raised the glass to his lips to take a drink, lowered it halfway without drinking, and then immediately lifted it back to his lips and drank. When both tells appeared at the same time, as they did tonight, Sethlan knew it was bad.

His irritation had been evident when they left Kyinth, but Dorlan had hidden it away, and had done an excellent job masking it as they slowly made their way back to the Southern Realm. But his irritation had resurfaced when news reached him that a powerful, out-of-season cyclone had practically destroyed Wrenda and Yarin. Now that he was back in the south, once again surrounded by his regents and their questions, he no longer attempted to conceal it.

When they arrived at Dunlor's mansion in Portstown, Sethlan was surprised to see so many regents present. It seemed every regent in the realm had descended on Portstown to welcome the chancellor back. He knew the real reason they were here, though, and it wasn't because they were glad to see him. With most of the provinces south of Eika and Baytown abandoned, and now potentially Wrenda and Yarin as well, they were eager for the news Dorlan brought from the emperor. Hantlo was overflowing with displaced citizenry and they wanted to know what the emperor was going to do.

Sethlan was constantly amazed that, even given the urgency of their situation, they spent so much of their time drinking wine and entertaining whores. Portstown's whores were not of the same quality as Hantlo's, but there were a few worthy of the chancellor, though barely. He thought briefly of Swanda.

The night began as a drunken revelry, but at last it transitioned to Dorlan catching his regents up on his trip to Kyinth—which was when Sethlan's real work began. Despite keeping busy ensuring the wine continued to flow, Sethlan kept an open ear. He listened for every tidbit of information that he might sell.

Dorlan reported to them that he'd updated the emperor on the continued deterioration of the Southern Realm. He'd urged His Blessed Highness that if he did not soon intervene, the south would go the way of the east and become forever lost to the empire. He'd explained to the emperor how cyclones, droughts, and fires were destroying the south, one province after another. However, in spite of Dorlan's dire urgency, the emperor remained unmoved, seeming more interested in the woman he planned to marry. Dorlan worried that Drakonias would rather lose the south than admit there was a problem.

Sethlan already knew all that and had passed it on to his true employer when they were in Croff.

"What's to be done, then?" asked a tall, thin woman. She had long brown hair, braided down to the small of her back, and wore a light blue robe tightly cinched at the waist, same as all the other regents in the great room. Sethlan recognized her as

Dreanna, one of the regents who had recently taken up residence in Hantlo. She was—or had been—the regent of the Southern Fingers province. Extreme drought and fires had scoured the islands five years ago. "My province is already lost," she continued.

"Nothing," Dorlan said.

"We must do something!" Dreanna shouted.

"And what do you suggest, little *sister*?" Dorlan said. It was clear to Sethlan that he was annoyed by the question.

"Obviously something is wrong," Dreanna said. "Why won't he do anything?"

Dorlan plopped himself down onto one of the many plush couches that adorned the great room of Dunlar's mansion. After taking a healthy swig of wine he said, "Honestly, I've come to believe that he doesn't know what's happening, and his inaction is because he doesn't know what to do."

"Perhaps it's time we look after ourselves," Drenan said.

"You would wish the wrath of our father upon us?" Dorlan said. He attempted another drink, but his glass was empty.

"You mean like Drashon?"

Dorlan beckoned to a woman nearby and shouted, "Sethlan! More wine!"

It appeared that Dorlan had decided to end that conversation in its tracks, which meant Sethlan would likely hear nothing more of consequence for the rest of the night. Dorlan was smart enough, Sethlan knew, to opt for another round of harmless debauchery instead of engaging his siblings in potentially treasonous conversation.

* * *

Sethlan woke to early morning light trickling through the small window of his tiny servant's room. He donned his southern servant's garb—a drab silk pull-over shirt and matching trousers—then retrieved the sealed envelope from under his thin mattress and tucked it into a pocket sewn on the inside of his trousers. Despite his doubts that he might learn anything of value last night, it had proven to be most informative after all.

Sethlan left his room and joined a group of servants leaving the mansion to run various errands. The servants' quarters were in the basement and had two exits: an internal staircase that led up into the kitchen, and an external one on the backside of the mansion. He filed up the external steps, in line with the other servants, and followed along as they made their way down the hill and into town. As they began to disperse and go their various ways, he entered a grocer on the main road. After all the other servants were out of sight, he left and proceeded to a whorehouse a little farther down the road.

The greeting room was empty except for one sailor passed out on a plush velvet couch, lying naked and face down, with a leg and an arm dangling on the ground. Sethlan walked across the large room and down the hallway, which was lined on both sides with doors.

When he was halfway down the long hall, the door at the back-right corner opened and Madam Swanda emerged. The madam didn't participate in the physical aspect of her trade, but Swanda dressed the part. Her hair was done up in an intricately woven bun and she wore a tight black dress covered in shimmering jewels. The dress revealed a surprising amount of leg as she walked toward him, a long slit on her left side opening with each step she took. Even though the dress modestly covered her, the sheerness of the fabric left little to the imagination. If it were any color other than black, all would be visible. She was getting on in years but, having never birthed a child, she still maintained a trim and tight figure.

"G'morning, Master Sethlan. It's a pleasure to see you." She stopped and held her hand out for him.

Sethlan took her hand in his and gently kissed the back of it.

"Business or pleasure?" she said.

"Business."

"That's a shame, dear. It has been some time since you and I last… did *business* together."

Sethlan smiled. Even though she owned the brothel and no longer took clients, Swanda occasionally came out of retirement for the right price—or person. He released her hand and proceeded the rest of the way down the hall, stopping at the door opposite the one Swanda had just emerged from. He pulled a small key from a different pocket in his trousers—hidden behind the belt—and unlocked the door while Swanda made her way down the hall knocking on each door to rouse her girls for another day of work. Before long, the lobby would once again begin to fill with patrons eager to begin their day with a poke.

He stepped into the small room, which was devoid of any furniture except for a plain armoire on the far wall. He opened it, then removed his plain shirt and trousers and exchanged them for a fine brown suit with stripes. From a shelf at the top, he retrieved a black wig and set it in place atop his naturally light-brown hair. He also pulled down a small jar, unscrewed the lid, and applied a small amount of goop to his upper lip and chin. Then he took a false mustache and long-braided goatee and secured them to his face. While he waited for the goop to set, he lifted the baseboard from the armoire to reveal several bags heavy with coin. He untied one of the bags, pulled out three drakes and a few smaller coins, then replaced the board. Finally, grabbing an ornately carved wooden cane from a hook, he left the room and locked the door behind him.

Sethlan wound his way around the scantily clad women now crowding the hall and headed out into the street. Verl's Mercantile, the outfit that controlled all the goods traveling in and out of Portstown, was located at the north end of the city, so he moved in that direction as quickly as he dared without attracting attention to himself.

The road widened as he approached Verl's. This was by design; as Portstown grew, so did the number of carts that lined up on the road waiting their turn to sell their goods. He passed all the carts and entered the mercantile by a side entrance reserved for those only looking to send small items, such as a letter. The side room was empty, so he walked right up to the counter.

"How may I help you?" a clerk said.

"May I speak to Verl?"

"Did you see the line outside when you entered? He's quite busy."

Sethlan reached into an inner pocket of his suit and pulled out a silver coin. He set it on the counter. The clerk immediately scooped it up and disappeared through a door without saying anything. A silver coin was more than the clerk would likely make all week; however, Sethlan had long since stopped cringing at how much it cost to move information. He paid what was required. After all, he was paid very well by his true employer.

The clerk returned and stood idly by, waiting for any other patrons that might enter the small room. Sethlan waited as well, in a somewhat awkward silence. After a few minutes, a bald man with a gray goatee—braided in the same fashion as the fake one Sethlan wore—entered the room.

"What can I do for you?"

Sethlan pulled the envelope and a drake from his suit and set them both on the counter.

"Where's it going?"

"Croff," Sethlan said.

"Who's the intended recipient?"

"A merchant named Jorgan."

Verl picked up the envelope and the gold coin, and they both disappeared into his tunic.

"It's… sensitive in nature," Sethlan added.

"One drake will ensure Jorgan receives it."

"And for it to arrive discreetly?"

"Will cost another."

The price at Verl's always varied between two and three drakes, depending on the thickness of the envelope Sethlan sent. He reached into his pocket, pulled out another coin, and placed it on the counter. Verl scooped it up and walked out without another word, leaving Sethlan standing at the counter. He looked at the clerk, who stared at the door behind him. When he turned to leave himself, the clerk said, "Have a nice day."

Sethlan quickly made his way back to the whorehouse, removed the wig and goatee, and changed back into his servant's garb.

"Come back soon!" Swanda called as he passed back through the greeting room.

With a wave, he stepped back out onto the busy street.

Running out of time, he hastily went to a warehouse on the southern end of town, where he placed an order for more wine to stock Dorlan's carriage for the remainder of the journey to Hantlo.

He hoped that the news of the boy would reach Jax in time for it to be of value. He hated wasting so much money and getting nothing in return. That was part of the job, though; the whole arrangement was a gamble. And, as risky as it was, it was a gamble he was willing to take. It was making him very rich.

CHAPTER 4

Hadie stepped into the small hallway and pulled the room's heavy door closed. Her head pounded right behind her eyes. She used the railing on the spiraling metal staircase to guide herself as she gingerly made her way down to the lobby. She'd been wrestling with her choices—whether she should stay in Portstown until after the chancellor's slow-moving caravan left and drink away the coins Drenan had thrown at her, or leave ahead of the caravan. Since she couldn't convince her body to go back to sleep—despite the hangover and early hour—she decided to leave.

When she reached the lobby, she rang the bell at the counter and waited for the innkeeper to emerge from his room. He appeared with his cheeks puffed out and lips pursed as he hastily chewed whatever he had crammed into his mouth.

"I've decided to leave," Hadie said. She set the key on the counter.

The innkeeper nodded, his mouth still full, and picked up the key. He walked back into the back room and returned with a clenched fist, then set three silver coins on the counter.

Hadie scooped them up. "Thank you."

The innkeeper nodded a couple of times in rapid succession,

still unable to speak. He rapped his knuckles on the counter and returned to his room.

Hadie pocketed the coins and left the inn.

She turned left initially, toward Hantlo, then turned back around and walked toward the north side of town. She kept a wary eye out for Drenan. Soldiers roamed the area, but as long as gray was the only color she saw, she would be all right.

She passed a large gap between buildings and the sound of hammering on metal caught her attention. She stopped and looked over at a building set back from the road. Dark smoke rose from the chimney on its soot-covered metal roof. Inside the wide entrance a man with thick arms and broad shoulders swung a heavy hammer with one arm, using a pair of tongs to hold a glowing piece of metal in place on an anvil with the other.

It was dangerous to travel the highways of Dradonia alone—especially for a woman who wasn't prepared to defend herself. Had she not been able to fend off unwanted advances, she would never have made it as far as she had.

She crossed the empty space separating the building from the road, passing between hitching posts on both sides. She stopped at the entrance to the recessed building.

The blacksmith noticed her and stopped hammering.

"You need something?" he said.

"A knife," Hadie said.

"What for?"

"Protection."

The blacksmith resumed his hammering. "From what?"

Hadie flinched when the hammer slammed into the glowing metal. "My ma always said to have something sharp on hand, for poking any man who tries to poke you without your consent."

"Smart woman," the blacksmith said after the hammer rang again. He gestured with the hammer toward the wall behind him. "Door at the back."

Hadie walked past him and flinched again when the hammer

rang once more. She opened the door and stepped into a small, dark room. A lantern hung from the ceiling, a small flame burning in it. She reached up and turned the little knob, further bathing the room in light.

Blades of various sizes and shapes lined the walls. Some of them were simply made, while others had elaborate designs etched into the metal or intricate twirling hilts. She wasn't interested in anything flashy, just something to protect herself. She selected a simple knife, similar in size to the one she'd left behind in Lonely Oak—thin, with a blade the length of her hand. She pulled it off the wall and tested its weight. Satisfied, she turned the lantern back down and left the room.

"How much?" Hadie said, holding the blade up.

"Half a drake," the blacksmith said without looking up or stopping his hammering.

Hadie reached into a pocket and pulled out two of the silver coins she'd gotten back from the innkeeper. She held them out toward the blacksmith.

The blacksmith stopped his hammering and took the coins from her, dropping them into a small pocket on the breast of his apron. "Sheaths over there are included," he said, pointing toward a counter along the wall with several drawers. "If you want something nicer, there's a leathersmith just down the road."

Like the knife, Hadie wasn't interested in anything fancy. She went over to the counter and, sifting through the drawers, selected a plain sheath made to be worn horizontally on the belt. "Thanks," she said. The blacksmith had already resumed his hammering, so she left clutching the sheathed knife in her hand.

Hadie didn't want to spend money on a fancy sheath but she did need a new satchel, so she pushed open the door to the leathersmith's shop and went in. A good satchel *was* something she was willing to spend extra money on, so she traded another half drake for a well-made one.

A few minutes later, with the remainder of her coins tucked

safely into an interior pocket of her new satchel and her knife hidden under her shirt on her belt, Hadie made her way to Verl's Mercantile, where she knew merchants would be lined up waiting to load and unload their wagons. When she arrived, she stopped and looked over the line of wagons pointed south. She picked one that looked to be in good repair and didn't have windows on the sides. She wanted to get to Hantlo as fast as she could, and merchant wagons with windows would be stopping in every town between here and there to sell their goods.

"Where ya headed?" she asked the plainly-dressed man just climbing into the seat of the first wagon that suited her.

"Buzz off," the man said.

Unfazed by his response, she moved down the line. On her travels north, she had learned that some merchants were amenable to hitchhikers and some were not. She took no offense when the merchants rejected her. If they didn't want her along, then they were probably not pleasant people in the first place. She repeated the question to each wagon that she deemed acceptable until she received a different response.

"What's it to you?" said the fifth man she asked.

"I'm headed to Hantlo and looking to hire a ride."

"Well, I happen to be heading to Hantlo, but I got no room for passengers. My wagon's loaded to the gills as it is."

"I can pay," Hadie said.

The man looked down at her curiously.

"Please."

"Walkin's free, lass."

"I know. It's just… I ran away from my ma and pa and, after drinking way too much last night, I finally realized how I must've hurt 'em by leaving. I need to be getting back home just as quickly as possible. By now they've got to be worried more than a cap'n sailing the gap in a storm with a drunken crew."

The man continued to study her. Finally, he said, "Climb up. It's late, and I need to be getting on."

"How much?"

"Keep your money," the man said. "You probably stole it from your parents anyhow."

Hadie looked down at the ground and toyed in the dirt with her foot, attempting to add some credibility to her story.

"You comin' or not?"

Hadie looked up at the man, nodded, and climbed up next to him. There was just enough room for the two of them to sit side by side on the narrow bench. "I could ride in the back, if you want," she said.

"Like I said, I ain't got the room. Wagon's loaded to the gills," the man said. "Name's Dennal, by the way."

"Jannie," Hadie said, providing the name she'd thought up on her way toward the mercantile.

Dennal snapped the reins and set his two-horse team into motion. "It's late enough as it is already, and I was hoping to put as many leagues between meself and the chancellor as I could."

"Why's that?"

"Have you ever seen how slow his caravan moves?"

Hadie thought about the time she'd spent traveling in that very caravan, but said, "No."

"If you get stuck behind it, it takes hours to make it 'round."

Hadie sat in silence as Dennal drove the team. As the day wore on, she mostly just answered any questions he asked or responded as briefly as she could when he attempted making small talk.

She knew she was taking a risk traveling with a stranger, but she needed to arrive in Hantlo as quickly as she could. With her knife, she knew she could take care of herself if she needed to— her mother had long ago seen to it that she knew how to handle a blade. However, the longer she rode next to Dennal, the safer she felt. He appeared to be a genuinely kind and simple man. And for that, she was thankful.

CHAPTER 5

Drenan rolled off the woman and sat up on the edge of his bed. She was a whore he knew well, and with all the distractions of the past month, he was pleased that he would have someone familiar warming his bed for the remainder of the excruciatingly slow trip back to Hantlo.

Now that they were back in the south, emissaries from the capital demanded his every waking moment. This late hour was the only time of the day he had left to himself. Many of the emissaries were just doing their jobs, but a few of the more eager ones were not-so-secretly vying for higher positions within the province. And since he was the regent of the Hantlo province, they went out of their way to try to please him. But they were the ones who annoyed him most. If he permitted it, he knew they would take even this late hour from him.

He rose to his feet and retrieved his robe from the end of the bed. After tying it around himself, he stepped out of the room. In the next room, his servants were busy in their nightly task of returning his dining room back to a presentable state. The continuous flow of revelers always left it looking like Hantlo did after a cyclone. The servants stopped working and bowed to him as he passed through. In the entry room, he stopped and looked at the cushion on the end of the couch to his left. Although the pattern matched the others, the cushion looked newer than the rest. As he walked out the door, he smirked at the thought of the poor girl who had died there while Danavin's get failed to save her.

Drenan was hoping to cool off a little from his physical exertions, but the evening air that greeted him was just as oppressive as it was during the day. After centuries of living in the south, he had known it would be, so he really wasn't surprised—but it was progressively getting worse. The days were getting hotter, and so were the nights. He might be eight hundred years Dorlan's junior, but even he knew something wasn't right. With half the realm abandoned, he wondered how much longer until Drakonias ordered the rest abandoned as well. He'd known since Kyinth the message that Dorlan would deliver to the other regents; now if he could only convince those with key influence to see things his way, he might be able to get Dorlan to agree. What was the point of remaining in the empire if the empire wasn't going to help when it was needed?

"Good evening, Your Majesty," his guard said, greeting him as he stepped down to the ground.

Drenan ignored the guard and looked up at the moon. It was almost full. It had been a month since the events in Lonely Oak, and only a few more days of travel stood between him and the comforts of his palace. These carriages were luxurious enough— they were nicer quarters than most people's actual homes—but he hated traveling. He was looking forward to ridding himself of them again.

The busyness of the last few days had distracted him from thinking about the tavern. However, standing out here in the dark, looking up at the moon, brought it to mind. He knew it might take time for Crin to find the Thornhill boy, but he'd yet to hear anything, which worried him. If both boys slipped through his fingers… He clenched his hands into fists, feeling the stretch in the scars covering the backs of them, and pushed back against his treasonous thoughts about the chancellor. For some reason Dorlan was determined to prevent Drenan from finally putting an end to Danavin's family.

Drenan decided to wait until he arrived in Hantlo before he did anything drastic. That gave Crin a few more days to make contact. In the meantime, he decided to pen a letter to Nera and find out why the Synod hadn't known Danavin had children. That was a huge lapse in her duties as head of the Synod, and she needed to be held accountable.

He enjoyed the light breeze for a while—small as it was, it gave some relief to the heat. When Drenan returned to his carriage, he demanded parchment and paper from the servants just finishing up in the dining room.

He sat at the table, eyeing Rennie's heavy breasts through her sheer garments as she retrieved ink, pen, and parchment from the sideboard. Drenan picked up the pen when she set the implements on the table and continued watching her as she poured him a glass of wine.

"Will there be anything else, Your Majesty?" Rennie said, nearly exposed to him.

Drenan motioned for her to leave with a flick of the pen, and she went and stood in the corner. He took a drink of wine then dipped the pen in the ink.

> *Dearest Aunt,*
>
> *It has come to my attention that certain loose ends exist from when last I served the Synod. I realized your need at the time and, as much ardor as I had in accepting the mission, it was still a favor. And now, the loose ends of which I speak have brought me great embarrassment.*
>
> *You know how I feel about loose*

ends, as well as my history with those that embarrass. Worse, these loose ends are once again causing problems for the empire—problems we thought eliminated with Danavin.

I realize the mission was twenty years ago, but I need answers.

Drenan

Drenan set the pen down and took a drink of wine. He reviewed what he had written, then said, "Cylinder."

Rennie left her corner and went back to the sideboard to retrieve a black tube, wax, and his seal. While he waited, Drenan reached under the table and touched the dragon bone inlaid into the wood. He siphoned some Energy into his Core and used it to dry the ink on the parchment. It discolored and looked slightly charred. When the ink was dry, he rolled the parchment tightly. Standing by his side, Rennie handed him the wax. He heated the tip of it until it softened then touched it to the parchment. Drenan handed the wax back to Rennie and she exchanged it for the seal. He pressed the seal into the wax and handed both the seal and the parchment to Rennie.

"Where to, Your Majesty?" Rennie said. She slid the parchment into the black cylinder and returned the wax and seal to the sideboard.

"Nera."

"Yes, Your Majesty."

Drenan finished off the glass of wine, then returned to the whore in his bed. He dropped his robe, lay down on the bed, and motioned to the woman to resume her work. As she climbed on top of him again, he closed his eyes and felt the backs of his scarred hands with his fingers. While she worked to arouse him anew, his mind turned to what his options were should Crin fail to capture the boy. He refused to let those boys slip from his grasp and would do whatever it took to ensure that didn't happen. Danavin paid for his crimes against the Regency with his life. But for killing Drenan's wife and daughter, Danavin's get will pay with *their* lives. No matter what the emperor had planned for them, Drenan would ensure they paid.

* * *

Sethlan stepped out of Dorlan's carriage with a handful of messages to deliver to the condors. As he crossed the camp and passed the fires, he looked around, half-expecting to see the boy from Lonely Oak and his friend, though he knew they weren't there.

As he approached Drenan's carriage, he saw Drenan's servant exit. She turned toward the birds as well, so he hastened his step—without running—to catch up to her. "Only one message tonight?" he asked her when he drew up alongside her.

"Yes," Rennie said.

"What's it say?"

"Dunno."

"Where's it headed?"

"Kyinth."

"To whom?"

"Nera."

Nera? Sethlan thought.

"You, on the other hand, have quite a few messages," Rennie said.

Sethlan looked down at the fistful of messenger tubes he held. "It's already my third trip to the condors."

"Is Dorlan really that much busier?"

"He just cares more about his realm than he does himself," Sethlan said.

They walked the remainder of the distance to the condors in silence. Sethlan wondered what Drenan could possibly have to say to the head of the Synod. The Synod was who decided the missions of the Black Sodality. Was there someone Drenan needed to assassinate? More importantly, he wondered what that sort of information might be worth. It was a good thing Rennie was the type of person that a type of person such as himself could trust.

CHAPTER 6

Javen's eyes opened and he stared blankly at the wooden planks above him. He sobbed in relief—the nightmare was finally over. He couldn't remember the last time he'd had such a vivid dream. Over and over Astora died any number of horrible deaths. Despite his efforts, he was never able to save her. He was always one step too slow. For a moment he thought only of the rough wood over his head. Then, all too quickly, images of Astora's lifeless body flooded his mind: her pleading eyes; the way she choked on her own blood as she gasped for breath; the horrible wound on her neck. He tried to push them away, but they continued to haunt him even though he was awake, as vivid dreams sometimes do. Then he realized he wasn't looking at the ceiling of the carriage Dorlan gave him back in Matis.

He tried to sit up, but his body protested. He became acutely aware of the aches in what felt like every muscle in his body. Worse, his head pounded as if he'd spent all night drinking Yolken's strong ale, and his hands and forearms itched. Slowly, he was able to coax his legs onto the well-worn planks of the floor and sat up. He scratched at his arms and weakly said, "*Hadie?*"

His head pounded so he squeezed his eyes closed and

pressed the palms of both his hands into his skull, just above his temples. He tried to remember what he'd spent the previous night doing, but he had no recollection of drinking. When the throbbing eventually abated, he opened his eyes and looked around.

He was alone in a small room. The floor and walls were of the same wood as the ceiling. An unlit oil lantern swung from the ceiling. There was a small desk against the wall to his right and an armoire to his left. He rose slowly to his feet and realized he was naked. He stumbled over to the armoire, which had clumps of grapes and vines carved throughout the wood. Inside hung three shirts and three pairs of pants, none of which belonged to him. They all swayed slightly on their hangers. Javen looked at them curiously, then the floor heaved beneath him.

Javen shoved the armoire doors closed and held onto the knobs. *What in the world?* he thought as he tried to steady himself. *Am I on a ship?* He had never been on a ship before, but he could think of no other explanation for why the floor beneath him might be moving. The floor lurched and threw him backward. He held onto the knobs and his momentum pulled the doors open. He fully expected to pull the armoire down on top of himself, but it didn't fall—it held his weight as he pulled against it. As he held on, arms outstretched, he noticed that the pigmentation of his hands and forearms didn't match the rest of his arms. They were pale, like they were after a winter of wearing coats.

What in Draego's Fire?

When he regained his balance he carefully stepped back over to the bed. The floor lurched again, forcing him to grab the wooden bed frame. He climbed onto the mattress and looked out the round window above the bed.

Water.

Except for hazy mountains way off in the distance, water was all he could see in both directions.

He was *definitely* on a boat.

"What in Draego's Fire," he said, sitting back down on the bed. Had he drunk so much he just couldn't remember getting on a boat? That *would* explain his pounding headache. But he was nowhere near water. The caravan was still days away from Portstown, which was the nearest body of water. And where was Hadie? He struggled to remember the last thing he'd done, but the only thing he could remember was… Astora.

It started coming back to him.

Fear.

Anger.

Desperation.

He remembered Drenan emotionlessly drawing a knife across Astora's throat. Drenan told him to heal her. But he couldn't use his gift. And Drenan knew that. Javen remembered begging Drenan to save her life while he tried to stop the blood flow. But Drenan had goaded him instead. *"Your brother, when confronted with a dying girl, used the gift that was his birthright and healed her. Are you telling me he is better than you?"* Javen remembered Astora's eyes pleading for help as she struggled to breathe. He remembered watching her life slip away and then Drenan callously walking away, telling him to return the next day for another lesson. And after that… he couldn't remember.

But the images of Astora overwhelmed him. As he scratched at his hands, a familiar feeling that accompanied too much drinking caused him to slide off the bed. He doubled over on the wood flooring and vomited. More and more he was beginning to think he had tried to drink away his grief. For a while, he didn't move. He just stared at the mess on the floor, spitting in it occasionally as his mouth filled with saliva, and tried not to think of Astora.

Javen wiped his mouth on the back of his hand when the nausea passed. He went back to the armoire and selected a shirt and a pair of pants. When he was dressed, he went to the door and tested the knob. It turned. He cracked the door open and peered out into a narrow, dimly lit hallway. He pushed it open farther and saw another door directly across from him. The door was open, so he stepped across the hallway and peered in. At least a dozen rope hammocks hung from the ceiling. There were also barrels in each corner as well as several small wooden chests. There was a third door at the end of the hall. It appeared statelier than the coarse doors leading into the other rooms and was adorned with the same carved grapes and elaborate vines as the armoire. At the opposite end of the hallway was a steep and well-worn staircase.

Javen decided to go up above and turned toward the stairs. He held his hands out to both sides, using the opposing walls to brace himself against the roiling of the ship, while he made his way down the short hallway. When he took his first step up the steep stairs, he heard a voice call out from behind him, "Master Javen! You're awake!" He turned to face a dark-haired man tying a sash around a plush white robe. He recognized the man as the other regent traveling in Dorlan's caravan: Devin.

"Where are we?" Javen said.

"Two days' sail from Portstown," Devin said.

Devin walked the length of the hall with his hands tucked into the pockets of his suit coat. Unlike Javen, he didn't rely on the walls for balance. He was as sure-footed on the ship as Javen was on land.

"Where are we going?" Javen said. His hands and arms felt like ants were crawling over them. He tried to resist the urge to scratch at them but couldn't.

"The feeling will pass. It's a side effect from the healing."

"What healing?"

"And we're going to Onta."

"Where's Hadie? Why are you taking me to Onta?"

"Come, join me in my quarters. There's plenty of time for questions, Master Javen. But for now, let's get you something to eat. I'm sure you're famished."

The mention of food made Javen painfully aware of the fact that he was indeed hungry. He followed Devin back down the hall and into the room at the end, again using the walls for balance.

The room was considerably larger and much brighter than the other two. There were large windows on both sides of the room, as well as at the back. In addition to all the windows, on the back wall was a pair of open side-by-side doors that led out to a small balcony. A chandelier was mounted in the middle of the ceiling with about two dozen small, unlit lanterns hanging from it. Elaborate moldings encircled the room, adorned with the same carven grapes and vines as the door, and each corner featured an ornate column carved from thick logs. As he stepped farther into the room, he noticed the furniture was much more elaborate as well. Everything—the armoire, the cabinets, the desk—was larger and elaborately engraved. Then the table dividing the room captured his attention.

Javen pulled back one of the many chairs surrounding the table and looked at the platters of food. One of them was piled with various fruits—apples, oranges, sliced melon, and strawberries—and the other held a small pig. As hungry as he was, he couldn't help but notice the curiously dark, almost black, wood of the table. He ran his hand across it, then noticed that the rest of the furniture in the room was made of the same material.

"Made from the finest wood in the empire," Devin said.

"What is it?" Javen said. He'd never seen anything like it before.

"It's made from the giant Kvorgan spruce. It's rare, and rather difficult to procure."

"It's very nice," Javen said, running his fingers over the grains of the dark wood.

"Help yourself to anything on the table."

Javen picked up a plate, which had a grape motif encircling the perimeter, heaped it with slices of pork, then filled the remaining space with fruit. He set the plate down, then inspected two decanters and a matching ewer sitting next to the platters. The decanters contained wine and the ewer, water. He chose the water.

When Javen sat down to eat, Devin sat on a large, curved couch set in the corner of the room. Javen picked up a green apple and bit into it. Its tartness exploded in his mouth, washing away the taste of bile. Before he got halfway through the apple, movement out of the corner of his eye drew his attention. He nearly choked on the apple when he saw it was a half-naked woman entering from the balcony. She had dark hair and olive-colored skin. Her hands were clasped at her belly and her arms supported a robe that hung openly around her waist, fully exposing her chest. Javen recognized her from Lonely Oak, and from their stay at the Blue Mountain in Matis: Karina, Devin's wife. He tried not to stare, but his eyes were drawn to her breasts like a moth to a lantern. Hadie would be furious if she knew.

"Greeting, Master Javen," Karina said as she walked up to him. "I was beginning to wonder if you were ever going to wake."

Javen averted his eyes, looked at his plate of food, and scratched at his arms.

"Rise and greet a lady properly," Karina said.

Javen looked over at Devin in question. Devin gestured toward Karina with a wave of his hand. Javen hesitantly pushed his chair back and stood, even though he didn't know the proper way to greet a half-naked lady. He awkwardly turned toward her but kept his eyes on his plate. Karina stepped closer and pressed her body against his. She cupped his chin and turned his head to face her. Then she wrapped her arms around him—one around his back, the other behind his head—and kissed him on the mouth. Javen was beside himself, but with her hands pulling him in as they were, and not wanting to forcefully shove her away, he was powerless to refuse. He felt like he was in one of Hadie's books.

When Karina finally pulled away, she said, "Caring for you as I have these past couple of days has made me anxious for you to awaken. I'm glad you finally have." She turned and walked around the table toward the couch, leaving Javen staring after her blankly. She sat next to Devin and crossed her legs.

The two strange individuals began speaking too quietly for Javen to hear so he awkwardly returned to his seat. When it became evident to him that they were done talking with him, he picked up the apple and took another bite. *That was really weird,* he thought. *She's his wife. Were the stories in* Lovers *true?*

When he finished a second plate and set his fork down, Devin said, "Pour yourself some wine and join us on the couch."

Javen wiped his mouth with a napkin, then filled a wide crystal glass with wine from one of the decanters. Devin and Karina were sitting together on one side of the curved couch, so he sat on the other side. He ignored the feeling of ants crawling on his arms as best he could.

"Do you know who we are?"

Javen nodded. "Devin and Karina Drake."

"Dorlan told me you were familiar with the family."

"My aunt made sure we knew who the Blessed were."

"Knowledge is a valuable asset," Devin said.

At the thought of his aunt, Javen felt pangs of remorse. He frowned and looked down at the wine glass he was holding in his lap.

"Dorlan told me what happened. My deepest apologies, Javen." Devin held his own wine glass up in Javen's direction and said, "To your aunt." Javen looked up and Devin took a drink.

Javen took a drink as well. "I wish she didn't have to die. My parents, either."

"Justice is often painful. But let us not dwell on the past," Devin said. "My wife and I were just—"

"Where's Hadie?" Javen said, regretting interrupting Devin the moment he spoke. Drenan would have berated him, if not worse, for being impertinent.

"Gone," Devin said, seemingly undisturbed by the interruption.

"*Gone? Gone where?*"

"This 'Hadie' you speak of—was the woman with you in the caravan?" Karina said.

"Yes," Javen said. "What happened to her?"

"She was a pretty lass. There were several nights I thought about inviting the two of you to spend the night in our carriage, but Devin said it was improper."

"Because you're married!"

"Actually, it was because you were not under his command. That's changed now, though, hasn't it?"

"So they're true?"

"Is what true?"

"The books Hadie read."

"What books are those?" Karina said with a wink.

Javen blushed and looked at Devin.

"Please," Karina said. "I truly am curious."

Javen looked back at Karina and said, "*The Lovers of Onta.*"

"Ah, yes." Karina placed her hand on Devin's thigh and said, "We're familiar with Rongin's work. What did you think?"

"Truthfully?"

"I hope for nothing less."

"I think half the reason Hadie insisted on reading them to me was that she enjoyed how much they embarrassed me." Javen tried to keep his eyes on Karina's. It was one of the hardest things he'd ever had to do.

"Why? Are you not experienced in the art of proper bedding?"

"Proper bedding!" Javen exclaimed. This really was too much. He looked away from them, feeling his face warming. He couldn't take any more of Karina's overt display. He took a deep drink of his wine.

"Well," Karina said, standing, "it sounds as though you gentlemen have a lot to discuss, so I'll leave you to speak in private. But worry not, Master Javen, I'll be just out on the balcony." Any confusion he might have had about what she meant was gone when she bent over in front of him and leaned in until her mouth touched his ear. With nowhere to avert his eyes, he squeezed them shut. "Perhaps one day Rongin will write a *Lovers* featuring the two of us," she whispered into his ear. Javen's eyes popped open in complete disbelief, but her breasts were mere inches from his face, so he immediately closed them again. She kissed him on the mouth, then said, "See you soon, Master Javen."

Javen breathed a sigh of relief when she walked away. She refilled her wine glass at the table, then sauntered back out onto the balcony.

"I suppose you're wondering what happened to your arms and why you're on a boat sailing for Onta," Devin said, continuing their conversation as if what had just happened was perfectly normal.

Javen tore his attention from the open doors Karina had walked through. He looked back to Devin and nodded.

"Dorlan has placed you into my care."

"I thought I was under Drenan's care?"

"You were. However, after what happened, Dorlan saw fit to transfer your care to me."

Javen thought about the sole horrifying time he'd met with Drenan for a lesson. The unsettling feeling in his stomach started building again, so he quickly changed the subject. "What happened to Hadie? Where is she?"

"You need not concern yourself with her."

"What does that mean?"

"It means that she's gone."

"She left?" Javen said. Suddenly, he was afraid she'd heard what happened and didn't want to be with him anymore.

"It was never Dorlan's intention for her to be with you in the first place, so he sent her away."

"What do you mean he 'didn't intend for her to be with me'?"

"Drenan was sent back to Lonely Oak to retrieve whomever it was that had Synthesized. You were obviously of interest, but why he went out of the way to bring her along as well, he has yet to say. Knowing my brother, his plans for her were likely similar to those for that other lass."

Javen cringed at the thought. Even though he hadn't originally planned on seeing Hadie for any longer than the time she stayed in Lonely Oak, he had grown attached to her. "Doesn't it matter what I might want?"

"Apparently, according to Drenan, she is the disgraced daughter of a Silk. A regent would never associate with the likes of her. You'll find that there are many more suitable choices once we arrive in Onta."

Javen hadn't realized that. He wondered why she never mentioned her parents were Silks. "But I'm not a regent."

"Presently, no."

"What are you saying?"

"I'm saying that if you're training is successful, I will escort you to Kyinth to meet the emperor."

Javen stared at Devin in disbelief. Was he dreaming? He couldn't even begin to explain what was happening to him. First, waking on a ship headed for Onta, not knowing how he got there; then the weird way Karina had acted; and now this. He had so many questions but didn't know where to start. So he simply said, "Why?"

"You succeeded in accessing your gift," Devin said. "So he wants to meet you."

Javen stared at Devin, dumbfounded. "I Synthesized?"

"Let's just say that you came into your ability… explosively. Which explains the new skin on your arms."

Devin explained to Javen the events that had taken place over the last several days—specifically Javen's response to Drenan killing Astora, and why he didn't remember anything that happened after.

"But I still don't understand why the emperor would want to meet me," Javen said.

"Your father was a rebel, but he was also a powerful Synthesizer. Naturally, the son of such a person would pique the curiosity of His Blessed Highness."

"But what would he want to have to do with me? I always thought the Regency dealt swift punishment to anyone associated with the rebels."

"Were you associated with the Order?" Devin said.

"No."

"Then there you have it."

"So then what *does* the emperor want with me?"

"As the head of the empire, Drakonias is the only one with the authority to elevate someone to the status of regent."

Javen's eyes went wide.

"Don't be so surprised," Devin continued. "That's how it's been done since the beginning of the empire. If you wish to become a regent, then you must stand before Drakonias."

"It's just—Dorlan asked me if I wanted to learn to use my gift," Javen said. "He didn't say anything about becoming a regent."

Devin moved on. While he talked, Javen reflected on the first time he'd met Drenan in the tavern, and how he'd felt a certain amount of foreboding toward him from that moment. As Devin explained that Drenan held a vendetta against Javen's family, the foreboding combined with the roiling of the ship made the sick feeling in his stomach return. He looked around for something to vomit in; unable to find anything, he ran through the doors at the back of the room, leaned over the wooden railing of the small balcony, and lost the meal he'd just eaten.

A soft hand ran through the hair on the back of Javen's head. He turned his head to the side to find Karina standing next to him.

"Everything will be all right, Master Javen," she cooed in his ear.

He turned from her and sent what remained in his stomach over the railing. When he was done, he leaned against the wooden rail until the nausea subsided. He wiped his mouth on his sleeve and turned to find Devin leaning against the doorjamb, arms crossed.

Karina offered him her glass, which he gladly accepted. He took a small drink and swished it around in his mouth, then spat it over the railing. He took another long drink and said, "So, what now?"

"Dorlan has tasked me with preparing you for your eventual meeting with Drakonias. When you're presentable, I am to escort you to the capital," Devin said. "You needn't fear Drenan. Though he may harbor ill will toward you, he will not openly trouble you—that is, assuming you choose to become a part of the Regency."

"So you're going to teach me to Synthesize?"

"I am. And, my methods are not as… bloody as Drenan's. I like to think that we are much more civilized in the west, and don't need to resort to such gruesome measures. We love proper wine and we love proper bedding. Death and pain are not the only methods to exert one's authority, despite what my younger brother seems to think."

Javen felt Karina's arm go around his back, then he gasped in shock when he felt her other hand get dangerously close to the waistline of his pants. The distraction made him forget about the itch in his arms.

"Karina requested the opportunity to welcome such a distinguished guest aboard our ship. When she's finished, come up and join me on the deck," Devin said. Then he left Javen with his wife, as though it were perfectly normal.

Karina reached up and pulled Javen's face down for a kiss. Then she lowered her arms to her side and let her robe fall to the ground. She pressed her body against his, wedging him against the railing, and kissed him for what seemed like an eternity, pausing only long enough to lift Javen's shirt up over his head.

"Have you ever bedded someone with six hundred years of experience?" Karina whispered into Javen's ear.

She took him by the hand and guided him into the room, over to the large bed whose corner posts extended from floor to ceiling. All thoughts of Hadie, Astora, or Drenan melted from Javen's mind as scenes from *The Lovers of Onta* began to unfold before him.

CHAPTER 7

Javen climbed the steep steps leading to the deck of the ship, still blushing. It took a lot to make him blush, but when he did, he grew excessively red in the face. He really wished he could go back to the cabin he had awakened in and hide there until the voyage was over, but he knew he couldn't. He hesitated at the door at the top of the steps, then pushed it open.

He emerged on the deck of the ship and immediately looked up in awe at the thick timber mast that reached high above the deck. It supported huge sails that were full of wind. He watched as two shirtless, sun-darkened men adeptly climbed up and down the mast and out onto the yards, making adjustments to riggings here and there. Watching them work so effortlessly at such a dizzying height made that now-too-familiar feeling in his stomach creep back, so he looked back down.

He was alone on the lowest of three decks. There were four sets of stairs, one in each corner, that led up to the higher decks in front of him and behind him. He slowly made his way to one set of stairs that led up to the aft deck, walking with his hand on the wall, then stumbled over to the railing and grabbed hold. As he made his way up the stairs, he looked over the side of the ship, which was a huge mistake. A bout of vertigo washed over him, forcing him to crouch down and wrap his arms around a railing post. When the vertigo passed, he climbed the remaining steps without looking up from his feet.

"That was quick," Devin said when Javen reached the top.

Javen felt his face flush. "I couldn't do it," he said, rubbing his arms.

Forcing himself off the four-poster bed was one of the hardest things Javen had ever had to do. Had Karina not been married, he would have had no qualms about bedding her.

"She's very pleasing, you know," Devin said. After a moment of hesitation he added, "And persistent."

"But she's your wife!"

"She's going to be quite cross—especially if you continue to rebuff her advances. I wouldn't expect her to give up until we have arrived in Onta and found you a proper lover. Maybe not even then."

The thought made Javen's stomach worse. It had been hard enough getting away from her just now; he didn't know if he could do it again. "How much farther do we have to go?"

"If the wind is favorable through the gap, it shouldn't be more than a few days."

Javen groaned and stared over the railing at the deck below. Onta couldn't come fast enough. "What's the gap?"

"You see those mountains?" Devin said, pointing off to the right.

"Yeah."

"Those are the southern Ontalis. We've been paralleling them since leaving Portstown, sailing just a few leagues offshore. The gap is when the sea narrows and squeezes through the Ontalis and the Island of Kvorga."

Javen's eyes lit up at mention of the island. "Are the stories true?"

"What stories?"

"I grew up sitting around the hearth in the tavern listening to fantastical tales about the Island of Kvorga."

"What sort of things did you hear?"

"All sorts of stuff. Lots about how animals there are bigger, faster, and meaner."

"Anything else?"

"Trees there grow enormously huge, unlike anywhere else in the world. Then there's the mysterious woman who lives there, Anivera. Supposedly she has her own dragon."

"Dragon?" Devin said with a chuckle.

"Yeah."

"Well, I can certainly say that *that* story isn't true. But most fables tend to be based on a modicum of truth. Take the Kvorgan spruce, for instance—they *are* bigger than the typical spruce, though the stories certainly exaggerate their real size."

"If that's true, then why not the story about Anivera?"

"Because for one, dragons no longer inhabit Dradonia."

No longer inhabit? Javen thought to himself. He'd always thought dragons were creatures of fable. "Are you saying dragons are actually real? I mean, besides Draego?"

"At one point in time they were, yes." Devin looked over at Javen curiously. "Did Dorlan never talk about this with you?"

Javen shook his head.

"Hmm, we'll have to remedy that soon."

Javen's mind raced with wonder. Dragons were real?

"But for now," Devin continued, "understand that the problem with stories is that, like rumors, they tend to grow and evolve over time."

"So all the stories about people who visit the island and never return—those aren't true?"

"They may be true to an extent—the island *does* have its dangers, and people have gone exploring and never returned. But it's not any different than, say, going up into the Ontalis unprepared."

That made perfect sense to Javen. Even the Mindons had

some dangers. Whenever he and Yolken had gone hunting in the mountains, they'd always made sure to take the proper precautions. The more he and Devin talked, the more he realized that Kvorga wasn't what he had grown up thinking it was.

"Enough about Kvorga," Devin said, changing the subject. "Let's get back to the issue at hand. You should know that customs are not the same in Onta as they are in the north."

"You mean with your wife?"

"That's part of it. If you wish to become a part of our society, then you must exercise care, and be willing to adapt to the cultural norms of whatever province you might find yourself in. Slights like that could very well get you killed.

Javen stared at the mountains in the distance, reflecting on Devin's words. The sun was just beginning to set, and the long light cast an eerie glow on them.

"Don't overly concern yourself with that matter for now," Devin said. "I'll speak to my wife if you're uncomfortable with our openness—though I can't promise she'll leave you be. Let's take advantage of what light we have left and talk about Synthesis."

Finally, something that made Javen feel like smiling.

CHAPTER 8

Javen closed his eyes and inhaled the fresh sea breeze. The smell of salt in the air was still new to his senses; it was something he could definitely get used to. His body ached, but in a good way. He had never particularly enjoyed working—and tried to get out of as much of it as possible—but for some strange reason he *did* enjoy the feeling the morning after a strenuous day. Not because he liked pain, but because it made him feel just a little bit more alive. The ache he felt now meant exactly that—he had awakened to a completely new level of existence, and his body would need time to adjust.

He knew he should be feeling complete elation at the positive turn of events, but the feelings that had overwhelmed him in the moments after Astora's death kept simmering at the back of his mind. Along with his thoughts of Astora was a desire to somehow right the wrong that had been done to her—to somehow make Drenan pay for his actions. And the people who were responsible for his parents' deaths—the same ones who were now corrupting Yolken—he wanted to make them pay, too. They needed to be stopped.

Javen closed his eyes and exhaled, clearing his lungs, then drew another breath. He listened to the water slapping against the side of the ship and waited for the sky to brighten. The freshness of the air and the sound of the water helped calm him.

He'd sneaked out of his room as soon as he woke in order to avoid any potential encounters with Karina. Devin had said that she would likely not give up on her advances toward him, and he'd been right. As soon as Javen shut the door to his room after he finished his lesson with Devin, she'd started knocking. Fortunately, he'd noticed that the door had a lock on it. Karina called to him softly but he'd insisted that he was too tired. Even so, she pleaded with him to open the door until Javen heard Devin say, "Let him be, love. He's had a long day. I'm sure he'll come around eventually."

Thoughts of Karina evaporated when the sky grew light enough for him to begin seeing their surroundings. He no longer saw endless water over the left side of the ship. Before him rose towering mountains. They dwarfed the Mindons, and they were close as well. He estimated the ship was no more than half a league offshore.

The Island of Kvorga, he thought. Despite what Devin had said, memories of the stories Kaylan's uncle had told around the hearth flooded into his mind.

He looked off the right side of the ship at the mainland. They were passing through the gap. He turned back to the island and studied it as the ship slowly passed it by. The giant trees rising from the ground were easily distinguishable. Birds soared high in the air, while others glided low over the water. They were too far away to see clearly, but by the shape of them, he guessed they were probably condors.

"Amazing, isn't it?" Devin said.

Javen looked over his shoulder and saw Devin joining him on the deck. "It is."

They stood in silence and watched the mountains drift slowly by until the sun stood full above the horizon.

"Even with this favorable wind," Devin said, "it will take

several hours to pass through the gap, and we can't waste it all standing here. Come, let me show you something I think you'll find just as intriguing as the fabled Island of Kvorga."

Javen followed Devin back down to the main deck, where Devin grabbed an iron loop lying flat in a recessed hole in the middle of the deck. He pulled up on the loop and lifted a large door, revealing a gaping hole. Javen walked up to the hole and hesitantly peered down into a large bay. A circular iron staircase led down into its depths, and Devin quickly descended. Javen followed and was assaulted by an unpleasant mixture of must and grease. He wanted to retreat to the smell of the sea above but forced himself to continue. The bay was filled with crates and barrels secured to the ground beneath webbed netting.

"Over here," Devin said as he walked around a stack of boxes.

Devin stopped next to a long, rectangular crate tucked into the corner. Javen waited as Devin pulled out a key and unlocked the locks on each of the four top corners.

"Help me lift the lid," Devin said.

Javen moved to the opposite end of the crate and together they removed the lid, tilted it to one side, and leaned it against the crate.

Javen stared curiously at a long, cylindrical, iron tube inside. It was wider at one end and smoothly tapered down at the other. It was mounted on a wooden structure with small iron wheels. Little wedges prevented the wheels from rolling around in the crate. "What is that?" he said.

"It's a relic from the war," Devin said, "called a Cannon. This is the only one not cached with all the other Machines left over from the war. I had to beg the emperor to let me keep it."

"Machine?"

"Machines are Energy-powered weapons we made during the war to help us defeat the Dragon King."

"What does it do?"

"You see the opening at the end, there?" Devin said, pointing to the circular opening at the smaller end. "That hole runs the length of the Cannon. It's called the ball chamber. A large iron ball fits inside. A rod is used to push the ball all the way back to this end," Devin said, pointing at the larger end, "and tamp it snugly into place. This end is where you fit the Power Cell." There was a small round wheel at the larger end of the Cannon, which Devin turned counterclockwise. When the wheel stopped, he pulled on the wheel and the rounded end of the Cannon swung open, revealing a slot inside.

"What's a Power Cell?"

"Oh, that's right… Dorlan didn't teach you about dragons."

Javen listened in rapturous amazement as Devin explained how the Regency had come to utilize dragon bones and scales to defeat the Dragon King. Dragon bones enabled Synthesizers to store Energy for use at night or when out of direct sight of the sun. They were also used to power Machines. Dragon scales were fashioned into armor that neutralized the effects of Energy. Javen understood now why his fiery attack on Drenan didn't harm Drenan—he was wearing his blue armor at the time.

"I've always thought the armor looked peculiar," Javen said. "It reminded me of fish scales, but I never once imagined that they were actually dragon scales."

"Being able to store Energy gave us a huge advantage," Devin said. "It was almost enough to end the war right then."

"What happened?"

"The Dragon King figured it out, which erased our advantage almost as fast as the tide had turned in our favor. But we can discuss the various strategic advantages and disadvantages we had throughout the war later, over a few bottles of wine."

Javen looked the Cannon over again. "What are those holes for?" he asked, pointing at two irregularly shaped holes about a foot from the end of the Cannon. They were just big enough that he could fit one finger in each, and they lined up along the length of the Cannon, about a hand's width apart.

"Warships were armed with a battery of Cannons ranging from as few as six to as many as a few dozen. The sides of the warships were lined with ports, and each Cannon was rolled into position so that its barrel stuck out through a port. Typically, every six Cannons had a Synthesizer assigned to them, and the Cannons under a given Synthesizer's command all had the same hole design. The Synthesizer had a two-pronged dragon bone key that fit into the holes. Between each hole," Devin said, pointing to the space between the key holes, "is a solid piece of iron dividing the ball chamber from the Power Cell. The key is used to connect the two chambers. With the Power Cell and the ball chamber connected with a key, the Synthesizer would use bursts of Energy to send the lead balls flying out the portholes, destroying whatever stood in their path."

"That's amazing!" Javen said. He'd never heard of anything like it before. The very thought of such a device was almost as unbelievable as the existence of dragons. "Have you ever seen one in action?"

"I have," Devin said. "I served in many capacities during the war, including at one point as the commander of a whole fleet of warships." Devin paused, and let Javen walk around the Cannon. Javen examined it closely, running his hands over it. "As I'm sure you are aware, the existence of such relics is unknown to the rest of the world. Even the crew of this ship doesn't know what's in this crate. And they know that if they poke their noses around, it will cost them their life. Other than myself and my wife, you are the only one on this ship who knows this Cannon exists."

"What are you trying to say?" Javen said.

"I'm sharing this knowledge with you as a token, if you will, of our willingness to accept you into the Regency. And of our hopes that, when the time comes, you will profess your complete loyalty to His Blessed Highness."

Javen thought about what Devin had said. If he wished to continue exploring this new level of existence, he knew he would have to choose one of two paths to follow.

He was still having a hard time believing his father had been a rebel—someone he had grown up being taught to deride. He had been young when his parents died; he couldn't remember them. Everything he knew about them was what his Aunt Selena and the other residents of Lonely Oak, like Deborah Browning, had taught him. But his aunt and Deborah had both turned out to be rebels as well, so he doubted whether anything he thought he knew about them was true. *Can I trust anything Selena taught us?* And now Yolken was mixed up with the same group.

Javen was familiar with the hushed nighttime conversations over tankards of ale in the pubs—there were those who believed the emperor was the true usurper and that the Order represented the true ruler. Sure, there were those who hated the Regency— old Relan came to mind—but everyone he knew who felt that way was either drunk or not right in the head. He had never agreed with any of them when they tried to drag him into their conversations; the Regency were the Blessed of the Dragon, after all.

No, Javen decided, he would not follow in his father's footsteps and risk meeting his father's fate. *He was responsible for getting my mother killed, too.* He resolved at that moment not to make the same mistake.

"Drenan spoke truthfully about my brother as well?" Javen already resented Yolken for so many things—among them, for winning Kaylan's heart. If he was mixed up with the Order now…

"You heard your aunt, did you not?" Devin said. "Dorlan filled me in on Drenan's report about the conflict in the tavern. He said your aunt swore that your brother was safe in the arms of the Order and out of the grasp of the Regency. We have no reason to think that he is not still in their clutches, or that it is not exactly as he wishes it to be."

"If I swear allegiance to the emperor, that would mean that the Order would be my enemy?"

"Yes. The Regency has strived for centuries to quell the last vestiges of the Dragon King's tyranny."

And if Yolken is one of them, then he will be my enemy as well, Javen thought. As he gazed down at the mysterious Machine and thought about it, he realized that nothing would really change. In a way, Yolken had always been an enemy of sorts. He had never thought this growing up, but now, looking back, he could see that they had always been at odds on so many things. To make it worse, their aunt had usually sided with Yolken in disputes, leaving Javen feeling less important or significant. It was always him against them. "For once," Javen murmured, "I'm in the right."

"Pardon?"

"I just realized," Javen said, patting the cold iron barrel of the Cannon, "that for once I'm the one in the right."

At that moment, Javen knew he was making the right decision. When the time came, he would swear his allegiance to the emperor. Then he would take revenge against the Order for killing his parents. He hoped that, before the time came, Yolken would realize that for once he'd made the wrong choice.

CHAPTER 9

The boat lurched, and Javen had to grip the crate to stop himself from falling. White-knuckled, he remained frozen in place as the roiling continued. He stared at the Cannon within its crate; it didn't move, even as he swayed left and right.

"Help me replace the lid," Devin said.

Javen lifted his eyes from the Cannon and looked at Devin, who seemed unaffected by the motion of the ship. He loosened his grip on the crate and quickly transferred his hands to the lid that leaned against it. He tried his hardest not to stumble, though he was having difficulty. Devin stood sure-footed, waiting for him to pick up his end. As soon as he stopped feeling like he was about to fall over, he lifted, and together they set the heavy lid back in place. He leaned on the crate, holding himself steady, as Devin replaced the locks.

"Come," Devin said when he finished. He walked steadily toward the spiral staircase leading up to the deck.

As the ship rocked, water poured down through the hole, soaking Devin as he climbed the stairs. Javen had managed to take only three wobbly steps by the time Devin disappeared through the hole. As he slowly made his way past the stacks of crates and gripped the rail of the staircase, he wondered how long it would take him to get used to the ship's unsteadiness. Just as he took his first step up, cold water poured through the hole and drenched him. He shivered as he slowly climbed the stairs. When he made it back up on deck, the ship rocked violently and threw him to the ground. While Devin closed the hatch, Javen crawled toward the door leading down to their sleeping quarters and used the handle to pull himself to his feet.

When he was upright, he became aware of a loud flapping sound behind him. He turned to find that instead of being filled with wind, the large sails shook violently. The ship rocked sharply to the left and a cascade of water rushed over the side. Some of the water flowed back off the ship through holes in the railing, but as the ship rolled to the right, the remaining water streamed across the deck.

After Devin closed the hatch, he walked surefootedly back up the stairs to the aft deck. Javen followed him, keeping his hand on the wall for support. He slowly made his way up the stairs and over to Devin. Dark clouds obscured the sky to the south and west, blocking out the sun. The Energy Javen felt from the sun had been reduced to a trickle. He watched as the crew fought to position the boat and sails to better weather the sudden squall.

"The biggest danger in sailing the gap is that the weather is very unpredictable and sudden," Devin said. "More boats have gone under here than anywhere else in the world."

According to one of the many tales told by Kaylan's uncle Jorgan, the Island of Kvorga was haunted by the ghosts of dead sailors.

"Even the most seasoned sailors know their best hope is to reef the sails and wait for the storm to pass," Devin said.

Javen gripped the railing tightly as the boat heaved again. He placed a hand over his mouth, looking down as a feeling of impending sickness washed over him. The feeling slowly passed and when it did, he noticed that the wood was two different colors. Where he stood it was brown, but where Devin stood, portions of the railing was black. He removed his hand from his mouth and ran his fingers over the area where the color changed. When his fingers touched the black-colored wood, Energy beckoned to him. He abruptly let go.

Devin smiled at Javen and placed his hands on the black portion of the railing. "It's dragon bone." The wind blowing in their faces stopped, then shifted to blow equally hard from behind them, once again filling the sails with air. "We are not like most sailors, you and I. I had this dragon bone inlaid here long ago for this very reason. I cannot afford to be at the mercy of the weather." Devin reached into his coat and pulled out a pair of the odd-looking eyepieces Javen had seen soldiers—known as Watchers—wear when regents passed through Lonely Oak. Devin handed them to Javen and said, "Here, try these on. Rather than trying to explain what I'm doing it will be easier if you can see for yourself. They're called Glasses."

Javen took the Glasses from Devin and fitted them over his eyes. Everything around him—the ship, the sails, the water, the mountains—turned different shades of gray, except for a rainbow of color that flowed like a river from Devin.

"Draego's Fire," he said in amazement.

"What you're seeing is Energy flowing out of me. I'm using it to redirect the headwind around the ship then back to fill the sails."

Javen watched the stream of colors flow from Devin toward the ship's bow. In front of the ship, the flows parted and streamed around the sides of the ship. Directly to their left and right, the flows ended. Devin used a second stream to form a sort of scoop that redirected the wind forward and toward the sails.

"It's amazing!"

"You try," Devin said.

"I—"

"Don't worry, I'll help you." Devin waited until Javen placed his hand on the dragon bone then said, "Draw Energy into your Core like we practiced yesterday—as much as you feel comfortable with. Then reach out with it and trace the pattern I'm making to block the wind."

The Energy Javen held in his Core oddly felt like it was a part of him, just as Devin had said it would. He tentatively reached out with it to trace Devin's flows, though his tendrils were minuscule by comparison. "I can't possibly do what you're doing."

"I have centuries of experience," Devin said. "Strength will come with time."

Javen gritted his teeth and with determination, drew as much Energy from the dragon bone as he could. It took him a while to get used to manipulating the Energy the way Devin was, but he eventually had a grasp on it. He mimicked Devin's work, albeit on a much smaller scale.

Rain pummeled the deck of the ship, but it didn't stop Javen from grinning. He knew he had a lot of work ahead of him if he wanted to be as skilled a Synthesizer as Devin. Yolken had often accused him of being lazy, and maybe he was. But that was just because he'd never really been interested in tending the bar or learning how to brew ale. But this... For the first time in as long as he could remember, he was looking forward to hard work.

CHAPTER 10

The next morning met Javen with even more soreness than the day before. He'd mimicked Devin's streams until the squall passed—and even attempted a second stream to make the scoops that redirected the air forward—and it had left him weak and tired. He'd wearily made his way back to his room, stripped off his wet clothes, and climbed into bed, falling asleep the moment he closed his eyes.

When he woke the next day, it was already light out—a common occurrence for him. But he knew he wouldn't get a tongue lashing from Yolken or his aunt this time. This time he deserved to sleep in past sunrise.

Javen sat up and found that his clothes weren't on the ground where he'd left them. Rather, he discovered when he opened the armoire, they were dry and hanging with the others. He looked at the door, but he'd been so tired when he stumbled in last night that he couldn't remember if he'd locked it or not. The thought of Karina coming into his room while he slept was a little unsettling, but if she had, at least she'd left him alone and let him sleep. He dressed himself, then went in search of food.

He walked the short hallway to Devin and Karina's cabin and slowly opened the door, peering in as he pushed it open, hoping Karina wouldn't be there. He stepped into the empty room and breathed a sigh of relief when he saw that the balcony doors were closed as well. He shut the door and walked over to the table that was never without food. He picked up a plate, loaded it up, then filled a glass with water. He hurried out of the room, back to his quarters, and locked the door behind him.

He could hardly keep his eyes open while he ate, so as soon as he finished, he climbed back into bed and went back to sleep.

Javen woke to Devin shaking him. He stood over Javen, wearing his blue armor. The armor still fascinated Javen, especially now that he knew it was made of dragon scales that had been fashioned to resemble a chiseled torso.

"We're arriving in Onta," Devin said. "Come, you don't want to miss it."

Javen rubbed his eyes and sat up.

"Don the suit in the armoire and meet us on the quarterdeck," Devin said as he walked to the door.

Javen stared after him, wondering what good it was to have a lock on the door if Devin had a key. Then he wondered if Karina had access to that key, and whether it was in fact her who had come in while he was sleeping.

He groaned as he stood, his body aching all over, and opened the armoire's doors. A finely tailored suit now hung next to the other clothing; it hadn't been there before. It matched the color of Devin's armor. Javen ran his fingers over the fine material. It was nicer than anything he had ever worn in his life. He put it on and went to join Devin.

On the main deck, Javen saw that they were sailing between a narrow inlet, flanked on either side by tall towers made from gleaming white marble. There were soldiers wearing gray armor in unevenly spaced openings going up the towers, as well as along parapets at the top.

He continued up to the quarterdeck and found Devin by the railing with the inlaid dragon bone. Karina was at his side. He glimpsed the curve of her right breast through the deep cut in her revealing blue dress. She winked at him and he quickly averted his eyes.

"Welcome to Onta," Devin said, gesturing with his arm toward the front of the ship.

The ship entered a large bay that stretched to the left and right. Other boats and ships sailed in the opposite direction, toward the sea, making a wide berth around them. A city stood in the distance, gleaming as white as the towers they had just passed. The ivory buildings were surrounded by a white wall, and in the middle of it all, a tall spire rose high into the sky. Javen had seen paintings of what some considered the most beautiful city in the empire, but none of them had come close to expressing Onta's true beauty.

Javen stared, enraptured, as the ship crossed the bay. As Onta drew near, he couldn't help but notice the decrepit buildings—made of wood and brick—crammed between the white wall and the water's edge. The sight detracted from Onta's beauty. As they drew closer to the dock, the spire slowly disappeared from view behind the wall, leaving Javen wondering at the stark contrast between the buildings inside the wall and those without.

The ship glided up to the long, stone dock, which was crowded with a throng of people. Sailors tossed ropes down to dockworkers, who used the ropes to guide the ship to its final resting point. When the ship came to a stop, another sailor opened a gate mid-ship and two dockworkers moved a wooden ramp into place. The crowd parted and dozens of armored men moved toward the ship; they formed two columns, resulting in a clear path through the crowd. When the soldiers were in place, a carriage pulled by two horses made its way toward the dock.

Hand in hand, Devin and Karina made their way toward the stairs to their left. Javen followed behind. Devin and Karina stopped at the top of the stairs and the crowd below erupted in cheers and fell to their knees. Devin continued down the stairs, but Karina held back. She took Javen by the hand, then followed her husband.

Am I hers to parade around? Javen wondered. From Hadie's books, he knew enough about Karina to know that by time they arrived at the palace he would probably be the talk of the city. Everyone would be wondering who the man with their beloved Karina might be.

They followed Devin down the gangplank. Devin paused at the bottom as he was greeted by a soldier, who bore an emblem resembling a cluster of grapes on the upper right side of the large oval plate covering his chest and stomach. The soldier opened the door of the carriage and held it while the three of them climbed in.

The carriage was much smaller than the ones they used to travel from Lonely Oak to Portstown. It was just big enough to sit four people on cushioned seats—two on each side, facing each other. It was colorfully decorated on the inside, bearing the carved vine and grape insignia of the Regent of Onta. Devin took the back seat, and Karina sat opposite him. Clasping Javen's hand even as he climbed into the carriage, she pulled him down on the seat next to her. Only when he sat next to her did she finally let go.

Karina pulled a tall, thin, crystal glass of wine out of a holder built into the side of the carriage. She handed it to Devin, then retrieved two more, one for herself and one for Javen. There was also a spot large enough to keep an open bottle of wine. Javen took a sip of wine, noticing that the crystal was etched with the same grape clusters that adorned everything.

The carriage lurched into motion. Javen looked out the window while he sipped his wine. The people who gathered behind the line of soldiers on the dock resembled the buildings packed outside the city wall—most of them looked run-down. They were sun-darkened, and for many of them, their teeth were either missing or black with rot. Children squatted low to the ground and peered up at the passing carriage through the soldiers' legs.

The carriage left the dock and proceeded down a road. The carriage slowed when they approached the base of the wall and Javen noticed a large group of people huddled together on the side of the road in a vacant lot. He leaned his head toward the window to get a better view. Many of them were laying on mats. Some were missing limbs—some only missing one, others more. Others had crooked legs, reminding him of Issa. Most of them had open sores covering their skin. Unlike the crowd at the dock who had shouted praises and cheers for the regent, this group pleaded for mercies. With a pang, Javen thought of the huddled group in the lobby of the Oak the night Dorlan had stayed in Lonely Oak, and how he had stopped to heal Issa.

A bearded man wearing a ragged cloak, squatting at the back of the group, caught Javen's attention. They briefly locked eyes, but then the man looked down and the hood hid his face.

The road made a sharp turn to the left, then followed along the base of the wall. Javen looked out the other window, past Karina, at the run-down buildings.

Karina placed her hand on his thigh and said, "You're going to love Onta."

Javen's gaze shifted back to Karina. She smiled and, with her other hand, traced the visible portions of her breasts in the deep cut of her dress. Javen blushed and looked over at Devin, who was focused intently on a stack of parchments he held with one hand while sipping wine from the glass in his other. Javen shifted his leg uncomfortably, causing Karina to remove her hand, then looked back out his own window.

The carriage followed the base of the wall until it arrived at a large gate. Javen craned his neck to look at the tall tower. The gate was open, but two rows of armored men guarded the entrance. Most of them wore gray armor, but there were also two men whose armor was blue and a woman wearing violet—regents.

The guards parted to admit the carriage. On the other side of the gate, the street widened as it proceeded into the city proper. The people lining the street here looked considerably better-dressed and in better general health than those outside the gate. No soldiers were present to keep them at bay.

Javen watched with great interest as the white-marble buildings passed by. They grew larger the farther they moved into the city. It was hard for him to believe that the entire city was made of marble when he lived his whole life in Lonely Oak, which resembled the buildings outside the wall.

They rode along for a while in silence. Devin studied his parchments and Karina drank her wine while Javen absorbed the sights of the unfamiliar city. When he finished his wine, Karina filled his glass anew.

"Will I get to meet Reago?" Javen asked.

"You will," Devin said. "Though the chancellor's company is not nearly as pleasant as ours."

"Is that why you and Karina are so much better-known?"

"What do you mean?"

"I mean, he's the Chancellor of the Western Realm, but all the stories I've heard are about you two."

Devin snorted behind his glass.

Karina placed her hand back on Javen's thigh and said, "What stories have you heard?"

"Well… I don't know… it's just… everyone knows who you are."

"It's true that it is Devin and myself whom our subjects adore."

"If we're going to be honest, love, it's you they adore," Devin said without looking up from what he was reading.

"He's being modest," Karina said, giving Javen's leg a rub. He was beginning to feel as though his face was as red as his wine. "The west loves you, dear."

"Doesn't that bother Reago?" Javen said.

"He quit caring long ago," Devin said.

"Why?"

"Who knows why my uncle is the way he is? He has been the subject of both curiosity and ridicule for some time now."

Huh, Javen thought, taking a drink of wine.

After passing several more cross streets, the carriage entered a large roundabout. They circled around a tall bronze statue and stopped in front of the palace. Javen peered out the window and up at the palace with awe. The center of the building, which was the base of the spire, extended out toward them in a half circle. Two rectangular wings, each with dozens of windows and balconies, extended from both sides of the spire. He craned his neck to look up at the tall spire rising high above the immense building; from inside the carriage, he could barely see the top of it.

A soldier opened the carriage door. Devin stepped out first, followed by Karina. Standing on the carriage step, she held her hand out for Javen. He took it, reluctantly, then followed her out.

Two rows of soldiers again formed a safe path to the entrance of the palace, one standing on each step. The steps were wide, requiring an extra stride on each before stepping up to the next.

They went through the enormous entrance and Javen stopped to take in the huge atrium. There were marble benches throughout the open room and six large doors on the far side. But what really drew Javen's attention was the large spiraling staircase. It started on the left side of the atrium and hugged the wall as it spiraled around the cavernous entry room. He walked to the center of the room so he could follow the stairs as they climbed. His steps echoed around him. Turning in a slow circle, he followed the curve of the stairs completely around the building. They continued to spiral repeatedly up the hollow interior of the palace, supported by huge columns at every quarter turn. Columns extended from the ground to the stairs, growing in height from left to right. The columns continued up with the staircase as the staircase spiraled higher. He counted at least a dozen floors before the stairs ended. However, the hollow inside of the spiral continued up to a dizzying height.

"Come," Karina said, joining Javen in the center of the large room.

Javen looked down at Karina when she again took him by the hand. He followed her as she led him across the atrium floor, their footsteps echoing harmoniously as they walked. He caught sight of Devin just as he disappeared through one of the doors on the opposite side of the room. The door reverberated loudly when it closed.

"That's the courtroom," Karina said. "There are a handful of emissaries who require his immediate attention, and then he'll be up to join us for dinner."

They started up the stairs. Javen glided his hand along the smooth stone railing as they circled the building. Still sore from Synthesizing with Devin the previous day, his legs began to ache.

As the stairs spiraled around the building, they arrived on a landing that led through a set of doors into the west wing. They walked across the landing, past the first of the large columns, to the stairs that continued on the opposite side. Halfway around the open atrium, they passed another landing with another set of doors leading into the east wing. With each circuit they made, the people milling around on the ground floor appeared smaller and smaller.

Javen counted their laps; after ten times around the spire, Karina turned to enter the west wing. Javen pulled his hand free from hers and looked over the rail at the ground floor far below. The immensity and magnificence of the building was mind-boggling. He peered up at the staircase and saw that it continued to spiral—there was one more floor above him on the opposite side. The stairs continued past that floor, which meant there was another floor directly above him on the west wing as well.

"That floor," Karina said, looking up at the floor opposite them, "belongs to Devin and myself. The one directly above us is Reago's. Come, let me show you your new quarters."

Karina led Javen through the two large doors and into a grand hallway with widely spaced wooden doors on both sides. Marble statues lined the spaces between the doors. As they made their way down the long hallway, Javen noticed that all the statues were of the same two people. After passing the fourth statue, he noticed a pattern. He stopped and looked back at the statues they had already passed. The man and woman started out standing alone. In the next set, they were closer together. By the third set, the two separate statues had become one statue with the man and woman standing close together. As they continued down the hall, the man and woman began to embrace—first with a hug and then a kiss. Then the woman began to remove the man's clothing and when he stood naked, he began to remove hers. After they both stood naked, the embraces became more intimate. The farther Javen walked down the hall, the more embarrassed he became.

After passing a statue where the man stood closely behind the woman with his hands covering her breasts, Karina stopped. She knocked on a door and waited. A female servant opened it, wearing nothing but a small wrap around her waist and sandals. The sight of her bare chest naturally drew Javen's eyes, but he quickly looked up at her face, embarrassed. She had brown eyes, a small nose, and full lips. Raven black hair curled down her back.

"This is Master Javen," Karina said to the scantily clad woman. "He is your new master. See that he wants for nothing."

"Yes, Your Ladyship," the woman said.

"In fact," Karina said, placing a thumb under her chin and

an index finger over her lips as if deep in thought, "just as soon as he has settled in, send Lannary up."

"Yes, Your Ladyship," the servant said again.

"Oshie here will see that you get settled," Karina said to Javen. "I'll come check on you later to see how you're doing and whether or not you found Lannary acceptable. Don't worry if she's not—I've got plenty of women in mind who might suit you." Karina kissed Javen on the lips and turned to leave.

Javen stared after Karina until the statue of the couple closest to his new quarters blocked her from view. Then he followed Oshie into his room.

"This is your sitting room, Master Javen," Oshie said.

The room had two couches and a few plush chairs. There was a hearth on one side and a long table on the other with several ewers, glasses, and decanters on it.

"Would you care for some wine?"

"Sure," Javen said.

Oshie sauntered over to the table. "What kind would you prefer?"

"Um… I don't know."

Oshie poured Javen a glass and handed it to him. "Here. This red is one of Karina's favorites."

"Thanks," Javen said, taking the glass. He took a sip and found that it was the same wine they'd been drinking in the carriage.

"The decanters are always full and rotated daily with wines from around the province."

With glass in hand, Javen looked the room over. Carved statues similar to those in the hallway occupied each corner of the room—three women and one man. The man appeared to stand aloof, unaware of the three women attempting to win his attention, each in her own way.

"This is primarily where you will entertain your guests," Oshie said.

Javen looked over at her. He immediately regretted it when his eyes went directly to her breasts.

Oshie noticed his struggle to avert his eyes and said, "It's all right, Master Javen. I'm not here simply to serve you. While you are a guest here, I am yours... completely. If you wish to look at me, you may. If you wish to touch me, you may. If you wish—"

"I get it, I get it," Javen said, holding up his hand.

"This floor and several of the floors below us are guest quarters for regents from around the realm and other emissaries visiting the capital," Oshie continued. "Should you wish to entertain any of them, you are free to do so. It is my responsibility to ensure that you are well-provisioned at all times. May I show you the rest of your quarters?"

Javen nodded. "Please."

Oshie stepped in front of him and walked toward the doors on the far side of the room. As she walked, he looked at her more closely. Her smooth skin was much darker than his, similar to Karina's. He guessed she was about his age or younger. Her black curls stopped halfway down her back. The sheerness of the wrap she wore around her waist permitted him to see the way her backside muscles flexed and relaxed as she walked.

A large table with a dozen finely carved wooden chairs, made from Kvorgan spruce, occupied the next room. The same four people stood in the corners of this room, only now the women had the full attention of the man.

"Your dining room," Oshie said.

She made her way around the table and opened the second set of doors. Javen followed her into the bedroom. There was a large four-poster bed against the wall to his right and an armoire to his left. Everything was immaculate and covered in the grapevine motif. A tub sat in the back left corner, steam rising from it. Javen blushed when he saw the single statue in the corner by the tub. The women, now fully naked, crowded around the man.

"Do you desire a bath?" Oshie asked.

Having spent the last several days on a boat where bathing had consisted of wiping himself down with a warm cloth, Javen desired a good scrub-down, so he nodded. He walked over to the vine-decorated armoire, removing his suit jacket on the way. He opened the armoire and sifted through the clothes hanging inside, looking for a free hanger. Finding one, he hung the jacket, then started to unbutton his shirt. He glanced over his shoulder and saw that Oshie was watching him intently.

"Yes, Master Javen?"

"Were you going to leave?"

"No, Master Javen. I am here to serve."

"Uh…" It was awkward enough for him being around her while she was mostly naked; he didn't know if he could undress in front of her.

Seeing his hesitation, Oshie said, "Would it please you if I turned around until you're in the tub?"

"Please, if you don't mind."

When Oshie turned around, Javen continued removing his shirt and pants, hanging them both in the armoire. He then removed his smallclothes and hurried over to the tub. He climbed into the nearly scalding water. He had hoped to hide his nakedness quickly, but instead, he had to slowly ease himself in.

Somehow, Oshie knew he was in, and she turned and walked over to the tub. With each step she took toward Javen, the more acutely he became aware of the fact that he was naked. He didn't know how she could walk around bare-chested as though it were perfectly normal. He put his hands in the clear water in an attempt to hide himself from the approaching woman.

"You aren't from the west, are you?" Oshie said when she arrived at the side of the tub.

"Why do you ask?" Javen said nervously.

"No reason," Oshie said with a giggle. She picked up a pitcher, knelt beside the tub, and began to dump water on

Javen's head. When his hair was sufficiently wet, she lathered her hands with soap, then scrubbed his head. After she rinsed his hair, she set to work scrubbing his back, arms, and chest. When she finished, she asked him to raise his arms so she could wash underneath. Javen felt exposed when he held his arms up, but Oshie didn't seem to pay any mind to that which he had been concealing.

When she finished rinsing under his arms she said, "Ahem."

Javen looked over at her. "What?"

She looked from his eyes down to the water and back. "You're only half clean, Master Javen."

He felt his face go flush. "I…"

"You will want to ensure you're fully clean before your guest arrives, Master Javen."

Javen hesitated, but then gave in. He slowly stood in the tub and used his hands to cover himself.

Oshie raised an eyebrow.

"What?"

"Hands to your sides, please."

Javen stared at the half-naked woman before him, then squeezed his eyes shut. If he was going to make it through this with any modicum of decency, he could not think about the fact that the woman cleaning him was naked as well. He groaned when he felt Oshie's scrubbing hands touch him.

"You may sit," Oshie said. "I'm through."

Javen splashed back into the water.

"Remain in the tub as long as it pleases you. I'm going to go get things ready for your guest."

"Oshie," Javen said, stopping her just before she disappeared through the door leading out of the bedroom.

"Yes, Master Javen?"

"Who was it that Karina spoke of sending?"

"Lannary, Master Javen."

"Yeah—who's that?"

"Have you never read *Lovers*?"

Javen blushed. "No." Hadie had read parts to him, but he'd never read any of the books himself.

"Next to Her Ladyship, Lannary is probably the most desired woman in the entire Western Realm. She is the subject of most of the *Lovers* printed in the last ten years."

"Oh," Javen said with a tinge of hesitation.

"I see. Well, I suspect you won't be disappointed."

Javen settled back into the water when the door closed behind Oshie. The tub was big enough that, with his feet against the opposite end, he could lay with all but his head and shoulders in the water. The warm water felt good on his sore muscles. He took a deep breath and closed his eyes. He didn't want to think about Yolken, or Astora, or Hadie, or Drenan. They were problems he would deal with in their own time. Right now, all he wanted to do was focus on where he was. He was in his own personal quarters in a beautiful palace in a beautiful city. And instead of catering to Yolken's needs, he had a beautiful servant who would be catering to his.

Javen let his mind wander until the water was no longer warm, at which point he stepped out, dried off, and wrapped himself in a thin robe Oshie had laid out for him. Figuring the view of the city had to be amazing from up where he was, he made his way out onto the balcony.

There were walls on both sides that blocked the view of the other balconies on his floor. However, over the top of the wall to the left, he could just make out the highest balcony on the opposite wing. *Devin and Karina's.* He stepped back a few feet and their balcony came into full view. It extended the length of the building and looked as though it wrapped around the side. Overhead, Reago's looked to do the same.

Javen made his way to the end of the balcony and peered over the waist-high wall. The view was just as he had imagined it would be. The city stretched out below, the buildings looking much smaller from this height. Past the wall, he could make out the tops of some of the bigger ships, and beyond that was a breathtaking view of the Onta bay. He rested his forearms on the top of the wall and absorbed the view, watching as boats and ships sailed in both directions. It became even more amazing as the sun began to set. It seemed to grow as it hovered over the horizon, and its color darkened, turning almost red.

The sound of someone clearing their throat made Javen turn around. He looked the balcony over, but didn't see anyone. He hadn't paid much attention to the balcony when he'd first walked out, but now he noticed that there were four lounge chairs, two on either side of the balcony, separated by large potted plants. Protruding from behind the plant on the left, Javen saw two bare legs, light cream in color. They rested one on top of the other, and were crossed at the ankles. He walked toward the lounge chair until the person concealed by the large plant came into view. With each step he took, more of a woman was revealed— and her legs were not the only part of her that was bare.

"You must be Master Javen," the naked woman said when Javen stopped in front of her.

Javen looked down at a woman whose beauty rivaled that of Karina. He tried not to stare, but couldn't help himself. She was laying on her side, propping her head up with an arm. The curve of her body from her head to her hips and on down her legs to her toes resembled the rolling hills surrounding Lonely Oak. She had long, flowing blonde hair that cascaded over her shoulder and partially obscured her heavy breasts.

"I am," he said.

"I'm Lannary," the woman said, extending her other hand out. The sultriness of her voice threatened to demolish Javen's inhibitions.

He stepped forward, took her hand in his, and kissed it lightly.

"It's a pleasure," he said.

"It will be," Lannary said. She gave Javen's hand a tug and pulled him down onto the chair. She sat up and kissed him deeply.

Javen pulled back, for some reason resisting her advances. Ever since he woke on Devin's ship he'd felt as though he was being emotionally torn in several directions. What Drenan did to Astora pulled him one direction, invoking in him dark thoughts of revenge. Yolken and Selena's betrayal pulled him in another direction, one of anger that left him wanting to scream and throw things about. And then there was his conflicting feelings for Hadie and Kaylan. He loved Kaylan but couldn't keep himself from thinking about Hadie. And then there was Karina. She was complicating things in a completely different—foreign—way.

"What is it?" Lannary cooed.

Javen looked into Lannary's blue eyes. He ran his fingers through her hair, brushing it back behind her shoulder. He studied her, realizing she was none of those feelings. She represented… an escape.

"Nothing," Javen said. He leaned forward and kissed her again. This time, uninhibited.

After a minute, Lannary broke off the kiss and pushed Javen back onto the chair. As she climbed on top of him and untied his robe, he noticed out of the corner of his eye that someone was standing on Devin and Karina's balcony. He looked past Lannary and saw Karina looking down at them. From this distance, he could just make out the smile on her face. Javen returned her smile, then turned his attention to the woman kissing his chest.

CHAPTER 11

Yolken made his way down the stairs to the main level of the
two-story house. He was surprised to find that his body
ached only slightly from the last day and a half of heavy
Synthesizing. The conditioning Jax put him through seemed to
have paid off in acclimating his body. When he reached the
bottom, he found Jax and Deborah already sitting at the table in
the kitchen at the far end of the house. It looked as though they
had just finished eating.

Jax's appearance took Yolken by surprise. Instead of the
traveling clothes and familiar leather coat he was never without,
Jax was wearing a finely tailored dark green suit. A round
brimmed hat, matching his suit, sat on the table next to his
empty plate.

"Late night?" Jax said.

"Kind of," Yolken said, fighting back a yawn.

"Not doing anything unbecoming, I hope."

"No," he said, feeling himself blush. "We stayed up talking,
is all."

"Leave him be," Deborah said. "You were young and in love
once yourself, Jax. Plates are in the cabinet, dear."

Yolken retrieved a ceramic plate covered in flower acrylics

and filled it with eggs and fresh bread from the stove. He was happy to be back in Deborah's presence, where there was always fresh bread. Deborah poured him a cup of tea as he took his seat at the table with her and Jax.

"You look like a Suit," Yolken said to Jax. Brall was the only person in Lonely Oak he'd ever seen dressed so finely.

"One must dress according to one's status within society."

"Which is what? I mean, besides the mysterious never-without-your-leather-coat wanderer?"

"Have you so quickly forgotten Kaylan's uncle, Jorgan?"

"You never wore anything like that when you were in Lonely Oak," Yolken said.

"That's because I would never wear them on such a long and dusty road. Clothing this fine is not meant for traveling."

"So what's Jorgan's place in society?"

"He is an esteemed businessman."

"What's your business?"

"I move the most valuable of products," Jax said. "Information."

"So you're a courier. How does that make you esteemed?"

"Well, first off, 'tis a vast empire, and information certainly doesn't move itself, so somebody has to do it. And I don't just move any information. I move information of particular value."

"We should probably discuss today," Deborah said, interrupting their banter. "What are we going to do about getting a meeting with the Council? They're not expecting you for at least another month."

"I'm going to go speak with Enif," Jax said. "When he finds out we're in the city, I'm sure he will convene the Council."

"Who's Enif?" Yolken said over his cup of tea.

"He's the High Councilman," Deborah said.

"What does that mean?"

"It means he is the highest-ranking member of the Council, and the leader of the Order," Jax said. "In total, there are nine members on the Council, each representing one of the children who remained loyal to Draeko. The Council makes all the decisions concerning the operation and direction of the Order. Every member gets a vote on the issues that come before them—such as the request you will make for help finding your brother. Try to keep in mind that even though every member will have a vote in the course of action to be taken—including our continued involvement—Enif is the one to convince."

"What do you mean your 'continued involvement'?" Yolken said.

"Deborah and I are members of the Order; our actions are dictated by the Council, just like everyone else."

"You're saying they may not let you help me anymore?"

"Correct."

"But you two are the only people I know here! What am I supposed to do if they send you off on some other errand?"

"I doubt it will come to that, dear," Deborah said.

"How do you know?"

"Because they are reasonable, that's why."

"What we do is not without risk, Yolken," Jax said. "The Council may very well order us elsewhere. It's your job to convince them otherwise—specifically, to convince Enif. His vote carries no more weight than the others'; however, his influence often affects how the others vote as well."

"All right," Yolken said, feeling horribly unprepared for the task before him. "Who are the other Council members?"

"Each member has a specific seat at the Council Table," Deborah said. "Enif sits in the center. You will be able to identify them based on where they sit. From your left to right their names are: Tabora Alon, Corin Foler, Dannl Kand, Rheena Drew, Enif Maldon, Aleena Harrin, Jerle Sage, Onig Frell, and Sherya Mernn."

Yolken forgot the names just as fast as Deborah was saying them. "How am I supposed to remember all those names?"

"No one expects you to, dear. They will understand that you are one and they are many. If they ask you questions, simply answer them. They know who they are, and for the most part are not so conceited as to need constant reminding."

"And these people will decide whether to help me rescue Javen or not?"

"They are our leaders," Deborah said.

"So that gives them the right to decide the fate of other people?" Yolken said. "How is that any different than the Regency?"

"The Order is designed to *prevent* it from being like the Regency," Jax said.

"But how are they different, if a few individuals can decide the fate of another?"

"Because Drakonias' rule is eternal. There is no choice. He is the emperor and always will be. He chose the chancellors and appointed the regents of each province without anyone getting a say in things. Unlike the Regency, the members of the Order get to choose our leaders."

The concept sounded foreign to Yolken. "I've never heard of such a thing."

"Of course you wouldn't have," Jax said. "The Regency isn't run that way. I won't go into the details, but every ten years the members of the Order get to pick who will sit on the Council for the next ten years."

"So there are new leaders every ten years?"

"Well… no. The system is not without its downfalls."

"What do you mean?"

"Unfortunately it has become customary to choose the most experienced members. So, most of the time, the same individuals get chosen."

"How is it any different from the Regency if the same people are always chosen?"

"The system is not perfect, and even though some members

have gained extraordinary influence—such as Enif—it's still better than Drakonias' Regency."

"How do you become the High Councilman?"

"Of those chosen to sit on the Council, the eldest becomes the High Councilman. For over a century, that has been Enif."

Yolken was beginning to wonder if there was any point in seeking help from the Order. "I fail to see how this is any different," he said.

"It's different because if a member proves unworthy of their post, they risk never being chosen to lead again."

"Has that ever happened?"

"It has."

"Hmm," Yolken said.

"And the only one instance of such a thing ever happening in the Regency is when Drakonias removed his son from a chancellorship—by murdering him."

Yolken's eyes widened in disbelief.

"I don't know why that surprises you, Yolken," Jax said. "Millions died as a direct result of choices Drakonias made—including the entire species of dragon."

"It's just—how could someone kill their own son? What kind of person—"

"The same type of person who was willing to kill their own father. As we continue to hunt for Javen, you must always remember the depravity the Regency is capable of. Let us hope that the Council agrees to help."

"Did my father ever serve on the Council?"

"He was chosen several times," Jax said. "But each time he refused."

"Why?"

"Because of your father's unusual strength and abilities with Synthesis, he believed that he could best achieve the goals of the Order not by telling others what to do, but by doing."

"It was very honorable of him, Yolken," Deborah said.

"Serving on the Council garners much respect from the other members of the Order, but your father managed to achieve much greater respect than all the Council members combined—much to the chagrin of many of them. It's funny how often new members of the Council succumb to their newfound positions of authority and believe that simple fact requires that they be respected. It didn't sit well with them when the Order respected your father more than them. They forgot that respect must be earned. Most of them came around to this. Those who couldn't, didn't last long on the Council. Now, finish your breakfast."

Jax pushed his chair back and rose to his feet. He donned the round hat and said, "All right, if there's to be any hope of convening the Council today, I must be off."

"How long will you be gone?" Yolken said.

"Couple of hours at most."

"Last night Kaylan talked about taking me out and showing me around a little."

"Not yet," Jax said. "Let me assess our risk first. Croff is teeming with Dalia's guards and Watchers. And, as far as we know, they haven't given up looking for you."

"Wouldn't Deborah know if they were looking for me?" Yolken said, turning to Deborah for help.

"I haven't heard anything," Deborah said.

"My answer is still no," Jax said. "I want to look into it myself. Just sit tight here; I'll be back soon."

Yolken wanted to object more, but Jax walked quickly to the door, not giving him the chance.

"What are we supposed to do now?" Yolken said, looking questioningly at Deborah.

"Well, you need to finish eating and I need to go to the market. Then just try to relax and enjoy some time catching up with Kaylan—assuming she ever wakes up. I swear, if you let her, she'll sleep longer than a bear in hibernation."

Yolken chuckled at the thought.

"I'll be back soon. Kaylan knows her way around the house. Have her show you the library if you'd like something to read."

Yolken had a mouthful of bread, so he just nodded.

Deborah grabbed a large burlap sack hanging on the back wall of the kitchen and left.

When Yolken's plate was empty, he went back to the stove and got seconds. When finished, he washed his plate and cup in the porcelain sink. He turned from the sink and stood for a moment in the kitchen, alone. He looked up at the ceiling as if he could see through it and the floor that separated him from Kaylan. Then he walked the length of the house, climbed the steps three at a time, and stopped at the first door on the right. He turned the knob quietly and gently cracked the door open.

Kaylan was still asleep, buried under a blanket. He snuck in, wriggled himself under the blanket, and snuggled up to her. She didn't wake, so he nibbled gently on her ear. That made her head turn toward him. "I don't think Mammy would approve of your being in my room," she said softly.

Yolken kissed her neck and shoulder. Between kisses he said, "She went… to the… market." He used the tips of his fingers to gently rub her shoulder, down her arm, and back up to her shoulder again, causing skin prickles to spring up on her flesh. Then he slowly began to feel his way lightly down her side, stopping as his hand crested her hip. He moved his hand back up slightly, then wrapped his arm around her stomach and squeezed her body tightly against his.

"Mmm," Kaylan said.

"Can I bring you something to eat?"

"Tea would be nice."

Yolken eased his arm from around her stomach and traced his fingers down to her hip again. This time he continued up and over her hip and squeezed her bottom before rolling off the bed as Kaylan exclaimed, "Hey!" and turned to swat him away.

He went back down to the kitchen and returned with a cup

of tea, which the kettle had kept nice and hot. This time he climbed the steps slower so the tea wouldn't slosh. When he entered her room again, she was sitting up in bed, pulling her hair into a tail behind her head. He looked longingly at her as her light nightgown clung to the curves of her body.

"What?" Kaylan said.

"Nothing," Yolken said. He set the cup and saucer on the small wooden table beside her bed.

"That wasn't nothing. Why were you looking at me like that?"

"Like what?"

"Like you wanted to—"

"Here," Yolken said, handing her the cup. After she had a few sips, he said, "What should we do while we wait for your mother and Jax to return?"

"I could show you around a little."

"Jax said he doesn't want me to leave the house. At least not until he can 'assess the risk.'"

"Well that doesn't leave many options, then."

"Your mother suggested you show me the library, but I'm not really interested in reading. I'm too anxious to concentrate on anything right now."

"What do you have to be anxious about?"

"I don't know. I guess I'm afraid."

"I don't think you have to be afraid, Yolken. You haven't done anything wrong."

"I know."

"What is it then?"

"What if they aren't willing to help? Jax keeps pressing the point that it's my job to convince them."

"I'm sure they'll help. Whatever it is you have to do to convince them, I'm sure you will do just fine," she said. "So, if you don't want to read, what *would* you like to do?"

"I don't know. We could just stay here."

"In bed?"

"Yeah." Yolken took the cup from Kaylan, set it back on the plate, then kissed her.

Kaylan engaged him, closing her eyes as he began to explore her body again with his hands. "Yolken," she said, breaking off the kiss.

"Yeah?"

"I'm hungry."

He groaned. "I'll be right back." He kissed her lightly on the lips then disappeared through the door a second time. He returned as quickly as he could with a plate piled with eggs and bread.

He lay down next to Kaylan while he waited for her to eat. As he looked up at the ceiling, his eyes began to grow heavy. He rolled onto his side, supported his head with his arm, and watched Kaylan. But his eyelids felt heavier by the second. Before he realized it, he was asleep.

CHAPTER 12

Yolken woke to a soft hand caressing his cheek. He opened his eyes to find Kaylan lying on the bed next to him.

"Jax has returned," Kaylan said.

Yolken sat up on the bed and said, "What happened?"

"You fell asleep."

"I guess the journey took more out of me than I thought." He noticed that Kaylan was now dressed in a dark blue, knee-length dress, cinched at her waist. Her hair was in a complex five- or six-strand braid. He couldn't even begin to imagine how she might have accomplished that. "You look really nice."

"Thank you," Kaylan said, blushing.

"How long have I been asleep?"

"Almost two hours. Come on, they're waiting for us downstairs."

Yolken yawned as he followed Kaylan out of the room. Jax and Deborah were waiting at the base of the stairs.

"Ready?" Jax said, shoving the bundled cloak concealing the Harachin sword into Yolken's hands.

Yolken accepted the bundle and said, "Now?" He was shocked that the meeting would be so soon.

"We have only a small window of time where the whole

Council will be in Croff. Several of them have business to attend to elsewhere and will be leaving in a few hours. Enif agreed to convene. If we don't go now, it might be at least a month before they're all present again."

Yolken didn't feel ready. And he didn't like being rushed. But he also didn't want to wait around in Croff for a whole month. He already felt like he'd lost so much time hiding up in the Mindons, so he nodded.

The group followed Jax as he led them through the city. As they walked, Yolken's nervousness grew. The city around him slowly disappeared until he felt like he was walking down a long, dark tunnel. Jax and Deborah were all he could see, and they were moving farther away. The only thing that kept him from succumbing to the darkness enveloping him was the warmth of Kaylan's hand. Then they stopped. Yolken slowly drew closer to them and watched as Jax knocked on a white door smeared with soot. A small window in the door opened and eyes peered out. Jax appeared to be conversing with the eyes but Yolken couldn't hear for the blood pounding in his ears. The window closed and they were left to wait. It seemed to take forever, like he was waiting for his brewing kettle to start boiling. Eventually, the door opened, and a stout man waved them in. Jax and Deborah stepped in and Yolken felt Kaylan's hand pull him forward.

"Yolken? Yolken!" Jax's voice echoed.

"Huh?" Yolken said.

"Are you all right?"

"Yolken, dear," Deborah said.

Yolken looked into Deborah's warm face. He felt the gentle weight of her hands on his shoulders, and the dark tunnel began to recede. He found himself standing in a warehouse.

"It's going to be okay, Yolken," Deborah said.

He nodded.

"Let's go," Jax said.

The warehouse reminded Yolken of Norin's, but on a much

grander scale. Instead of crates stacked haphazardly as they were at Norin's, the cavernous inside of this building featured rows of huge shelves.

The stout man returned to a rickety wooden seat next to the door. It creaked as he sat and Yolken wondered how it supported his weight.

Jax led them into the depths of the building, guiding them through the rows of shelves piled with goods. He stopped in front of a crate guarded by two men and identified himself. The two men grabbed hold of the crate and pulled it away from the wall, revealing a hidden staircase.

When they were all below ground level the two men covered the staircase back up. At the bottom, they entered a hallway that stretched straight ahead and to their right. It was illuminated in both directions by a series of lanterns fitted into brass sconces. Jax turned and followed the hall to the right. He stopped in front of a set of double doors.

"Kaylan and I'll wait for you down in the lounge," Deborah said.

Yolken looked at her in disbelief. "You're not coming in with me?"

"Only those specifically called to stand before the Council are permitted within the chamber," Jax said.

"But..." he said, looking at Kaylan. She looked as shocked as he was. He wanted her at his side.

"I'm sorry, dear," Deborah said. "You'll do fine. We'll be right out here."

Kaylan hugged Yolken and said, "Good luck. I love you."

"Unwrap the sword and strap it on," Jax said. "But don't touch it. They know the Harachin sword is a powerful dragon bone so you wouldn't want to give them the impression you're threatening them."

"Then why bring it at all?" Yolken asked as he strapped on the belt.

"Because it'll convey to them who you are."

Yolken looked a little confused.

"The sword will testify that you are your father's son."

"I'll take the cloak, dear," Deborah said.

Yolken handed her the cloak. Kaylan gave him one more hug, then she and Deborah walked farther down the hall until they disappeared around a corner.

"When instructed to do so, present your request," Jax said. "Then answer whatever questions they might have for you."

"All right," Yolken said. The dark tunnel threatened to return as he felt his pulse quicken. He placed his hand on the hilt of the sword and felt the pulse of Energy, a calming presence between the metal twines. Jax looked at him crossly, so he removed his hand. His nerves returned.

"No touching the sword."

"I won't."

Jax knocked on the right-hand door.

An attendant—a young girl wearing a plain white cassock—opened the door and ushered them in. She shut the door behind them and said, "Just a moment, please."

The girl crossed the room and exited through a door to the side of a curved white platform. It was about six feet tall and curved toward them in a semi-circle. Behind the platform, at the top of a dais, sat an empty chair.

Yolken followed Jax as he walked up to the platform and stopped in front of it. "What's that?" he said, pointing up to the chair.

"The Dragon Throne," Jax said. "Well, a replica, anyway. No one ever sits in it. It represents the fact that the Order does not acknowledge the rule of Drakonias. Now, as they enter, try not to be too nervous. And whatever you do, do *not* touch the sword."

"Telling me not to be nervous is like telling old Relan he can only have one," Yolken said.

Jax smirked. "Just remember that these people have the same mission your father did. They are our friends."

Yolken swallowed hard and waited. He could almost feel the Energy in the Harachin sword beckoning to him. Its presence in his Core would be a welcome relief to his nerves, but he resisted. He focused instead on the mysterious throne looming overhead.

The side door eventually opened again and individuals filed out. Yolken counted them as they stepped up onto the platform—nine. Each of them wore a yellow cassock, with a thick band of darker yellow cloth with green embroidery encircling their necks. He looked closely at the embroidery on the darker cloth as they stepped up one by one onto the platform and realized the design was of dragons.

The Order of the Dragon.

For Yolken's entire life the Order of the Dragon had always been something people whispered about over mugs of ale. Although it had never happened in Lonely Oak, it was rumored that discussing the Order could get you killed. So no one did—except occasionally old Relan, but only when he was really drunk. To Yolken, though, they'd been just stories meant to frighten children into respecting the Blessed, no different than any other story Kaylan's uncle told around the hearth. But then he had awakened one day in the cabin high up in the Mindon mountains where Kaylan's mother and uncle identified themselves as members of the Order, and suddenly the stories had become real.

Once the Council members were all in position on the platform, they all simultaneously sat. Yolken tried to remember their names, but he couldn't remember any of them other than Enif. Even after they were all seated, the waiting continued. He watched them patiently as they looked down at him. A few of them turned to each other and murmured. Enif—the bald man in the middle, his dragon embroidery brilliant gold in color— stared down at Yolken with a furrowed brow.

Yolken felt the weight of the Harachin sword tugging at his side. He clenched his fists, fighting back the desire to grip its hilt.

The furrow on Enif's brow eased, then he spoke. "Greetings, young Thornhill. My name is Enif Maldon. I am the High Councilman. It is a most unusual occurrence to admit someone unaffiliated with the Order into our headquarters. But you are Danavin's son, and Danavin was a valued member of the Order. Even so, we are bypassing layers of protection that must usually be observed before someone is permitted to speak to even one Council member, let alone the entire Council. So it goes without saying that it is with great risk that we have granted you an audience. Thankfully for you, Jax can be quite stubborn. Now, several of us have places to be, so out with it."

"Uh… thank you for seeing me," Yolken said.

Enif waved a dismissive hand. "What is so important that Jax insisted we convene?"

Yolken looked over to Jax in confusion. He'd assumed they already knew why he was here—or at least they should. Wasn't that the whole point of Deborah and Kaylan leaving the cabin—so that they could lay the groundwork with the members of the Council for getting the help he needed to rescue Javen?

"Formalities," Jax whispered. "Everyone must state their business."

Yolken turned back to the Council and said, "I need your help. My brother has been taken prisoner by—"

"Yes, yes," Enif said. "The circumstances which transpired were, admittedly, most tragic. Lael was a valuable member of the Order."

"That tavern has proven most troublesome," one of the Council members on the far right said.

Yolken looked over at her: a thin woman who wore her hair in a bun.

"Agreed," said another.

"Perhaps it was a mistake after all to keep the boys there," said yet another.

"Danavin's plans were foolish," Enif said. "And a waste of resources."

"But now he's used his gift," said a female Council member on the left, down at the end. She was pretty, Yolken thought. She wore her hair in a long braid that draped over her shoulder and down the front of her cassock. It reminded Yolken of how Kaylan typically did her hair. She also looked younger than most of the others.

"An incredible way to discover your abilities," a Council member, three to Enif's right, said. This one was a man with a mustache and a pointy goatee, and long hair hanging loose around his face.

Yolken wished he'd had the time to memorize their names. His head was spinning.

"Simple healings are troublesome enough," the man said. "But that... that was most difficult, indeed."

"Yes, incredible!"

"Agreed."

"Such skill is unheard of."

"Especially someone untrained!"

The room filled with the chatter of eight Council members. Only Enif sat quiet. He looked down at Yolken, who thought it felt ominous. His hand twitched at his side, and he wanted to take hold of the Harachin sword for comfort.

"Enough!" Enif said, his voice loud enough to overcome the chatter. He looked crossly at the men and women sitting on both sides of him. When they quieted down, he turned back to Yolken and said, "As I've already said, what happened was tragic. Unfortunately, our laws prevent us from engaging in rescue missions—especially for outsiders."

Yolken's stomach roiled like he'd drunk too many strong ales. The Harachin sword beckoned. It took every ounce of self-control to ignore the soothing Energy he knew awaited him.

"Everyone in the Order knows that to be a member comes with great risk," Enif continued. "They acknowledge this when they take their oath, and again every time they accept an assignment. It is this law—in part, along with many others—which has kept the Order safe for so long."

"What law?" Yolken said, his voice quavering.

"That the lives of other members are not to be risked rescuing a member who gets caught."

And just like that, Yolken realized he had failed. He'd never had a chance. He turned to Jax, wondering why he'd even brought him here—made him go through this—when there was a law against the very thing he was coming to request. Why even waste his time coming to Croff? He could have been out there looking for Javen himself.

Jax pointed toward the platform with a tilt of his head.

Yolken turned back to the Council, sitting above him on their elevated platform, and thought. Jax had brought him here for a reason. And he didn't think Jax would deliberately lead him astray. He'd said that he would need to convince them for help. Was there a chance they would break their own law to help him? Besides leaving empty-handed, he didn't have much to lose by finding out. He chose to be bold. He chose to ignore Jax's advice about touching the sword and what it would mean if he did. He placed his hand on the hilt of the Harachin sword and said, "Is that why you let my parents die? So that *you* would be safe?"

Enif's eyes went wide.

A few of the other Council members gasped in shock.

They're afraid of me, Yolken thought. From the corner of his eye, he saw Jax look at him, but he kept his eyes on Enif. Yolken's body began to tremble, so he tensed his muscles as best he could to stop from shaking.

"We did *not* let your parents die," Enif said. He looked warily at the sword. "Did you think if you came here and threatened us that we would lend you our help? Your father certainly knew the risks; they were his laws."

"So you left him to die. My mother, too."

Enif sighed.

Yolken could tell Enif had been agitated from the moment he had entered the chamber, and he knew his remarks were only making it worse. When he had agreed to this meeting, he probably hadn't expected Yolken to question them, let alone threaten them. He let go of the sword and fought against the urge to clench his hands into fists. He wanted to appear at ease, even though he felt like losing his meal.

"Your father," Enif said, pausing and letting out a small sigh of relief, "was the one who Synthesized that day. It was his choice to meet in Lonely Oak. It was also his choice to charge the bone there. So it was his fault that the Regency found him."

Yolken looked up at Enif, furrowing his own brow. "What are you talking about?"

"It was your father's choice to leave the Order. Unfortunately," Enif said, looking to his right, "Tabora felt we owed it to him to be present when we confirmed Detron's death."

Yolken was so confused. Who was Detron? And what did he or she have to do with his father?

"We wouldn't have known about any of it were it not for him," the woman at the end said.

At least Yolken knew one of their names now. *Tabora.*

"Which is why I agreed," Enif said.

"Reluctantly," Tabora added.

"Even so. It was his choice to do it in Lonely Oak, where we couldn't offer the same protections as here," Enif said. "And if there were Watchers in Lonely Oak that night, then they already knew where he was."

"I'm sorry for what happened to your parents, Yolken," Tabora said, her voice soft.

Yolken looked over at her. Her eyes were green, like

Kaylan's. They glistened with moisture and seemed to glow as they played off the color of the embroidery around her neck.

"I was present with your father in Lonely Oak the day Detron met its fate," she said.

Its?

"I'm positive Jax and Deborah have already told you this," she continued, "and please believe me when I say that I speak for the entire Council and every member of the Order when I say that we all grieved the death of your parents. What happened after our meeting was a tragedy. When we found out the Synod had located your father we sent Jax to warn him. We shouldn't have—"

"Because it broke Danavin's own law by putting Jax at risk," Enif said.

"But we did," Tabora said. "We owed it to Danavin. But he chose to stand his ground."

"All of this is beside the point," Enif said. "The fact is that we do not engage in rescue missions. Not for members of the Order and certainly not for outsiders."

Yolken had no idea what all that talk about Detron was about—he would have to ask Jax—but he realized he was not going to be able to use the guilt of something that had happened twenty years ago to convince them to help. He needed to shift tactics. "I know the death of my father was a tragic loss to the Order."

Enif looked down at Yolken without replying. Others on the podium shifted in their seats.

"Perhaps, then," Yolken continued, "my brother and I can be of value to the Order." He didn't yet know if he wanted to pledge his life to the Order like his father had—like Jax, Deborah, and his aunt had—but if doing so helped him rescue Javen then he would certainly be more inclined to consider it. "Perhaps the two of us can replace him."

Enif snorted. He placed a finger on his lip and tapped it

lightly. "First you attempt to intimidate us, now you barter with us?"

Yolken said nothing, instead looking hopefully at the other eight individuals seated above him.

"Jax did say he has progressed well with his training," one of the other councilmen said.

Enif removed his hand from his mouth and said, "Is the same true with your brother? Has he succeeded in using his gift?"

"I… I don't know," Yolken said. This wasn't going as he had planned. He couldn't give up, though. "Until the morning I healed Issa, neither of us had ever Synthesized."

"Well," Jax interjected, "that's not exactly true. Yolken *was* using his gift before he healed Issa; he just didn't realize it yet. So if he was using his gift, then it is possible his brother was as well."

"I don't know exactly how this works," Yolken said, "but if I'm able to use my gift, isn't there a good chance that Javen will be able to as well?"

Enif looked from Jax to Yolken. "Your value—or potential value—does not change the fact that the Order does not engage in rescue missions."

"Perhaps," Tabora interjected, "given the uniqueness of this situation, we could put his request to a vote?"

Yolken watched as Enif looked over at Tabora crossly.

"We did it for his father," she added.

"Very well," Enif said. "Let us vote as to whether we will authorize once again breaking the law of the Order of the Dragon, put members at risk, in an effort to rescue the second son of Danavin." Enif paused then issued the first vote, "Nay." He held up his arm and pointed at Tabora.

"Aye," Tabora said.

Enif proceeded from member to member, each casting their votes when it was their turn.

"Nay."

"Nay."

"Aye."

"Nay."

"Nay."

"Aye."

"Nay."

Silence hung in the air. Yolken had failed.

"By a vote of six to three," Enif said, "the Council denies your request for help."

Yolken hung his head. He couldn't convince them to budge from their position. He didn't know what else he could say—he had all but pledged himself to their cause and they'd still voted against helping him. He looked up and watched as Enif rose to his feet and stared down at Yolken. The others rose as well and began to move toward the steps at the end of the podium.

Enif's gaze shifted from Yolken to Jax.

Yolken looked over at Jax, who was staring straight ahead at Enif.

"Even though our laws prevent us from intervening, and our vote affirmed it," Enif began, causing the other members to stop and look back at him, "I believe there is someone who might be able to help you."

Yolken felt a tiny amount of hope return, and he looked up eagerly. Enif's statement had caused confused looks to wash over the faces of the other eight Council members. They seemed to be as interested in hearing what Enif had to say as he was.

"Who?" he asked.

"Go to the Island of Kvorga and find a woman named Anivera. Perhaps she can help you where we cannot."

CHAPTER 13

Yolken's head spun as he watched the Council file out of the chamber. Their business with him completed, they left without bidding him goodbye. Those he had hoped would aid him had instead left him with more questions than answers. After the last of the Council members went through the side door, Jax turned and left as well. Feeling helpless, Yolken followed.

Yolken trailed after Jax, who walked quickly down the hall in the direction Deborah and Kaylan had gone. When they stepped into the large room filled with tables and couches, he exclaimed, "The Island of Kvorga! We have to go to the *Island of Kvorga?*"

"I'm sorry, Yolken," Jax said, facing him. "We tried."

"What's this about Kvorga?" Deborah said.

Yolken looked across a table laden with meats, cheeses, and fruits at Deborah, who was sitting on a couch with someone Yolken didn't recognize. Kaylan was sitting by herself on a separate couch with a plate of food. They all rose to their feet.

"They want us to go to the Island of Kvorga!" Yolken exclaimed.

Kaylan set her plate down. "Is that where they think Javen

is?"

"No. They want me to chase a fable."

"What do you mean?" Kaylan said.

Yolken watched as Deborah and Jax exchanged a look. They seemed to be communicating something to each other. "What is it?" he said.

"What do you mean?" Jax said.

"You're looking at each other as if…" Yolken paused, then said, "as if you expected this."

"To be perfectly honest, dear," Deborah said, "this *is* pretty much what we expected."

Yolken looked between the two of them, confused—angry, even. "You expected that instead of helping me directly, they would send me halfway around the world chasing a fable?"

"What fable?" Kaylan said.

"If you already knew the Council wasn't going to help me," Yolken continued, "why did you lead me to think otherwise?"

"There was always the chance that they would make the same decision with you as they did with your father," Deborah said.

Yolken furrowed his brow. He wasn't satisfied with the outcome of the meeting, but he had no other option but to trust what Deborah said. There was nothing he could do to change the Council's decision.

"What fable?" Kaylan said again.

"They told me to find Anivera and ask her for help," Yolken said.

"The old woman?"

"They're sending him to find Anivera?" said the stranger standing next to Deborah.

"We doubted the Council would help you directly," Jax said, "but I didn't expect them to send you to Kvorga."

Yolken glared at Jax.

"And yes," Jax continued, looking at the stranger, "they have sent him to find Anivera."

"Yolken, this is Piter," Deborah said.

Yolken looked over at the man briefly. His hair was in two long braids that draped over his shoulders and onto his chest.

Deciding he didn't really care who this man might be, Yolken returned his attention to Deborah and Jax. He needed answers. "First, tell me who, or what, Detron is."

Deborah and Jax exchanged another look.

"Detron is—" Deborah started.

"Not important," Jax finished. "What's important is that the Council has provided you with a path to finding Javen."

"By chasing a fable halfway across the world?" Yolken said, exasperated.

"Yes."

"What was the point of coming here if you already knew that's what they were going to do?"

"We didn't know for sure," Deborah said.

"Right," Yolken said. He was really beginning to get irritated with them. "I had to convince the Council… my time could have been better spent if I'd just gone searching for Javen myself."

"We came here because it was the only option that provided even a sliver of hope," Jax said. "And for us to directly aid you without the consent of the Council would have been a direct violation of the oaths we made when we joined the Order. As hard as this might be to grasp, it was truly the best—the only— option available to you. Had you gone after your brother yourself, you would now be either dead or in the hands of the Regency—which is just as bad."

"So my only hope lies in a children's story?" Yolken said. It was unbelievable, really. "How is that any better?"

"Every fable is based on some—"

"—modicum of truth," Yolken finished for Jax. "I know. So you're saying there really *are* dragons on the island?"

"No."

"But Anivera is?"

"That's what the Council thinks."

"Why?"

"Because the evidence suggests as much," Jax said.

"I always thought those were just stories to scare us," Kaylan said. "I never imagined they might have been real."

"The stories themselves aren't true," Jax said.

"So let me get this straight," Yolken interjected. "The best help the Council can give me is to send me all the way to Kvorga in hopes of finding someone who they aren't even sure exists?"

"Unfortunately, yes," Jax said.

"This has to be one of the most ludicrous things I've heard!" Yolken exclaimed, throwing his hands up. "I might as well go there hoping to find dragons! Surely dragons would be willing to help." He shook his head and turned to leave. If the Council wasn't willing to help him, then he wanted nothing more to do with them. He would find Javen on his own if he had to.

"Yolken, wait," Deborah said as his hand touched the door handle. He stopped, took a deep breath, then turned to face them.

"For all we know, the stories you all heard growing up about that island may indeed be entirely fictional. We may not know whether or not Anivera exists, but we do know there's a strange power at work on the island. The unfortunate truth is that, despite the laws, the Order is too weak and spread too thin to be of any real help with Javen. And the reality is that you have nowhere else to turn. If there is even the remotest chance that you might be able to use the power that enchants Kvorga to free Javen from the clutches of the Regency, then don't you think it's worth it?"

Yolken looked from Jax to Deborah to Kaylan, and even to the stranger, Piter. He studied them and thought about how to proceed. "You all feel this is the best chance I have of finding Javen?"

"We do," Deborah said.

"Jax?"

"I do."

Yolken looked at Kaylan. Her opinion mattered the most to him. "What do you think?"

"What other choice do we have?" Kaylan said.

None. Other than going it alone, he had no other choice.

Yolken looked at Piter. "What about you? Do you think this is what I should do?"

"Deborah's filled me in on what has happened to you and your brother. Jax and Deborah have spoken truthfully. This is the best the Order has to offer. Although the last time someone attempted to locate Ani—"

"It is decided, then?" Jax interrupted. "We go to Kvorga?"

Yolken looked warily at Jax, then at Piter.

"This is truly your best option," Piter affirmed.

"Then it is decided," Jax said. "Let's go back to the house and make our preparations."

Yolken nodded his agreement. He was ready to be away from the Council and he was certainly ready for a glass of his ale. Probably several.

CHAPTER 14

And what about us?" Deborah said. "Did the Council give approval for us to continue helping Yolken?"

Yolken looked up briefly from the half-drunk cup of ale sitting before him on the table.

"They didn't say otherwise," Jax said. "So we should leave before they have a chance to."

"What's our plan, then?" Deborah said.

"We leave for Onta as quickly as possible."

"What about Yolken?"

"What about him?"

"How does he fit into our little… family?"

Jax looked at Yolken pensively. He took a drink of his ale and said, "Maybe they should marry."

Yolken hadn't been paying attention to what Jax and Deborah had been talking about since leaving the Order's headquarters. Instead, he'd been stewing over the unbelievable turn of events. "What's this?"

"We're going to be on the road for quite some time, so my thought is that since you're already in love, you should marry. That way you wouldn't have to pretend to be anybody other than who you are—newlyweds."

"Perhaps you're right," Deborah said, looking first at Kaylan—who sat next to Yolken at the table in the kitchen—with a smile, then at Yolken.

Kaylan grinned broadly at Yolken.

"Wait. What are you talking about?" Yolken said, still trying to catch up.

"Weren't you listening?" Jax said. He looked annoyed. "While we're on the road, we'll need believable stories to cover the true purpose of our trip. I can easily get past the prying noses of Regency patrols as Kaylan's uncle, and Deborah is her mother, but no one will believe that you're just a friend traveling the country with a beautiful—and unmarried—young woman. I think it best, if we wish to remain unnoticed, that the two of you marry."

Yolken blushed as he finally comprehended. Now he understood the reason for the grin on Kaylan's face. "I…"

Kaylan took his hand in hers and said, "What do you think?"

Yolken hesitated. Everyone was looking at him expectantly. He stood and led Kaylan over to the couch in the sitting room. He took her other hand and held them both up to his chest so that she stood close to him, looking up into his eyes. "Kaylan… I love you very much and want nothing more than for you to be my wife. It's just… I don't want to do it like this. Given Javen's feelings toward you, I think it's important that we seek his blessing before we marry."

Kaylan's eyes glistened.

"You understand, right?"

She nodded. "No, I understand. You're right." She rose up on the tip of her toes to kiss him lightly on the lips. "I didn't think of that. He would be really hurt if we married without him there."

Yolken breathed a sigh of relief. The last thing he wanted to do was hurt Kaylan. "I love you so much."

"Me too."

Yolken hugged her, then they returned to the kitchen.

"So you'll marry?" Jax said.

"No," Yolken said. "Not right now. It's important to both of us that we have Javen's blessing and that he's present when we marry."

"Hmm," Jax said.

"Couldn't we pretend to be siblings?"

"You don't look enough alike to pass as siblings."

"Well, what about cousins, then?"

"Yolken, we're going to be on the road for a very long time. Do you really want to spend the entire time pretending to be related?"

Yolken realized the point that Jax was making. "No."

"Well, there you have it," Jax said. "I still think that the two of you marrying would be the most believable way for the four of us to travel together."

"I understand, but we're going to wait."

"Then, at the very least, you can pretend to be married. So long as no one monitors your… nightly activities, we should be fine."

Kaylan and Yolken both blushed.

"I have just the thing!" Deborah exclaimed. She disappeared through the house and up the stairs, returning just as fast. She reached out, took Kaylan by the left hand, and slid a thin silver ring onto her third finger.

Kaylan held her hand up to get a better look at the ring. "What's this?"

"It belonged to your grand-mammy," Deborah said. "I never married, so I never had a use for it."

Kaylan smiled as she inspected the ring closely, spinning it around on her finger.

"We'll have to find something for the lad as well," Jax said to Deborah.

"Does no one care about what I think?" Yolken said.

Jax, Deborah, and Kaylan looked at him and waited for him to continue.

"Well?" Jax finally said.

With no other options coming to mind, Yolken said, "I suppose we could pretend to be married, if you think it'll help."

"That's settled," Jax said. "I'm going to go make our final arrangements. I hope to be on the road first thing tomorrow."

"I'll fix some supper," Deborah said.

"Mmm, one last home-cooked meal before road fare slowly kills our palates," Jax said. "That and a jug or two of Yolken's ale. The Dragon knows I'll miss that!" Jax finished off what remained in his glass and rose from the table. "I'll be back shortly," he said before leaving.

Yolken picked up his glass of ale from the table and drank, then went over to the barrel against the back wall and pulled on the stopper, filling his glass anew. He sat down at the table next to Kaylan, who had poured herself a cup of tea. "It's kind of fun to imagine being married to you."

"I know," Kaylan said with a smile. "I can't wait until we really get married."

"So we're promised, then?" Yolken said quietly.

Kaylan blushed and looked over at her mother standing by the stove. "Aren't you going to ask my mammy?" she whispered back.

"I figured we already had her blessing since it was sort of her idea."

"You still need to ask."

"Okay," Yolken said. He set his glass down and stood.

Kaylan grabbed him by the arm. "Now?"

"Why not?" He kissed her then turned to Deborah. "Missus Browning?"

"Yes, dear?" Deborah said over her shoulder.

Yolken waited until Deborah put the knife she was using to chop vegetables down and turned to face him. "Might I have the hand of your daughter in marriage?"

Deborah grinned broadly. She looked at Yolken then at her daughter, whose face was beet red. Directing her attention back to Yolken she said, "Of course, dear."

CHAPTER 15

Devin's thoughts turned to wine as he finished attending to the emissaries from the Turnig province. Turnig was a remote enough province that every few decades an uprising escalated enough to require the chancellor's attention. On the surface, the uprisings never seemed to be related, but Devin knew that the same people were always responsible—the Order of the Dragon. Darek, the provincial regent, had the situation under control, as usual, so Devin put the meeting behind him.

He climbed the stairs, passing his floor, and continued the last half-circle around the spire to the end of the staircase. Before arriving on Reago's topmost floor, Devin took a moment to suppress the tinge of annoyance he felt at even having to meet with the emissaries. The Turnig Province should not be his concern. As chancellor, Reago should have been the one dealing with them.

Devin walked the long hallway, passing door after door—each one guarded by two men in gray armor wearing Glasses—until he reached the double doors at the far end. Unlike every other floor of the palace, Reago's hallways were not decorated with the statues Karina had commissioned long ago.

He knocked on the door and waited. A modestly dressed

woman opened the door, and Devin caught a glimpse of the space between her breasts as she bowed deeply.

"He's on the balcony," the woman said.

Devin passed through the many rooms of the suite and proceeded outside. The balcony wrapped around the building, giving Reago an unobstructed view to the north, west, and south; Devin's own balcony was similar, only on the east side of the palace.

He found Reago standing by the waist-high wall facing the setting sun, with his hands clasped behind his back. Tendrils of smoke rose above his head from the pipe in his mouth. Devin looked at the untouched glass of wine sitting on the wall with disgust. The pipe seemed to be the only indulgence Reago still maintained. His tobacco was shipped to Onta from the very province now under revolt.

"We have returned from Kyinth, Your Highness," Devin said, addressing the only man who superseded his own authority in the west.

Reago puffed on his pipe, not responding to Devin's greeting.

Devin clenched his fists in annoyance. Reago seemed unconcerned that the man who shared his residence had returned. "There were emissaries from Turnig waiting upon my arrival. They indicated that they have been waiting for an audience for nigh on a month."

Reago puffed on his pipe again.

"Another rebellion has begun." Nothing. No reaction from Reago. "At this point, Darek doesn't believe it will amount to much."

Another cloud of smoke exited Reago's mouth.

Devin stood quietly, staring at the sun as it inched slowly below the horizon. Reago's lack of interest in matters within his own realm was bothersome. But at the same time, it had given Devin considerable sway within the realm. At one point, he even had approached Drakonias with the hope that something could be done about it, but Drakonias had refused to entertain the idea of having his younger brother replaced. Devin had realized that doing so would probably cause more problems than it would solve anyway—he remembered the debacle with Sheal—and, in the end, his uncle's lack of attention had the effect of giving Devin the power he wanted. His siblings and cousins governing other provinces in the realm occasionally protested at the arrangement; however, with the capital under Devin's direct control, they were powerless to do anything about it.

"I presume you are aware of the events regarding Danavin's children?" he said.

Smoke emerged from Reago's nostrils.

"Javen, the younger of the two, is here. I've been given the task of training him. Drakonias wishes him to become a regent. He thinks that using Danavin's children in such a role will be a psychological blow to the Order, one that rivals their actual loss of Danavin."

Reago reached up with his right hand and removed the long-stemmed pipe from his mouth. He turned to Devin and said, "What does it matter?"

"What do you mean? It matters greatly. Were it not for the continuing annoyance of the Order, revolts—such as the ones in Turnig—would not be so common."

Reago turned his gaze back to the setting sun and said, "None of it matters. Regardless of whose children may or may not be for or against us, we're all going to die anyway." Reago returned his pipe to his mouth.

Devin shook his head and left Reago standing alone. His uncle had been this way for a century now. If he wanted to waste away alone in his quarters, brooding, it was fine with him. When he spent all his time alone in his rooms, it gave Devin pretty much unlimited control of the realm—and he was perfectly content with that arrangement.

CHAPTER 16

Javen stifled a yawn as he climbed the stairs to Devin and Karina's quarters. He'd missed the meal he was supposed to have eaten with them last night—Lannary had refused to let him go, promising Devin and Karina wouldn't mind—and he'd barely gotten any sleep. He wasn't going to complain, though; he'd enjoyed himself immensely.

Oshie had been in and out of his quarters throughout the evening and morning, attending to their needs. She ensured they never wanted for food, wine, or fresh towels. Her presence made Javen uncomfortable, especially since Lannary eyed her longingly every time she came into the room. So, sitting at the small round table on his balcony eating their mid-day meal—him wearing a thin robe and Lannary wearing nothing—he'd blushed after reading a note the half-naked Oshie had delivered.

"Who's it from?" Lannary said.

"Karina."

"What's it say?"

Javen summarized the note, not wanting to share Karina's extremely suggestive words with Lannary.

"Hmm," Lannary said with a purr in her voice. She closed her eyes and said, "Karina is an exquisite lov—"

"You've said," Javen cut her off. Lannary opened her eyes and looked at Javen. Karina's ogling of them over the balcony, the words of her note, and Lannary's repeated comments on Karina's bedding skills all made him think the two of them were plotting to get them all together. "No offense, Lannary, it's just... the openness with which you westerners express yourselves is a bit much for me."

"I'm not offended, Master Javen," Lannary said. She picked up a fresh strawberry and bit slowly into it. "Let's eat. We need our strength."

Javen stabbed a strawberry on the platter with a fork and thought, *even the way they eat is sexual.* And her voice—it was as intoxicating as fine Ontan wine.

While they ate, Javen thought about the note and added it to the list of things westerners sexualized. In her flowing script, Karina had managed to put together words that, alone, were completely innocuous, but together, combined to imply an unending string of innuendos. All of it to convey the simple message that she wouldn't permit him to miss another meal with her and Devin—regardless of how much he was enjoying his time with Lannary. His new lover was of course invited to join them, she reassured him—in fact, she encouraged it. Fortunately for Javen's sake, Lannary fell asleep after their post-meal session in the tub. It was hard enough to make it through a meal with Lannary or Karina separately; he doubted he could survive a meal with both of them together.

He walked down the long hallway on the top floor of the east wing, which was decorated very similarly to the floor on which he now resided. Surprisingly, despite the night and day he'd spent accompanied by the second most famous lover in the realm, the farther he proceeded down the hall, the more he felt his desires rise within him. The statues were too much—they left nothing to the imagination.

He stopped just short of the large double doors carved with

the now-familiar vines and grapes at the end of the hall and looked closely at the statues on either side of the doors. They were identical to each other, just viewed from opposite sides. The man lay on his back with the woman straddling him. He had a look of intense concentration on his face, and her head was thrown back in the throes of passion. He went red in the face when he realized who they were.

"And where is your lover, Master Javen?"

Javen jumped. He hadn't been expecting to hear Karina's voice. He had been so transfixed by the statues that he hadn't even heard the door open. "She's asleep."

"Hmm," Karina said. She turned to the statues flanking the doors and said, "I remember when these were made. The sculptor did wonders capturing not only the moment, but the entire experience." She looked back up the hall at the rest of the statues.

"Are the statues on my floor of actual people, too?" Javen said.

"They are. In fact, all the statues in the palace are. The sculptor had a real talent."

"Had?"

"He died a century ago. If you like these," Karina said, stepping behind Javen, "you should take the time to admire the sculptures on the other floors. Lannary has been begging me to commission a set of her, but I've yet to find another sculptor with the skill necessary to complete them to my satisfaction."

"There have been no sculptors in the last thirty years," Javen said, guessing at Lannary's age, "talented enough to carve a statue of two people? How much skill does it require?"

"There are many wonderful sculptors, but none have proven capable of capturing the essence of the bedding experience exuded by the couple and maintaining that essence for months afterward, while working the rock."

"Oh."

"Does Lannary please you, Master Javen?" Karina said.

"Yes, very much. She made me miss dinner last night."

"It looked to me like you didn't mind too much." Karina turned him around. "There are others," she said, tracing his lips with her fingers. "Many more that I think might please you. Just let Oshie know, and she will see to it that you have everything… everyone… you want."

Javen blushed.

"Come, dinner awaits." Karina led Javen by the hand into her private quarters.

They walked straight across the large entry room and past several side doors, then made their way through Devin and Karina's bedroom, which held a bed big enough to comfortably sleep a dozen people, and out onto the balcony. Devin sat at a table adorned with food, drinking red wine from a crystal glass. He rose to his feet when Javen and Karina appeared on the balcony.

"Please, sit," Devin said. "I trust you found your first night in Onta pleasing?"

"More than I could have imagined," Javen said, sitting at the table. He stifled a yawn, then picked up the glass of wine already waiting at his seat. After he took a drink he said, "Tired, though."

"I imagine you didn't get much sleep," Karina said.

Javen shook his head.

"Your training will be quite vigorous, I'm afraid," Devin said, "and it will take some getting used to your new home. Synthesizing is like bedding in many ways—it's fun, it's exhilarating, it's pleasing—but it's exhausting if you aren't acclimated to it. When we get done here, I'll teach you a little trick to help increase your stamina in both of your gifts. Karina tells me she has quite the lineup prepared for you." Devin took a sip of wine. "Just remember that your primary reason for being here is to become proficient in Synthesis. You will spend your mornings with me, then you're free to spend the rest of the day how you see fit—just don't forget the importance of sleep. Even my trick is no substitute for proper rest."

Javen nodded again and took a drink of his wine. He looked over at Karina, who was wearing a blue dress that hugged her neck tightly. It wasn't low-cut like the dress she had worn when they disembarked from the ship, but it didn't need to be—he could see most everything the dress might have otherwise meant to conceal. She smiled, causing him to blush and turn his attention to his food.

While he sipped his wine and ate his food, he thought about the future relations Karina had planned for him. His mind slowly wandered across the many girls he'd bedded in the past. As their faces flickered by in his memory, he paused on the thought of Astora. He remembered the one time they had hastily bedded in the loft of her father's barn. But when he imagined himself looking down at her, lying under him on the soft hay, both her throat and the hay were drenched in blood. He gagged on his food.

Karina placed a hand on his arm. "Are you all right?"

Javen nodded and pushed the thought of Astora away.

Kaylan came to mind next. Even though he'd fooled around with a lot of girls—both local and those passing through Lonely Oak—it was always her that he had truly loved. The night of the festival, he'd wanted nothing more than to spend it with her. But that night he had learned she loved Yolken instead.

Then he'd met Hadie. He couldn't explain it exactly, but there was something about her that captivated him.

"You offer me all these women," he said, putting his fork down, "but what I really want is Hadie."

"Not her again," Devin said with a sigh.

"What?"

"I told you, she is not befitting a regent."

"I agree," Karina added. "Pretty as she was, she doesn't suit you."

"Shouldn't I be the one who gets to decide that?" Javen said.

"With all the fine lovers Karina has lined up for you," Devin said, "why would you possibly desire her? I've already told you that she's nothing but the disgraced daughter of a Silk."

"I don't care about that," he said.

"Gentlemen," Karina interjected. "We didn't invite Javen here to bicker over a lass. Javen, if after a week you still desire this… Hadie, then my sweet husband will send for her, won't you, dear?"

"Javen?" Devin said.

Javen thought about Karina's proposal. He really had been enjoying his time with Lannary, but there was something about Hadie that he couldn't quite put his finger on. "I want you to send for her now," he finally said.

Devin looked over at his wife and said, "Fine."

Karina pursed her lips. "Let's finish our meal. I'm sure Master Javen will need to get back to Lannary soon."

CHAPTER 17

Dennal's merchant wagon made much better time than they ever had traveling in Dorlan's caravan. Hadie found it ridiculous that most people could travel farther on foot in a day than the Blessed did in their extravagant carriages. She wondered how they had any time to govern when they wasted so much time in those things. Their extravagant travel accommodations were a display of their grandeur, she knew, but she thought it showed they cared more about themselves than about those they ruled.

Sitting next to Dennal on the hard bench, Hadie quietly planned her revenge. The intensity of her thoughts tamped down her pain smoldering like morning coals. Not wanting to stoke the embers back to life, she tried her best to not think of Javen. Fortunately, the ninety leagues separating Portstown and Hantlo went by quicker than Hadie had thought they would.

Dennal proved to be a pleasant travel companion. After the first day, Hadie warmed up to him and began to engage him more in conversation, which served to help keep the slow-burning coals from flaring back to life. She almost forgot about the knife she wore on her belt at the small of her back.

Hadie knew they were getting close when the dense trees on

the right gave way to steep cliffs. As the wagon lumbered along, she stared at the Kvorgan Sea stretching out far below. The distant sound of waves crashing against the cliffs was just audible over the noises from the horses and wagon.

The peacefulness of the view and the heat of the sun beating down on them combined to make Hadie tired. She rested her head against Dennal's shoulder, closed her eyes, and slowly fell asleep.

She woke to Dennal gently elbowing her, and the sound of the horse's hooves clacking on smooth stone. When she came to her senses, she realized they were traveling down a familiar road. She recognized the buildings that rose up around her, made from smooth brown stones, and knew they had arrived within the limits of Hantlo proper. She'd slept through the outlying villages where the buildings were mostly wooden structures.

Hadie didn't need to see the villages to remember that all the buildings were of poor quality and stood haphazardly. Because the city stood high above the sea, it was protected from the widespread flooding caused by the increasingly frequent cyclones; however, the storms' strong winds often knocked most of the buildings in the villages down. When the storms come, the poor who lived there flocked to the stone buildings of the city for protection. The Blessed typically helped with the cleanup, but then the poor were left to rebuild on their own. The new buildings that went up were always as flimsy as those that had been blown down.

If they continued down this road, the smooth stone buildings would slowly begin to give way to slightly larger buildings made from similarly colored granite. The street would eventually merge with three others in the center of the city, forming a roundabout where a statue of the emperor stood in the center. The street to the right led to Dorlan's palace, which stood on the cliffside and overlooked the Kvorgan Sea; the street to the left led to Drenan's smaller, but equally opulent, palace. When Dorlan's caravan finally reached Hantlo, locals would pack the circle to greet them. By the time that happened, she hoped to have her plan in place.

Hadie quietly watched the city she'd so recently left behind pass by as Dennal navigated the paved street. Prior to reaching the statue of the emperor at the center of the city, he turned onto a street branching off to the left. Hadie knew he was heading toward one of four warehouse districts.

"Are you sure I can't pay you?" Hadie said. "The money's mine, I assure you."

"No, lass."

"Thank you for your kindness, Dennal. I really appreciate it."

"The pleasure was mine," Dennal said. "Now, be off to those parents of yours."

"Thanks again," Hadie said. She hugged Dennal, then climbed off the slow-moving wagon.

"Take care, lass," Dennal called down.

Hadie waved up to him then turned to follow the road back the way they had come. She rejoined the main road leading into the city from the north and followed it toward the city center. The statue of the emperor came into view, but before she reached the roundabout, she determinedly turned down a side street.

Half an hour after parting with Dennal, Hadie stopped in the middle of a road where dozens of women—and a few men— were loitering around the entrances of the buildings that lined both sides of the street. A sheen of perspiration covered her skin. Every single one of the men and women she could see wore variations of the sheer house garments that were common in the south. However, except in the H district, it was *not* common for southerners to wear them outside.

As a child, she and her friends used to collapse on the

ground in laughter every time a traveler took their advice and visited the H district. *If you visit only one place while you're in Hantlo, the H district should be it.* Whatever the H was meant to represent, it certainly did *not* stand for Hantlo.

As she walked down the street, Hadie tried to avoid looking directly at the men and women who crowded it. None of them worked for the woman she was looking for, so she didn't want to give any of them the wrong impression. They betrayed their low status in the district by the fact that they were milling the street looking for patrons. Sonja's women did not have to look for work—patrons came looking for them.

Hadie moved slowly, trying to determine which building might belong to Sonja. They all looked the same. Each house was made from the brown granite common to Hantlo. Each one had stone steps leading up to a porch, which was covered by the overhanging roof that ran the width of the house. The door on every house was red.

Despite her efforts to ignore them, both male and female prostitutes attempted to draw her attention. She waved each of them off in turn until, finally, a house came into view that was different from the others by virtue of both its size and the lack of loitering whores. *Patrons come looking for her,* she thought.

Hadie stopped in front of the house, which stood out on the drab street like a finely dressed regent in a crowd of beggars. The first level was made from the same granite as those surrounding it, but overlapping cedar shingles adorned the walls above that. Round pillars, carved to resemble marble columns, supported the roof of the long porch. The only other resemblance the house shared with the others on the long street was the red door. She stared at it for a long time, considering what she was about to do, then strode up the steps.

She paused at the door and considered turning around and walking to the southwest district of the city, where her parents lived. Perhaps Lyoll was right; maybe there were plenty of other men out there for her. With her hand hovering inches above the handle, she thought of Javen. Her feelings for him—the smoldering coals below the bed of ash—flared. She thought of each night she'd spent with him, from the night they had met at the festival in Lonely Oak until the morning Drenan had stolen him away. She thought about not only the times they'd bedded, but also every other moment they'd shared together. She smiled at the thought of him blushing as she read to him from *Lovers of Onta,* or when they'd walked through Matis together, or the evenings they had spent together around the campfire with Lyoll and Ganip. As the coals burst into flame with a fresh round of desire for the man, she remembered why she was about to enter this brothel.

Would Javen approve? Hadie wondered. It didn't matter; if her plan gave her even the slightest chance of reuniting with him, it would be worth it. And even if she never reunited with Javen, she would at least have avenged Astora and Javen's aunt.

With both fear and determination, Hadie opened the door and stepped inside.

CHAPTER 18

Hadie entered a large, high-ceilinged room dimly lit by oil lanterns hanging on the walls. The air was thick with the smell of burning incense. Scarlet paper with intricate patterns covered the walls, and several plush, velvet couches—which matched the walls—sat around the room. All of them were empty except one. When the door closed behind Hadie, a voluptuous woman dressed in a tight corset and a red skirt rose from the couch to greet her.

Hadie waited as the woman made her way around the couches. The woman ran her fingers lightly over the plump back cushion of a couch as she walked behind it, then repeated the strokes across her bosom, which fought to spill over the top of the crimson corset. Her hair was woven into a tight bun at the top of her head, leaving her neck free to display the gold necklace she wore.

"Do you have an appointment?" the woman asked, stopping before Hadie.

"No," Hadie said.

"Hmm," the woman said. She lightly brushed her bosom again with her fingers. "You *do* know we rarely accommodate anyone without an appointment, don't you?"

"I—"

"Is there someone in particular you have come to see? I could look at their schedule to see when they're available next, but you must know that we book out days in advance."

"I..." Hadie started again, "I was hoping to speak with Madam Sonja."

"She does not take clients," the woman said.

"I'm not here to—"

"Then what business could you possibly have with her?"

"I wish to speak to her about..." Hadie trailed off. She didn't want to come out and say what it was she was planning, so she thought about how to phrase her question.

"Yes?"

"I... have a proposition for her."

"A proposition?"

"Yes," Hadie said.

"What sort of proposition?"

"I... I wanted to talk to her about..."

Hadie didn't know exactly how to answer—especially to a woman she didn't know. She couldn't tell the woman what she really wanted, because she knew her plans were treasonous. If the wrong people found out, she would likely end up dead. She settled for saying, "I wanted to talk about working for her."

"You have experience whoring?"

Hadie shook her head.

"This is the premiere brothel in all of the southern realm. Madam Sonja is not in the habit of hiring whores off the street—especially if you have no experience. The reputation she has spent two decades building would be ruined if she were to send you to one of her most esteemed patrons and you failed to please them to the level that is expected of Madam Sonja's whores."

"May I at least talk with her?" Hadie said. "Please?"

"With whom do you think it is that you speak?"

"You're—"

"If you are not willing to be forthcoming with what you want, then why should I be forthcoming about who I am?"

"I..."

"Come, sit," Sonja said. She gestured to the couch in the back corner of the room, where she had been sitting when Hadie entered.

As Hadie followed Sonja around the couches, she looked up at paintings on the wall—women wearing a range of clothing, from corsets and pleated skirts to nothing at all. The painting behind the couch Sonja sat on resembled the madam, only younger and thinner. Hadie sat on the opposite end of the couch from Sonja.

"Now, tell me what it is that you really want of me," Sonja said. "I'm guessing you aren't really interested in entering the profession."

"How do you know I don't want to become a whore?" Hadie said.

"I've been in the business a long time, lass."

"Lyoll sent me here," Hadie said, deciding to answer Sonja's question.

"*Lyoll?*" Sonja said. She brushed her fingers across her bosom a few times, then said, "How does a girl such as yourself know a man like Lyoll?"

Hadie spent the next several minutes explaining to Sonja how she knew Lyoll, and how she had come to find herself sitting in the brothel of the most respected madam in the realm. She left out most of the details, however, since she still didn't fully trust Sonja.

"So you are here simply seeking information about this man you claim to love?"

"Yes, ma'am."

"Madam."

"Yes... Madam," Hadie said.

"Information is not cheap, you know," Sonja said.

"I have gold."

"How much?"

"A few drakes."

"Hmm," Sonja said. She brushed her bosom again. "Information on the whereabouts of this man is all that you seek?"

"Yes, ma… dam," Hadie said, correcting herself.

"Why don't I believe you?"

Hadie hesitated.

"Ah, you see, your hesitation tells me you're lying."

"I—"

"Why should I help someone who isn't even willing to be honest with me?"

Hadie looked down at her hands. She took a deep breath. "I want more than information."

"What else could you possibly think I can provide you?"

Hadie looked around the room hesitantly.

"Fear not, lass," Sonja said. "Nothing you say will ever leave this room."

Hadie looked over at Sonja. Her words were reassuring, though she knew it could be a ploy as well. Lyoll had told her who some of Sonja's clients were, and anything she said could end up being repeated directly to them. Hadie doubted she could ever know whether this woman was trustworthy, but she also believed Lyoll wouldn't intentionally send her into harm. Her plan was dangerous. If she ever intended to execute it, it would not be without risk. And trusting a woman she did not know was going to be but one of many risks she was going to have to take. She thought about Javen—the man she loved—and knew he was worth it. Even if it meant she might die a traitor's death.

Hadie took a deep breath. "Once I know where they have taken Javen, I'm going to kill Drenan."

CHAPTER 19

Sonja traced the tips of her fingers across her bosom several times.

Hadie waited patiently, trying not to fidget.

"Why ever would you wish to murder the Regent of Hantlo?" Sonja said. "What has he done to you?"

Hadie sat in silence. To explain why she wanted to kill Drenan would require her to open up to Sonja—to be completely honest with her. She picked at her fingernails.

"It doesn't really matter, I suppose," Sonja continued. "He is, after all, a truly horrible person. If I had a choice, I would not send my girls to him. They come back battered more often than not." Sonja stood and said, "Come. If we are to continue this conversation, we must have a little more privacy." She clapped her hands loudly.

A beaded curtain hanging in place of a door clacked as a thin woman entered the room. She had red hair, pale skin, and was dressed like Sonja. "Madam?"

"I'll be unavailable for the next little while. Please attend to the lobby and bring some wine to my room."

"Yes, Madam."

"I believe there are a few patrons due to arrive soon."

"I'll bring the wine, then see to their preparations."

"Thank you," Sonja said. "Come… um…" Sonja paused and turned toward Hadie. "I didn't catch your name."

Hadie thought about providing her with the name she had given to Dennal, but instead she said, "Hadie."

"Hadie, you said?" Sonja said with a quick flick of her fingers across her bosom. "And what is your last name, Hadie?"

"Umm…"

"No. It doesn't matter. Come, Hadie, we'll continue this conversation privately."

Hadie followed Sonja through the beads into a long hallway lined on both sides with doors. At the end of the hallway, Sonja followed a set of stairs on the left. They climbed three flights, then headed down another hallway, also lined with doors, back toward the front of the brothel. At the end, Sonja opened a door and held it for Hadie.

Hadie stepped into a large room with three windows: two facing the street outside and one facing south. She walked over to the south-facing window and looked out. The chancellor's palace towered in the distance over the sprawling city. The late afternoon sun made it gleam like a beacon, guiding the ships in the sea far below as they approached the city. She looked left and was just able to make out the top of Drenan's palace on the far side of the city.

"Come, sit," Sonja said from behind her.

Hadie joined Sonja on a large plush couch occupying the center of the room.

The redheaded woman entered the room with a tray holding a decanter and two glasses. She set it on the table in front of the couch, then left, shutting the door behind her.

Sonja poured a glass of wine and handed it to Hadie, then poured herself a glass as well. After Hadie took a couple of sips from her glass Sonja said, "Did you know that His Majesty, the Regent of Hantlo, has an insatiable lust for women? He has a drive I've seen in no one else. Truth is, he's quite perverse and I don't particularly like doing business with him. The first time one of my girls returned abused, I tried to end our association."

"You tried?" Hadie said. She fidgeted at the mention of Drenan abusing Sonja's whores. It made her think of Astora.

"He wouldn't permit it." Sonja brushed her bosom several times. "You know, I endure endless ridicule because of my business. As esteemed as I am, this is not the west, and the Silks do not associate with whores—at least not publicly."

Hadie's father was a Silk—a member of Hantlo's wealthy class—so she knew exactly what he and his associates thought of whores.

"Even though I am just as wealthy as they, I will never be considered a Silk. What's more, if you survey the other brothels on this street, you will find that I didn't become as wealthy as I have by catering to peasants. No, I became rich because the rich come to me. They scorn me by day and solicit my brothel by night."

"Why are you telling me this?" Hadie said. She didn't really care what people thought of Sonja or how she made her money. She just wanted her help.

"Because, even though the Regency and the Silks bring more gold to my business than I know what to do with, I am not in the business of permitting my girls to be abused. If anyone has reason to kill Drenan, it would be me. Now, tell me why it is that *you* wish him dead."

It was Drenan's servant, Rennie, who had told Hadie what happened to Astora. And, until now, those whispers of a servant were the only evidence she had about what had happened. She had decided on her course not because she could prove Drenan had killed an innocent girl—although killing Javen's aunt was reason enough—but because Drenan had humiliated her by forcing her to stand naked before him, and for taking Javen away from her. Hearing Sonja speak, though, solidified in her mind the reality of what had happened to Astora and the true monster that Drenan was.

"He murdered an innocent girl from the small village where I met Javen," Hadie said.

Sonja looked curiously over at Hadie. She sipped her wine and brushed the tips of her fingers over her bosom with her free hand.

While Sonja sat considering Hadie's proposition, Hadie shared more of her experiences with the man. She told how he had stripped her and held her with his gift, leaving her unable to move while he threatened her. She explained how their journey together in the caravan had begun with Drenan killing Javen's aunt.

"Ah, now your plea makes a little more sense," Sonja said. "You neglected to mention all of this earlier."

"I didn't know if I could trust you," Hadie said. "So you understand?"

"I am not unfamiliar with the forced groping of men either, lass. I've made my living by allowing the scales to claw at me. Truthfully, from the very beginning I feared that Drenan would one day hurt me. In the end, it turned out to be my girls. Still, he has made me very rich. Going along with your plan would have financial ramifications on my business."

"Didn't you say you had more gold than you know what to do with?" Hadie said.

"I did."

"If gold is not an issue for you, then why not help?"

Sonja sat quietly and sipped her wine.

"What kind of person brutally kills a young girl?" Hadie said. "Drenan delivered Javen to me, unconscious and covered in blood, with not the least sign of care or concern for the girl he'd just murdered."

Sonja stroked her bosom.

"He killed Javen's aunt simply because she tried to protect

Javen and his brother from him."

"Now why would Javen and his brother need protection from Drenan?" Sonja said, her fingers freezing.

"He…"

"What did you say happened to this lover of yours?"

Hadie hesitated. How much should she tell Sonja? She needed Sonja's help. And if she lied, even a little bit, Sonja would probably back down—maybe even turn her in. If Hadie was going to get the help she needed, she could hold nothing back.

"Javen's brother had their gift and—"

"You mean the Blessed's?"

"Yes. And Drenan was trying to force it out of Javen."

"So, this lad of yours is Blessed… You're asking me to get mixed up with rebels?"

"*Rebel?* Javen's not a rebel," Hadie protested.

"How else do you explain his having their gift?"

Hadie could sense Sonja's hesitation. It was dangerous to talk about rebels, let alone associate with them. But their conversation had been dangerous since the beginning, so she didn't see why that mattered now. "I don't know. But they told him he had it and he was struggling to use it. So Drenan *killed* Astora trying to force him to."

"I see," Sonja said.

"Then, when Javen tried to attack Drenan," Hadie continued, "something happened to Javen that left him unconscious for days. When we arrived in Portstown, Drenan took Javen away and I haven't seen him since."

"And how is it that you know all this?"

"Drenan's servant told me." Hadie said. "She said she learned it from a whore."

"Ah, yes. Two things will loosen a man's tongue: wine and a woman in his bed." Sonja sipped her wine and looked thoughtfully at Hadie, making Hadie nervous. Finally, she said, "I'm guessing you don't intend to bed the man, so tell me what it is you propose."

"Lyoll sent me to you because he said that if anyone could get the information I needed, it would be you. I'm willing to pay whatever it costs, and if I don't have enough, I'll earn it somehow. Once I find out where they sent Javen, I was hoping you could get me into the palace so I can kill Drenan."

"And how do you propose to do that? Not everyone has access to the regent."

"*You* do," Hadie said.

"Ah. And what if, after you kill him—assuming you're successful—they come after me?"

"Why would they come after you?"

"Because I'm responsible for my whores, especially those who visit the Blessed."

"Wait," Hadie said, realizing what Sonja was suggesting. "But I'm not a whore."

"How else do you think I'd get you into Drenan's palace?"

"I'm not a whore! And I'm *certainly* not bedding him!"

"Perhaps not. But if you want my help, you will have to learn to play the part, else you won't ever get close enough to him to kill him. At least not with my help."

"But he knows me. He knows my father. So even if I did 'play the part', he'd recognize me."

"Then, if I agree to help you—*if*—we'll have to ensure that he doesn't, won't we?" Sonja's fingers flicked across her bosom as she studied Hadie.

Hadie nervously drank her wine while she waited.

"Tell you what, lass, let me see what I can find out about your lover. Since Drenan is not yet back from his trip to Kyinth, it will buy me some time to think about this fool plan of yours." Sonja finished off her wine. "In the meantime, if you're going to be convincing you will need some lessons, and," Sonja said, looking Hadie over, "some refining. Now, stand up and let me have a look at you."

"What?"

"Drenan expects women of very specific… attributes. I can't very well send you to him if you are not what he desires," Sonja said. "Now, if you want my help, stand up and take your clothes off."

Hadie hesitated at first, but then gave in. She was, after all, alone in a room with another woman. It wasn't as though she was about to strip in front of a man she didn't know. She set her glass down and rose to her feet. She looked questioningly at Sonja, but Sonja gave no indication that she might have been bluffing. Hadie lifted her loose-fitting blouse up over her head, dropped it to the floor, and quickly covered her breasts by crossing her arms over them.

"Pants, too."

Hadie started to protest, but then let out a sigh and reluctantly unbuckled her belt. She pushed her pants down to her ankles, pushing her smallclothes down with them. When she stood back up, she covered her breasts again. She waited awkwardly, knees slightly crossed, for Sonja to say she could put her clothes back on.

Sonja set her empty glass on the ground and sipped from Hadie's half-full glass while looking Hadie over intently. She took her time, which made Hadie fidget uncomfortably. When she downed the last of the wine in Hadie's glass, Sonja set the glass down next to her own and stood. She took a few steps toward Hadie and looked her up and down, inspecting every inch of her bare skin. "Arms to your side, please."

Hadie kept them in place for a moment, then reluctantly dropped them to her sides.

Sonja inspected Hadie's breasts closely then walked slowly around her. When she stopped behind her, Hadie turned to find her staring down at her backside. Sonja grabbed Hadie's bottom and squeezed, making her flinch.

Hadie turned her head and stared through the two windows

on the far side of the room, wishing she was somewhere else. She'd rather be getting chastised by her father for behaving poorly at a gala than being inspected by a stranger like she was an animal being sold at market.

Sonja let go of her bottom, but before Hadie could sigh in relief she reached around from behind, grabbed both of her breasts, and squeezed firmly. Hadie fought the urge to reach up and remove Sonja's hands; when Sonja let go on her own, she finally let out a sigh of relief.

Sonja snorted through her nose slightly as she returned to the couch and sat back down.

"What?" Hadie said.

"You're smaller than he prefers," Sonja said, her eyes fixed on Hadie's breasts.

"If I don't plan on actually undressing in front of him, does it really matter?"

"I suppose not, though we will have to fix you up to give the appearance that you're larger."

"Uh," Hadie said, hiding her breasts under her arms again. She'd always thought she had nice breasts—Javen certainly liked them.

"Don't get me wrong, darling, you have excellent breasts, and had you the experience, I'd hire you into my services. It's just that Drenan is very particular, and if we're going to do this, we'll have to make you appear desirous to him."

Hadie didn't like the idea of having to pretend to be someone she wasn't, but when she thought about it, she realized that was exactly what she was doing. "Can I get dressed now?" she said, feeling insecure about herself.

"Why? Does the lack of clothing make you uncomfortable?"

"I'm just not used to being looked over like a horse at market."

"If you're going to do this, you must be able to convince others that you are not only a whore, but one of *Sonja's* whores.

You must learn to exude nothing but confidence when you are naked, no matter who might be ogling you." Sonja retrieved her glass and refilled it from the decanter on the table. After she had several drinks, leaving Hadie standing in front of her, she said, "I will inquire after your lover. In the meantime, join Ursella in the lobby. Tell her she's to instruct you on how to properly greet my patrons."

"I have to bed them?" Hadie said with exasperation. She was *not* a whore. And she didn't intend on becoming one.

"No, lass, that is not the job of the greeter. Your job will be to… prepare them before their appointments. You won't be whoring yourself, but you must learn to play the part. Drenan has spent many lifetimes with whores and he is very keen. As you are presently, he'll know you're an imposter the moment you set foot into his quarters. Now, be off. We'll talk gold once I know more."

Hadie picked up her pants and began to put them back on but stopped when Sonja said, "You won't need those while you're here." Hadie looked up, mouth agape. "You must learn to be confident in yourself. There'll be no need for clothing until then. When you're ready, we'll fit you into something befitting of Sonja's. Leave those behind. You can have them back when your business here is done."

Hadie considered taking her clothes and leaving right then. But finally, she dropped them on the floor and went to find Ursella. When the door closed behind her, she hid herself as best as she could, hoping she didn't cross paths with anyone on the way.

CHAPTER 20

Sauntering around in front of men proved to be much harder than Hadie had imagined it would be. She hated every moment of the experience. Every time an unfamiliar man gazed at her with lust in his eyes, she felt like losing her meal. But she forced herself to let them gaze. She knew she had to if she wanted Sonja to help her.

Sonja gave Hadie a room in the brothel. She kept the only clothes Hadie owned, so she had nothing to wear except a slip she found laid out on the bed—it was for sleeping in, Sonja said, not for whoring. Hadie worked through the nights and only returned to her room as the sky began to brighten. She slept until mid-afternoon and then spent the entire night working the lobby.

Ever since her private meeting with the Madam, she'd wanted nothing more than for Sonja to let her wear something—even if it was a corset, like the rest of the women in the brothel—but Sonja continued to refuse, saying she could wear a corset only when she was ready.

"I'm ready," Hadie insisted again. She had spent every waking moment for five days without clothing.

"You're not."

"Why? The last couple of days I've felt much more comfortable with myself."

"Your movements are rigid, your back is stiff, and your face conveys no desire for my patrons."

"I *don't* desire them."

"Until you do, or at least until you learn to pretend that you do, you aren't ready. If you ever hope to get close to Drenan, you must learn to convince these men that you want them."

Hadie sighed. She hated having to pretend she was a whore when every aspect of her screamed she was not. The only eyes she wanted on her were Javen's. But she forced herself to improve. Even though she hated it, she wanted—needed—Sonja's help. If this was what she needed to do to get that help, she would do it.

Hadie practiced the techniques Ursella taught her—how to move seductively and bend over at just the right angle as she poured wine. She learned to bury the revulsion she felt when she positioned her breasts just so in front of a patron while she filled his glass. She forced herself to imagine that she wanted to bed each man she served. She learned to speak to them with her eyes and entice them with her body.

As much as she hated them, the ogling eyes were not the worst part of it. It was the waiting. Drenan had yet to arrive in Hantlo; she had to wait for him to return before Sonja's whores could glean the information she needed. She wanted Javen to wrap his arms around her, to shield her from the eyes of these men and take her away—she didn't care where, just so long as they were together, and not in the south. So until Drenan returned, Hadie committed herself to doing what was needed to convince Sonja to help. She forced herself to acclimate to the lifestyle.

On the morning of her ninth day at Sonja's, as she lay in bed staring at the crimson-papered ceiling, someone knocked on her door.

"Come in," she said.

The door opened and Ursella poked her head in. "Dorlan and Drenan are arriving today."

Hadie popped out of bed with excitement. She hastily prepared the room for the day's work and made her way toward the lobby. She wouldn't learn anything about Javen today, she knew, but it was a step in the right direction—she was moving again.

"Hadie," Sonja said, stopping her at the top of the stairs.

Hadie turned around as Sonja approached her with her clothes in hand.

Sonja handed Hadie her clothes. "Return once the procession is over."

She looked down at them in confusion for a moment. Hadie had forgotten that by law, all business ceased any time the regent or chancellor returned from a journey—if loyal citizens were not otherwise occupied, they were free to crowd the streets and welcome the Blessed home. She'd always thought it telling that there had to be a law requiring them to do it.

Excitedly, Hadie pushed her legs into her pants. "Just remember," Sonja said as she worked at buttoning them closed, "it will take time before we learn anything. Patience and time."

"I'm tired of waiting," Hadie said impulsively. "Just send me to the palace."

"Then your lover will forever be lost to you," Sonja said. "A whore needs to seduce her way into a man's confidence if she wishes to reach into the depths of his being."

"I thought you said a man's lips were loosened when a woman shared his bed?" Hadie said as she put on her shirt.

"I did, and they are. But a whore cannot be forthcoming. She must wait, bide her time, build trust, and hope that her patron's lips eventually loosen enough to let sensitive information slip. Now, I must go. I mustn't keep His Majesty waiting."

"You're going to see him?"

"Of course, lass. Your duty as a citizen is to stand on the streets and inflate his ego by cheering his return. My duty is to ensure that today his ego is not the only thing that's inflated."

Hadie blushed as Sonja walked past her. She followed Sonja down the stairs and into the main lobby where many of the other whores were already gathered.

"Go and greet the Blessed," Sonja said. "Be back by sundown." Sonja looked the women over, running the tips of her fingers across her bosom, then said, "Kitt and Panny, come with me."

Sonja waited while the two whores made their way toward the door, then she led the way outside.

Hadie followed the others as they exited. Sonja, Kitt, and Panny climbed into a carriage pulled by two horses. When the carriage pulled away, she followed the rest of the women up the street. Whores from the other brothels joined them as they made their way. The crowds grew with every street they turned onto.

Sonja's whores stopped where their street merged with the main road entering Hantlo from the north. Crowds lined both sides. Hadie waited with the others and listened to the chatter. Most of those around her complained about losing pay or business because of this charade. Others were legitimately excited about the rulers of the southern realm returning.

Hadie simply welcomed the reprieve from being ogled all day.

They waited in the heat for what felt like hours. Nobody knew exactly when the procession through the city would take place, and as miserable as it was, it was much safer to be early than to be late and miss it. When the procession finally commenced, a calm swept over the crowd followed by cheering as the first row of soldiers came into view.

Row after row of soldiers—a dozen across, all of them wearing gray armor with swords at their hips—marched by. Every third row had a soldier who wore those mysterious spectacles. They were always around when the chancellor was out in public. They also had black daggers on their hips.

The row of twelve soldiers gave way to six: three on either side, leaving a gap in the middle. After a few of these rows passed, the first of two carriages rolled by. The cheering of the crowd escalated in intensity as the carriages came into view. Dorlan and Drenan had exchanged their large traveling carriages for smaller ones. Two men sat in the seat in the front, one driving the horses and both wearing spectacles.

After the carriages passed, the rows of twelve guards returned and the cheering died down. The crowds of onlookers spilled out into the street and followed the Blessed. Music filled the air as they neared the center of the city—the first sign of the festival celebrating the Blessed's return. By the time the tall bronze statue of the emperor came into view, the crowd was moving at a crawl.

Hadie pushed her way into the roundabout and turned left. The festival, she knew, stretched from palace to palace. But she wasn't interested in joining in with the revelers as she had in Lonely Oak. Instead, she passed by several groups of musicians and merchants selling street-side food and various other wares. She skirted around dancers, passed several groups of invalids and those offering up prayers to the Great Dragon, and made her way toward Drenan's palace.

It took Hadie the better part of an hour to navigate the crowds, but she eventually found herself standing at the iron gate blocking the way to the palace grounds. Worshipers crowded around her and pleaded with the guards at the gate to let them through so they could offer their adulations directly to the Blessed. But only the rich, Hadie knew, would be permitted inside. There was a good chance her father was there. If not here, then at Dorlan's palace.

Ignoring the worshipers, Hadie looked past the rigid guards, through the gate. The carriage would have recently passed through the gate, down the long, tree-lined entrance, and delivered Drenan to his home, where he would be safe, hidden away from those he ruled. It was all but impossible for someone such as herself to see the inside of the palace. Only Silks and those on official business were allowed inside. She no longer had, or wanted, her father's aid, so the only way she was going to ever see the inside of that palace again, and accomplish what she had come here to do, was with Sonja's help.

Hadie turned from the palace and made her way back through the crowd. A new sense of resolve filled her. She would do whatever she needed to do—be exactly who Sonja said she needed to be—in order to gain entrance to Drenan's palace and end his life.

CHAPTER 21

When the wheels of Drenan's lumbering travel carriage began to roll smoothly across the paver stones of Hantlo instead of the rough dirt roads that crisscrossed the empire, the carriage stopped. His personal guard opened the door and Drenan, dressed in his blue dragon armor, stepped out of the carriage that had been his home since they'd left Kyinth. The guard ushered him to a smaller carriage parked nearby. He climbed inside the smaller carriage and sat down in the sole open seat. He looked over the three women occupying the other seats, all of them wearing crimson corsets that pushed their ample bosoms up, then turned his gaze out the window.

"I trust Ylonna has satisfied you since your return to the south, Your Majesty?" Sonja said after the carriage got under way.

Drenan ignored her and stared vacantly out the window.

"I've brought several new girls into my employ since you've been gone," Sonja continued. "These are two of them."

Drenan looked at Sonja again. When she saw she had his attention, she rubbed one hand on the thigh of the woman sitting next to her and the other on the thigh of the woman sitting across from her. He looked at each of them briefly then looked back out the window.

Out of the corner of his eye, he saw Sonja brush the top of her breasts with her fingers. Having known Sonja for a long time, he knew the gesture—she was either nervous or pensive. He turned and looked at her, and she increased the pace with which her fingers moved. *She's probably worried I'm not pleased with the women she brought.*

Drenan watched closely as Sonja reached down into her corset, between her squeezed-together breasts, and pulled out a small knife. He eyed her closely as she pulled it from its sheath and cut the cords cinching the corset of the woman sitting next to her. When all the cords lacing up the front of the tight corset gave way, the corset burst open. "Kitt, here, comes with very high recommendation from Gretcha's in Onta. And Panny," Sonja said, repeating the process on the corset of the woman sitting next to Drenan, "is southern through and through. However, she traces her roots back to the east."

Drenan eyed the chests of the two women briefly, but he wasn't in the mood. He was agitated, and not interested in what Sonja had to offer. Again, he noticed from the corner of his eye when the madam started brushing the tops of her bosom.

The carriage rolled smoothly through Hantlo. It turned right as the paved road merged with the large roundabout at the center of the city and slowly rounded the tall bronze statue of the emperor. Drenan stared at the crowds with about as much interest as he had shown the whores. He normally reveled in the attention of those who put their days on hold to come out and worship him—even if the law required it—just as he normally couldn't get enough of Sonja's whores, but his mood had soured considerably since leaving Portstown.

The carriage finished its circuit around the emperor and followed the packed street to the east, parting ways with Dorlan's carriage, which left the roundabout to the west.

Every morning since leaving Portstown, Drenan had

expected news from Crin. He anxiously awaited word that Crin had captured or killed the Thornhill boy. However, he had heard nothing. He would have preferred to hear that Crin was unable to locate the boy than to hear nothing at all. Never had he been so agitated as he had grown since losing his grasp on both the Thornhill boys. Not even losing his aunt Deanna had bothered him this much.

When the carriage passed through the wall surrounding the palace and stopped in front of the main entrance, he opened the door and stepped out without waiting for his guard to open the door for him. He left the whores behind without a second thought and marched up the steps and through the oversized front doors. A dozen servants awaited him on the inside; they hurried to keep up as he walked straight across the atrium and up the wide staircase leading to his quarters.

"A message from Onta, Your Majesty," one of the servants said hastily, holding a rolled parchment for him to take.

Could the boy have fled all the way to Onta? he wondered, snatching the paper from the servant. He read it as he climbed the steps, then crumpled the paper in a fist and threw it to the ground. *Devin wants me to send Phenor's daughter Hadie to Onta? What in Draego's Fire could he possibly want with her?*

After climbing the long staircase, passing the curved offshoots that led to each subsequent floor, he arrived at the top floor of the palace. He went straight into his room through the doors Rennie held open. Frustration filled him. He clenched his fists, feeling the scar tissue on the back of his hands stretch. He needed an outlet, a way to vent. He turned back to Rennie, who waited anxiously at the door, and said, "Send up the whores I left in the carriage."

CHAPTER 22

Sonja sat in the dark corner of the entry room, her fingers lightly stroking her bosom, and reflected on her debriefing with Ylonna. The girl had spent half a month with Drenan, yet she had garnered almost nothing of use. The only thing Ylonna said was that Drenan wasn't happy, and that he seemed distracted. She'd hoped that Ylonna would have learned the location of Hadie's lover, but Ylonna swore Drenan never mentioned him.

Sonja was disappointed, but that was how it went. She sometimes went months without learning anything useful from her whores.

She sipped wine and eyed Hadie. The girl's plan was foolhardy, she knew, but in her heart, Sonja wanted to help her. She couldn't bring herself to do it, though. The risk was too great. She had hoped that Hadie would realize this on her own and leave, making the decision easier, but the girl seemed stubbornly intent. Each day Sonja waited for Hadie to announce she was leaving—her discomfort at showing her body was evident—but each day she remained. Worse, the girl was improving, making Sonja believe that she might not give up.

The morning hours passed slowly. Kitt and Panny should

have returned by now. Drenan's disinterest in the women and obvious state of agitation in the carriage worried her. She'd learned long ago that he was systematic in two ways: He never rejected the opportunity to bed a new woman, and he didn't keep them longer than it took to satiate his immediate desire. So, when he had stormed out of the carriage and left both girls behind, she didn't know what to do. It had never happened before. Was she supposed to leave and take the whores with her? Would he be angry? Should she leave them behind in case he desired them later? Not knowing what to do, she'd told the driver to wait. When a guard returned to the carriage and retrieved the whores, her fear had abated some, but on the carriage ride back to her brothel, it began to grow. Something wasn't right, she knew, and she sat in the lobby of the brothel all night, worrying over their safety.

The front door opened, and Sonja shot to her feet. A young girl walked hesitantly through the door. A lump rose in Sonja's throat as she recognized the plain, light tan clothing of a palace servant. She crossed the room quickly and met the girl who stood nervously by the door. "May I help you?"

"I… I have news for Madam Sonja."

"Speak, girl; I am she."

"I… I shouldn't be here…" the girl said.

"No one will ever know, lass. Why have you come?"

"As I left the palace this morning to run errands, I saw guards carrying the bodies of two women out of the palace. They threw them into the back of a wagon."

"Did you know these women?"

"No, but I saw their clothes when they came into the palace yesterday."

"And? What were they wearing?"

"Red corsets, Madam."

Sonja felt the blood drain from her face. She was accustomed to Drenan periodically abusing her whores, but he had never killed them before.

"I'm sorry, Madam."

"Thank you for coming," Sonja said. She pulled a gold coin out of a hidden pocket on her corset and pressed it into the servant's hand.

The servant snatched her hand back and the coin clattered to the floor. She curtsied and left.

Sonja shut the door behind the servant and picked up the coin. She turned to look at Hadie, who was tending to a patron. Confidently, Hadie bent slightly as she poured wine into the man's glass, giving him a close-up view of her breasts. She straightened and spun around, showing him her backside, then sauntered over to the next patron.

Sonja nodded her approval and returned to her couch. She watched Hadie attend to several more patrons who came in over the next hour and thought about Kitt and Panny. For years, she had endured Drenan's abuses because she was afraid to confront him. But what she would *not* do was let her fear of the vile man make her accept the murder of innocent whores.

Sonja watched Hadie move with confidence from one patron to the next.

She made up her mind.

CHAPTER 23

Deborah and Jax walked side by side in front of Kaylan and Yolken. Their boots kicked up fine dust from the dry road. Yolken had never realized that traveling was so dirty. As tempting as it was, he resisted the urge to complain. He distracted himself by thinking about the signpost they had passed when the road split, shortly after leaving Croff, right before an old stone bridge spanning the Croff River. One sign, with an arrow pointing straight ahead across the bridge, said, "To Onta." Another sign with an arrow pointing left said, "To Hantlo." But then he realized that thinking about the crossroads was stupid—every time he did, a pang of homesickness washed over him. He wished they could have followed the road to the left, back to Lonely Oak, back to his tavern.

Instead he reflected on the stories Deborah told, about what life was like before the edict of 295 that banned the use of dragon bones, and tried his best to ignore the itch of the sun's Energy beckoning to him. Deborah didn't like talking about the past—she said it was better to live in the present—but had agreed to because Jax had specifically told Yolken to ask her about it.

Her stories really did make Dradonia sound like a different

world. The thing she was most animated about was ovens. Although she had never run a bakery before her assignment in Lonely Oak, she reminisced about how baking was so much easier with an oven powered by dragon bones. Yolken had always thought a good wood-fired oven worked wonders, but Deborah insisted it was because he didn't know about how much better they were before.

She remembered going to the repository once a week as a child, to exchange empty bones for charged ones. Of course, back then, she'd said, nobody knew they were dragon bones. How they worked was a mystery to everyone but the Regency; all they knew was that they provided great convenience to the citizens of the United Realms.

The wonders before the ban were endless: from the Bulbs that illuminated rooms in place of lanterns to the transports called Trains that moved people between cities in a fraction of the time. Deborah talked at length about a trip she remembered taking in her childhood, from Arinin to Turnig, to see the ocean. That was the first Yolken had heard about where Deborah was from. He'd known she was from the west, but that was it.

Whereas Jax reveled in the opportunity to tell stories, Deborah did so reluctantly. Her stories ended far too quickly— like musicians at a festival just beginning a lively dance tune, then abruptly stopping.

Yolken looked over at Kaylan and smiled at her. She smiled back with tired eyes. He was tired, too. It was almost one hundred leagues from Croff to the base of the Ontali Mountains, and the fourteen days it took them to travel the valley separating the Mindons and Ontalis was almost unbearable. It started out pleasantly enough; the road followed along the north fork of the Croff River, but the sun beat down on them relentlessly. There were almost no trees to grant the occasional respite except a few right along the river, off the road. Any break from the sun forced them to leave the road to go down to the river, and traveling alongside the river would have made their progress unbearably slow. The builders of the road certainly hadn't considered the comfort of travelers when they'd plotted the road's course. Whenever a wagon passed by and churned up dust, Yolken found himself yearning to slip over to the water's edge until the dust settled.

Yolken carried his cloak in a bundle on his shoulder. He knew Jax had small dragon bones woven into the hems of his tattered coat, but even so, he couldn't understand how Jax could bear wearing it in this heat. Yolken wished he could Synthesize, as they had done when they'd run from the Mindon Falls to Croff, to help stave off his weariness. He even wondered if he could transfer Energy to Kaylan to help her as well. But Jax refused to let them Synthesize—doing so on the road wouldn't be safe. But that didn't stop Jax and Deborah from talking endlessly to Kaylan about it, having her perform what looked to Yolken like stupid exercises, hoping she could access the dormant gift within her. But he wondered if her catalyst needed to be something big, not these menial exercises. She wasn't even subconsciously using it like he had been before he'd healed Issa. But he'd been using Synthesis without knowing what Synthesis was, so he wondered if subconsciously Synthesizing was even possible since she already knew about it.

While he walked and Deborah talked, Yolken absentmindedly played with the ring on his left hand. With his thumb, he turned it around and around. Even after nearly fifteen days on the road, pretending to be married to Kaylan, the ring still felt foreign. Sharing a bed with her in the cramped room of an inn or out under the stars was difficult. The feel of her warm body cuddled up next to him each night made his desire to be her husband stronger every day. He questioned the wisdom of his decision to wait to marry her. Kaylan's gentle assurance that one day they *would* wed helped—that, and the constant presence of her mother. He certainly wasn't going to bed her with

Deborah nearby. He settled for the closeness, whispered words, and gentle kisses they exchanged nightly. He didn't know which was worse: feeling the constant beckoning of the sun's Energy and not being allowed to draw it in, or feeling Kaylan's body next to him at night and not being able to bed her.

The arrival of the Ontalis brought with it two things: the west and—more importantly—shade. The sight of them drawing near was both welcoming and exciting. Jax assured them that once the road entered the Karin Valley, there would be plenty of trees to shade them from the sun. They were all eager to be able to travel in a little more comfort—or at least in a little less discomfort.

Not only were they looking forward to less intense days under the sun, but Yolken and Kaylan also brimmed with excitement about leaving the Northern Realm. The Ontalis and the west had always been a point of intrigue to Yolken. He knew the mountains represented the border between the realms and that Lonely Oak was not that far from them, but even on clear days, they weren't visible, not even from the western slope of the Mindons. As close as the mountains might have been, they were still far away. Their proximity became real when they first appeared in the distance—first as a small line of blue dividing the fields from the sky, and then a slowly growing wall.

Despite their fatigue, the now continuous view of the approaching mountains filled both Yolken and Kaylan with excitement. Both of them had left the area surrounding Lonely Oak, but it had always been either to the north, east, or south— never to the west. There was nothing west of Lonely Oak except an endless sea of wild grass. The border to the Southern Realm was not that far away, but it was farther than most residents of Lonely Oak ever went. To most of them, anything south of Matis might as well have been the south—most had never even been to Matis. There was just no reason to travel so far away when everything they might ever want or need could be found in either Matis or Edis. The idea of leaving the Northern Realm was both foreign and exciting to the young couple.

The Ontalis grew closer and the Karin Valley became distinguishable. There were three distinct ranges that made up the Ontalis—the northern range, southern range, and western range—and the Karin Valley was what separated the northern from the southern. In the end, crossing the border came and went without notice. Had Yolken not known that the beginning of the Ontali range represented the border between the north and the west, he wouldn't have realized they'd crossed the border. There was no sign or any other marker, and the first town they went through, nestled right where the foothills began, reminded Yolken of home. It seemed to him that the only border that existed was the one drawn on maps.

"I thought it would feel different somehow," Kaylan said. She sounded disappointed.

"Me, too," Yolken agreed. He felt let down—like the anticipation of tasting a new ale creation, only to find out it hadn't fermented.

The hype of traveling to a different realm had definitely been exaggerated in their minds. The only real change was the welcome relief from the sun. The elevation increased as they made their way deeper into the valley, and tall pine trees gradually came down from the mountains to greet them. Before long, the road wound through the forest and the weary group welcomed the shade.

"I wonder why it's called the Karin Valley," Kaylan said after they were almost a day's travel into it.

"I haven't any idea," Yolken said.

"The valley is named after the Regent of Onta's wife," Jax said over his shoulder.

"Karina?" Kaylan said.

"The desire of every Ontan," Jax said.

Yolken looked over at Kaylan and saw that she was blushing

intensely.

"What?" Kaylan said, looking away.

"A fan of *Lovers of Onta,* are we?" Jax said.

"No!" Kaylan said.

"I thought *Lovers* warmed the hearts of lasses throughout the empire?"

"I wasn't allowed to read them."

"Why would you keep her from such fine literature, Deborah?" Jax said wryly. He was obviously enjoying himself.

"Fine literature?" Deborah didn't look amused.

"At any rate," Jax continued, "I believe one book in the collection is titled *Karina's Valley.*"

"Jax, please," Deborah said.

"We *are* in the west and on our way to Onta, Deborah."

"Tell me," Kaylan said.

"Go ahead, Jax," Deborah said with a sigh.

"Well," Jax began, "according to what is written in that particular piece, Devin thinks the space between his wife's breasts resembles a great valley, so he named one after her."

Kaylan blushed a deep red.

"Get used to it, lass," Jax said. "I'm sure you'll see and hear much worse before we're through with the west. And Deborah?"

"Yes, Jax?"

"I think it's time you stop shielding Kaylan. She's a grown woman now."

"Don't remind me."

CHAPTER 24

With the cooler temperatures and protection from the sun, Jax sped up their pace, adding a few leagues a day to their travel. They largely traveled through forested terrain, but even when they found themselves in a meadow, such as they were now, the temperature was never as oppressive as it was before reaching the Ontalis. Before Yolken knew it, they had traveled another eighty leagues, and what little novelty there was from being in a different realm had worn off.

"We should reach the west end of the valley in another day or so," Jax said.

"Will it get hot again?" Kaylan said.

"Not like before. We'll be in the sun again, but shortly after we leave the valley, the road will begin to follow the east fork of the Ontali River. And unlike with the Croff, a nearly continuous breeze blows across it. It'll feel marvelous."

Two merchant wagons traveling in the same direction passed them as the sun dipped below the mountains. In unspoken routine, Yolken, Kaylan, and Deborah covered their mouths with strips of cloth; Jax used the arm of his coat. Passing wagons didn't bother them for long when there was a breeze, but at present the air was calm. The dust hovered over the road as it slowly settled back down. Jax walked off the road to get out of it, and the others followed. They paralleled the road, walking through thin brush, until the dust settled.

They walked alongside the road, the air slowly becoming clearer as the dust settled. Then Yolken noticed they were catching up to the wagons. *That's odd,* he thought. Merchant wagons kept a much swifter pace and they never passed them on foot—it was always the other way around. Occasionally, they came across merchants who had passed them earlier in the day, then stopped in a town to sell their goods. They usually packed back up and left once they had sold everything the townsfolk were willing to buy, but if it was late in the day, they tended to stay put. Spending the night in a town was much safer than being out in the open.

"Do you see that?" Yolken said.

"I do," Jax said.

"What?" Kaylan said.

"The wagons ahead have stopped," Yolken said.

"That's odd," Deborah said, speaking Yolken's thoughts aloud.

"Indeed," Jax added.

"What do you think it means?" Yolken said.

"A broken wheel would be my guess," Jax said. "Or maybe a horse threw a shoe."

"Could be bandits," Deborah said. "When was the last time we saw a patrol?"

"It's been a few days," Jax said. "Keep close."

"This pass is notorious for banditry."

"I'm surprised we haven't come across a band already."

"Notorious?" Yolken said. He certainly hadn't known that. "It seems like there would be more patrols here if the Regency knew it was teeming with bandits."

"There used to be, but things change."

"Perhaps we should steer clear," Deborah said.

"At this point it wouldn't matter," Jax said.

Yolken looked from the wagons ahead to the edge of the meadow a few hundred paces south of the road.

"If there are bandits up there," Jax said, "then they likely won't be alone. There's strength in numbers. Now, shh, I want to pay attention to what's ahead. And, Yolken…" Jax stopped and turned toward him. "No Synthesizing."

"I know," Yolken said. "We've already discussed this."

"Perhaps we should stay right here," Deborah said.

"We don't even know if it *is* bandits," Jax said. "If it's a wheel or a horse they might need our help."

Jax moved forward. The others followed. As they inched closer to the wagons and the dust from the road continued to settle, it became clear to them that men on horses blocked the path of the wagons. Jax crouched on the ground and gestured with his hand for the others to follow.

"What should we do?" Yolken said.

"For now we—" Jax began, but screams pierced the air, cutting him off.

They watched in horror as a man on horseback roughly wrenched a woman from the seat of the rear wagon. She hit the ground hard, then the man slid off the horse next to her. He climbed on top of her as she struggled to free herself.

Someone hidden on the other side of the wagon yelled, "Stop! You're hurting her!"

The bandit ignored the plea and hit the woman roughly with the back of his hand.

"We have to help her," Deborah said.

"I agree," Yolken added. "We can't just sit here and let him hurt her."

"Let me handle it," Jax said. He gripped the corner of his coat and rose to his feet.

One of the rough-looking men on horseback looked in their direction and yelled, "Hey!" He let out a shrill whistle and spun his horse in their direction.

The man sitting on top of the woman looked up at his companion first, then over toward them. He turned back to the others blocking the forward advance of the wagons and signaled for them to follow. A half dozen bandits split away from the group and rode toward the bandit who first noticed them. The man straddling the woman stood and signaled another to come and hold her. When she was secured, he mounted his horse and rode toward Jax and his companions.

"Do nothing," Jax said tersely. "I will handle it."

The group stood close together as the men on horses drew near. Jax maintained his grip on the frayed corner of his coat and Yolken unslung the rolled-up cloak from his back. He planned to heed Jax's warning, but he wanted to be ready in case whatever Jax had planned didn't work. The men on horseback surrounded the group and waited until their leader arrived.

The leader rode into the circle made by the other bandits and, pulling his horse to a stop, looked down at the group. He smiled broadly, revealing a mouth full of rotten teeth.

"What have we here?" the leader said as he slid off his horse. He pushed past Yolken and grabbed a lock of Kaylan's hair. He pulled her hair roughly toward his dirty face and inhaled deeply.

"Don't touch her!" Yolken exclaimed.

The man looked over his shoulder at Yolken. "What did you say?"

"I said don't touch her."

The bandit turned to face Yolken. He kept his grip on Kaylan's hair, forcing her to follow him awkwardly as he pivoted. "Or what?"

Yolken remained silent, waiting for Jax to do something.

"I said, or what?"

Yolken stared the bandit in the eyes. "Or you'll wish you hadn't."

"Ha! You hear that? This one talks tough." The bandit

stepped uncomfortably close to Yolken and said, "What exactly are you going to do?"

Yolken smelled the man's foul breath.

"Look," Jax said, "my niece's new husband, here, is just a little protective of his bride. We didn't mean any offense. So if you don't mind, we'd like to be on our way."

"Newlyweds, eh?" the bandit said. "Well, s'far as I can tell, she's mine for the taking. I imagine, then, that your new nephew probably could use a few pointers from someone with a little 'sperience, no? And the best way to gain some 'sperience," the bandit said, pulling roughly on Kaylan's hair, "is by watching."

Yolken reached into the folds at the end of his bundle. He touched the hilt of the Harachin sword and drew Energy into his Core.

"Easy there, lad," the bandit said. "I'd take that hand back outta there, were I you. You wouldn't wanna go doing nothing stupid."

Yolken obeyed and removed his hand from the bundle.

"Hand it over," the bandit said, gesturing toward Yolken's bundle.

Yolken handed it to the filthy man.

When the bandit had Yolken's bundle in his hand, he said to his men, "Hold these three while I teach these young ones a thing or two about proper beddin'."

Three men slid off their horses and drew thin swords from the scabbards at their hips. They pointed their blades at Jax, Yolken, and Deborah.

The leader turned back toward Kaylan and forcefully pushed her to the ground. He dropped Yolken's bundle on the ground then began to unbuckle his belt. "You ready for some real beddin', lass?"

Yolken looked past the bandit at Kaylan. She stared up at the bandit, fear in her eyes, and tried to scoot away using her elbows and heels. She might not have been his actual wife yet, but he loved her as if she were, and he wasn't about to stand idly by while that disgusting bandit had his way with her.

Feeling beads of sweat beginning to trickle down his forehead, Yolken looked from Kaylan to Jax. Jax returned his look, shook his head slightly, then reached into his coat and turned back to the bandit. Yolken ignored Jax and reached out with a tendril of Energy from his Core. He directed it into the bandit's boot.

The bandit had his belt unbuckled and was working at unlacing his pants. However, his hands froze and he lifted his right boot off the ground. The sole was smoking.

"What the—" He yelped when it burst into flame. He began dancing around frantically and stomping his boot on the ground.

The men guarding them stared at their leader, transfixed. The bandit's efforts were futile. The flames on the boot only grew bigger.

Yolken cut off the Energy fueling the fire and quickly gathered water from the air. He directed the water toward the boot and the fire went out with a hiss.

The bandit looked down at his boot, which was now sopping wet. He looked up with fear in his eyes. The two men guarding them lowered their swords and began slowly backing away.

"Let's go!" the leader exclaimed. He hobbled back to his horse and, placing his left boot into a stirrup, climbed back into the saddle. Ribbing his horse forcefully, he took off at a gallop toward the cover of the forest. The other bandits sitting on their horses turned and followed. The men guarding Yolken, Jax, and Deborah hastily sheathed their swords, climbed onto their horses, and fled with the others.

Yolken turned from the fleeing bandits and helped Kaylan to her feet. She hugged him tightly and sobbed into his chest. "It's okay now," he reassured her.

"I-I-I was afraid they were going to…"

"I would never have let that happen," Yolken said. "I promise I'll never let anything happen to you. Ever."

CHAPTER 25

Well, that didn't go as I had hoped," Jax said. He had a tinge of irritation in his voice.

"What do you mean?" Yolken said, growing irritated himself. "There's no way I was going to let them have their way with Kaylan while I stood by and watched."

"That's not what I meant, Yolken. Of course I would never have let anything happen to her. But in the interest of not attracting attention to ourselves, I was hoping to resolve things before it required Synthesis."

"What else could I have done?"

"We could have offered them gold," Jax said. He pulled a bag from his coat and held it up. "Bandits are very easy to buy off. The one thing stronger than their carnal desires is their thirst for gold. And if gold wasn't enough to get them to leave us alone, *then* we could have resorted to other options."

"You were going to pay them off?"

"I was about to. I had my hand on my purse when the bandit's boot started to smoke."

"I... I didn't know," Yolken said. "I'm sorry."

"I'm not," Kaylan said. She hugged Yolken tightly.

Jax sighed through his nose, then turned and walked toward

the merchant wagons.

"I would have done the same thing," Deborah whispered to Yolken as the three of them followed Jax.

When they arrived at the wagons, a man with a long, pointy goatee was hugging the woman the bandits had been abusing.

"Thank you so much," the woman said. She showed signs of a bruise growing on the left side of her face near her eye. "I thought certainly that—"

"Don't worry about it," Jax said dismissively.

"No, we're truly indebted to you," the man said. "Not only would they have taken turns having their way with my wife, but they would have made off with our goods, leaving us broken. Name's Keb Hewer of Tieger." He let go of his wife and offered out his hand.

Jax took it into his own and shook it. The merchant then offered his hand to Yolken, Kaylan, and Deborah, and introduced his wife, whose name was Tessie.

"My name is Laura," Deborah said when Jax didn't offer their names in return. "And this is my daughter Jula and her new husband Neffin." She gestured at each of them in turn. Pointing at Jax, she said, "And his name is Shen. Pardon his manners."

"We saw what you did," Tessie said.

"We did nothing," Jax said with a glare toward Deborah.

"Don't worry," Tessie said. "We won't be telling anybody."

"It's just the two of you?" Deborah said.

"Aye," Keb said. "I drive the forward wagon and Tessie drives the rear."

"Why don't you have guards?" Kaylan said.

"Can't afford 'em," Keb said. "Sell-swords have exploited the opportunities they've had since the Regency scaled back their patrols. The valley's reputation hasn't helped matters either."

"Isn't that all the more reason to hire them?" Yolken said.

"If we did, we wouldn't be able to afford to do this anymore. More merchants make it through here unharmed than don't, so we take the risk."

"Seems foolish to me," Jax said.

"Is there anything we can do in return for your help?" Tessie said.

"No," Jax said. "We're quite fine, thank you."

"Please," Keb said. "We don't have much money, but at the very least let us give you a ride. Where ya headed?"

"No thank you," Jax said again.

"Shen," Deborah said. "A little rest would be beneficial."

"I agree," Yolken said.

"Me, too," Kaylan said.

"Give us a moment," Jax said. He stepped away from the merchants and the others followed. "This is not a good idea," he whispered.

"So long as we maintain our identities, how can it hurt?" Deborah whispered back.

"They saw what Yolken did."

"They also said they wouldn't say anything."

"You believe them? They're merchants."

"So?"

"So they would say anything for the right price."

"Aren't you a merchant?" Deborah said.

"Exactly. So I know everything has a price."

"Come on, Jax," Yolken said.

"Fine. But know that I do *not* think it's a good idea."

"Thank you, Jax," Deborah said, sounding relieved. She walked back to Keb and Tessie and said, "We would love a ride."

"Excellent!" Keb said. "Where ya headed?"

"Onta," Deborah said.

"Well, then, you're in luck! That's where we're headed."

"You're welcome to ride with us as far as you wish," Tessie said. "There's plenty of room."

"Why don't the men ride with me and the ladies ride with Tessie," Keb said.

"Sounds like an excellent idea," Deborah said.

"Let's be off then," Keb said.

Yolken and Jax followed Keb to the lead wagon.

Keb climbed up to the simple bench and sat in the middle. "There's room for one on either side of me," he said.

Jax climbed up and sat next to Keb on his left. Yolken walked around the boxy wagon, which had shuttered windows on the sides and a door at the back, and climbed up onto the right side of the bench. By the time Yolken took his seat, Keb had the reins in his hands. He gave them a firm shake and the two horses jerked the wagon into motion.

"Thanks for the ride," Yolken said. He was as relieved for a break as Deborah had sounded. He found himself wishing there were still Trains so traveling wouldn't be so wearisome.

"It's the least we could do for your help," Keb said. "What's in Onta, anyway?"

"We're—"

"—seeking different opportunities," Jax finished for Yolken. "After my niece wed young Neffin, here, we decided to sell what little we had in Terin for what we hope to be bigger and better opportunities in Onta."

"Terin, you say? If I remember correctly, that's the small town just this side of the border with the north?"

"That's it," Jax said. "We've had a series of poor crops, and each year it's been getting harder and harder to make do. Given all the talk of bumper crops on the other side of the mountains, we thought we'd give it a try. After all, we had nothing but more poverty in our futures in Terin, and I'd hate for these young'uns to start their life together in such conditions."

"Can't say I blame ya," Keb said.

"It is not without risk that we accept your offer," Jax said. "I don't think I can express this point enough."

"As Tessie said, we won't be telling anybody. It would be foolish to go around turning on those who come to your aid. Draego knows, Dradonia needs more people like you."

Jax snorted.

CHAPTER 26

Keb and Tessie stopped in every village they passed. Despite the delays, Yolken knew they were still traveling faster than the four of them would have had they declined Keb's offer. The stops were frequent, though typically short. It didn't take long for Keb and Tessie to set up their wagons and for the locals to peruse their goods. Most of the towns were no bigger than Lonely Oak—many of them smaller—so everyone who wanted to come look quickly got their chance. As soon as the last local stepped away from the wagons, Keb and Tessie shuttered the windows, closed the door, and set off again.

Traveling with Keb and Tessie removed much of the unpleasantness of traveling. If gold wasn't an issue—and it didn't seem to Yolken that it was, the way Jax always talked about information not being cheap—then Yolken didn't know why they didn't buy a horse and trailer for themselves. He had never traveled before, but he'd quickly learned that walking on a dusty road day after grueling day was not the way to do it. The thin pad on the seat left his backside sore, but it was much better than slogging along all day on foot. Rather than waking tired and sore each morning, Yolken began to enjoy each day more and more.

They had left the Karin Valley behind, and now traveled between the southern Ontali range and the east fork of the Onta River. The mornings were calm and cool; as the day began to warm, without fail, a steady breeze rose from the west, carrying cool air with it.

Jax's mood reminded Yolken of when they'd fled from the cabin in the Mindons. He sat on the bench, stewing to himself and smoking his pipe. Keb, it turned out, could spin tales every bit as well as Jax. So, while Jax stewed, Keb passed the time by telling tales about love—most of which involved Karina Drake—and harrowing escapes from menacing bandits. He also told stories about the Regency's heroic squelching of various rebellions.

As villages came and went, and the merchant couple proved true to their word, Jax slowly relaxed and began telling tales of his own. Jax and Keb took turns, becoming more animated with each tale they told, almost as if they were competing with each other. Yolken just hoped they didn't ask him who he thought was best.

Their tales began to center around the great bridge that spanned the Onta River. Yolken had seen paintings of the bridge, and its grandeur was known throughout the empire. He knew they were close to reaching it, and he was growing excited at the prospect of seeing the immense structure. Jax was in the middle of an especially enthralling story about the battle between Drakonias' army and the evil forces of the Dragon King, in which the original bridge spanning the Onta River was destroyed, when they rounded a copse of trees and the bridge came into view. Jax stopped speaking and Yolken gasped.

The bridge was enormous. Two large towers, rectangular in shape, guarded the base of the span. From there it arched high in one smooth curve up and over the water, then down again to similar towers on the north side of the river.

"Drakonias had this bridge positioned here not long after

the end of the war," Jax said. "It has stood in its present state since the inception of the empire."

"He positioned it here?" Yolken said, looking past Keb at Jax.

Keb looked at Jax, seemingly with equal curiosity.

"It is hard to tell from this far away, but that bridge is one solid piece of stone."

"You mean it was put there?" Yolken said. "How?"

"It must be the work of the Blessed," Keb answered for them both. "There's no natural way anyone could ever move a structure that big."

"You're right, Keb," Jax said. "The war with the Dragon King left much of the empire in ruins, so Drakonias secured his power by putting the empire back into working order. This bridge represents one such example. This particular structure, if I remember correctly, was carved from the mountains north of Kyinth, then transported here by a legion of Blessed."

"I've crossed that bridge hundreds of times," Keb said, "and never once considered that it wasn't constructed right here like every other bridge."

"Have you ever seen a bridge like this before?"

"Well, no, not exactly. But I don't know anything about bridge building, so I didn't think it was any different from any other bridge, I suppose."

"Imagine the hundreds of people who cross this bridge every day and never appreciate its true wonder."

"How is such a thing even possible?" Keb wondered.

"What's *not* possible for the Blessed of the Dragon?" Jax suggested.

"I suppose you're right," Keb said. "How do you know so much about it?"

"Before becoming a farmer," Jax said, "my father spent several years as a merchant such as yourself. He had the privilege of traveling to Kyinth on a regular basis, so he heard quite a few stories that don't tend to circulate around much."

The two wagons continued to lumber closer to the immense structure. The closer they came, the more amazing it became. The typical support structures that held bridges in place were absent from this one. The span curved smoothly over the water with no support whatsoever. Yolken had always wondered how this was possible when he'd seen paintings of it, and now he knew. It was truly amazing. He wondered if Kaylan was experiencing the same awe at the sight of the bridge that he was.

The wagons approached a large crowd gathered around the right tower, drawing Yolken's attention from the bridge. "I wonder what's going on," he said.

"Probably a hanging," Keb said.

"Hanging?"

"'Tis a common occurrence here."

"It is?"

"Since this is the juncture of two major roads, patrols use this location to execute those found guilty of breaking Regency laws. You know, thieves and bandits. They hang the dead bodies to remind the people who pass by of what can happen to those who break the law." Keb pulled the wagon to a stop just before the horses reached the crowd.

From where he sat on the elevated seat, Yolken could see over the top of the crowd to the gallows built at the base of the tower. A filthy man stood in the center with a noose around his neck and his arms secured behind his back. He was flanked by two men wearing shimmering gray armor. A third armored man stood facing the filthy man, holding up a roll of parchment before him. With a loud voice, he read a list of laws the man was guilty of breaking.

Yolken's breath caught when he recognized the man with the noose around his neck. "Jax..."

"What?"

"That's the bandit."

"So it is," Jax said with a frown.

Yolken watched the bandit intently; he didn't seem to be afraid that he was about to die. Then his heart began to race when the man turned his head in their direction.

The bandit's eyes grew wide, then he yelled at the top of his lungs, "Rebel!"

The armored man standing opposite the bandit stopped reading and lowered the parchment.

The bandit stared, transfixed, at Yolken. When the soldier began to read again, the bandit again shouted, "Rebel!" This time he took two steps in the direction of the wagon and stopped only when the noose around his neck prevented him from taking a third.

The soldier lowered his parchment again; the bandit turned to him and said something that Yolken couldn't hear. He gestured with his head toward the two wagons.

"It's time for us to be on our way," Jax said with just a hint of fear in his voice. "Let's go, Keb. We've all seen hangings before."

Keb nodded and snapped the reins.

"Stop those wagons!" the soldier with the parchment shouted at a group of soldiers standing at the base of the gallows.

About a dozen soldiers pushed their way through the crowd until they blocked Keb's advance. The soldier who had been reading the parchment rolled it up and walked down the steps at the side. He made his way through the crowd, which had parted to allow him through. The other two soldiers standing on the gallows remained at their positions on either side of the bandit. When the soldier arrived at the wagon, he looked each of them over, then looked behind them at the wagon driven by Tessie.

"What's your name, lad?" the soldier said.

Yolken looked over at Jax, who nodded slightly. He turned back to the soldier and said, "Neffin, sir."

The soldier pointed at the bandit on the gallows and said,

"Have you ever seen this man before?"

"No, sir." Blood pounded in his ears.

"Have you come across any bandits in the last few days?"

"No, sir." He hated lying.

"This man has accused you of being a rebel."

"R-r-rebel? No, sir. I-I-I'm not a rebel."

"Hmm… He has confessed to accosting two merchant wagons a few days back. Says you ran his party off by setting his boot on fire."

"And you believe him?" Jax said. "He's a thief."

"His boot *is* burned."

"Perhaps he fell asleep too close to the fire."

"Hmm," the armored man said. "He seems certain he knows this lad."

"Sir, we are but simple merchants traveling to Onta to sell our goods," Jax said. "Had we encountered bandits we would have reported it just as soon as we saw you here, no? That is the law. We're grateful you and your men look out for us merchants. Our livelihoods depend on it."

The soldier studied the three of them for a moment. He looked back at the wagon behind them, then over at the bandit. Turning back to them, he said, "Be on your way."

Keb urged the wagon back into motion.

The bandit started to scream. "Rebel! Draego's Fire, he's a rebel!"

The soldier motioned to the others standing on the gallows next to the bandit; the one on the bandit's left moved a lever. The floor dropped out from underneath the bandit, silencing his screams.

Yolken, Jax, and Keb rode in silence until the majestic bridge disappeared from sight behind them.

"I'm sorry I Synthesized," Yolken eventually offered.

"We were lucky that soldier opted to take the word of a merchant over that of a bandit," Jax said. "Let it be a lesson to you about our need to remain absolutely hidden."

CHAPTER 27

The gleaming white walls of Onta stood before Yolken. Between him and the walls arched a bridge similar to the great bridge that spanned the east fork of the Onta River. Yolken looked ahead at the wide span of smooth stone arching up before him. The horses' hooves clacked loudly, and the wagons slowed as they started their ascent. The Onta River became visible as the wagon rose above the surrounding countryside.

"Welcome to the land of wine," Jax said.

"You've never been to Onta before?" Keb said.

"The lad hasn't."

The wagon approached the crest of the arch. A pure white, needle-like structure pierced the horizon and slowly came into view. As the wagon reached the top of the bridge, the spire stretched higher and higher. When the bridge no longer obstructed their view, Yolken could see the tops of buildings nestled behind the wall. They were as white as the tower that rose majestically over them.

As the wagons descended the other side of the bridge, Yolken stared up at the guard towers built into the wall. They depicted carved scenes of sprawling vineyards. There was a small balcony about halfway up each tower with armored guards standing on them. One of the soldiers looked in their direction as he surveyed the slow-moving line of wagons.

They passed between the towers and into the capital of the Western Realm. A wide paved square surrounded by white marble buildings greeted them on the other side. The road continued straight ahead on the far side of the square, and another followed along the base of the wall to the left.

Keb guided the wagon to the left and followed the road along the wall. "The warehouse district is this way," he said.

"Then it appears to be time we parted ways," Jax said. "We're headed for the West Gate."

Keb shielded his eyes and looked up at the afternoon sun. "Farmers have probably concluded their business for the day."

"Aye," Jax agreed. "We'd like to find lodging in the area and settle in so we'll be ready to greet them first thing in the morning."

"It's been a pleasure," Keb said, offering his hand first to Jax, then to Yolken.

"Indeed," Jax agreed.

"I thoroughly enjoyed myself," Yolken added.

"The pleasure has truly been mine," Keb said. "And rest assured, lad, your secret is safe with me and Tess."

"Thank you."

Yolken and Jax climbed off the wagon, leaving Keb alone on the bench. Yolken waved up to him, then met the others between the two wagons. He waved up to Tessie as she urged her horses back into motion.

"So, the West Gate?" Yolken said as Tessie's wagon passed by.

"South Gate, actually," Jax said. "They thought we were coming here to farm, remember? The South Gate leads to the docks. This way," Jax said as he started across the large square.

They reached the far end of the square, then continued on the road farther into Onta. The beauty of the buildings amazed

Yolken.

"Can you believe this?" he said to Kaylan.

"It's gorgeous," Kaylan replied. "Croff was nothing like this. There were nicer areas, but most of it was dingy and old. This city looks pristine."

They followed the road as it led west, toward the spire, which grew in immensity as they approached it. When the road reached a large roundabout, Jax cut through the traffic to the island in the middle. A bronze statue of a man stood in the center of the island, facing the spire. Yolken recognized the man from his visits to the Dragon Shrine in Lonely Oak: the Emperor of the United Realms.

Jax looked up at the palace. "The home of the Chancellor of the Western Realm and Regent of Onta," he said. He pointed up to the top of the left wing of the building and said, "That balcony is Reago's residence, and that one," he said, pointing to the topmost balcony on the right wing, "belongs to Devin and Karina."

Yolken turned back around and looked at the statue again.

Drakonias stood facing the entrance to the palace. He wore scaled dragon armor resembling a chiseled chest and a cloak that rippled out behind him as if a breeze blew it. With his right hand, he gripped the Dragon Scepter, which was the likeness of a dragon winding its way up a tall staff. The detail of the dragon was amazing. Yolken noticed Drakonias gripped the scepter at a portion of the staff visible near the dragon's underbelly.

"As amazing as it is," Jax said, "we'd best be on our way. I'd like to hire a boat and be out of the city before the day's out."

"Good idea," Deborah said.

The roundabout had exits to the west, east, and south. Jax headed toward the road leading south. Deborah, Kaylan, and Yolken followed. Deborah walked up alongside Jax and they began to discuss hiring a boat. Yolken and Kaylan followed them, hand in hand, admiring the brilliance of the city.

One thing Yolken noticed as they walked through the city was that people in need were conspicuously absent, unlike in every village they'd passed through from Croff to Onta. Even Lonely Oak had them. But not a single person they passed as they walked down the marble street lined with marble buildings looked anything but prosperous. He peered down alleys and side roads as they passed them, but never saw anyone huddled in a corner or otherwise looking like they didn't belong.

"What's the matter?" Kaylan said.

Yolken shook his head. "Don't you think it's strange that nobody here seems to be in need?"

"I hadn't noticed it."

"I haven't seen a single person who didn't look like they had at least as much money as your uncle," Yolken said, looking ahead at Jax.

They passed through the heavily guarded South Gate of the wall surrounding the city. The road turned left and followed along the base of the wall, and their surroundings immediately changed. The buildings outside the wall were not the gleaming marble of those inside the wall—rather, they were run-down and made from wood and brick. Not only did the buildings change, but the condition of the people did as well. They no longer wore fine suits and dresses, but clothes resembling the buildings that now surrounded them—dirty and ragged. Yolken realized it was all a façade.

Yolken stopped at a vacant lot at the base of the wall where the road turned right, heading south. Scattered bricks were all that remained of the building that had once stood there. A large group of people crowded the area; many of them lay on mats, while some sat against the wall of the adjoining building. As Yolken realized why there were no beggars on the street within the walls, his heart sank. The sight of so many people huddled together stirred within him a feeling he remembered experiencing once before.

Kaylan pulled on his arm. "Come on. We're going to lose Mammy and Jorgan."

Yolken gave into Kaylan's pull and they hurried to catch up with Jax and Deborah. They soon found them standing outside a building with a large loaf of bread carved on the door. The docks were visible a little farther down the road.

"Why don't you all stay here and look for something to eat, while I go secure a boat," Jax said.

"Sounds good," Deborah said. Jax started down the road, and she looked in the satchel she had slung over her shoulder. She turned to Yolken and Kaylan and said, "We should definitely restock before we leave the city—who knows what Jax will find down there."

"Do you mind if we have a look around?" Yolken said.

"Just don't go far," Deborah said. "Kaylan, hand me your bag."

Kaylan unslung her bag from her shoulder and handed it to Deborah. Deborah took it from her and ducked into the bakery.

Yolken took Kaylan by the hand and said, "Come on."

"Where are we going? Mammy said not to go far."

"Just back up this way a little," Yolken said. He led her by the hand back up the road toward the wall. He stopped in front of the group gathered in the empty lot.

Yolken looked down at the people lying helplessly on mats crowded near the street. Some of them were asleep, but those who were awake looked up at him curiously. Most people passing by, he figured, ignored them. As he looked down at them, he realized why they crowded along the street—they weren't allowed to beg in the city, so they picked the next best spot. And they weren't simply the poor begging for money; every single person crowded into the lot had some sort of ailment. He knew they were here to beg for mercies from the Blessed, who likely frequented this road connecting the palace and the docks. Their look reminded him of Kristana's look when Issa had fallen from the oak tree. They were looking at him with hope.

"What are we doing here?" Kaylan said.

"I was thinking," Yolken said, "why would they choose to gather in this lot?" Shielding his eyes, he looked over at the bright sun hovering just over the ramshackle buildings. "Why would they choose to sit here under the hot sun? There must be cooler, shaded spots somewhere else. Why here?"

"I don't know."

"I think this road," Yolken continued, pointing back toward the gate and then down to the docks in view below, "is often traveled by Blessed traveling to and from the city."

"So?"

"So, even though this spot exposes them to the harshness of the sun, it also puts them in direct view of the Blessed." When Kaylan looked at him in confusion, he added, "They're hoping that the Blessed will heal them." Yolken let go of Kaylan's hand and knelt beside the closest person to him—a woman with twisted legs.

"Yolken," Kaylan said, "I don't think this is a good idea. Jax told you not to use your gift. What if someone sees you?"

"They won't," Yolken said. He unslung his pack and set it on the ground, then reached inside the rolled-up end and touched the hilt of the Harachin sword.

"How can you be sure?"

"Perhaps there are Watchers milling about, but if I don't draw from the sun, and I don't let Energy leave the body," he said, "they won't see anything." He reached toward the woman and said, "Do you mind?"

She sat up on her mat. "Are you one of them?"

"Who?"

"One of them Blessed?"

"Sort of," Yolken said.

The woman studied him for a moment, then tentatively nodded.

"Try to relax," Yolken instructed. He looked down the road in both directions to ensure there were no armored men in sight, then pulled Energy from the sword. He ignored the feeling of sweet relief at having Energy flowing through him as he directed it into the woman's leg. The memory of what he did for Issa flooded back into his mind, and he knew exactly what he needed to do.

The woman cringed in pain as her crooked leg involuntarily straightened.

Kaylan gasped.

Yolken let go of the woman's leg and she eased herself back down to the ground as the pain abated. Yolken gave her a moment to recover, then moved his hand to her left leg. He repeated the process and she sat back up abruptly as another pang shot through her, then lay back down when Yolken finished. When she recovered, he took her by the hand and helped her to her feet. She placed her hands on his shoulders to steady herself.

Holding onto him for support, the woman looked down at her legs. She looked up at Yolken, whose eyes were mere inches from her, and whispered, "Bless you." She tried to move her legs and wobbled unsteadily.

Yolken reached up and took the woman by the hands. He motioned for Kaylan to come help him. She moved closer, and Yolken placed her hands into Kaylan's. "It will take some time to let your legs get used to working, so go easy," he said to the woman.

She nodded.

Yolken turned from her and looked down at the others crowding the side of the road. All eyes were on him, each of them pleading with him. His heart ached for those who were missing limbs; he knew there was nothing he could do for them. But although he was not able to replace their lost limbs, he did what he could for them.

He knelt beside an old man who was missing both legs below the knees. He wore only a filthy rag around his waist. Sores oozing green pus covered much of his blistered skin. Yolken placed his hand on the man's forehead and sent tendrils of Energy into him. He felt around with the Energy in search of what caused the sores. He identified an unfamiliar organism feeding on the man's skin and used Energy to burn the organism everywhere he found it, careful not to further damage the man's body. He traced every inch of the man's skin with Energy to ensure none of the organism remained, then set to healing his sores. "Bless you!" the man exclaimed, looking up at Yolken, then closed his eyes as a sigh of relief washed over him.

Yolken moved from person to person, checking the road often to ensure it remained clear, until he had done what he could for every person in the square. Many of them had the same skin affliction as the man missing his legs, so he eased their unnecessary suffering. While he worked, those he had healed slowly left the lot. Soon, only four people remained—those with missing limbs. Tears welled in his eyes. He wanted to help them.

A woman missing her entire left arm touched his shoulder and whispered, "'Tis all right, lad."

Yolken's tears let loose. "I wish there was more I could do," he said.

"You've done more here than has been done in twenty months."

Yolken stood and looked down at the few remaining in the square. He reached into a side pocket in his satchel and pulled out all the money Jax had given him. He divided it up between them, then turned once again to Kaylan, who stood by looking at him with glistening eyes.

Kaylan reached out and took Yolken by the hand, pulled him close, and hugged him.

"Please don't say anything to Jax," Yolken said. "When he finds out, he'll be furious."

"I won't."

CHAPTER 28

W**here have you two been?"** Deborah said when Yolken and Kaylan arrived back in front of the bakery. She stood under the overhang with two bulging satchels.

"We just went for a little walk," Yolken said.

Deborah gave Kaylan her satchel back and said, "Jax should be back any minute now, so keep near."

"We will," Kaylan said. She turned and slid her hand behind Yolken's head and pulled him down until their faces almost touched. "I love you," she said, then kissed him gently.

While they waited for Jax to return, the three of them perused nearby shops with roadside displays. Yolken wondered who would ever buy the trinkets that many of them sold. He stopped in front of a shop selling jewelry and looked at the various necklaces, bracelets, rings, and earrings on display. "Do you want anything to remember Onta by?" he asked Kaylan.

Kaylan shook her head. "I've never much liked jewelry. This is the only thing I need," she said, holding up her left hand. Yolken smiled and kissed her. They moved on and she added, "When we marry, we'll need to get you a real ring. I don't want you wearing that cheap thing Jax found for you."

They stopped in front of a food market and Deborah bought

dried meats and hard cheeses to fill Yolken's satchel. Then they found a bench to sit on near the bakery and waited for Jax to return. Yolken picked a strip of dried meat seasoned with crushed peppers from his satchel. After only a couple of bites, he found himself drinking water from his flask and wiping sweat from his brow.

"Draego's Fire," Yolken said, wiping his brow. "I don't know how much of this I can eat."

"Don't worry," Deborah said with a smile, "I bought some without the peppers as well."

"There you are," Jax said, walking up to them. "I found a schooner that will take us as far as Ronig."

"Where's that?" Yolken said. He wiped his brow again as the sweat continued to bead.

"What have you been doing?" Jax said sternly.

"Don't worry," Deborah said. "It's just peppered beef."

"Ah, they do grow a hotter variety here, don't they?" Jax said. He laughed and slapped Yolken on the back. "Ronig is a fishing town south of here. It's the closest point to… our destination."

"They won't take us all the way?" Kaylan said.

"I haven't broached the subject yet," Jax replied. "I figured it's a request best made when we are not in a city filled with Blessed. Let's go; the captain won't wait all day."

Yolken drank more water as they made their way down to the docks. The road came to a T, branching left and right as the buildings gave way at the water's edge. They stopped at the sloping ramp leading down to a dock and gazed at a large moored ship. It had a thick mast with huge, furled sails.

"The *Vineyard*," Jax said, gesturing toward the ship. "Devin's ship. Majestic, isn't it?"

"It is," Kaylan and Yolken both agreed.

"Ours is down this way," Jax said, gesturing to the left.

They followed the road built along the top of a stone seawall, passing several docks that jutted out into the water; several ships of various sizes and shapes were moored to each one. Jax made his way down the sixth dock from the *Vineyard*'s.

Kaylan hesitated at the top of the ramp.

"What's the matter?" Yolken said.

"I've never been on a boat before."

"Neither have I."

"Aren't you nervous?"

"A little," Yolken said. "We'll do it together, okay?"

Kaylan nodded.

Hand in hand, they made their way down.

Jax and Deborah waited for them about halfway down the floating dock, next to a ship half the size of the *Vineyard*. When they were close, Jax walked up the ramp and onto the ship. Deborah waited for Yolken and Kaylan, then the three of them followed Jax.

When they caught up with Jax, he was talking with a shirtless man. A cloth was secured over the man's head with a thin rope, and extended down the back of his head so that it covered his neck.

"This is Captain Urgil," Jax said, introducing them. "He has graciously given his quarters to us while we're on board."

"How very kind of you," Deborah said.

Urgil bowed deeply. "Anything for the right price, ma'am," he said with a wink. "Master Shen will show you to your quarters. I'll be seeing to casting off."

Jax led them across the deck while Urgil barked orders at his sailors. They descended steep, narrow steps leading underneath the deck at the back of the ship, then proceeded down a short hall and through the solitary door.

"Our quarters for the next few days," Jax said. He unslung his satchel and tossed it on the floor.

"How much did it cost?" Deborah said.

"Does it matter? It was either here or share the berth with the rest of the crew."

"I suppose you're right."

"Can we go back up and watch as we pull away from the dock?" Kaylan said.

"Yes, dear," Deborah said. "Leave your things here; I'll get everything arranged as best I can."

Yolken and Kaylan unslung their satchels and tossed them onto the room's sole bed. Yolken set his rolled-up cloak that concealed the Harachin sword on the bed next to his satchel. "Where are we all going to sleep?"

"I already took care of it," Jax said. "Urgil will bring us a couple of mats once we're out of the bay. Now be off or you'll miss it."

Yolken took Kaylan by the hand and they hurried back up to the deck. Men worked busily tossing ropes over the side to dockworkers. When the ship was no longer secured to the dock, the men dispersed to other areas to further ready the ship. Some began to climb the mast in the middle of the deck; others ran up to the front where there was another smaller mast. Yolken and Kaylan watched eagerly as the ship slowly moved away from the dock. A shrill whistle caused them both to turn, and they saw Urgil waving at them from atop the back deck, gesturing for them to join him.

They took the stairs leading to the upper deck and joined Urgil, who stood along the front railing, supervising the entire goings-on. A man behind him had one hand on a giant wooden wheel.

"The view is much better from up here," Urgil said.

Once the ship cleared the docks, it began to move faster. Behind them, the city slowly grew smaller as they pulled farther into the Onta bay. They marveled at the tall spire, rising high above the city like a beacon guiding sailors home. The shores stretched out around them like the wings of a hawk enshrouding its young, leaving only a small opening between the two tips of land.

From their position at the front of the deck, they watched the sailors work as the ship sailed toward the inlet. White marble towers stood at the end of each arm, opposite each other. Yolken could just make out men standing on both towers. The glistening light from the setting sun reflected off their armor.

They moved to the very back of the ship once they reached open water and watched as the inlet grew smaller. The water of the open sea was considerably choppier than the waters in the bay, and Yolken's stomach began to feel unsettled. He leaned over, braced his forearms on the railing, and rested his forehead on his hands.

"What's the matter?" Kaylan said.

"I'm not feeling all that good."

Kaylan placed her hand on his back.

It was a familiar feeling. And it was growing. He remembered it distinctly from the last time he drank too much ale. The feeling right before he… Yolken lifted his head and leaned over the railing. He opened his mouth and let fly the dried meat that had recently burned his mouth. As he readied himself for another expulsion, he realized it was going to be a long trip to Ronig.

CHAPTER 29

Lannary reclined opposite Javen in the tub, submerged up to her neck. "Let's go sailing," she said.

"I thought you wanted to take a carriage out to that winery you're so fond of?" Javen said.

The last month had been a whirlwind. Javen's Synthesis lessons with Devin were progressing well. His mornings alternated between meeting with Devin on his balcony and conditioning his Core on his own. The rest of his days were filled by the never-ending stream of women Karina sent his way. He had all but mastered the technique Devin taught him on how to use his gift in bed, and combined with his increased stamina from his regular conditioning, he met every challenge Karina sent him.

Oddly enough, for reasons he still didn't understand, Lannary didn't seem to mind. She often asked after his other lovers, wanting to know more about them than he was comfortable sharing, and seemed to know most of them—at least by name, if not more intimately. The first time she had suggested that they invite one of them to join the two of them for food and bedding, he had blushed furiously.

"I changed my mind," Lannary said. "I still want to take you there, but I've decided that today I want to go sailing."

Javen climbed out of the tub and wrapped a robe around himself. The thin material clung uncomfortably to his wet body. He enjoyed watching the same thing happen to Lannary and the other women he bedded, but didn't care for the sensation himself. He crossed to the door dividing the bedroom from the dining room, leaving a trail of wet footprints behind, and pulled on a knotted rope hanging next to the door. He then went over to the armoire to pick out some clothes. "What does one wear while sailing?"

"Whatever you wish," Lannary said, rising from the tub. She gestured at her body with both hands and said, "I plan on wearing this."

"You're going to ride through town like that?"

"I'll find something *appropriate* to wear down to the docks, but once we're at sea, we won't be needing our clothes anymore. Well… at least I won't."

Javen blushed and turned from Lannary. He sifted through the armoire, looking for something to wear. He picked a simple green shirt made from silk, and light brown pants. He pulled on the pants, then turned back to watch Lannary dry herself with a towel while he buttoned the shirt.

Oshie appeared in the doorway. "You called?"

"Are there any boats we can take sailing?"

"Yes, Master Javen. There's a whole fleet of ships to suit whatever need you might have."

"Good. We wish to go sailing today."

"How long did you plan on being gone?"

Javen turned to Lannary in question.

Lannary stepped out of the tub. "Just for the day."

"I'll see to it that arrangements are made," Oshie said. "Will there be anything else, Master Javen?" Javen shook his head, so she bowed and left.

Javen finished buttoning his shirt and sat on the bed while

Lannary went to the armoire to choose some clothes. He actually wouldn't have minded if she rode to the docks naked. She was, after all, one of the most beautiful women he'd ever met. He enjoyed being with her. When he was with her, he wasn't thinking about Hadie.

In her own way, Hadie was equally as beautiful as Lannary. And despite how much he enjoyed his time with Lannary, she didn't invoke within him the captivation he felt for Hadie. Ever since he'd given up hope of being with Kaylan, his feelings for Hadie started to grow. Every day he hoped Devin would find her. He would trade Lannary and all the other women if only he could be with her again.

For now, he pushed the thought of Hadie out of his mind and watched Lannary closely as she picked out a short dress that matched his shirt. She turned toward him before she stepped into it, then pulled the dress up until the bottom hem reached the middle of her thighs. The upper portion of the dress was simply two strips of silk, each about a hand wide, that crossed at the middle of the back. He smiled as she stretched the material from the sides up and over her breasts. Once she had the dress in place, it left a wide gap down to her navel.

Javen rose from the bed and held his hand out for her. As she crossed the room, the tight fabric stretched across her thighs. She took his hand and they made their way out of his quarters and through the palace.

A small, two-passenger carriage awaited them at the base of the marble steps outside. When they were seated, Lannary handed him a glass of wine. There were two things he had not been without since arriving in Onta: wine and someone to bed. As the carriage pulled away from the palace, he chuckled.

"What?" Lannary said.

"Nothing." He leaned over and kissed her to distract her from asking more questions. He didn't want to tell her that what he really wanted was some of his brother's ale. She had no love for ale. In Onta they drank wine. The Blessed drank wine, not ale. He'd heard it all before, so he didn't want to hear it again. Kissing her worked.

As the carriage made the final turn toward the docks, Javen glanced out the window over Lannary's shoulder and sat up. He stuck his head out the window of the door and shouted, "Stop!"

The driver tugged on the reins and brought the carriage to a stop. Javen handed his glass to Lannary, pushed the door open, and climbed out.

"Where are you going?" Lannary called after him.

Javen ignored her and walked around the back of the carriage. He stopped when the lot at the base of the wall came into view. The beggars who normally crowded the lot were largely absent. He crouched next to a man who was missing both his legs at the knees.

"Where is everyone?" he said.

"Gone."

"Where?"

"They left."

"Why?" Javen pressed.

"Someone came along and healed them."

Javen looked down at the man, surprised. Devin had completely ignored the large group of people when they'd arrived in Onta. He remembered finding it a bit strange; he'd thought that Devin's majestic return from his travels would have been the perfect opportunity to shower his blessings on his subjects. *Dorlan certainly didn't miss an opportunity to display his power*, he thought, remembering little Issa. In the time that he had been in Onta, Blessed had come and gone—he'd even gone down to the docks with Devin to meet a few of them. And they had all shown the same indifference for the beggars as Devin.

"Who healed them?" Javen said.

The man shrugged.

That's odd, Javen thought. Even though he had trouble

believing it was a Blessed that healed them, it had to have been. Who else could it be? They were the only ones with the gift. But if it had been a Blessed, the man would have known—they were easily identifiable. He stared down at the man.

If it wasn't a Blessed, then it had to have been… At the very least it had to have been a rebel.

The man looked up at Javen with a tinge of fear in his eyes. "What do you want?"

"Was it the Blessed?" Javen said.

The man shook his head.

If it wasn't the Blessed, then there were rebels nearby. Javen rose to his feet and returned to the carriage. "Take us back to the palace!" he shouted at the driver before climbing back in.

"What's the matter?" Lannary said.

Javen shook his head. Even though he'd been bedding her for the last month, he didn't feel comfortable discussing this with her. With Hadie, it would have been different—he trusted her. Lannary was just a… someone Karina probably paid to pleasure him.

The road wasn't wide enough for the driver to turn the carriage around, so he turned down a side road and drove through the ramshackle buildings, eliciting shouts from several people as they jumped out of the way. They emerged on the main road, close to the gate leading through the wall.

Javen downed the wine in his glass and stared out the window, considering the implications of what he might have just discovered.

CHAPTER 30

Ursella was unlike the other girls working at Sonja's. They all had one job—to bed Sonja's clients. Ursella, however, never bedded anyone. Instead, Hadie learned, she was essentially a servant—she did Sonja's bidding, whatever that happened to be. And since Hadie had come to Sonja's, her job had been primarily to train Hadie. She still did other errands and tasks for Sonja, but she spent the bulk of her day with Hadie. As Hadie learned what Ursella's job was, she knew she was being trained to take over for her.

"It's how everyone wanting to join the brothel starts," Ursella said.

"So you're not a whore?" Hadie said.

"I am, just not here. I used to work at another brothel down the street; when Sonja started hearing my name float around amongst the madams, she brought me here. But before I can start bedding her clients, I have to earn my spot."

Ursella was eager to move on, Hadie knew, so she taught Hadie her job well. Once Sonja was satisfied with Hadie's performance in the lobby, she started giving Ursella patrons of her own. Hadie thought Ursella almost looked excited when she guided her first client through the beaded doorway—the whores for the most part didn't *enjoy* being whores, they did it because they had to. And whores made a lot more money than the girls who served wine, prepped patrons, and cleaned rooms.

Hadie wondered if Ursella knew she was only here temporarily. Not wanting to disappoint her, she kept her plans to herself. However, as soon as she found Javen and killed Drenan, she was going to leave. She knew this, and Sonja knew this. Even though she had grown accustomed to the ogling eyes of patrons, she had no interest in being a whore. She couldn't imagine letting these disgusting men have their way with her.

As she poured wine wearing a tight crimson corset laced up the front, she often thought about the morning Sonja had pulled her into her private quarters. Hadie had stood naked before Sonja, wondering if she had done something wrong, while Sonja brushed the tops of her bosom with the fingers of her left hand.

"Once we learn where your lover is, I will assist you in killing Drenan," Sonja had said.

Then, without any sort of explanation as to how or why she had decided to help, Sonja sent Hadie off to Ursella to be fitted with a corset.

Hadie had knocked eagerly on Ursella's door. It wasn't until she'd tried on the fourth corset that she learned what had happened to the whores Sonja had taken with her to herald Drenan's return. She still remembered being unable to stop herself from gasping in horror. The numbness she'd felt as she stared at her reflection in the mirror while Ursella dressed her was still vivid. While Ursella worked, she'd described all the whores who had returned from the regent battered and bruised over the years.

"I can't believe she keeps sending us to him," Ursella had said as she worked. "I'm tired of tending to the poor girls when they come back beaten. Maybe this will finally get Sonja to stop."

"Maybe she doesn't have a choice," Hadie said, thinking about her conversation with Sonja.

"What do you mean?"

"Have you ever considered that maybe Sonja keeps sending whores to Drenan because he makes her?"

"I never thought of that. There!" Ursella exclaimed. "Finally!"

Hadie stared at herself in the mirror. She almost didn't recognize herself. She wore a thick, pleated skirt that hugged her waist tightly. It extended to the ground and hid her feet. Even after such a short time at Sonja's, it was odd to look at herself and not see her naked reflection. The corset squeezed her tightly, making it difficult to inhale fully. Crisscrossing red laces cinched the corset closed in the front, but despite its tightness, a gap the width of her hand remained, leaving a visible path from her navel to her breasts. The corset squeezed her breasts up, giving the appearance that they were about to spill out the top.

"Bend over as if you're pouring wine," Ursella said.

Hadie did. "Wow," she said, gawking at herself. "I look amazing."

"You truly do. You'll drive the men insane. Now, if you lift your leg like this," Ursella said, lifting her leg up at an angle, "you'll really drive them wild."

Hadie turned to face the mirror sideways and lifted her foot up on a stool. The folds in the skirt fell away, revealing her stocking-covered leg. The black stockings stopped halfway up her thigh and were held in place by a length of silk tied to a loop woven to the inside of the skirt, near the waist.

"If you combine showing them a little leg with a look at your chest, you will do well in preparing them for their appointments."

"Won't I seem… boring… after traipsing around for a month completely nude?" Hadie said.

"You might think that, but you'll find the exact opposite to be true."

"Really?"

"Have you ever been with a man before? I mean, aside from whoring?"

"Yeah," Hadie said, blushing.

"Haven't you ever noticed that they get just as excited about the *prospect* of bedding you as they do the *actual* bedding?"

Hadie nodded.

"Then you know that if done right, you can almost leave a man fully satisfied without ever having to take your clothes off."

"Almost?" Hadie said.

"Almost."

Hadie looked at herself in the mirror and imagined how Javen might react if she teased him while she wore this, then denied him any further access to what she concealed. She imagined he would not be too pleased.

"Hadie," Sonja said, bringing Hadie's mind back to the present. She looked up at Sonja who stood near the beaded door. "Come with me."

Hadie set down the wine bottle she had been uncorking, with the screw half twisted into the cork. She followed Sonja through the brothel and up to Sonja's private quarters. It had been a full month since she'd last spoken privately with Sonja. Anticipation grew within her as they walked.

"I've located your lover," Sonja said as soon as the door to her room closed behind Hadie.

"Where is he?" Hadie said. She could hardly contain her excitement. Was she actually going to see Javen again?

"He's in Onta."

"Onta!" Hadie exclaimed in disbelief.

"It seems that his care was transferred to the Regent of Onta when the two of you were in Portstown. He was seen being taken to the regent's ship moored at the docks."

Hadie remembered seeing the ship there the night she ate dinner with Lyoll. Her excitement at the prospect of reuniting with Javen faltered. Onta was a world away—much farther away than she had traveled before she met Javen. She thought about how many drakes she had and how many might be left after she paid Sonja for her help.

"How much do you think it would cost to buy passage on a ship?" she said.

"Lass, I know how much you've been hoping to find him, and I know you hoped he would be here in Hantlo, but were I you, I would forget about him. I hate to say it, but he's likely already forgotten about you."

"Why do you say that?" Hadie said. A sense of hopelessness crept up inside of her. She tried her best to ignore it.

"I'm sure you know who the Regent of Onta is?"

She knew. She'd read *Lovers of Onta.*

"And his wife?" Sonja continued.

"What are you saying?"

"You said the Regency is interested in your lover, no?"

Hadie nodded.

"It seems to me that they have taken him under their wing. If that's true, then how do you think Karina is going to treat him as a guest in her palace?"

Hadie knew what Sonja was getting at, but she refused to think about it. After she'd killed Drenan and paid Sonja for her help, she was going to Onta, whether she had the money to or not.

"What now?" Hadie said.

"If you're still up for it, we move on to the second part of your plan."

"When?"

"Tonight."

CHAPTER 31

Hadie gazed out the window of the carriage as it carried her through the city, toward the Regent of Hantlo's palace. The past few hours had been a whirlwind of activity that never permitted Hadie to recover from her shock. She'd figured she would have days to prepare for what she had to do, but instead she had had only hours. And in that brief time, her attention had been pulled in two different directions, leaving her little time to think about what she was preparing to do.

She'd never killed anyone before, let alone a regent. They were the Blessed of the Dragon. They weren't immortal, but close enough. They didn't age like everyone else, and they used their gift to heal each other. She'd tried to mentally prepare herself while she waited for Sonja to decide whether she was going to help or not, but wishing Sonja would help turned out to be completely different from hearing her actually *say* she would help. And too quickly she'd gone from thinking about killing Drenan to actually planning to kill him. Her fantasy became reality, but without enough time for her to prepare herself mentally.

She was having difficulty breathing—and not because of the corset. The passing scenery blurred as she reflected on those last few hours.

Sonja placed a small leather bag, heavy with gold coins, into Ursella's hands and said, "What is said in this room you must never speak of."

Ursella took the bag and nodded.

"Now help me get her ready."

"Ready for what?" Ursella said.

"She's going to work at the palace tonight."

Ursella looked surprised, but took Hadie by the hand and led her to the tall mirror in the corner of Sonja's room. Hadie knew what she must be thinking. Only the most experienced whores worked in the palace and Hadie had only just come to Sonja's. She wasn't even one of Sonja's whores yet.

Ursella positioned her in front of the mirror and lit the lanterns that hung on either side of it. She adjusted them so they burned brightly, then turned her attention to Hadie. After unlacing the ties on the back of Hadie's skirt and the lace strings holding up her stockings, Ursella pulled the skirt to the floor. Next, she worked quickly to unthread the lace cords that cinched the corset in the front. When it fell to the floor, Ursella motioned for Hadie to step out of the skirt around her feet. Hadie complied, and Ursella kicked the skirt and corset out of the way.

"Her breasts need to look bigger," Sonja said.

Ursella looked down at Hadie's chest, making Hadie suddenly aware of her reflection in the mirror. She crossed her arms over her chest to conceal herself as a wave of insecurity washed over her.

Ursella grasped her hands, gently moved them to her sides, and looked at her intently for a moment. Then she crossed the room, opened the armoire against the wall and sifted around in a drawer at the bottom. When she returned to where Hadie stood, she had two pouches in her hands.

"What are those?" Hadie said.

Holding one in each hand, Ursella pushed them up against

the underside of Hadie's breasts. "Sheep stomach."

Hadie gagged. "Sheep stomach! What's it for?"

"To make your breasts look bigger."

Ursella frowned and went back to the open drawer at the bottom of the armoire. She returned the two pouches to the drawer and pulled out two more that were slightly bigger and smiled with satisfaction when she held them up against Hadie's breasts.

"Occasionally, we're asked to attend events hosted by His Majesty," Sonja said, "and I don't always have enough girls who meet his criteria, so I came up with this idea. By making these little pouches and filling them with water, I can make any girl look bustier than she really is."

"But won't he just find out when they're bedded?" Hadie said.

"Those who wear these are assigned to non-bedding duties."

Hadie shook her head in disgust.

"One thing I've learned over the years," Sonja continued, "is to never let Drenan become unsatisfied."

Next, Ursella sifted through the crimson corsets hanging in the armoire until she found what she was looking for. She pulled the front of the corset open, slid the pouches into pockets sewn on the inside, then pulled the corset from the hanger.

Hadie held her arms straight out from her sides while Ursella reached around her and pulled the corset tight around her torso. Hadie held the corset against her body as Ursella began to work at tying the lace that held it closed, starting from the bottom. When she got about halfway up, Ursella stopped and said, "Hold these." Hadie held the laces tight so they wouldn't loosen while Ursella reached inside the corset and pulled Hadie's breasts in and up so they sat on top of the pouches hidden inside. When she had them positioned where she wanted them, Ursella took the laces back from Hadie and finished cinching the front closed.

After Ursella finished cinching the corset, she returned to

the armoire, opened another drawer, and sifted through it. While she stooped down in front of the armoire, Hadie took the opportunity to take a peek in the mirror. She looked at herself straight on first, then turned from side to side.

"Go ahead, give them a squeeze," Sonja said.

Hadie hesitated.

"Go on," Sonja urged.

Hadie felt weird, but she reached up and cupped her enlarged chest—gently at first, then she gave them a firm squeeze. To her surprise, through the corset it felt as if her breasts were as big as they looked.

Ursella returned from the armoire and handed Hadie a small piece of black silk.

"What's this?" Hadie said.

Ursella looked down at Hadie's bare bottom.

Hadie looked at the cloth in her hand. It was a pair of silk undergarments with no leggings. "You've got to be kidding me. What about the skirt I've been wearing the last month?"

"That would never do for Drenan's visitors," Sonja said. "Put it on, we haven't all night."

Hadie bent over and stepped into the undergarment, then pulled the small piece of material up. It fit snugly over her bottom and stopped short of her thighs.

Ursella knelt in front of her and pulled Hadie's stockings up firmly on her right thigh and tied the silk cords to the bottom of the corset. She did the same on her left leg.

When Ursella finished, Hadie once again examined herself in the mirror, inspecting her newest article of clothing. The cloth concealed her bottom, but little else.

"Sit," Ursella said, placing a padded chair immediately behind Hadie.

Hadie sat.

The moment her silk-covered bottom hit the chair, Ursella began to fidget with her hair. As she worked, tightly weaving

Hadie's hair into an intricate bun using more pins than Hadie had ever imagined possible, Sonja went over to her desk. She retrieved something from a drawer then came and stood in front of Hadie.

"This is what you will use to rid Dradonia of that vile man," Sonja said. She held up a pin featuring a flower made from tiny gems. "It's laced with a very deadly poison."

Sonja spent the next several minutes explaining to Hadie the routine that Drenan followed with each woman sent to bed him.

"He will be sitting in his chair. Stand before him and begin to remove the pins from your hair, moving provocatively, just as Ursella taught you. When you pull out the pin with the flower, lean in to give him a close-up view of your breasts. Then, instead of setting it down with the rest, stick him in the neck with it. The poison will not take long to do its job."

"Won't he be able to just use his gift to heal himself?"

"You needn't worry about him using his gift."

"Why not?"

"I have studied the Blessed for a long time now and know that even they are not without limitations."

"All right," Hadie conceded. She once again remembered the last words Drenan had spoken to her: "*If I ever see you again, I promise that I will do more than simply look at you.*" Fear swelled in her constricted chest as she realized her plan wasn't going to work. "So you don't think he'll recognize me?"

"You said he threatened to rape you, no?"

Hadie nodded.

"Then perhaps that's a good thing. When he recognizes you—*if* he recognizes you—"

"Why wouldn't he recognize me?"

"You saw yourself in the mirror. You aren't the woman you were when you first stepped into my brothel. And if his servant does her job, he'll be quite inebriated before he lays eyes on you. But even if he does recognize you, he'll realize he's beaten you—

that by taking Javen from you he's driven you into whoring, the most detested occupation in the empire. His lust for you will become insatiable as he realizes he has complete control over you. He will revel in the opportunity to humiliate you."

As sick as it made her to think about it, Hadie knew Sonja was right. And if she succeeded, it would be she who reveled in his humiliation. The Blessed who was killed by a whore.

"After you stick Drenan with the pin, you are to do exactly as his servant says. She is the only one who can get you safely out of the palace."

"What then?"

"That is completely up to you, lass. I'll ride with you to the palace, but once you step out of the carriage, we will never meet again."

"So you're leaving Hantlo?" Hadie said.

"I won't live to see the sun rise if I don't."

"What about your girls?"

"Ursella will see to their safety once we leave."

Ursella looked up from what she was doing and glanced at Sonja.

"I will compensate them sufficiently that they can leave Hantlo and never need to whore again," Sonja said.

Hadie's gaze out the window of the carriage returned to focus as the carriage passed through the open gate in the wall surrounding the palace. The last time she had been here was at the gala he'd thrown for himself just before he left for Kyinth—not long before she decided to leave Hantlo herself. Silks had come en masse to bid him a pleasant journey, and she had been her father's begrudging guest.

Closely-spaced poles bearing blazing torches illuminated the roadway, leaving the grounds behind the torches dark. As the carriage stopped in front of the steps leading up to the palace entrance, Hadie closed her eyes and took as deep a breath as the corset allowed.

"You'll do fine, lass," Sonja said, patting her on the leg. "Are you sure you want to go after that lover of yours?"

Hadie opened her eyes and said, "I am."

"The best of luck to you then. Remember, when you're finished, listen to Rennie. She has your gold and will get you safely out of the palace."

"You don't want me to pay you for your help?" Hadie said.

"No, lass. After all, it is *you* who is helping *me*. I've even given you a little extra," Sonja said with a wink. Looking past Hadie at the guard approaching the carriage, she said, "Now, be off with you."

The door opened and Hadie took the hand of the guard when he offered it and stepped down out of the carriage into the wet night air. She felt exposed, as though everyone in the city were staring at her. Never in her life had she dressed like this, not even in private, let alone out in full view of the public. The southern house garb was revealing, no doubt, but dressed as she was, it meant but one thing—she was a whore about to do some bedding. Everyone who saw her would know what she was about. She turned to Sonja, and Sonja blew her a kiss.

Then the guard closed the door and the carriage pulled away.

CHAPTER 32

Drenan looked over the railing of his balcony. The light of the city was a fraction of what it had been before Drakonias' infamous edict. Two rows of torches illuminated the pathway leading to the entrance of the palace. The carriage carrying his pleasure for the night had just arrived. From this height, and in the poor lighting, he couldn't make out enough detail to determine who it might be. Madam Sonja had hinted that it might be someone new.

He watched the whore emerge from the carriage and disappear into the palace. Rather than returning to his quarters to greet her upon her arrival, he watched the carriage pull away from the palace and exit through the gate, back into the city. Torchlight illuminated the streets surrounding the palace walls, so he watched as the carriage merged with the other carriages and carts crowding the dimly lit road. He watched it until he lost it in the masses.

He looked down at the empty glass in his hand and picked up the bottle of western wine sitting on the ledge. Tipping it over, he filled the glass anew. Devin had brought plenty of it on their journey, and Drenan had been quite pleased when he'd agreed to part with what remained when they arrived in

Portstown. It was expensive, and in short supply in the south, so it was worth it. Devin was, after all, boarding a ship stocked to the gills with it as well as returning to the realm of wine, so it wasn't as if he needed it.

The flapping of wings to his right drew his attention away from the city below. A condor emerged from the darkness held at bay by the torches burning on the wall behind him. Its wings flapped quickly as it stretched out its feet to alight on a wooden perch. Drenan frowned. Condors sent directly to his personal quarters never brought with them good news.

With the glass of wine in his hand, he walked over to the large bird as it settled into position, arriving next to it just as it finished tucking its wings against its body. Drenan set the glass of wine down on the ledge and pulled the rolled-up piece of paper from the bone tube attached to the condor's leg. He unrolled it and read it.

> *Dearest brother,*
>
> *Do you remember the saying Father often repeated when we were young? Come, quickly! What you lost in the north can be found in the west.*
>
> *Devin*

Drenan crumpled up the paper in his fist and thought about the saying of which Devin spoke: *When a dragon hunts its prey, it descends quietly from on high; whether night or day, it rains fire from the sky.*

For the first time since he'd sent his bastard in search of Danavin's get, Drenan smiled.

* * *

The guard climbed the torch-illuminated steps, leading Hadie into the palace.

Hadie took as deep a breath as she could.

At the top of the steps, they walked through two large wooden doors made from several thick planks fitted tightly together. The wood was smooth and glossy, with no carvings of any sort, and encased in a silver frame. They had to be at least ten paces tall. Every time she had passed through them with her father, she'd imagined it probably took an entire tree to make a single plank.

She stepped through the doors into the atrium, and its cavernous size overshadowed the immensity of the doors. The guard walked straight across the open floor on a wide rug to the staircase on the opposite side. The rug gradually grew wider as they got closer to the staircase. On the way, they passed several marble statues of both people and animals positioned along the edge of the rug. The staircase was widest at the base, and arched out in a half-circle, narrowing as it led to each successive floor of the long palace.

Hadie was acutely aware of everyone looking at her. She felt as if she were on display, traipsing through the palace wearing the obvious clothing of a whore, and she worried what those whose eyes lingered might be thinking about her.

But the moment she put her foot on the first step leading up the long staircase, it no longer mattered what those milling about the atrium thought, because the reality of what she was about to attempt finally hit her. Since she had arrived in Hantlo, killing Drenan had largely been fantasy. Even as she'd stood in Sonja's room, while Ursella prepared her physically and Sonja instructed her on what she was to do, it hadn't seemed real. She'd hardly been able to think while the carriage rolled through the city, and now, as she took step after step up the granite staircase, the immensity of what she intended to do washed over her. It was larger than the wooden doors that always amazed her; larger than the atrium she had walked into; larger than even the grand staircase she was ascending. Each step she took made her fantasy more of a reality. She was about to have her revenge for what Drenan had done to Javen. Revenge for what he had done to Sonja and her girls. Revenge for what he had done to Astora and

Selena. Revenge for what he'd done to her.

Hadie passed several sets of stairs that curved off the main staircase. She didn't pay any attention to them or the floors they led to. Instead, to help keep her nerves at bay, she focused on the shimmery overlapping ovals covering the armor of the guard who walked two steps ahead of her.

Despite her best efforts, she began to doubt her plan. She doubted whether she could actually pull it off. Drenan was Blessed, and the Blessed had lived for millennia. Surely someone had attempted to kill him before. Why should her plan—as simple as it was—be successful when there were surely others, better trained and better prepared, who had attempted before and failed? Surely something had happened to him to leave him covered in scars.

She also feared what Drenan would do if he recognized her. What if Sonja was wrong? What if he killed her like he did Panny and Kit? No, she forced herself to conclude, his lust for her would preclude his desire to hurt her. If he was going to kill her, it wouldn't be until after he'd had his way with her.

She forced the doubt out of her mind. It was too late to turn back now so it didn't matter. She had set in motion a plan irreversible—if she fled now she would die, and Sonja was already gone. No; only one of them would see the sunrise. As she climbed higher into the palace, she hoped it would be her.

At the top of the stairs, Hadie stopped behind the guard as he rapped on one of two gilded doors with his fist. She fidgeted with the taut laces crisscrossing up the front of her corset as she waited. The door opened and the guard stepped aside. Hadie took a deep breath and stepped into the room.

"His Majesty will be right in," Rennie said. She showed no visible sign of recognizing Hadie. "Would you care for some wine?"

"P-please," Hadie said. Her stomach roiled.

Rennie shut the door and crossed the room to a table that

held several bottles of wine. While Rennie worked, the brilliant blue armor just to Rennie's right caught Hadie's attention. It hung on a wooden frame to the left of a fireplace, which had a small fire burning in it. The last time she had seen Drenan— when he'd used his gift to rip her clothes off and manhandle her—he had been wearing that armor.

In front of the fireplace sat two high-backed, velvet chairs. Hadie swallowed a lump in her throat as she recognized it as the spot where she would shortly end the life of the second most powerful man in the realm. Even farther to the right, sharing a wall with the door into the room, was Drenan's bed. With a sense of disgust, she looked away.

Rennie returned to where Hadie stood and handed her a glass of wine. "I'll let His Majesty know you're here." She walked to the set of double doors on the opposite side of the room and disappeared through them.

Again, Hadie fidgeted nervously with the lace on her corset with her free hand. She looked briefly at the tapestry hanging on the wall to her left, but her nerves soon took over to the point that she could no longer concentrate on anything. Instead, she stared at the open set of double doors Rennie had walked through.

She raised the glass nervously to her lips and took a sip. Before she could swallow, Drenan stormed through the open doors, his right hand clutched in a fist. He walked straight over to his armor and began hastily removing his clothing. "Prepare my things!" he barked.

Rennie trailed after him, trying to help, but he brushed her aside. He slipped on the leggings and buckled the breast piece around his chest; then, without even noticing Hadie standing next to the tapestry, he stormed out of the room, slamming his hands against the doors to push them open.

Rennie rushed over to Hadie and grabbed her by the hand, saying, "Come, we haven't much time."

Rennie led Hadie to the door and one of the other servants took the glass of wine from her as she passed them by. Outside the door, Rennie entered a side door, which led into a small area with a spiraling stone staircase.

Panic welled inside of Hadie as they made their way down. They passed a door each time they completed a circle down the stairs, finally stopping in front of one that looked the same as the others. "Wait here," Rennie said, then opened the door and went through it.

What felt like an eternity passed as Hadie stood alone in the stairwell, wondering, not knowing what was happening.

"What's going on?" she said when Rennie returned.

Rennie shoved a heavy purse into Hadie's hand and said, "His Majesty is leaving the city."

"Why? What happened?"

"I don't know. I must get you out of the palace quickly so I can see to the necessary preparations."

At the bottom of the staircase, they entered a large kitchen with several stoves and large wooden tables. It bustled with activity. Drenan's petite servant pulled Hadie through the kitchen and out a door leading to the palace grounds. Once outside, Rennie jogged quickly down a straight path that led through a garden, pulling Hadie after her by the hand. At the base of the wall, Rennie unlatched a narrow door and opened it. "I'm sorry," she said, beckoning Hadie to step through.

Hadie looked at Rennie in confusion.

"Please, hurry."

Hadie stepped through the door and it slammed shut behind her. She turned and looked helplessly at the closed door. A wave of pent up emotions washed over her as she realized that her opportunity to kill Drenan had come and gone. With Sonja fleeing the city, there was no one remaining who could help her.

She turned and leaned against the door. Since the moment Sonja had told her that today she would be killing Drenan, she had been hit with a barrage of emotions. Fear. Anxiety. Determination. Revenge. Doubt. And now, failure. Her opportunity missed, and no longer in immediate danger, the emotions collapsed in on her. She burst into tears and slid down the rough wood until she sat on the ground. She pulled her knees up to her chest, wrapped her arms around them, and cried.

CHAPTER 33

Hadie felt a hand on her shoulder and an accompanying soft voice say, "There, there, lass. Everything'll be all right."

Hadie lifted her head from her arms and wiped her eyes with the back of her hand. She looked up at the silhouette of a person standing over her.

"Might I offer you a future apart from whoring?" the male voice said.

"What?" Hadie croaked.

"There's nothing to be ashamed of, lass. Many have come through this gate before you, and those who accept my offer end up living much better lives. My name is Teff," the man said, holding out his hand, "and I own a factory in the southeast quad. Work in my factory comes with decent wages, warm food, and a bed. What do you say?"

"No, thank you," Hadie said. She pushed herself to her feet and ignored the man's extended hand. She crossed her arms over her breasts, feeling exposed in the corset and ridiculously small piece of undergarment.

"Suit yourself. Should you change your mind and find yourself in the southeast quad, look me up. My offer remains standing to all those who wish to accept it."

"Thank you," Hadie said.

The man turned from her and walked down the alley between the palace wall and the building standing next to it.

She walked quickly in the opposite direction. She emerged at the end of the alley on the road that paralleled the front wall of the palace. She didn't know where to go, so she turned right and followed the nearly empty road, hugging the purse Rennie had given her tightly to her body. She felt doubly exposed, walking scantily-clad through the city and carrying a bag heavy with gold.

Hadie's awareness lapsed as she walked. She became less cognizant of her surroundings until she wandered mindlessly through the sleeping city, not knowing where she was. She didn't care anymore. The streets were largely empty, but even as she passed the occasional night wanderer, she gave little thought to her safety. She received an occasional glance or open gawk but nothing more. No one bothered her.

When night began to give way to day, she finally stopped. In the pre-dawn light, she stared ahead and found herself standing at the foot of the stairs leading up to the doorstep of Sonja's brothel. She stared up at the door, not knowing why she had come here. With nowhere else to go, she climbed the steps. She half-expected the door to be locked since Sonja had fled Hantlo, but when she turned the knob, the door opened.

Hadie walked into a dark lobby. She crashed onto a couch and lay down, curling up on her side. She closed her eyes and tried not to think about what had happened, but it was impossible. She had been so close; she'd been in the same room as Drenan. Hadie reached up to her hair and felt around until she felt the pin with the flower on it. She pulled it out and dropped it to the ground. *So close,* she thought, closing her eyes.

The ceiling creaked faintly. Hadie opened her eyes. She picked the pin back up and sat up. Standing, she groped her way through the lobby—she was familiar with the layout of the couches—to the beaded doorway. She felt her way down the length of the hallway, keeping her hand on the wall, until she reached the stairs at the end.

She slowly climbed the stairs, pausing on the second floor. The hallway was dark. Seeing no light under any of the doors and hearing nothing, she continued up the stairs. She stopped on the third floor and, finding it equally deserted, continued up to the fourth. Light peeked underneath the closed door at the end of the hall—Sonja's room.

Hadie silently made her way down the hallway, holding the pin in her hand. When she stepped up to the door, she pressed her ear against it and listened. Someone shuffled around inside. Hadie placed her hand on the knob and thought about how to proceed. Should she turn around and leave, or see who was in there? If it was Sonja, she wanted to tell her what happened. Maybe they could come up with another plan to kill Drenan.

She turned the knob.

Ursella looked up from behind Sonja's desk, eyes wide. "What are *you* doing here?"

"I…" Hadie started. She looked over at a metal bucket in the center of the room; a fire was burning in it. "What are you doing?"

Ursella walked around the desk with a handful of papers and tossed them into the bucket. "Burning Sonja's records."

"Why?"

"So the regents can't find her or any of the girls. Her client lists include the names of which girls they prefer; she wanted to protect their identities."

"Oh. Well, you can stop." Hadie stepped farther into the room while slipping the poisoned pin back into her hair.

"Why? What happened?"

"Nothing. No one will be coming for Sonja or any of the girls." Ursella looked expectantly at her. "I'll tell you about it in the morning. I'm exhausted." Hadie turned from Ursella, intent on finding a bed, but stopped. She turned back around and asked, "How much have you burned so far?"

"I just started."

Hadie hurried over to the desk and looked down at the open drawer. It was stuffed with sheets of parchment. She rifled through them, pulling individual pieces up to look at the names at the top. They appeared to be organized alphabetically. She skipped clumps of pages until she found the letter she was looking for, then she flipped through them one by one. She froze on a page when she saw the name she was looking for, and pulled the parchment completely out. Unlike the other sheets, there were no names or particular bedding preferences listed on this one. The only thing besides the name was an address.

Hadie folded the parchment and went over to the armoire. She held the folded parchment in her lips as she began to unlace the corset she wore. When it fell to the floor, she opened the armoire and pulled out her pants hanging inside. She pulled them on over the thin undergarment, then grabbed her shirt.

"What are you doing?" Ursella asked as Hadie buttoned her shirt.

Hadie shook her head. When she finished, she grabbed her satchel, folded the parchment again, and shoved it in a pocket. "Take care," she said to Ursella as she hurried out the door. On her way through the lobby, she picked up the bag of gold she had left on the couch when she went to investigate the sound upstairs.

By the time Hadie left the H district, the sun was just creeping over the horizon and the city was coming to life. She walked with determination toward the address scrawled on the parchment.

Day was in full swing when she arrived at the narrow street in the northeast district. Hadie walked between the closely-spaced houses lining both sides of the street. She stopped in front of a house indistinguishable from the others—it had three square windows, one on top of the other directly over the door, and its tan color matched the others. She looked at the number painted vertically on the right corner. She didn't have to pull the parchment out of her pocket to know it was the one.

Hadie took a deep breath and walked up to the door, which was set only a couple of paces back from the narrow street, and knocked. Tears welled in her eyes as she waited. When the door opened, she looked into the eyes of the red-haired man who answered.

"Lass, what are you doing here? How did you find me?"

Hadie stepped through the door, buried her face in the man's chest, and sobbed, "Oh, Lyoll!"

"It's… it's okay," Lyoll said, patting her back hesitantly. "Ganip!" he yelled. "Put on some tea! We've got company."

CHAPTER 34

The sun reflected off the dozens of pins in Hadie's hair as she cried into Lyoll's chest.

"There, there, lass," Lyoll said, patting Hadie on the back. "Come in, come in."

Hadie sniffed and followed Lyoll into the house.

"Sit over here," Lyoll said. He gestured to a worn sofa against the wall.

Hadie did as he instructed, and Lyoll sat next to her. She heard loud footsteps tromping around above her. The footsteps moved toward the rear of the house. Stairs squeaked as feet quickly descended them. A gangly boy sprang through the empty doorway on the far side of the room, catching the jamb with both hands to stop himself quickly.

"Who's here?" Ganip said. With a quick look in her direction, he exclaimed, "Hadie! What are you doing here?"

"Put some tea on, will ya?" Lyoll said.

"Yeah, sure." Ganip spun and disappeared through the door.

"I'm sorry to bother you," Hadie said. "But I didn't have anywhere else to go."

"You're not bothering us," Lyoll said. "But what's happened to you? No, no," Lyoll quickly added, "you've obviously been through a lot. Let's wait until you have some tea to help calm yourself down a little and then you can tell us what's happened."

"Do you have any of that whiskey of yours?" Hadie asked.

"Uh… sure. Lemme go get it." Lyoll rose from the couch and went through the door Ganip had appeared and disappeared through.

Hadie removed the jewel-encrusted pin first and slipped it into a side pocket on her satchel, then began removing the rest of the pins from her hair, setting them on the small table at the end of the couch.

Lyoll returned a moment later and set two small glasses on the short table in front of the couch. He sat back down next to Hadie, uncorked the large jug he held in his other hand, and poured some of the light-brown liquid into both glasses. He set the jug on the table and handed one to Hadie.

Hadie upended the glass and coughed when the liquid burned her throat. She held her glass out and said, "More."

Lyoll refilled Hadie's glass. "Have you eaten, lass?"

Hadie shook her head.

"Go easy, then."

Hadie leaned back on the couch and cradled the glass in both hands. She took a deep breath and took a sip.

Lyoll sat next to Hadie and sipped on his glass quietly.

After a few minutes, Ganip came back through the door carrying a tray in his hands with a teapot and cups on it. "What? No tea?" He set the tray on the table.

"She wanted something a little stronger," Lyoll said.

"Well, it's too early for me to start hitting that stuff of Lyoll's, so I'm gonna have tea," Ganip said. He pulled a wooden chair from the corner of the room and set it on the other side of the table from the couch. He poured himself a cup of tea, leaned back in the chair, and put his feet up on the table. "It's sure good to see you, Hadie. What are you doin' here anyways? I thought I'd seen the last of you."

"Give her a moment to get her wits about her, Ganip," Lyoll said.

Hadie took a few more sips from her glass then breathed a deep sigh of relief. "I went to Sonja like you told me to…"

"And did she agree to help you find that lad of yours?" Lyoll said.

Hadie nodded. "It took a while, but she eventually learned that he was put on the Regent of Onta's ship in Portstown and sent to Onta."

"Onta!" Ganip exclaimed. "Why'd they send him there?"

"I don't know," Hadie said. She took a sip of her whiskey and pulled a few more pins out of her hair.

"I'm so sorry, lass," Lyoll said. "I know how much you liked the lad."

"I *love* him, Lyoll," Hadie said. She pulled pins from her hair to stop herself from curling up in a ball on the couch and crying. "You have to understand why I couldn't just abandon him." She set a few more pins down. "Anyways, that's not all Sonja agreed to help me with."

"No?"

"She also… it's just… I hate him *so* much…" Hadie wiped tears from her eyes with the sleeve of her shirt. "I couldn't let him get away with what he did to that poor girl."

"Who?" Lyoll said. "What girl?"

"He murdered her in cold blood just to goad Javen into using his gift."

"Who are you talking about, lass?"

"Drenan."

"He… is that what happened to the lad?" Lyoll said.

"You told me to go to Sonja because she could help me find Javen, so I did. But by the time I arrived in Hantlo, I decided there was something else I wanted her help with too." She took another sip of her drink then stared into her cup, silently debating with herself whether she should admit what she had done. If anyone found out she had attempted to murder the Regent of Hantlo, she would hang—people hung simply for talking about such things in the wrong circles. The only other people who knew about it were Sonja, Ursella, and Rennie, and they were all complicit, so she didn't have to worry about them saying anything. These two, though—they *worked* for the Regency.

"What?" Ganip said.

"Don't rush her," Lyoll said.

"You were the only two to treat us kindly while we were in the caravan, so I trust you not to…"

Lyoll placed his hand on Hadie's back. "Lass, whatever it is, you don't have to worry about anything you say going beyond these walls."

Hadie looked over at Lyoll, completely trusting him, and said, "I tried to kill Drenan."

Ganip spewed tea all over the table and fell over backward in his chair.

"You… tried… to kill… Drenan," Lyoll said slowly. "Wha… what happened?"

Ganip picked himself up off the floor and righted the chair.

"Too many have suffered under Drenan, so I decided it was time to end it."

"But you don't simply decide to kill a regent!" Ganip exclaimed. "Draego's Fire… they're Blessed of the Dragon!"

"Shh, keep it down, lad," Lyoll said. "No sense in alerting the whole neighborhood—unless you want to see a rope around her pretty neck, that is."

"Sorry," Ganip said. "It's just…"

Lyoll waved for Ganip to be quiet. He turned to Hadie and said, "You're saying Sonja agreed to help you kill Drenan?"

Hadie nodded. "She said she's put up with him abusing her whores for years; when he killed two of them, she decided she'd had enough."

"Why would he kill her whores?"

"I don't know why, but he had his servants dump them off like garbage. He's a monster, Lyoll."

"I know, lass, but killing him? That's not such a great idea."

"I know it wasn't, but after what he did to Javen and that poor girl from Lonely Oak, I had to do something." She took a drink from her cup. "Anyway, I had my opportunity and missed it. I didn't have anywhere to go, so I came here."

"Tell us what happened, lass."

Hadie recounted everything that had happened since her meal with Lyoll in Portstown, beginning with buying a new knife and finding a merchant to ride with to Hantlo, all the way up to standing in Drenan's room with a poisoned pin in her hair and watching her opportunity storm away. She took several drinks of Lyoll's whiskey as she spoke.

When Hadie finished, Lyoll said, "What now?"

"At first I went to Sonja's. I don't know why… maybe I thought I'd get another opportunity. But she's gone and not coming back. That was part of the plan all along. She was done with that life. Even when she hears that nothing happened, I doubt she'll return. I think she got the break she's wanted for a long time."

"I agree," Lyoll said. "She's not coming back."

"How do—?"

"Because I know. So… what now?" Lyoll repeated.

"First, I need some sleep," Hadie said. "And then… then I'm going to Onta. And I want you to come with me."

Ganip spewed tea from his mouth a second time.

CHAPTER 35

Hadie woke slick with sweat, her head pounding. She knew she should have heeded Lyoll's advice about drinking so early on an empty stomach, but just as in Portstown when Drenan had taken Javen away, she didn't care.

She rose from the bed and collected her clothing, which lay strewn across the floor. She was grateful that Lyoll had let her sleep in his bed—the door had a lock on it so she'd slept naked with the windows open. Her efforts were futile, though; there was no escaping Hantlo's sweltering heat and wet air.

Before putting her clothes back on, she picked up the small towel Lyoll had given her on her way up to the third floor of his tall and narrow house, and dunked it in the bowl of water he'd also provided. After wringing it out, she used the cool, damp towel to wipe her sleep away. When she was dressed, she stepped over to one of the windows and looked outside. The rows of houses were situated facing north and south. This far south, the sun's path through the sky was high enough that it never shined directly through the windows. Judging by the light and the way the buildings had a red hue to them, she guessed it was early evening.

Hadie descended the stairs slowly. She knew she'd asked a

lot of Lyoll to come with her to Onta. She was grateful that, instead of outright saying no, he offered to think about it and said they'd talk about it more after she'd slept. She didn't know why she wanted him to come with her—she was perfectly capable and had the gold to travel there herself—but for some reason it was to his house that she'd gone. Lyoll and Ganip were the only people in Hantlo she felt she could trust. Everyone else she knew was a Silk, or associated with Silks.

If Lyoll and Ganip said no, she would understand. Either way, her mind was made up: She was going to Onta. She just hoped they would come along.

At the bottom of the last flight of stairs, Hadie stepped into the kitchen. Lyoll and Ganip were both at the small table hunched over plates of food. A small potted flower with yellow petals sat on the table between them.

"Grab a plate," Lyoll said without looking up.

Hadie opened a cabinet with peeling paint and retrieved a plate. She used the large wooden spoon sitting next to a pan on the stove and dished herself up a heaping pile of the sauce-drenched pasta. She found a fork in a drawer and joined Lyoll and Ganip at the table. She looked at the yellow flower a little more closely. The yellow petals had veins of red running through them.

They ate in silence. Ganip occasionally looked over at her from the corner of his eye. When Lyoll and Ganip finished, they sat back in their chairs and waited quietly.

"Lyoll," Hadie said, setting her fork down when her plate was empty, "I know asking you—"

"Yes," Lyoll said. "My answer is yes."

Hadie grinned broadly. "I didn't think you would agree."

"So long as the chancellor is holed up in his palace, we are of no use to him."

"But what if he should need you?"

"There are other teamsters in the city. In fact, with all the regents from the southern provinces here, Hantlo is positively swarming with them. Besides, maybe what little influence I have within the Regency will be of some use."

Hadie looked at Lyoll, confused.

"Once we get to Onta, you're gonna need to get access to the lad. And you can't very well stroll into the palace and demand his audience."

"I… I don't know what to say," Hadie said. "Except, thank you."

"Think nothing of it, lass. Ganip and I have been going stir-crazy sitting around doing nothing. We'll leave with the tide first thing in the morning."

* * *

In a dark room, Hadie woke to the sound of knocking on the door.

"Just a moment," she called out.

"Time to go," Lyoll called back.

Hadie climbed out of the bed and stumbled to the lantern hanging in the corner. She struck a match and lit it, then turned the knob to bathe the room in its soft light. She collected her clothing and quickly put them on, not bothering to wipe herself dry first; the wet air prevented her from ever being dry anyway. She buckled her belt around her waist and unconsciously felt for the knife at the small of her back. She picked her satchel up from the foot of the bed and slung it over her shoulder.

She doused the light, then joined Lyoll and Ganip on the bottom floor. They each had a small leather pack slung over their shoulders. "What time is it?" she said.

"An hour or so before the tide lets out," Lyoll said. He opened the front door and held it as Ganip and Hadie walked through.

The streets of Hantlo were still largely asleep. They made good time as they navigated their way toward the north road. It was much busier than the smaller side streets, even at this early hour.

Hadie glanced to her right when they passed the street leading toward the H district. She'd failed, but she was glad that experience was over. The idea of being a whore still made her sick. She felt bad for all the women who depended on the lifestyle to survive. She felt the bag of gold in her satchel and wondered how much Sonja had given each of them. She had only been at Sonja's for a short time, and her bag contained more gold than she would have thought was fair. She hoped that each woman had received at least as much, if not more. If they did, it would be plenty for them to start fresh.

They rounded the bronze statue of the emperor in the middle of the large roundabout at the center of the city just as the sky began to show hints of dawn. Hadie looked up at the larger-than-life replica of the man who ruled over all of Dradonia. His armor shimmered in the light of the lanterns illuminating the roundabout. The plates covering his chest and stomach resembled the descriptions of the emperor's physique. She wondered if he was actually as muscular as the stories depicted. In his right hand he gripped a thick scepter, intricately carved into the serpent-like creature of legend. The scepter was about two-thirds the height of the emperor.

Lyoll exited the roundabout following the south road. Ganip and Hadie followed a half-step behind. It slowly grew lighter as they made their way toward the docks.

As they approached the south end of the city, the grade of the road increased, causing them to descend relative to the surrounding buildings. The buildings rose higher around them as they made their way toward the docks. Every few dozen paces, a narrow set of steps carved into the rock led to streets up above. Before long, the height from the road to the buildings became so great that the steps were replaced with bridges. Ahead and high above them, Hadie could see the end of the city approaching.

At the end of the towering cliffs Hantlo was built on, the road turned abruptly to the left and continued down the side of the cliff. Hadie hadn't been down this road for several years, so she stopped to look up. The city was built right to the very edge of the rock wall and the granite buildings were visible peering over the edge from fifty paces above them. She looked over the metal railing on the right side of the road at the Hantlo river, flowing another two hundred paces below them.

Hadie felt a gentle hand on her shoulder.

"Come, lass," Lyoll said.

She turned from the river and followed Lyoll down the road. They walked along the railing, keeping clear of the wagons moving slowly down. Along the wall, horses labored to haul wagons up. The smell of fish wafted by each time a wagon passed. Walking with her hand skimming the top of the railing, Hadie could see the docks stretching out below.

"Do you think we'll be able to find a ship?" she said.

"There are always ships sailing between Hantlo and Onta, so I'm sure it won't be difficult," Lyoll said. "Ultimately it'll depend on how much comfort you desire for the voyage and how much you're willing to pay."

"I have gold," Hadie said, feeling the bag through her leather satchel again.

"Then we won't have a problem," Lyoll said.

"We should hire a whole schooner," Ganip said.

"Are you paying?" Lyoll said.

"No, but—"

"No, but then you don't have a say, do ya?"

"I was only saying…"

"I don't have enough gold to hire a whole ship, anyhow," Hadie said.

"Ganip and I can make do staying in the berth," Lyoll said. "No sense wasting money on the likes of us. But I suggest private quarters for yerself."

"I don't see why I have to stay with the salts," Ganip protested.

"Because you're a teamster, lad. And teamsters don't get private quarters."

"Not now, we're not teamsters," Ganip said. "We're—"

"My escorts," Hadie said. "And if you want to stay in my quarters, you're welcome to."

"We'll be fine," Lyoll said. "A lass needs her privacy."

As they descended the road carved into the side of the cliff, the smell of fish grew stronger. It reminded Hadie of their arrival in Portstown—her last day with Javen. Before long, instead of looking down at the ships moored at the string of docks, Hadie was looking up at their tall masts.

The road broadened at the bottom of the canyon and continued farther for another few hundred paces. Wagons lined the edges, in queue to either drop off goods or pick them up. They waited in rows in the center of the road as well.

Lyoll led them around the railing that ended at the bottom of the road and back up the wide stone walkway paralleling the road. The docks continued to the west almost as far as they did to the east. "Wait here," Lyoll said when they approached a line of benches. "I'll find us a ship."

Ganip plopped onto one of the wooden benches and Hadie sat next to him. She leaned back and rested against the cool rock, watching as Lyoll made his way down the walkway. He stopped to speak with someone at each dock he passed that had a moored ship, then continued on.

"Are you sure you wanna do this?" Ganip said.

Hadie took her eyes off Lyoll, who was now several docks down, and looked over at Ganip. He picked at one of several red blemishes on his cheek.

"I mean, I get that you love Javen and all, but with him bein' mixed up with the Blessed, I don't know that it's all that smart. You know firsthand they don't respond well to people interfering in their affairs."

"I'm not worried about the Blessed," Hadie said. She looked

back toward the docks to find Lyoll again. "It's not as though they'll hurt me for telling someone that I love them."

"Lyoll told me that they said if they ever saw you again, they'd kill you."

"That was Drenan, and he's nowhere near Onta."

"I suppose," Ganip said. "But if what Lyoll said about yer fella bein' mixed up with the Regent of Onta is true, then isn't it likely he's already found another lover?"

Sonja's words rang through Hadie's head. *I hate to say it, but he's likely already forgotten about you.* Her eyes blurred as they filled with tears. She reached up and used her sleeve to wipe them away.

"I… I'm sorry," Ganip said. "I didn't mean to upset you."

Hadie shook her head. "It's not your fault."

"I just wanted to make sure you really wanted to be doin' this… goin' to Onta and all."

"Thanks, Ganip," Hadie said. She refused to believe that Javen had forgotten her so easily. "I'm sure." She wiped her eyes again.

"What's going on?" Lyoll said.

Hadie looked up and saw Lyoll approaching.

"Nothing," she said.

"You didn't go upsettin' the lass, did you, Ganip?"

"I didn't mean to."

"It wasn't his fault," Hadie said. "He was just trying to be helpful."

"I found us a suitable ship," Lyoll said. "If you're sure you want to be going to Onta, it sails in an hour."

"I'm sure," Hadie said again.

She stood and adjusted her satchel at her side. She had never loved anyone before and couldn't simply abandon Javen. She would never be able to forgive herself if she didn't go. And, if she got to Onta and it turned out that he had moved on, well… she would deal with it then.

"Let's go," she said.

CHAPTER 36

Lyoll led Hadie and Ganip down the walkway paralleling the Hantlo River.

"How much did it cost?" Hadie asked after they passed the third dock.

"Five drakes for you," Lyoll said.

"And for you and Ganip?"

"It's covered."

"I'll pay," Hadie said. "I'm the one who asked you to come with me."

"I know, lass, but you needn't worry about it."

"Thanks, Lyoll." Hadie reached into her satchel and felt her way into the heavy purse. She fished out five coins and handed them to Lyoll. "Here you go."

Lyoll took the coins from Hadie without a word. He turned at the fifth dock they passed and led them down the sloped ramp.

There were two ships moored at the dock, one on either side. Hadie eyed them both curiously. She had been sailing with her parents before, but had never been on anything this large. Her father traveled often and she had many sad memories of carriage rides to the docks with her mother to drop him off—it always meant she wouldn't see him for months. She had just as many memories of gleefully returning to the docks to pick him up on his return.

Lyoll climbed the gangplank of the ship on the right, and Ganip followed him. Hadie studied the ship a moment longer before following, wondering if it was one her father might have used. It looked much more weathered than any he had ever traveled on. She watched large hoists lower a crate into the bowels of the ship, then she climbed up the gangplank.

"Welcome aboard *Onta's Desire*," said a sun-darkened man. "Name's Cam." He held his hand out to Hadie and she shook it. "It's a pleasure to have you aboard, miss. Lyoll here did his best to barter his way into my own cabin, including offering to put the lad here to work, but we couldn't come to an accord."

"Hey!" Ganip protested. "Who said I—"

"As it is, miss," Cam continued, "I've got a cabin that'll suit you perfectly. Lyoll can show you the way, as I've got preparations that need seeing to." Cam bowed slightly to Hadie, then redirected his attentions to readying the *Desire*.

"I'll show you to your cabin," Lyoll said.

"What about us?" Ganip said.

"We can't very well share a cabin with the lass, so it's the berth."

"The berth…"

"What's wrong with that?"

Ganip looked around at all the sailors busy readying the ship for its voyage and sighed.

"You spend most of your time sleeping with horses, and you're worried about sleeping with sailors?" Lyoll teased as they crossed the deck toward the stairs leading down to the cabins.

"The smell's different."

"The smell?"

"Horses don't stink like—"

"Have you ever smelled yerself?" Lyoll said. He led the way

down the steep, narrow steps. He stopped in front of a door on the right side of the hallway and opened it.

"What about that one?" Ganip said. He pointed at a matching door opposite the one Lyoll opened.

"Already been let," Lyoll said.

"Fine."

"You don't have to come, you know."

Hadie walked through the open door and unslung her satchel. She set it on the small bed and looked around. The room wasn't big, but she honestly would have slept with the sailors in the berth; she knew how to take care of herself. And Lyoll was with her. She knew he would never allow anything to happen to her.

"You're welcome to stay here with me," Hadie said. "It's tight, but there's enough room for all of us."

Ganip's eyes widened and he opened his mouth to speak, but Lyoll stopped him by saying, "Nah, lass, it's as I said—a woman needs her privacy. Come on, lad," Lyoll said, gesturing toward the door, "leave the lass be."

"I'm not staying," Hadie said. "I want to watch us set sail."

Lyoll nodded.

Hadie followed Ganip out the door. When they climbed back up onto the deck, several sailors were working at closing the large bay doors in the center of the deck. She followed Lyoll to the back of the ship, out of the way, and watched.

Hadie looked up at the city perched high above them on the edge of the cliff. For the second time in only a few months she was leaving the city that had been her home. She hadn't planned on returning when she'd first left, but she also hadn't planned on falling in love with someone who would bring her back. Now that she was leaving a second time, she hoped it was for good. Once she found Javen, there was no reason for them to return. They would be in a new realm, far from the problems plaguing the south. She heard enough stories in the short time she had been back in Hantlo, working with Sonja, to know that Dorlan was rapidly losing control of the realm. She was honestly surprised that the docks weren't overflowing with people wanting to flee; it probably all came down to money.

The ship began to pull away from the dock, and Hadie gazed up at Hantlo for what she hoped was the last time. As the ship pulled out into the river and turned west, she looked back up the canyon walls to the east. The canyon turned sharply left at the far end of the city and formed the eastern border of the city as well. She turned around and watched as the ship approached an imposing bridge arching over the canyon. The latticework of metal visible underneath it glinted in the sun rising over the canyon wall behind them.

Being here brought so many memories to mind. Sailing with her parents as a child; taking carriage rides across the bridge and into the rolling countryside on the south side of the canyon from the city—both were fond memories. Her eyes moistened as she remembered convincing her father to stop the carriage so she could look over the side of the bridge. The memory of seeing the tiny ships sailing below was vivid. As the ship passed beneath the bridge, she mentally became the little girl running across the bridge when the ship disappeared underneath to watch it appear again on the other side. A feeling of guilt washed over her for leaving her mother behind.

Hadie turned around and watched the bridge slowly drift away. Ganip and Lyoll wandered the ship while they crossed from river to sea, but she stayed where she was. Dorlan's palace came into view, towering over the city built on the cliffs. Its majesty testified to his power. But unlike the tenaciousness of the rocks upon which his palace was built, which steadfastly endured the increasingly destructive weather, his rule was crumbling. She was indeed glad to leave it behind.

Hadie leaned against the railing and closed her eyes. She concentrated on the feeling of the ship slowly rising and falling in motion with the sea. *Onta's Desire.* She knew who the ship was named for—Karina—but she thought about Javen. *Hadie's Desire.*

Hadie imagined warm arms wrapping around her waist and a strong chest pressing against her back. She sighed when she envisioned the arms squeezing her tight. The hug loosened and she turned around. She opened her eyes and looked up into Javen's blue eyes. She wriggled her arms up between his and ran her hands through his dirty blond hair. Wrapping her hands around the back of his neck, she pulled his head down to her and kissed him deeply.

Javen broke off the kiss and took her by the hand. He led her down the steps and into the depths of the ship. He opened the door to her room and led her inside. After shutting the door and turning the lock, he took her by the hand again and walked over to the bed. He turned, kissed her again, then sat on the bed.

Hadie took her loose blouse by the hems with both hands and lifted it over her head. She unbuckled her belt and bending forward, toward Javen, she slid her pants down to her ankles. After stepping out of them, now wearing only the small silk undergarments she'd worn the night she went to kill Drenan, she began to move in the manner Ursella had taught her to whet the appetites of Sonja's clients. Only now, she was using her new skills to whet the appetite of the man she loved.

Hadie stepped close to Javen and leaned forward. She pressed close, making him lean back onto his elbows. She leaned farther, placing both her hands on the bed on either side of Javen and one knee on the wooden bed frame. She kissed him, then pulled away. As she slowly stood, he followed her, his mouth remaining less than an inch from hers. When he sat up again, she grabbed hold of his shirt and lifted it over his head, revealing his muscular frame.

She stepped back again, moving seductively. When he tried to follow her off the bed, she pushed against his chest to keep him seated. She danced for several minutes, occasionally leaning in close or lifting a leg up onto the bed frame next to Javen.

Hadie closed her eyes and leaned in for another kiss.

"You okay?"

The sound of lapping water replaced that of Javen's breathing. She opened her eyes and looked down at the wake spreading left and right behind the ship. Her face flushed at the sight of Lyoll standing beside her.

"Ah," Lyoll said with a smirk. "Thinkin' bout the lad?"

Hadie was too embarrassed to answer. Instead, she looked at the dwindling cliffs.

"Love is a curious thing. 'Twill make you do things you wouldn't never do otherwise."

"You mean like go to Onta?"

Lyoll looked over at Hadie and shrugged his shoulders.

"You said you've been in love before. Didn't you ever do anything you wouldn't have otherwise done?"

Lyoll laughed out loud. "Aye, lass. My whole life has been a result of doin' something foolish for love."

Hadie was surprised by his answer. "What?"

Lyoll leaned over the railing and looked back toward Hantlo. "I once followed a lass—more beautiful than the chancellor's palace, she was—from our home in the Fingers to Hantlo. We weren't exactly poor—my family made a decent living crabbing—but she refused to marry someone and spend the rest of her life in the Fingers. So when she announced she was leaving the Fingers for the riches of Hantlo, I followed her."

"What happened?"

"Well, I ended up hiring on as a teamster, and she became a whore."

Hadie looked over at Lyoll. He continued to gaze out over the water. "You mean Sonja?"

Lyoll nodded. "She eventually found her riches, but it was the end of us. I couldn't remain with her while she whored, and she wasn't willing to quit. 'The money's too good,' she always said."

"I'm sorry, Lyoll." She felt compelled to comfort him as he had her.

"It was a long time ago," Lyoll said with a shrug.

"Why didn't you go back home?"

"I couldn't."

"Why not?

"When you leave your family like that, you can never return."

Hadie thought about her parents. When Lyoll left her side, she stood there, wondering if they would take her back if she went home. It didn't matter, though, because she wouldn't be returning.

Hadie remained at the back of the ship and watched her home shrink into the distance. The pain she felt at failing to kill Drenan shrank with the city. Before long, the only thing distinguishable from the cliffs was Dorlan's palace. But even that soon disappeared. Then, the cliffs. When all she could see was water, she turned her back on her past and looked forward to her future.

Her future with Javen.

CHAPTER 37

Sethlan sat at the small desk to the side of Dorlan's throne. He scanned the crowd gathered in the throne room and sighed. It was going to be a long day. Being gone from the realm for so long tended to have that affect. There was nothing to be done about it, unless Dorlan decided to quit early, leaving petitioners unheard, so he picked up his pen, dipped it in the inkwell, and waited to record the first petition.

The people who crowded the throne room looked travel-worn. They were not locals—those would fall under Drenan's jurisdiction. Residents of the Hantlo province only appeared in court at the palace when their petitions went unheard or unresolved at the Regent of Hantlo's court.

Dorlan entered the room through the door at the back of the dais, clad in orange armor. When he appeared beside his throne, the din in the room quieted and the petitioners fell to their knees. Dorlan sat, and the crowd rose to their feet. He looked over at Sethlan and nodded.

Sethlan had compiled a list from the line of people gathered outside the throne room before they were permitted in. Now he called out the first name. "Gregan Nashor!"

A man and woman separated themselves from the crowd.

Gregan walked with his arm around the waist of the woman, who was large with child. He stopped at the bottom of the dais and they both bowed their heads.

"Speak your request," Dorlan said.

"Our c-crops didn't survive 'til harvest, Your Highness, and my wife is w-with child, so w-we left our home in Hunva with the rest to come here. Now, she is about to give birth and w-we don't have the money for a proper inn. W-we sleep in an alley and as much as I hate to beg from you, I can't permit my child to be born in sewage. Please, Your Highness, have mercy on us, O Blessed of the Dragon." Gregan bowed.

Dorlan gestured to his left where tables were set up behind a row of armored guards and said, "Speak to my Secretary of Coin at the first table."

"Bless you, Your Highness," Gregan said. Both he and his wife bowed then shuffled toward the guards.

Dorlan looked over at Sethlan again and Sethlan called out the next name, "Rik Tanger!"

The morning inched by slowly as Sethlan read off name after name and Dorlan heard request after request. Some he helped—those whose need he deemed to be greatest—but most he turned away. Sethlan knew the status of the treasury and knew Dorlan couldn't very well help everyone.

As petitioners made their requests, Sethlan recorded them in the ledger. He also made mental notes when he deemed the information valuable. Dorlan had held a meeting with his regents from around the realm the day after his return to Hantlo, but Sethlan hadn't been permitted to attend. However, over the last half-month, he'd gleaned everything he needed to know about the state of the realm from the requests of the petitioners.

This summer season had been especially brutal to the eastern provinces. Many of them joined the southernmost provinces and abandoned their homes, moving west. In his most recent communication with Jorgan, Sethlan had named three additional cities that were completely abandoned. He also reported that, from what he could tell, the reservoirs north and west of the Ginbon River still had water, so those provinces still held. However, their resources were strained because of the influx of those fleeing the easternmost provinces. All told, it sounded to him as though half of the Southern Realm was now abandoned. Dorlan's face betrayed what Sethlan knew to be true. In the time it had taken Dorlan to travel to Kyinth and back seeking help from the emperor, he'd lost another quarter of his realm.

A door at the back left of the chamber opened and caught Sethlan's eye. He watched as a courier ran up behind the row of tables and stopped behind one of the guards. The courier got the attention of the guard, who then stepped aside to permit him to walk to the base of the dais. The courier bowed and waited.

Dorlan gestured to the courier, and he hastily climbed the steps, knelt before Dorlan, and held out a rolled-up parchment. Dorlan took the parchment from the courier, broke the wax seal, and unrolled it.

Sethlan watched the chancellor intently as his eyes flicked back and forth, trying to ascertain his feelings.

Dorlan rose to his feet and rolled the parchment up. The crowd fell to their knees. "Sethlan," he said, turning toward the door at the back of the dais, "come with me."

"Yes, Your Highness," Sethlan said. He set the pen on the desk and followed Dorlan through the door, held open by a guard.

Dorlan handed Sethlan the parchment after the door closed behind them and said, "Find out where he's gone."

"Yes, Your Highness," Sethlan said with a bow. He walked alongside Dorlan as he made his way toward his personal chamber. When Sethlan unrolled the parchment, all it said was that Drenan had boarded his ship and set sail in the night.

"The realm is crumbling around us and he leaves?" Dorlan said.

Sethlan didn't answer—it wasn't his place. But he listened.

"What in Draego's Fire could be more important than his duties here. I swear…"

"I'll find out where he went, Your Highness," Sethlan said.

Sethlan turned as they walked and bowed, then stopped. He watched Dorlan walk away for a moment, flanked by two guards, then turned and headed in the opposite direction. He needed to get over to Drenan's palace as quickly as he could. Dorlan was obviously unhappy about the news that Drenan had left, so Sethlan didn't want to add to his displeasure. That, and he needed time to send messages of his own.

CHAPTER 38

Yolken opened his eyes when he heard the sound of a closing door. Kaylan lay on her side next to him, facing the wall. He turned his head to see Deborah setting a tray on the wooden dining table, worn by years of use, in the center of Captain Urgil's quarters. She walked over to the bed, sat down on the edge, and dabbed Yolken's forehead with a warm towel.

"How are you, dear?" she said.

"A little better," Yolken said.

The last two days had been completely miserable for both him and Kaylan. Neither of them handled being on a ship well at all. Yolken had never recovered after losing everything he'd eaten over the stern of the ship. After slowly making his way back down to Urgil's quarters, he had gone straight to bed, hoping that after he slept he would feel better—but it hadn't turned out that way. To make matters worse, while he slept, Kaylan had fallen to the same fate. Since then, neither of them could bring themselves to get out of bed.

"I'll be glad when we finally get to Ronig," he said.

"We aren't going to Ronig," Deborah said.

"What?" Yolken pushed himself into a seated position.

"Come over to the table and eat and I'll explain."

Deborah helped Yolken up. After a wave of nausea passed, he slowly made his way to the table. The usually amazing smell of Deborah's cooking made him feel like vomiting again. When he did nothing but look at the steaming bowl of soup, Deborah insisted that he eat, so he forced the soup down, gagging with each bite.

After Yolken had slurped down half a dozen spoonsful of the hearty soup, Deborah said, "Jax convinced Urgil to take us directly to Kvorga."

"How'd he do that?" Yolken said. "I thought Urgil refused to go there."

Deborah had told Yolken that Urgil was quite furious with Jax for not telling him about his true intentions until they were a day's sail from Onta.

"He did, initially. But Jax can be quite persuasive when he needs to be."

"How much did it cost?"

"He won't say. The good news is that we'll be there shortly."

"Really?"

"The two of you have slept practically the entire voyage. Now, eat. You need your energy." Deborah turned back to Kaylan and woke her with a gentle touch. "Time to wake, dear. We're almost there, and you need to get some food in you."

Yolken finished eating, and even though he didn't feel good, he found comfort in knowing this journey was about to conclude. He rose from his seat, went over to sit on the bed, and kissed Kaylan on the top of her head.

"Go on up, dear," Deborah said. "We'll join you just as soon as we're ready."

Yolken made his way slowly to the door and up the steep steps. He gripped the railing on both sides to hold himself steady as the ship rocked. Fresh sea air greeted him on the deck.

When he found Jax and Urgil, Jax said, "About time you get out of bed."

"Ugh," Yolken said, shaking his head.

"I don't believe I've ever known a man and a woman to spend so much time lying next to each other and not bed one another." Jax elbowed Yolken in the ribs.

Yolken ignored Jax and stared straight ahead, past the mast and full sails of the ship, at the towering mountains.

The island of Kvorga.

The mountains drew Yolken's attention away from an overly jovial Jax and the churning in his stomach. He wondered how they were supposed to find a single person on such a large, mountainous island. He still had trouble coming to grips with the idea that a fictitious woman living on an island shrouded in mystery could possibly be the best hope for him finding Javen. But his only other option was to face the Regency alone. And despite his reservations, he'd come too far and invested too much time to turn back now, even if the odds of them finding her were worse than those of finding a dragon. He hoped Jax and Deborah knew what they were doing by bringing him here.

Yolken leaned with both hands on the smooth wood of the railing, transfixed by the once-fantastical island that was slowly growing larger before him. Kaylan and Deborah soon emerged from below deck and joined them at the railing.

Yolken hugged Kaylan and said, "How're you feeling?"

"Like I'm about to lose the soup Mammy forced me to eat," Kaylan said. Her normally radiant face looked ashen.

"Me too."

"How much longer?" Deborah said.

"Not long," Jax said.

"Where are we going to moor?"

"Nowhere," Urgil said.

Deborah looked at Jax and said, "I thought you said he was going to wait for us?"

"I said no such thing," Urgil said. "I intend to put you in the dinghy and put as much sea between me and this cursed island as I can before the sun sets."

Deborah looked at Urgil with the kind of look Selena used to give Yolken when he was about to get in trouble. "You're leaving us with the dinghy? How are we supposed to make it back to Ronig in a dinghy?"

"Not my problem, ma'am. The original deal didn't even include my taking you this far. But Shen wouldn't leave me be. So here you are. How you get off the island is your problem."

"Jax!" Deborah exclaimed.

"I'll figure something out," Jax said with a terse look.

"I'll be below deck readying our things," Deborah said with a scowl.

Yolken watched as Deborah left, then looked worriedly at Jax.

"The only other way to get here would have been to buy a boat," Jax said, looking straight ahead at the island. "That would not have been very practical. And since no sailor would willingly sail it here, we would either have had to coerce them to do it against their will or sail it ourselves. Which," Jax continued, turning to look at Yolken and Kaylan, "I'm doubting the two of you would have been up to, given your state over the past few days. This was the only option."

Yolken and Kaylan stood silently, holding onto the rail while the ship pitched and rolled in the swells as the island slowly grew larger.

Jax bickered on and off with Urgil, attempting to convince Urgil to remain anchored off the island until they returned, but he had no success. The closer the ship sailed toward the island, the more Urgil fidgeted.

Urgil began to bark orders and motion with his hands at sailors around the ship when the shores of Kvorga grew near. Waves crashed against the island's rocky shores. However, Urgil steered the ship toward a sandy spot devoid of the perilous rocks. A forest of enormous trees stretched almost down to the water. The sails began to furl and the ship slowed. Sailors on the right side of the ship were fastening the dinghy, which had previously lain hidden upside down under a tarp, to a boom. Using winches, they raised the tiny boat up and over the side railing, then positioned it against the side of the ship level with the main deck. As the ship continued to slow, it turned sharply to the left.

"End of the line," Urgil said.

They made their way to the main deck. Yolken quickly grew apprehensive about the dinghy—especially the thought of having to cross the Kvorgan Sea in it. Was such a thing even possible?

"We'll pay you double if you anchor here for a month!" he heard Jax shout to Urgil.

"A full month?" Urgil spat. "No!"

"Triple!" Jax shouted.

"No!"

Deborah joined them on the main deck and handed everyone their things. Jax donned his coat, and Yolken mentally cursed himself when Deborah handed him his rolled-up cloak concealing the Harachin sword. He had meant to recharge it while they were at sea, but hadn't been able to because of his sickness.

"I am a man who specializes in the acquisition of information," Jax said to Urgil in one last desperate attempt. "And I hear that the *Vineyard* may soon be in need of a new captain."

Urgil looked at Jax with curiosity. "And how could you *possibly* know that?"

"Your trade is to perfect the sailing of ships, is it not?" Jax said.

Urgil simply stared at Jax.

"Mine is the acquisition of information—valuable information," Jax continued. "I save it, file it away, and trade it for the right price."

"What are you saying?" Urgil said. "That you can somehow convince His Majesty to appoint me as his next captain?"

"Let's just say that I know the right people and can plant a good word should the need arise."

Urgil looked guardedly at Jax for an uncomfortable amount of time. Finally, he said, "Triple the gold *and* captain of the *Vineyard*, and I will return to this spot in one month."

"Captain of the *Vineyard* should the need arise," Jax added.

"But the need will arise, no?"

Jax winked. "One month," he said, holding out his hand. Urgil shook it.

Urgil led them to where the dinghy hung over the side of the ship. He opened a latch and swung a small gate inward. Jax climbed into the dinghy first, and Yolken followed, stepping over a small gap between the deck of the ship and the side of the dinghy. Yolken set his things on the bottom of the boat, then turned to help Kaylan and Deborah in.

Jax directed Yolken and Kaylan to sit on a plank at one end of the small boat and Deborah to sit on the other end. Then he sat on the middle plank, reached under the board, and picked up two oars. The dinghy was lowered fitfully down the side of the ship toward the water.

"One month!" Urgil shouted down at them.

"One month!" Jax shouted back.

"Kind of steep, don't you think?" Deborah said.

"I had to do what I could to secure a ride off the island, didn't I?" Jax said.

"You don't think Anivera can get us off?"

"I don't want to depend on her. Last time someone asked for her help she said no, remember?"

Yolken listened to them curiously. Just as he was about to open his mouth and ask a question, the bottom of the dinghy hit the water. They all reached out frantically and gripped the sides of the boat to steady themselves.

"Get the ropes!" Jax shouted.

Yolken gathered his wits about him and unhooked the slack ropes hooked at his end of the dinghy.

After Deborah had the ropes unhooked at her end, Jax pushed against the side of the ship with the oars. As the little boat drifted slowly away from the ship's hull, he put the oars in the water and aggressively rowed to put distance between them and the ship. He turned the dinghy so that his back faced the island.

"What was all that about Devin needing a new captain?" Yolken said.

"I specialize in the trading of information, Yolken, so I keep my ears open at all times," Jax said. "It just so happens that while I was down at the docks securing our passage, I heard rumor that Devin's current captain is ill."

"And what was that about Anivera refusing to help?"

"Let me concentrate on getting this thing ashore, will ya?"

Yolken and Kaylan huddled together while Jax rowed with a steady cadence. The rising and sinking of the dinghy as it rode the swells felt more intense than it ever had on the ship. Yolken stared past Jax at the trees rising high above the beach. He could see exactly where Jax was rowing as the dinghy crested a swell, but then the beach disappeared when they descended back into the valley of water. The island was a little closer with each swell they crested.

Excitement filled Yolken. He was ready to be done with boats, and he was about to land on the island that until today had simply been the subject of endless tales. As Jax continued to steadily row, he thought about the stories Jax used to tell him, Javen, and Kaylan when they were younger. Many of them had been about the old woman he was now hoping would help him rescue Javen from the Regency.

"She is older than the Blessed," Kaylan's uncle had said so

many years ago, "but her gift was not the gift of the Blessed. Her gift stems from the island itself. She was not born there, but once she visited the island, she received her gift and never left. Older than the great Kvorgan spruce that grows, she has long, scraggly white hair and walks doubled over with a mossy cane. Her skin hangs loose on her bones and she has a knobby nose. However, despite her old body, her eyes remain sharp. Looking at them brings even the Blessed to their knees."

In other stories she was the mother of Dradonia and the source of its life and power, and instead of being old, she was eternally young; in those tales, men avoided the island because if they saw her they would instantly fall in love with her and never leave. And, in still others, she was the mother of the Dragon King, driven mad when he marooned her on the island for speaking out against his tyranny. She was condemned to immortality and anyone who attempted to rescue her would join her in her fate.

The stories were as many as the mountains were tall. But the one thing they all had in common was that she was dangerous and to be avoided at all costs. For centuries people had avoided the island for fear that even one of the tales told about it might be even partially true.

Despite knowing the stories couldn't possibly be true—especially about her eyes being able to bring the Blessed to their knees—a twinge of fear crept into Yolken at the thought of meeting her. He was doing exactly what he had grown up hearing Kaylan's uncle say should never be done.

CHAPTER 39

The dinghy pitched down sharply as the swell transitioned into a wave and crashed around them. Warm water cascaded into the boat, soaking everyone. Jax dropped the oars onto the floor of the dinghy then jumped out the side. "Help me!" he shouted at Yolken.

Yolken climbed out of the dinghy on the opposite side from Jax into the knee-high water. Together they pulled the boat the final distance to the shore, not stopping until the boat was safely out of the water.

The sun shone down on them, so Jax and Deborah began drying themselves with Synthesis. Remembering the technique he had used to dry his boots, Yolken did the same. It was with great relief that he felt Energy flowing into him again.

Soon, Kaylan was the only one still wet. "Not fair!" she exclaimed.

Yolken wondered if he could use Energy to dry her as he did himself without burning her. Afraid to try—he didn't want to risk hurting her—he opted for a different technique he was familiar with. He reached out with Energy and collected water from her body as he did when he filled his water flask. When she was dry, he used a small amount of Energy to lightly squeeze her backside.

"Hey!" Kaylan exclaimed.

Yolken kissed her lightly on the lips and said, "Love you."

"Don't do that," Kaylan said.

"Why not? You've never protested to me grabbing your backside before."

"Because it's weird. I can't see it; it's not you."

"It *is* me, though. Energy is a part of me now."

"Please, Yolken," Kaylan said.

"All right," Yolken agreed, pulling Kaylan in for a hug.

Jax grabbed his coat from the boat then stretched the small of his back. "What I wouldn't give for some Rejuvenation," he said.

"Your gold couldn't buy that secret?" Yolken asked as he pulled his things from the boat.

"That's a secret Drakonias keeps closely guarded, lad. Of all the value your father had to the Order, the knowledge of Rejuvenation was one of his biggest assets. Without him, we grow old while Drakonias and the Regency remain young."

Yolken pondered that as he set the satchel in place on his shoulders. He unbound the Harachin sword from his cloak and reattached the sheath to his belt. While he put his cloak on, he turned his attention to the tall trees standing ominously before them. "Where do we begin?" he said. "We can't possibly search the whole island in a month."

"No," Jax said.

"Do you know where we are?" Deborah said.

Jax pointed out at the water. "Directly across the water from us is Ronig." Turning back toward the trees standing before them, he said, "Most of the stories about the island occur in these mountains."

"But the whole island is covered in mountains," Yolken said.

"Not the whole thing." Jax reached into his satchel and pulled out a rolled-up parchment. He untied the cord securing it, then unrolled it to reveal a map.

They all crowded around Jax to look at it. None of the maps of Dradonia Yolken had ever seen were of such detail. Hundreds of small lines curved all over, giving a sort of shape to the mountains.

"See here," Jax said, pointing at the map. "There are areas on the southern portion of the island not covered in mountains."

"Still," Yolken said, "there's way too much ground to cover."

Kaylan pointed to little red marks on the parchment and said, "What are these?"

"Do you know how to read topography maps?" Jax said, looking from her to Yolken.

Yolken and Kaylan both shook their heads.

"This is where we are," Jax said, pointing at the map. "See how the lines are spaced here, and how, as you move farther inland, they get more bunched together?"

"Yeah," Kaylan said.

"They represent the rise and fall of the ground. The closer they are together, the sharper the rise."

While they talked, Yolken kept his hand on the hilt of the Harachin sword and secretly pushed a steady stream of Energy into it. Healing all those people in Onta had drained it considerably. "This is amazing," he said as he began to make sense of the tiny lines covering the map.

"Now, to answer Kaylan's question, I've spent decades scouring every detail from every story about the island that I could find. These marks," Jax said, pointing at the many red marks on the map, "represent where I think each of them occurred. Notice anything?"

"They all seem to be concentrated around these lines," Kaylan said, pointing at the map.

"It's a mountain," Yolken said.

"Yes. If Anivera is real," Jax said, "my guess is that she lives on this mountain."

"So that's where we'll go," Deborah said.

"Yes."

"Then let's be off."

Deborah and Jax slung their satchels over their shoulders and started toward the woods.

Before following them, Yolken looked up at the trees towering over them. They looked very similar to the pines that grew in the Mindons, except they were much larger. The trunks were so thick that if the four of them held hands and tried to encircle them, they would be unable to reach even halfway around them. He estimated it would likely take a dozen people to do it. Craning his head back to look up at the tall trees, he guessed they were at least a hundred paces tall, dwarfing even the tallest pines of the Mindons. They were densely packed for their size, creating a canopy that blocked the sun from reaching the floor.

"They're unbelievable," Kaylan said.

Yolken nodded his agreement then looked for Jax and Deborah. They were disappearing into the shadowed undergrowth, so he pulled Kaylan by the hand and they moved quickly to catch up with them.

Once they were in the shade of the trees, the warm, wet air cooled significantly. The undergrowth was surprisingly thin. Almost nothing grew—only widely spaced shrubs and a thick mat of fallen needles covered the forest floor. There were, however, very large mushrooms growing around the bases of the trees—large enough that he thought he might be able to curl up underneath some of them.

The openness of the forest floor allowed them to travel swiftly, the only thing slowing them as they moved into the depths of the forest being the need to wind around the thick tree trunks. As they walked, the typical sounds of a forest complemented the surrealism of walking amongst giants.

Despite his best efforts, Yolken's mind wandered to the

stories Jax used to tell about the island. Most of them didn't have happy conclusions. Allowing his worries about meeting the fabled woman to distract him, he didn't see Jax abruptly stop. He bumped into him, then looked up to see Jax gripping the bone fragments woven into the hem of his coat.

With his free hand, Jax pointed about a third of the way up the trunk of a tree ahead and to their right.

A mountain lion clung vertically to the tree, its body pointing down. It was looking directly at them. It didn't look any different from any other mountain lion, except that it somehow gripped the trunk without falling. When its muscles tensed, Yolken reached down and grasped the Harachin sword, drawing Energy into his Core.

Suddenly the lion leaped from the tree to another one about twenty paces away. "How in Draego's—" he began, then stopped when Jax waved at him.

Jax kept his eyes fixed on the large cat as it slowly inched its way down the tree. When the cat neared the base, a flame appeared in front of Jax. The flame quickly spread from side to side, creating a barrier between them and the predator. The cat hesitated. When it tentatively extended one of its front paws down another foot, the flames flared, making the creature pause. It turned and quickly climbed back up the tree. About halfway up the tree, it leaped back to the tree where they had first spotted it. From there it leaped to another tree, and after two more jumps, it disappeared from their view.

"The stories are true, then?" Yolken said, amazed by the cat's unnatural agility.

"We wouldn't be here if there wasn't at least some truth to them," Jax said. "And I imagine that the deeper we move into the island, the more likely we are to encounter animals like that cat."

The cat's amazing demonstration increased Yolken's confidence in the actual existence of Anivera. He had put Jax's earlier comment to Deborah about Anivera refusing to help out of his mind, but now he wondered if there was more to her existence than they had been letting on. He pushed the Energy in his Core back into the sword.

Jax started walking again and said, "Stay alert. Be ready to Synthesize should another lion—or anything else—prove to be stealthier than that one was."

For three days, they moved deeper and climbed higher into the forests and mountains of Kvorga. They saw numerous different animals, many of which seemed, like the mountain lion they had encountered, to be gifted with unnatural abilities. At first, it didn't make sense to Yolken, but the more he thought about it, the more he wondered: If Draego had chosen to bless the Dragon King and his descendants with Synthesis, why couldn't he have also blessed other animals—besides dragons— as well?

"Do you think all these animals have the gift?" Yolken said.

"It's a gift for sure," Jax said, "but I can't tell if they're Synthesizing."

"But they're obviously not normal. If they do, where do you think they got it?"

"What's the common theme in all the stories about Kvorga?" Jax said.

"I don't know," Yolken said.

"Think about it."

"That it's a mystery," Kaylan said.

"Exactly," Jax said. "Which means my guess is as good as yours."

"There's no official record about the island?" Kaylan said. "I mean, besides the stories?"

"No. Even someone such as myself—a procurer of information— has never come across anything that explains the origins of the stories—let alone the mysterious gift of the animals that live here."

"What about the trees?" Ever since he'd first seen them, Yolken had been wondering how they could grow so tall. "Are they gifted as well?"

"Could be," Jax said. "They do seem to defy nature. Have you noticed that most of these trees have survived a fire or two? Almost every single one has severe burn scars," he continued, pointing to the bases of several of the trees that surrounded them.

"Trees in the Mindons don't survive like this," Yolken said.

They were now high into the mountains. Kaylan wore Yolken's cloak; Yolken warmed himself when he needed to with Energy. Every now and then, they caught a glimpse of the snow-covered peaks that continued to rise above them. But as breathtaking as the mountains were, the view they occasionally caught of the sea below and behind them surpassed their grandeur.

On a rocky ledge devoid of trees, providing an amazing view of the waters below, Jax took out the map and cross-referenced their location. He looked from the ledges that surrounded them and traced his fingers on the map. "I think we're right about here," he said, pointing at the map. They all took their eyes off the cascading view to look where he pointed. They were nearing the center of the red marks that peppered the map.

Yolken traced his finger around the valley that rose up on either side of them and the still-higher mountains to the south. "So you think she's somewhere in this valley?"

"Yes. All the credible stories about her occur somewhere in this valley," Jax said.

"The valley is pretty big," Deborah said. "How do you propose we search it?"

"We could split up," Yolken said.

"No," Jax said. "I don't think that's a good idea. I suggest we head straight up the valley until we reach the foot of this mountain," he said, pointing at the highest peak on the map. "If we don't find her, then we can talk about which side to search next."

"How long do you think it will take to reach the base?" Yolken said.

"My guess would be," Jax began, rising to his feet and turning to face the mountain to the south, "at most, another…"

Deborah, Kaylan, and Yolken simultaneously looked up to see why Jax had stopped speaking. He stared, transfixed, toward the snow-covered mountain. A mountain lion stood on a boulder about five paces away from them. Yolken wondered why Jax did not simply scare the lion away with fire as he had done previously, but then he realized why. An old woman, hunched over at the waist, stood next to the boulder. She made an indiscriminate noise and the cat jumped down from the rock and sat next to her.

CHAPTER 40

Yolken stared curiously at the hunched woman standing by the boulder. She made no move in their direction. Unlike in the stories—where Anivera wore ratty clothes covered in mildew and walked with a moss-covered cane—her simple clothes looked well-made and relatively clean. Her cane looked like a carved piece of wood and was moss-free. She did, however, look every bit as old as the stories indicated. Her liver-spotted skin sagged, and her hair was thin, white, and wild. Everything about her spoke of age.

The large cat flicked its tail, but otherwise didn't move. *Is it her pet?* He kept his hand on the hilt of the Harachin sword, ready to Synthesize should the lion decide to leap in their direction.

Nobody said anything or moved for what seemed like an eternity. Yolken wanted to approach her and petition her for help, but he recognized Jax's authority over their group, so he waited for Jax to make the first move. They were the intruders, so he wondered if she was waiting for them to speak first.

Finally, Jax spoke. "Your pet thought to make a meal of us."

Jax thinks it's her pet as well, Yolken thought. *So it'll probably only attack us if she instructs it to.* He considered removing his hand from the sword, but he had no idea whether this mysterious woman could be trusted. Until now, no one in the Order knew whether she even existed, so they couldn't possibly assume she was a friend of the Order. Given the stories, she didn't appear to be a friend of anyone—especially the Regency. Maybe that was why the Council thought she could help.

"She was not there to eat you," the woman said in a cracked voice.

"What then?" Jax said.

"To assess the threat."

"What threat?"

"It is not every day that three Synthesizers visit Kvorga," the woman said. "Why have you come?"

"We are looking for Anivera," Jax said.

"And who might that be?"

"Some say Anivera is the source of the mysteries enshrouding this island—mysteries such as that cat," Jax said, pointing at the mountain lion.

"And what do you want with this… Anivera?"

"We seek her help."

"For what?"

"First tell me if you are the woman whom we seek."

"How many hunchbacked women do you think inhabit Kvorga?" the woman said wryly.

"It's a large island…"

The woman looked thoughtfully at Jax. "I am she," she finally said.

Yolken let out a sigh of relief. At least the largest unknown aspect of their journey had ended. Until now, he hadn't even known if the mysterious Anivera existed. Now that he knew she did, and that she did possess some sort of power, he intended to win her support. "I need your help rescuing my brother," he said.

The woman turned her head slightly to look in his direction. "Of what help can I be to you?"

"You have great power."

"As do you."

Her response left Yolken not knowing how to proceed.

"His brother is a prisoner of the Regency," Jax said. "The three of us are no match against the Blessed."

"Ah," the woman said, "you're rebels."

"I am Jax Karven, and this is Deborah Browning," Jax said, gesturing toward Deborah. "And, yes, we are members of the Order of the Dragon."

"What about the boy?"

"What about him?"

"Is he not also a member of this… Order?"

"No," Jax said.

"Why not?"

"Yolken has only recently come into his gift."

The woman stared at Yolken. He became uncomfortable when she began to walk toward them, never taking her eyes from him. The mountain lion followed at her side. She stopped a couple of paces away and continued to stare into his eyes. Her eyes were clear and sharp—not clouded, as were the eyes of the aged people he knew in Lonely Oak. They flicked briefly to the sword secured to his belt. She looked from Yolken to Jax and said, "Rebels don't need my help." She turned and started away from them.

"We've grown incredibly weak!" Jax said.

Yolken sensed a thread of desperation in his voice.

"The rebels have always been weak," Anivera said over her shoulder.

"Even more so now," Jax said. "We recently lost a valuable member—Yolken's father."

Anivera continued to shuffle away.

"Danavin," Jax added.

She stopped.

"Danavin was the only real strength the Order had," Jax said. He looked over at Yolken. "But the Regency finally succeeded in killing him."

Anivera turned around.

Does she know who my father is? Yolken wondered.

Anivera stared at Yolken like she was sizing him up. Yolken wanted to avert his eyes from her intense gaze but he forced himself to return her stare. She made a strange noise, and the mountain lion sprang into a run and disappeared into the woods.

Growing impatient, Yolken said, "Please, help me."

"He must be of considerable value," Anivera said, turning toward Jax.

"What do you mean?" Yolken said.

"And if I am to lend you the aid of… the mysteries of Kvorga, then I need to assess for myself exactly how valuable he is."

"Is that really necessary?" Deborah said, speaking for the first time since the meeting began.

"Is what necessary?" Yolken said.

"It's deplorable," Deborah said.

"It's what I require," Anivera said.

"We'll do what she wants, if it means she'll help us," Jax said.

"Don't you think Yolken should get to decide?" Deborah said.

"Decide what?" Yolken said.

"She wants to test you," Jax said.

"What's wrong with that? Didn't you say the Order tests people?"

"Yes… but I'm guessing she's not intending on utilizing the Order's more *refined* methods."

"And he is at the very least entitled to know what that entails," Deborah insisted.

"We didn't come all this way to refuse her help," Jax said.

"No, but Yolken *gets* to decide."

"Fine," Jax said tersely. He turned to Yolken and asked, "Do you remember what happened when you first Synthesized? How it left you drained?"

Yolken nodded.

"The result of her test might be similar to that."

"It will be exactly like that," Deborah said.

"You mean it'll leave me unconscious?" Yolken said.

"Possibly."

"It's cruel," Deborah said. "The Order completely changed how we test people after Drakonias—"

"If you refuse," Anivera said, "then I insist you leave Kvorga and never return."

Yolken turned to face the old woman. "If I let you test me, will you promise to help me?"

Kaylan hugged Yolken tightly from the side.

"I make no such promise," the old woman said. "But if you do not permit it, then my answer is no."

Yolken studied Anivera. He had no other options. Jax was right; they had come here for help, and if he refused this woman's demand, then he had accomplished nothing but wasting valuable time. He wanted his brother out of the clutches of the Regency and if this was what he had to do to get the help of this woman, then he would do it.

"Fine," he said.

"Are you sure about this, Yolken?" Kaylan asked quietly.

"What other choice do I have?"

"We don't know this woman. Why should we let her perform some test on you?"

"I will not hurt the boy," Anivera said.

"That's a lie," Deborah said, "and you know it."

Kaylan looked at the woman in surprise.

"True, it is both mentally and physically draining. More so than some are capable of enduring," Anivera said. "But if the boy is truly the son of Danavin, then he will survive."

"But there's a chance he might die?" Kaylan said.

"Life is not without risk, child," Anivera said. She looked

from Kaylan to Yolken, then to Jax. "But you already know that, otherwise I suspect you wouldn't have come here. That is, unless it is *you* who are the cruel ones."

"The Order does not cook people from the inside out," Deborah said tersely.

Kaylan and Yolken both looked at her, wide-eyed.

"He's strong enough," Jax said.

"Kaylan," Yolken said, looking down at her. "I have to do this… for Javen. I'll be okay."

"How can you know that?" Kaylan pleaded.

"Because, ever since I discovered this gift, I've done things I never thought possible. I believe I can do this. I *need* to do this."

"I know. It's just… I love you and I don't want anything to happen to you."

"I love you too, Kaylan Browning," Yolken said. He leaned down and kissed her. She hugged him tightly, then he turned to face Anivera. "Let's get this over with."

"Come with me," Anivera said. She turned and hobbled slowly through the woods with the aid of the cane.

Yolken followed immediately behind her, and Kaylan, Deborah, and Jax followed behind him. They stopped in a clearing where the light of the sun penetrated through the giant trees to the ground.

Anivera turned to face Yolken and said, "Remove your things."

Yolken removed his satchel and water flask and handed them to Kaylan. Next, he unbuckled the sword belt and gave it to Jax.

"Something about this boy," Jax said, talking past Yolken, "tells me you will find that he is even stronger than his father."

"That is not possible," the old woman said.

"I know it's not supposed to be possible," Jax said. "But I've been with him since he first Synthesized, and I've had this nagging feeling that I can't shake."

"Hmm," Anivera said. Directing her attention back to Yolken, she said, "The test is simple. I will direct Energy into you. Your only task is to absorb it into your Core. At no point are you permitted to disperse any of it."

Yolken nodded.

Immediately Yolken felt the press of Energy. It felt different than the Energy from the sun that flowed around him when he stood in its light, or the beckoning of Energy from the Harachin sword. Energy stored in the sword and other dragon bones was under pressure and pushed against him when he was in contact, but he had to let it in. The Energy flowing from Anivera pushed its way in against his will. Sweat began to form on his forehead. Within a few heartbeats, a sheen covered his face and arms. His body was heating up.

He was experiencing exactly what happened if he held Energy in his Core too long. His intuition was to redirect the Energy Anivera was pushing into him into the ground, but she had said not to. He had to do something, though, or he knew the Energy would burn him up. Anivera had said she wouldn't let that happen, but if he didn't pass her test, she wouldn't help. So, he collected the Energy rapidly raising his body temperature and began to redirect it into his Core. *Easy enough,* he thought. After a moment, his temperature returned to normal. Until his Core grew full, he could store it there. However, as Anivera continued pumping Energy into him, he quickly began wondering how long it would take his Core to reach its max.

The flow of Energy from Anivera increased. Its force felt like a huge weight pushing down on Yolken. He had a hard time standing under the weight and fell to his knees. Kaylan gasped behind him. His Core reached its limit and as Energy spilled out into his body, his temperature started rising again and he began to sweat and feel nauseated.

Just before delirium set in, he remembered stretching his Core when he had first started conditioning. He stretched it the same way now, and forced more Energy in. It went in, but much more slowly, so his temperature continued to rise, but not as fast.

Under the strain, Yolken fell onto his backside. He held himself in a sitting position with his arms bracing his body behind him, but soon the weight overcame him and he fell back onto the ground. He frantically ripped his shirt open, popping the buttons off in his haste to expose more of his skin to the cool air.

Kaylan appeared above him and fell to her knees. She lifted his head and positioned herself under him, so his head rested on her lap. Sweat poured profusely from every inch of his body, soaking his hair and drenching his clothes. Deborah also approached, and she tore a large strip from the hem of her dress and handed it to Kaylan, who used it to mop sweat from his face.

Anivera continued to push Energy into Yolken. Despite Kaylan's efforts, Yolken's face remained soaked in sweat. He was pushing Energy into his stretching Core as fast as he could, but Anivera's relentless assault crushed him to the ground. He desperately wished she would stop. He almost cried out that he'd had enough, but he couldn't give in. He *had* to pass her test. He *had* to rescue Javen.

The world around Yolken darkened. The weight grew to be too much. No matter how much he pushed, he couldn't keep up. It was simply too much. His vision narrowed. The trunks and tops of the trees around him vanished. Kaylan's face disappeared. Soon, the only thing he saw in the narrow band of vision that remained was the hunched-over woman standing at his feet.

Blackness consumed the rest of his vision. Unable to continue, Yolken placed both of his hands on the ground at his sides and pushed the Energy in his Core out as fast as he could. The ground around his hands burst into flames, and he succumbed to the blackness.

CHAPTER 41

Y olken!" Kaylan screamed, shying away from the fire. Water appeared out of nowhere around her and doused the flames with a loud hiss.

Anivera knelt down beside Yolken and placed two fingers on the side of his neck. "He lives, child," she said to Kaylan, who started shaking uncontrollably. Seemingly satisfied, the old woman stood up and said, "It is as you suspected, Jax. This boy's strength eclipses that of his father."

Jax stared transfixed at Anivera, not knowing what to think. He'd had his suspicions, but deep down he had believed they couldn't be true. He looked down at Yolken lying unconscious on the ground, his head resting in Kaylan's lap, and said, "How is this possible?"

"I don't know," Anivera said. "This is not how the gift is supposed to work."

"So you're willing to help?" They desperately needed her help. He wouldn't leave without it, no matter what it took.

Jax watched Anivera look down at Kaylan, and followed her gaze with his eyes. Kaylan was now sobbing as she cradled Yolken's head. Jax watched her as she gently combed Yolken's wet hair with her fingers, then looked back at Anivera. She looked to be studying Yolken pensively. She looked back up at Jax and said, "Something tells me you haven't come here simply wanting my help rescuing his brother."

Jax shook his head.

"Then why have you come?"

"Because the Order needs your help."

"I've already refused the Order's plea for help once," Anivera said. "When this boy's father came here. Have you so quickly forgotten?"

"Quickly?" Jax said. "It's been over three hundred years!"

"And nothing has changed. What makes you think I'll help now, when I've already refused once?"

"Because our need is urgent," Deborah said.

"And because of what you've just learned about Yolken," Jax said, pointing down at Yolken. Then he pointed up at the sun. "And if not because of him, then because of that."

Anivera looked up at the sun shining through the trees, then down at Jax. "What are you talking about? Speak plainly."

"If nothing is done," Jax said, gesturing upward again, "the sun will destroy us."

Anivera stood silently looking at Jax and Deborah. Even Kaylan's eyes were on her now.

"That's why it is changing," Anivera mumbled to herself.

"Yes, Deanna," Jax said, answering her thought. "And *you* are responsible."

CHAPTER 42

Yolken's eyes opened. He was looking up at Anivera. The look on her face, he thought, betrayed fear.

"Will you help us put an end to this evil that has doomed us all?" Jax said from behind him.

Anivera did not respond.

"Yolken!" Kaylan said.

Deborah knelt beside him. She and Kaylan helped him sit up.

He looked at the burned ground around him. "What happened?"

"You dispersed the Energy into the ground when you passed out," Deborah said.

"Well?" Jax said.

Yolken looked up at Anivera. His head was pounding. "Did I pass?"

She stared down at Yolken. Without answering, she visibly began to change. Yolken stared in bewilderment as the time-aged, loose skin on her hands, arms, neck and face—those parts not covered by the garb hanging loosely over her frame—began to smooth out and tighten. The liver marks that splotched her skin faded and disappeared. The thin wiry hair that covered her head thickened and lengthened, its white color changing to a shimmery black. Her stooped frame, which forced her to rely on a cane to walk, straightened. The swollen joints of her bony fingers straightened and lost their swelling.

The transition took only moments, but it stretched on for what seemed like several minutes as time seemed to slow during the process. When it was over, a young woman stood before Yolken, the ravages of time melted away. The only part of her that even hinted that she was the old woman who had, moments ago, stood over him were her eyes.

"What in Draego's Fire…" Kaylan said.

Yolken had never heard her curse before. His surprise momentarily made him forget the pounding in his head.

"Yes, you passed," the young woman said. "And yes, I will help."

Jax breathed an audible sigh of relief.

"Who are you?" Yolken said, his gaze still fixed on the young woman.

"Yolken," Jax said, "meet the Emperor of the United Realms' little sister, Deanna Aliza Drake—your aunt!"

"Help me up," Yolken said. Deborah and Kaylan helped Yolken stand. He leaned heavily on them, feeling drained. "*Deanna*? I thought she died?"

"I'm very much alive," Deanna said.

"We were taught that you were executed alongside your father, that it was justice for you betraying Drakonias."

"We've discussed this, Yolken," Jax said. "Much of what the Regency has taught is not as it really was."

"History has a way of favoring the victorious," Deanna said. "I came here long ago to hide from my brother. After a while, I learned that I could better hide myself if I permitted myself to age. Come, let us walk to my cottage. I imagine Yolken could use a rest."

"He'll need something to eat," Deborah said. She retrieved

Yolken's satchel and water flask and carried them for him.

Yolken didn't feel all that well and wasn't hungry. Kaylan took him by the hand, and they fell into step behind the others.

Deanna started peppering Jax and Deborah with questions about the Order and the Regency, so Yolken and Kaylan dropped back a little.

"You scared me," Kaylan said. "The thought of something happening to you…"

Yolken pinched the bridge of his nose and said, "I'm never letting anyone do *that* again. My head is throbbing."

"No you're not!" Kaylan emphatically affirmed. "I don't want you getting yourself killed over some test simply to prove your worth. You don't have to prove yourself to anyone, Yolken."

Deborah held out Yolken's water flask and said, "Here. Drink."

Yolken gladly accepted it. He removed the lid and drank healthily. "It worked, though," he said as he replaced the lid. "Finally, someone is going to help us."

Kaylan wiped her eyes. "I didn't like seeing you suffer."

Yolken hugged Kaylan.

They walked the remainder of the way to Deanna's cottage in silence. When they arrived, Yolken fought the urge to lie down and fall asleep. He sat heavily in the only chair at the table inside, and it was all he could do not to doze off while Deanna prepared a meal.

Jax pushed a couple of chests to the table so the others would have somewhere to sit.

When Deanna set bowls of soup on the table, Kaylan blurted out, "So how old *are* you?"

Deanna smiled. "Well, let me think… I was born in the fifteenth year of King Jhoran."

Yolken looked up at Deanna in confusion.

"King Jhoran?" Kaylan said. "Who's that?"

"There's plenty of time to talk about this—"

"Indeed," Jax said.

"But in short," Deanna continued, "at my birth I was pledged to marry his eldest son. That year would later become known as the year forty-one of the Previous Era. I was second-born to my father Draeko Dairion Drake, behind my brother Drakonias."

"That makes you…" Kaylan said.

"One thousand six hundred and one," Deanna said.

Yolken's amazement at sitting across the table from the infamous Deanna Aliza Drake was overshadowed by his desire to get rid of his headache. But something Deanna had said didn't make sense. "How can I be your nephew? You supposedly died shortly after your father."

"Well, to be precise, you're my great-nephew," Deanna said.

"Great-nephew?" Yolken said. That still didn't make sense.

"How much of your heritage has Jax told you about?"

"I know that I'm very distantly related to the emperor," Yolken said; "that we all are."

"That is true. Everyone who can Synthesize is, to an extent, related," Deanna said. "But you're not *distantly* related to the emperor."

"What do you mean?" Yolken's fatigue and headache were forgotten.

"I'm assuming Jax didn't tell you that your father fought alongside me during Drakonias' war?"

Yolken shook his head. "He… he couldn't have. Jax said my father was just a little older than him," Yolken said with a look at Jax, "and the war was four hundred years ago."

"It would seem that *Jax*," Deanna said, "has misrepresented things about your father."

Yolken looked crossly at Jax. "You lied about my father?"

"I didn't lie," Jax said.

"Jax…" Deborah said.

"I may have misrepresented a few things, but I didn't lie."

"You didn't tell him who his father was, did you?" Deanna said.

Yolken was not in the mood for this. "I know who my father was!" he exclaimed. He clearly remembered the day he woke in the cabin up in the Mindons. It was when he discovered everything he grew up learning was a lie. Nobody turned out to be who he thought they were. Not his aunt, not Deborah, not Kaylan's uncle Jorgan, not his parents. It was then that Jax told him his father's name wasn't really Orwyn Thornhill. "His name was Danavin Hippolyte Drake."

Deanna looked tersely at Jax. "You didn't tell him his full name?"

Yolken looked surprised. "What do you mean? Jax?"

"Tell him," Deanna said to Jax.

"His full name was Danavin *Drae* Hippolyte Drake," Jax admitted.

"Drae?" Yolken said.

"Orwyn was Drae's son?" Kaylan said. She sounded as surprised as Yolken.

"Yes. Orwyn was Drae's son, making him my nephew," Deanna said. "And that makes you my *great*-nephew."

He looked at Jax and Deborah with agitation. "Why would you keep this from me? Wait—if you're my great-aunt," Yolken said, looking back at Deanna, "then the emperor is… my great-uncle?"

"Yes."

"And the Dragon King…"

"Was your great-grandfather," Deanna finished for him.

"You didn't think to tell me any of this?" Yolken said, looking at Jax again. The pounding in his head added to his agitation.

"Would you have believed us?" Jax said.

"You should have at least given me the opportunity to

decide for myself instead of lying to me."

"I didn't lie. I said your father was a little older than me. I just didn't say how much."

"Well, you certainly didn't tell me the truth," Yolken said. "At least not all of it."

Jax shrugged.

Yolken pinched the bridge of his nose. "So what's the plan?" He didn't want to wait any longer than necessary to rescue Javen. He knew that the longer he was in the Regency's clutches, the greater the chance was that they would corrupt him.

"First, let me apologize for testing you," Deanna said. "I needed to know exactly how strong you were."

"Why?" Yolken said.

"Because I have abstained from most contact with the realm for four hundred years. I was not about to get mixed up with my brother again for just anyone."

"So… you wanted to see if I was worth it?"

"To be perfectly blunt, yes."

"If you already knew who I was, then why did you have to test me?" Yolken said.

"You claimed to be Danavin's son, so I needed to know if it was true. As you now know, your father was my nephew. Did you know that your father found me after I went into hiding, and that he too sought my help?"

Yolken looked confused. He looked back and forth between Deanna, Jax, and Deborah.

Did they know that? he thought. *They couldn't have. They didn't even know if she was real. Surely Jax would have known if my father had met her.*

"What did he want?" Yolken finally said.

"Even after everyone else was dead—Drae, Lio, Bathsheth, and Esli—your father refused to give up. He was determined to not allow Drakonias to get away with his evil deeds."

"But you refused."

"Yes."

"Why?"

"For the same reason I disappeared after Drakonias murdered our father: I was done fighting. Too many people had already died as a result of Drakonias' war. I decided I didn't want to be responsible for any more unnecessary death."

"But you're willing to help now?" Yolken said. "Why? If you weren't willing to help my father, then why are you willing to help me?"

"Because I now understand the threat we face."

"So you'll come with us?" Jax said.

"No," Deanna said.

"Then how can you possibly be of any help?"

Everyone sat around the table waiting for her to answer, but she just sipped her tea. Yolken stared at her, trying not to be prematurely disappointed.

"Well?" Jax said.

"There's something about you, Yolken, that doesn't make sense," Deanna finally said.

"What?" Yolken said. His disappointment changed to confusion.

"And I want to take you to meet someone who might be able to tell us why."

"What are you talking about?"

"You are stronger than you should be."

"What? I don't understand."

"Remember what I taught you about one's strength in Synthesis?" Jax said. "How it diminishes with each subsequent generation?"

Yolken nodded.

"You are stronger than your father, Yolken," Deanna said. "And that shouldn't be."

He stared at Deanna, not sure what to think.

"What's more, you are stronger than me. Probably

Drakonias, too."

Jax's eyes widened. "He's stronger than the emperor?"

"I can't be sure. I've never tested Drakonias, but I've seen him Synthesize enough to know what he's capable of. Which is why I'm going to take Yolken to someone who knew my father."

"Your father?" Jax said. "Who?"

"No!" Yolken shouted.

"No?" Jax said. "You obviously don't understand the implications of what she's saying."

"You're right. I don't. But I came here to get help rescuing Javen and I've wasted enough time as it is chasing after people." Yolken glared at Deanna. "I submitted myself to your test. You said you were going to help me and now you're saying you won't. I'm not going anywhere with you."

"He isn't far," Deanna said. "After a night of rest I'll—"

"I don't care. I'm not inter—"

"Yolken—"

"No!" Yolken shouted again. "I'm not interested in knowing why I am the way I am; I simply want to find Javen!"

"Yolken, I'm taking you to meet a dragon."

CHAPTER 43

The setting sun moved behind the marble guard tower as *Onta's Desire* sailed into the Onta bay, turning the tower into a giant silhouette. The tower on the opposite side of the inlet gleamed brightly. Hadie stood at the front of the ship with Lyoll and Ganip and watched eagerly as they sailed toward the beckoning spire rising high above the storied city. It was where the man she loved now lived.

"I know what you're thinking," Lyoll said.

"What?" Hadie said.

"That you can just march right into that palace and call for Javen. Well, it's not going to be that simple. They don't permit people to walk in and out as they wish."

"I know."

"Okay. I just wanted to make sure—"

"I understand, Lyoll."

Lyoll nodded. "Sorry, I—"

"You don't have to apologize, Lyoll. You're looking out for me, I know."

"Over the years I've garnered a certain amount of… influence… with the teamsters, so I'll do what I can to help."

"You don't have to."

"I didn't come for nothing," Lyoll said.

"I mainly wanted the company," Hadie said, "but I appreciate any help you can give." Then, turning and looking at Lyoll, she said, "You have influence with teamsters in Onta?"

"The lad and I have traveled here numerous times with Dorlan and Drenan, and when they get here, they need carriages. Of course, we don't bring our own, so it's been my job to ensure their needs are met while they are here."

"Oh," Hadie said.

Hadie watched as the ship approached the city. Lyoll and Ganip's interest faded—they had been here before—so they started milling around the ship. But it was her first time, and the pristineness of the buildings rising behind the white wall intrigued her. As the sun inched closer to the horizon, the line separating light from shadow moved up the spire. It was about halfway up when the ship pulled into the docks.

"Come, lass," Lyoll said from behind Hadie. "We need to hurry if we're going to make it through the gates before they close for the night."

Lyoll handed Hadie her satchel and they moved toward the center of the ship. They walked off the ship the moment the gangplank was in place.

Hadie and Ganip followed behind Lyoll as he walked briskly up the dock and onto a crowded street leading toward the wall. "Come on," he said, and turned down a side street to the left. Lyoll led them down the much less crowded street, which was lined on both sides with ramshackle buildings. After several blocks, he turned right and once again moved toward the wall. They joined a street at the base of the wall and merged with the line of people moving toward the gate. Those in line protested but there was nothing to be done. All up and down the street, ahead of them and behind them, the same thing was happening.

They drew closer to the gate, and Hadie watched as the guards inspected each person or wagon attempting to gain entrance to Onta. They permitted most to enter, but turned several away—those who resembled the rundown buildings outside the wall. When it was their turn, the guards inspected the three of them and let them pass.

Hadie looked around in awe as they entered the city and walked down the marble-paved street. The sound of loud gears groaning into action startled her. She looked over her shoulder and saw the enormous metal gates closing.

"We'll find an inn over by the West Gate for tonight," Lyoll said, "and then tomorrow we'll find something outside the city."

"*Outside* the city?" Hadie said.

"You'll eat through your money faster than a cheap whore can satisfy a man if you stay inside the walls," Lyoll said. "Look around. This city devours gold."

"Makes sense."

They walked toward the spire in the center of the city. It was almost completely dark by the time they arrived at the roundabout with a statue of the emperor in the center. Hadie moved toward the statue, out of the way of those passing through, and looked up at the spire. Dozens of fires on the rooftop of the two rectangular arms of the palace flickered, illuminating the spire. Hadie stared at it, then scanned the many balconies of the wide palace. A few of them had people milling near the edges, but it was impossible to make out if any of them was Javen.

"Come, lass," Lyoll said.

Hadie closed her eyes for a moment, feeling that she was close to Javen, and turned from the palace. She followed Lyoll around the bronze statue of the emperor and down the road toward the West Gate. When the wall came into view, the road broadened into a large square lined by several white buildings. Lyoll walked over to one of them, which had a stable attached, and went inside. Hadie looked up at the sign before following him in: the Plump Grape.

Five drakes for a room. More than twice as much as the Blue Mountain—and for a ground-floor room. The innkeeper called it a suite. Lyoll sent Ganip off to check with other inns. He reported back that all the other inns were equally as expensive.

"'Tis Onta, my friends," the innkeeper said. "The pearl of the empire!"

"It's fine," Hadie said.

Hadie paid and received a key. The suite was actually two rooms—a sitting room with a couch, and a separate bedroom.

"We'll see you in the morning," Lyoll said once Hadie was safely inside.

"Nonsense," Hadie said. "This is big enough for all of us."

"Good, 'cause I'm tired of sleeping with horses," Ganip quipped.

Lyoll peeked through the door dividing the sitting room from the bedroom and gestured toward a couch at the foot of the bed. "Do you mind?"

Hadie shook her head. "No. One of you can sleep on this couch." She pointed at the couch in the sitting room, "and the other on that one. It'd be rude of me to bring you all this way and make you sleep on the floor when there's a perfectly good couch."

"Help me, lad," Lyoll said. He walked over to one end of the couch at the foot of the bed and waited for Ganip to join him. Together they lifted the couch and moved it into the sitting room.

"You don't have to do that," Hadie tried to protest, but they were through the door before she got the words out.

An attendant knocked on the door and took orders for food. Hadie wasn't very hungry, so she only ordered bread and cheese. Lyoll and Ganip, however, were determined to eat good food and drink fine Ontan wine until they got their money's worth.

"Get some rest," Lyoll said when Hadie finished her small meal. "Tomorrow's a big day."

Hadie stood and said, "See you in the morning." She eyed the small table covered in trays of food for a moment, then grabbed the half-full bottle of wine by its neck and took it with her to her room. She was in Onta, after all.

CHAPTER 44

Hadie sat on the waist-high wall surrounding the bronze statue of the emperor and looked up at the palace. For three days she'd walked the city hoping to catch a glimpse of Javen in the bustling streets, but always ended up back here. The moment they'd settled into an inn outside the city's West Gate, Lyoll had gone to visit with the palace teamsters and quickly learned that Javen was indeed living in the palace. Several of them even reported having taken him on carriage rides out into the vineyards.

She knew he was in there. She tried not to think about the rest of what the teamsters had reported to Lyoll—about Javen always being accompanied on his rides by a woman—and scanned the many balconies. She didn't know which one was his, and even if she did spot him, it wasn't as though that would accomplish anything. The only way she was going to reunite with him was if she went in. And she hadn't come all the way to Onta simply to walk its streets and stare at the marble walls of the palace.

Hadie hopped off the small wall and strode confidently toward the steps leading to the palace entrance. She walked between two carriages stopped at the base of the stairs and stepped up onto the marble curb. She joined with others—dressed much more nicely than she was, in their trim suits and elegant dresses—as they climbed the wide steps. She walked closely behind a couple, hoping to sneak past the guards standing on both sides of the open doors at the top of the steps. She made it two steps through the doors and looked up at an enormous spiraling staircase when a hand grabbed her by the arm.

"Where do you think you're going?"

Hadie tried to pull her arm free of the guard's firm grip, but he held on tightly. "I'm going to visit someone," she said.

"Who?"

"Master Javen."

"Not dressed like that, you aren't."

"But… he's expecting me."

"Sorry," the guard said, "can't let you in lookin' like that."

"But…"

"Come on." The guard tugged on Hadie's arm and pulled her back through the doors. Once outside, he let go.

Hadie looked back through the doors then turned to the guard. "Would you be willing to send him a message for me?"

"I'm not an errand boy," the guard said. "Now get outta here."

"Please?"

"I'm about this close to showing you the inside of a cell," the guard said, holding his finger and thumb close together.

"Fine," Hadie said with a huff.

As she made her way back down the steps, each taking two strides to cross, she tried to remember if any of the markets she had visited over the past few days sold clothing. She wanted to buy something readymade instead of hiring a seamstress—she didn't want to wait that long. A market not far from the West Gate came to mind, so when she stepped back onto the road, she walked briskly toward it.

The market was a narrow road lined on both sides with shops with completely open fronts. Many of them had fabric awnings stretching out into the street, covering their tables laden with wares. She walked down the street, scanning the shops on both sides, until she found the one she was looking for. It was sandwiched between two shops with awnings. One of them sold what looked to be expensive satchels and purses—though everything in Onta was expensive—and the other, jewelry.

Hadie walked between the two awnings into the shop with dresses of various shape and elegance hanging on racks.

An attendant walked over to Hadie and said, "Can I help you?"

"I've been invited to attend a midday meal at the palace and need something proper to wear," Hadie said.

"Do you know with whom you'll be dining?"

"Master Javen," Hadie said without hesitation.

"Oh my…" the attendant said.

"What?"

"It's just—you're so lucky. Midday meal, you say?"

Hadie nodded.

"I know just the thing." The attendant turned to a rack against the back wall and selected a yellow dress embroidered with flowers.

"What do you mean I'm lucky?" Hadie said.

"Ever since His Majesty and Lady Karina returned from their journey, Master Javen has been the talk of the city."

"He has?"

"Mmm-hmm." The attendant held the dress up to Hadie's front and said, "Perfect."

Hadie took the dress from the attendant, held it up in front of herself, and looked in a mirror. It was low-cut down the front and the bottom hem stopped at the middle of her thigh.

"Care to try it on?" the attendant said.

"Sure." Hadie took it into a small room and tried it on. Just as the attendant said, it fit perfectly. She put her own clothes back on and exited the small room. "How much?"

"Two drakes."

Hadie reached into her satchel and procured the coins. She handed them to the attendant and said, "Thank you." She folded the dress over her arm and turned to leave. She took one step out of the shop and froze, then backed up a few steps and hid herself behind a rack.

The attendant walked over to Hadie. "Is something the matter?"

Hadie shook her head.

"Well then, what are you—" the attendant started. "Oh. Do you know who that is?"

A woman with long blond hair, cream-colored skin, and breasts that strained the tight fabric of her dress was perusing the purses at the next shop over. A man with dirty-blond hair, wearing a light green silk shirt, stood next to her, looking off into the distance.

"That's Lannary," the attendant said. "Do you think… is that Javen?"

Hadie crouched behind the rack of dresses, hiding herself as much as possible. "I… I don't know," she lied. It *was* Javen. Her heart raced at the sight of him.

"Everyone's been talking about him. Women have been lining up to get on Karina's list of potential lovers. The rumors must be true, though."

"What rumors?"

"That he prefers Lannary," the attendant said. "Oh my…" she said, fanning herself with her hand. "You *must* be lucky to have made it on her Ladyship's list."

Hadie fought back tears. Sonja's words echoed in her head again. *"I hate to say it, but he's likely already forgotten about you."* The woman—who was picking up purses, looking them over, then setting them back—*did* look familiar. She matched Ronig's descriptions in *Lovers* perfectly. She was the subject of his last five books. "Do you think he's… bedding her?"

"How could he not be? That's Lannary. *I'd* bed her if I had the chance."

He's likely already forgotten about you…

Sonja was right.

Hadie suddenly felt incredibly stupid. She had come all this way, was standing mere paces away from the man she loved, and she knew at that moment that he didn't love her. He was bedding the most famous lover in the empire, next to Karina herself. Javen had already forgotten her. Who was she, anyway? Nobody.

Hadie stared at Javen, who looked uninterested in the purses Lannary was looking at. She eventually turned from the table of purses and slipped her arm into Javen's. Together, they walked down the narrow street, away from Hadie. She inched out of the shop just quickly enough to keep sight of Javen's back. She longed to run after him and declare her love for him. She didn't care if he was bedding Lannary. She didn't care if he was bedding Karina. But she couldn't make herself do it. She felt too stupid. She should have listened to Lyoll all the way back in Portstown. She should have turned around and headed north again. She'd ignored Sonja's advice, too. She should have listened to her as well.

When Javen disappeared from her sight her tears began to flow freely. She dropped the dress and ran down the street in the opposite direction from Javen.

"Miss!" the attendant called. "Your dress!"

Hadie didn't care. She had planned to wear the dress to go see Javen, and now she wasn't. Ever.

She ran all the way back to the West Gate, down the road winding between vine-covered trellises, to the inn she was staying at with Lyoll and Ganip. She pushed open the front door and hurried through the scattered tables to the stairs on the far end.

"Lass?" Lyoll said, rising from the table when she passed him and Ganip. "Lass!"

Hadie slammed the door to her room and fell onto the bed. She curled into a ball and cried uncontrollably. Someone knocked on the door and she heard a muffled, "Lass?"

"Go away!" she shouted.

"Are you okay?" Lyoll's muffled voice said.

"I said go away!"

"We'll be right out here if you need anything," Lyoll said.

Hadie didn't respond. She cried. And eventually, she fell asleep.

* * *

Hadie sat at the table with Lyoll and Ganip, her eyes puffy and red. Lyoll signaled to the innkeeper's wife, who was bustling about the lobby tending to the needs of their patrons. When she came over, Lyoll ordered a plate of food for Hadie.

"What happened, lass?" Lyoll said.

Hadie stared blankly at Ganip's half-empty plate.

"Did you find Javen?" Lyoll said.

Hadie nodded.

"What happened?"

"I want to go home," Hadie said. "Today."

"All right," Lyoll said. "Just as soon as you've eaten, we'll go to the docks and find a ship."

The next few days blurred by. Hadie hardly remembered boarding a ship and sailing back to Hantlo. Hantlo was the last place she wanted to be… no, the *next to* last place she wanted to be. All she knew was she wanted to get as far away from Onta as possible, as quickly as possible. She hadn't even wanted to wait until Lyoll could find a ship with an empty cabin, so they had boarded the first one sailing for Hantlo. Lyoll attempted to persuade the captain to allow the lady to have his cabin, but he insisted that if she wanted personal quarters she could find another ship. Hadie didn't care. She climbed into an empty hammock hanging in the berth, where the crew slept, and left it only to relieve herself.

"Thanks for watching over me," Hadie said as they trudged back up the steep road carved into the cliff up to Hantlo. Lyoll and Ganip had taken turns sitting in the berth the entire voyage. "You didn't have to do that. I can take care of myself."

"I know you can, lass," Lyoll said. "But we done it anyhow. What now?"

"I don't know," Hadie said. "Right now, I don't really care."

"Love's a tricky thing, lass. A tricky thing. But you'll regain your bearings, I promise ya."

"Thanks, Lyoll."

Hadie followed Lyoll and Ganip back to their house, and Lyoll invited her to stay with them if she wanted.

"Thanks," she said.

Ganip bounded up the stairs and Lyoll busied himself in the kitchen. "You hungry?"

Hadie felt antsy, not hungry. "Thanks, but I think I'll go for a walk."

"All right, lass," Lyoll said. "I'll have something hot for you when you return."

Hadie nodded and left.

She wandered the city aimlessly, not paying any mind to where she was going. The sun slowly arced overhead, and flickers of familiar places flashed through her memory: the statue of the emperor, the gates leading into Drenan's palace, the alley outside the palace wall where Rennie had left her, the gate blocking the tree-lined road to the mansion she'd grown up in, places she used to play with her friends as a child, markets she had gone shopping in with her mother.

Any time a thought of Javen crept into her mind, she pushed him away. She imagined him bedding Lannary and Karina. The thought now disgusted her. She was angry with him—even hated him for forgetting her so quickly.

The flickering images stopped. She stood in front of a large house with a covered balcony made from the brown slate common in Hantlo. It had round pillars carved to resemble marble columns supporting the porch cover. Rising above the first level of the house were three more levels covered with cedar shingles. The house was much nicer than those crowding the street on either side, and the only resemblance it shared with them was the iconic red door.

"Hadie?"

She looked to her left and saw a scantily-clad woman approaching. She looked familiar, but Hadie couldn't quite place her.

"What are you doing here?" the woman said.

"I…"

"It's me, Ylonna, from Sonja's," the woman said with a gesture toward the house.

"Sorry," Hadie said. "I recognized you but couldn't remember your name."

"It's all right," Ylonna said. "What are you doing here?"

"I… I don't know. I was just out for a walk and ended up here. What about you?" Hadie said with a glance at Ylonna's clothing. "I thought Sonja paid everyone so they didn't have to do this anymore."

"She paid us all very well when she left, but it's all most of us knew, including me."

"So you all kept whoring anyway?" Hadie said. "Even though you didn't have to?"

"Not all of us," Ylonna said.

"Oh."

"Anyway, I've gotta go. Mustn't keep the clients waiting. Madam Rita is ever as much a stickler for promptness as Sonja was, if not as refined."

"All right."

"See ya, Hadie."

"See ya." Hadie watched her walk away, then called after her. "Ylonna!"

The woman turned around. "Yeah?"

"Do you like it at Rita's?"

"She has a strict policy about clients not beating us, so at least I don't have to worry about that anymore."

"Which one is Rita's?"

"Fourth one down on the left."

"Thanks," Hadie said.

"Sure," Ylonna said. She smiled then continued down the road.

Hadie watched her until she disappeared into the house she indicated, then redirected her attention to Sonja's. Several whores wandered by and offered her their services as she stared at the house.

"I miss working for Sonja," a woman said.

Hadie turned and recognized another woman she remembered from Sonja's.

"You would have been a great whore, you know," the woman said.

"I—" Hadie started. "I miss working for her, too."

"You're welcome to come work with us. I'm sure Madam Geena would take you in; you've got a great figure."

"Thanks," Hadie said, feeling herself redden. "I'll think about it."

"You should."

The whore—whose name Hadie couldn't remember—sauntered off.

Hadie thought about what she'd said, but she wasn't interested in whoring. The only reason she had come to Sonja in the first place was to get help finding Javen and to kill… Hadie thought of something. She had missed her opportunity to kill Drenan, but what if…

She walked up the granite steps and turned the doorknob. It opened. Hadie confidently strode in.

CHAPTER 45

Javen opened the door and walked into his empty quarters. It had been half a month since he'd talked to the beggar in the empty lot, and three days since he had last seen Lannary. Their parting still reverberated in his mind.

"So?" Lannary had said, slipping her arm into his as he walked through a market near the palace. "I'm still dying to hear what it was that made you decide to return to the palace so hastily the other day. I'm still disappointed that we didn't get to go sailing."

"I said I don't want to talk about it," Javen said.

"Well, I think I have a right to know, since whatever it was was more important than our trip."

Javen yanked his arm free of Lannary's and shouted, "I said no!"

Lannary shied back.

"I'm sorry," he said. "I just need to be alone for a while." He'd turned from Lannary and walked away from her.

He instantly regretted yelling at her. He'd been on edge since he reported to Devin his thoughts about the healed beggars. Worse, for some reason Drenan was in Onta. But neither of those things gave him an excuse to yell at Lannary. It wasn't her fault. He returned to the palace and went straight to his quarters.

Since then, he had spent a considerable amount of time walking alone through the streets, hoping to—and yet at the same time hoping *not* to—catch a glimpse of Yolken. There was no way he could know it was Yolken who healed all those beggars, but he couldn't shake the feeling that it was. What time he didn't spend walking the streets alone, he spent standing on the balcony and looking down at the city. Oshie occasionally came with messages from Lannary begging forgiveness, but he continued to ignore her—even though he felt bad for yelling at her.

Javen leaned on the cool marble wall and looked out over the city. After reporting to Devin what he suspected had happened to all the beggars in the now-empty lot, he had wrestled with a mix of emotions. Even though he knew he was in the right for going to Devin, he felt as he often had as a boy when he had run to his Aunt Selena and tattled on Yolken for something he had done. He remembered, as a boy, enjoying each opportunity he had to get his brother in trouble, and then immediately feeling bad about it after. Now he couldn't help but feel as though he had just tattled on his brother to Devin. And he didn't even know for sure it was him. He shook his head to push the thought away; this was different. This was not simply boys being naughty. The Regency was the law and Yolken was actively rebelling against it. He'd simply done what he had to.

Despite the fact that he knew he had done what was right, Javen continued to doubt. He looked down at the city wondering if Yolken was out there. If Yolken was in the city, and the Regency succeeded in finding him, Javen wondered what they would do to him. Would they kill him? Or would they give him the opportunity to pledge his allegiance to the emperor? He certainly didn't want his brother to get himself killed. Drenan's presence worried him. Whereas Devin seemed to be kind-hearted and open to the idea of welcoming Yolken into the

Regency as he had with Javen, Drenan was not. Drenan hated both him and his brother, Javen knew. And he was worried that Drenan would convince Devin to kill him.

He continued to scan the city, even though the people milling around below were too small to identify. His eyes drifted to the bay at the southern end of the city. It was full of ships moving both toward the city and away. He wondered if Yolken was on one of the ships moving toward the inlet that protected the bay from the open waters of the Kvorgan Sea. If he was on a ship, where would he be going?

When he wasn't thinking about Yolken he thought about Astora. He wanted to confront Drenan about what he did to her, but the very thought gave him an upset stomach. Javen was determined to hold Drenan accountable, but he wasn't ready. He didn't want to ruin his chance at becoming a regent. Thankfully he'd managed to avoid running into him. Seeing Drenan would not end well, Javen knew.

He wished Hadie was here. With everything that had happened over the last couple of weeks, he felt alone, isolated. And he missed her. None of the women Karina kept trying to send to him could give him what he needed right now. But Hadie could. Part of him wondered if Devin was deliberately not bringing her to him. Perhaps Karina had convinced him not to.

"Master," a now-familiar voice said from behind him.

Javen turned to find Oshie standing a few paces away. "What is it, another message from Lannary?"

"No, Master Javen."

"What, then?"

"Your presence has been requested in His Highness' quarters."

Reago? Javen thought. "What for?"

"I don't know, Master. I am but here to serve."

"Sorry," Javen said.

"No need to be sorry, Master."

"When?"

"Immediately, Master."

"Thank you."

"I will take you if you wish," Oshie said with a bow.

Javen nodded.

Oshie led him back through his quarters and into the hall. Normally he would have admired her backside as it moved under the thin fabric of her skirt, but instead he stared blankly ahead wondering why the chancellor had summoned him. He had been in the city for a while now and had yet to meet him; Devin had been right when he described Reago's reclusiveness.

At the end of the long hallway, they joined the stairs that circled around the inside of the spire and turned left. They climbed the marble steps, which were mostly covered by a green carpet embroidered with vines, and passed Devin and Karina's floor, continuing up to the final level. Oshie stopped on the landing and gestured for him to continue. He stopped and waited for her to lead the way, but she said, "I am not permitted on His Highness' floor."

"Not at all?"

"No, Master." Before turning to leave, Oshie said, "Is there anything, or anyone, you wish to have awaiting your return?"

Javen shook his head. Since he'd sent Lannary away, the only person he wanted to be with was Hadie, and Devin still hadn't found her.

"As you wish," Oshie said with a bow. She quickly made her way back down the stairs.

Javen started down the hallway and instantly noticed two significant differences from the other levels of the palace: There were no statues, and each door he passed had two armored guards, wearing Glasses, stationed before them.

At the far end of the hall, a woman stood next to the double set of doors; she opened the door on the right when he drew near. Her modesty gave Javen pause. Unlike any other servant in the palace, she did not expose herself in any way. She wore modest clothing. For once, he didn't blush when he looked at someone. He must have stared too long because he saw her begin to fidget and grow uncomfortable. He said, "Sorry," and entered Reago's quarters.

Reago's residence mirrored Devin and Karina's in its structure. However, the large greeting room lacked the statues just as the hallway had, and the tapestries decorating the walls depicted simple landscapes instead of the lewd physical acts found in Devin and Karina's.

He walked through Reago's bedroom and out onto the balcony. Three men gathered next to the wall. Several wine bottles and glasses sat on the ledge. Devin stood on the right; another man stood on the left with a smoking pipe in his mouth. Javen figured he had to be Reago—he had never seen him before, but every description he had heard of the man included a pipe. Unlike Devin, or any of the other Blessed he had come across, gray tinged Reago's otherwise black hair and lines of age etched his face. The third man had his back to Javen and he couldn't see who he was. He also noticed another man standing in a corner on the far side of the balcony, under the guard of two men wearing gray armor.

Devin saw Javen approach and turned to greet him. "Welcome, Javen."

Reago and the third man turned to greet him as well.

Javen froze when he saw Drenan's face. It was all he could do to not draw Energy in from the sun and attack him. He was much stronger than he was the last time they'd met. But Drenan was wearing armor. He would have to wait. He would wait.

Reago took the pipe from his mouth and said, "So, this is him."

"Javen, meet His Highness, Reago Draeko Yarin Drake, Chancellor of the Western Realm," Devin said.

"Your Highness," Javen said, bowing slightly with a tinge of fear in his voice. He eyed Drenan, wondering what he was doing here. He had hoped never to see him again—at least not until he'd plotted how he was going to kill him.

"I've heard a lot about you," Reago said. "And your brother. In fact, Devin can't stop talking about you. Your bloodline is quite pure, from what I understand."

Drenan shifted, causing Javen to look directly at him. He looked visibly agitated at Javen's presence.

Javen turned back to Reago and said, "I… I understand my father was your nephew."

"And cousin to these two," Reago said.

The comment made Drenan shift again. "Cousins, yes, but a century and a half younger and less experienced," Drenan said sharply.

"Even so," Reago said, "his blood is equally as pure as that which flows in your veins."

Is Reago intentionally trying to rile Drenan?

"Perhaps," Drenan said. "But he is dead, is he not?"

"True," Reago said. He placed his pipe into his mouth and toked it back to life.

"We have not gathered to debate the purity of our lineages, gentlemen," Devin interjected. "Now that Javen has arrived, let us discuss what we intend to do about what Javen has discovered."

"I fail to see how this has anything to do with a boy who continues to go unpunished for violating Regency law," Drenan said.

"I don't recall the solicitation of your opinion in the matter," Reago said.

"My opinion," Drenan shouted, "matters not! It is the law that matters, and this boy violated it! I refuse to pretend that he is somehow one of us!"

"Enough!" Devin shouted. Then, speaking more calmly, he said, "We've already discussed this, Drenan. Javen is under my authority and will take part."

"I came all the way here," Drenan said, staring icily at Javen, "only to find out he doesn't even know if it *was* his… brother."

"Well, if you'd have apprehended him as Dorlan sent you to do," Reago said, "Devin wouldn't have needed to bother you. I'm sure you were quite busy whoring."

Drenan turned his icy glare on Reago.

"If it *was* his brother," Devin said, "and you *do* want to take part, you must accept Javen's participation."

Drenan's icy glare returned to Javen.

"Do you accept this?" Devin asked.

Drenan continued to stare at Javen, then finally nodded.

"Good," Devin said. He gestured to the guards to bring the man in the corner over to them. "The reason I've called this meeting is because this morning I learned that the individual who healed the beggars boarded this man's ship."

"And who is this?" Drenan said when the guarded man stood before them.

"This," Devin said, "is Urgil. Go ahead, tell them about your latest… cargo."

"S-several days ago a man by the name of Shen purchased travel on my ship for himself and three others."

"Four?" Javen said. "What were their names?"

"The second man's name was Neffin and the two women went by Laura and Jula."

"What can you tell us about them?" Devin said.

Urgil began describing the four individuals.

Javen's eyes went wide. It *was* Yolken. He recognized the others as well: Kaylan, Missus Browning, and Kaylan's Uncle Jorgan.

"Shen appeared to be in charge; he spent most of his time attempting to coax me into taking them to Kvorga or talking to the older woman, Laura. The younger two wore marriage rings and spent most of their time together in my cabin."

"Kvorga!" Drenan exclaimed. "Why were they going to Kvorga?"

"I… I don't know," Urgil said.

Yolken and Kaylan got married? Javen thought, furrowing his brow.

"I gather, then, that Kvorga is not where you originally agreed to take them?" Devin said.

"No, Your Majesty. He originally bought passage to Ronig."

"Why did you agree to take them to Kvorga instead?"

Urgil hesitated a moment before answering. "Because he offered to pay me triple, Your Majesty."

"Anything else you can tell us that might be of value?"

Urgil looked down at his feet, then he looked back up at Devin as though he remembered something. "Just before I dropped them off, the woman, Laura, accidentally referred to Shen by another name."

"What?" Devin said.

"Jax, Your Majesty."

Drenan's eyes narrowed.

"You know the name?" Devin asked Drenan.

Drenan peeled his white gloves off and clenched his hands into fists. "He is the one who gave me these."

"Kaylan's uncle?" Javen exclaimed.

"So you recognize the individuals your brother is traveling with?" Devin said.

Javen nodded. "The older woman's name is actually Deborah Browning. She owns a bakery in Lonely Oak. The younger woman is her daughter Kaylan, and the other man is Kaylan's Uncle Jorgan—at least that's what I thought his name was."

Devin turned back to Urgil. "Anything else?"

"Yes, Your Majesty. I agreed to return a month later to pick them up."

"Excellent!" Devin said. "You will honor the contract."

"Yes, Your Majesty."

"If you have nothing else, you're dismissed."

Urgil shook his head. Devin nodded to the guards and they led Urgil away from the group and through the double doors into Reago's bedchamber.

When the door closed behind them, Devin turned to Javen and asked, "Had you any idea this Deborah Browning or Jorgan were associated with the rebels?"

Javen shook his head. "My brother and I grew up with Kaylan. We've known her and Missus Browning our whole lives."

"And what about this uncle of hers?"

"He didn't live in Lonely Oak, but he visited periodically. We used to love sitting around the hearth in our tavern with cups of hot cider listening to his tales."

They're married? Javen thought again.

"And you had no idea they were rebels?"

Again, Javen shook his head. "I didn't even know my aunt was a rebel. As far as I knew, they were just good people—just like us."

"What sort of relationship did your aunt have with them?"

"They were friendly with each other. Lonely Oak was small enough that most people were. My aunt knew most people in the town, since most of them came to the tavern. Jorgan used to stay late into the evening talking with my aunt after we were sent to bed."

"Did you ever hear what they were talking about?"

"Not really. I always thought he stayed for the ale. By the time we went to bed he'd have drunk several mugs while telling his tales."

"And you recognize this… Jax?" Devin asked Drenan.

"I've been looking for him ever since he gave me these scars," Drenan said.

"Do you suppose he is the one who took the boy the night

you went to the tavern?"

"I don't know. The whore didn't say where the boy had gone or who took him."

"My aunt was not a whore!" Javen shouted.

"Was he around when your brother healed the girl?" Devin asked Javen.

Javen nodded. "He showed up in town the day Dorlan arrived."

"Who helped the boy escape Lonely Oak doesn't matter," Devin said. "They're helping him now, so they're obviously rebels."

"What could they possibly be doing on Kvorga?" Drenan said.

"I have no idea. What's important is that we be prepared when they return. According to Captain Urgil, Shen… Jorgan… Jax—whatever you want to call him—purchased passage on his ship the same day the boy healed the beggars, which was a little over two weeks ago. So we have roughly two weeks to finalize our plans."

"And what are you planning?" Reago said, taking his pipe out of his mouth and finally joining the conversation.

"Drenan and I have been discussing various options since his arrival," Devin said. "But, in short, we're going to apprehend the boy and kill the others."

Javen's eyes went wide. "All of them?"

"The fewer rebels wandering about, the better," Devin said.

"But," Javen stammered, "but, how do we know for sure they're rebels?"

"Because of the simple fact that they are abetting your brother."

"I can see how Missus Browning and Jorgan might be, but Kaylan can't possibly be a rebel."

"And why not?"

"She… she just can't."

"It sounds as though you care more for this girl than your own brother," Drenan said. "Perhaps you're jealous that he is bedding her and you are not? Maybe we should keep her alive long enough to bed her, then kill her."

Javen looked at Drenan with fear. Draego's Fire, he hated him. But he was right. From the moment Urgil had said they were married he had been able to think of nothing else. The person he wanted more than anyone else—even more than Hadie—had married his brother. Devin had agreed to look for Hadie, but had yet been unable to find her. And now, maybe Javen had an opportunity to be with Kaylan instead.

"Ah, so it *is* true," Drenan said with a sickening sneer.

"Please," Javen begged Devin, "can we spare her?"

"We?" Drenan said.

Ignoring Drenan, Javen continued, "You've said I can have any woman I want. Well, I want her."

Devin looked at Javen. "I will consider it."

"Whatever your plans," Reago said, "you will not harm the boy or the girl."

"Fine," Devin said with a cross look at Reago.

"Jax is mine," Drenan said.

"Done. Care to join me in my quarters? We can make plans with wine and some proper… scenery."

"That sounds delightful," Drenan said.

"Come, Javen," Devin said. "You are to be a part of this as well."

Drenan and Devin both bowed slightly to Reago, then turned to leave.

Javen bowed as well and followed them.

"Remember," Reago said, "you are not to harm the boy or girl."

Devin did not turn to acknowledge Reago, but his step faltered slightly at his words. Javen knew from his conversations with Devin that he was accustomed to doing pretty much whatever he wanted, because Reago rarely made decisions when it came to the administration of the realm. It probably irked him to have Reago intervene now, but Javen was glad that he had.

He followed silently behind, glad that Devin wanted to include him in the planning. He wanted to ensure that Kaylan—and, if at all possible, his brother—remained unharmed. He felt betrayed by Yolken, but that didn't mean he wanted him to die. In actuality, he didn't want anyone to get hurt... except Drenan.

CHAPTER 46

Yolken stared at Deanna in disbelief. *Dragons are extinct. Did Jax lie about that, too?* He glanced over at Jax and Deborah. They both looked to be just as confused as he was.

He looked back at Deanna. "A… a dragon?"

"Yes," Deanna said. She took a sip of her tea.

"Wait," Jax said. "What do you mean your father *knew* a dragon?"

"My father knew a dragon."

"I didn't think any dragons survived," Deborah said.

"Neither did I," Deanna said. "But one did. And I intend on taking Yolken to meet it." She took another sip of tea. "But first, rest. Yolken will need his strength."

"I can't possibly sleep now!" Yolken protested. But the truth was he could barely keep his eyes open.

When the meal was done, he lay down on a makeshift mat and Kaylan snuggled next to him. Deanna, Jax, and Deborah stayed at the table talking. His anticipation reminded him of the night before the winter moon festival when he, Javen, and Kaylan used to sleep by the crackling fire in the hearth while the adults—their aunt, and Kaylan's mammy and uncle—would stay up late into the night talking. It was always hard to fall asleep.

They would chatter and giggle amongst themselves, often drawing the ire of the adults. He wondered how they expected him to sleep after Deanna had declared that she was going to take him to meet a dragon. But then sleep came.

When he woke, Deanna, Jax, and Deborah were already up and at the table—or perhaps they had not slept. He woke Kaylan and they joined them. Deborah set a plate of hot food before them.

"Drakonias hadn't changed when Danavin came here on his fool's errand," Deanna said.

Joining them in the middle of the conversation, Yolken wondered what they were discussing.

"And from what you've said, it's apparent he hasn't changed from then to now. So, my traipsing into his palace on behalf of the Order will accomplish nothing except to anger him."

"What?" Yolken said through a yawn.

"That's exactly what you came here for, is it not?" Deanna said to Jax and Deborah.

"No!" Yolken exclaimed. "We were sent here to get help rescuing my brother!"

Deanna looked from Yolken to Jax and Deborah. "Is that so? Did the Council send you here simply to solicit my help in finding this boy's brother? Or did they think that if they placed this boy before me, it would somehow convince me to intervene with Drakonias?"

Jax and Deborah looked at Deanna without response.

Yolken looked at both of them, waiting for their reply. When they continued to sit and stare at Deanna, he said, "What is she talking about?"

"The Council *did* send us here to seek your help to find Javen," Jax finally said. "However, we also need your help dealing with Drakonias."

"I refuse to involve myself with him, just as I did when Yolken's father came and made the same request."

"Why?" Jax said.

"Because it will accomplish *nothing*."

"If we do nothing," Jax insisted, "then—"

"That does *not* mean I'm unwilling to provide what help I can," Deanna said. "Something bigger than Yolken's brother and Drakonias is happening, and I think taking him to see the dragon offers us the best chance of finding out what."

"Can we all come?" Jax said.

"You're welcome to accompany us as far as the entrance to the cave where the dragon lives if you wish, but I will take only Yolken in to see it."

A look of disappointment washed over Jax's face.

"Let's be on our way, then," Deanna said.

The excited group followed Deanna out of the cottage. They walked south toward the mountain at the end of the valley where they'd found Deanna.

"What exactly did you mean when you said your father *knew* a dragon?" Jax said

"I spoke plainly enough," Deanna said. "My father knew a dragon."

"Okay, then. *How* exactly did he know a dragon?"

"That is a tale worth the telling," Deanna said. She took a drink of water from her flask then began, "My father, Draeko, took a secret with him to his grave. It was something he shared with no one, not even his children. Even my brother doesn't know what I'm about to share with you."

* * *

I still don't fully understand the motives my brother had in revolting against our father. For over a thousand years, my family ruled peacefully over all of Dradonia. Our subjects revered us, worshiped us even. While they lived and died, their generations coming and going, we lived on, never aging. Our family was unique. All that changed when Drakonias revolted.

My father felt obligated to stop my rebellious brother. The

war lasted for a little over thirty years, and left millions dead. The people who had worshiped us began to lose faith in us when we enslaved them and forced them to fight our war. The war concluded when my father, for reasons unknown, surrendered to Drakonias.

Those of us who had remained loyal to him and fought alongside him couldn't figure out why he had surrendered. He refused to explain his decision except to say that it had to be so.

Drakonias assumed our father's throne and began his rule by mercilessly executing our father; then, to consolidate his power, he executed everyone who wouldn't pledge loyalty to him. The people, powerless as they were, had no choice but to submit to his rule. However, it was not so with those of us who remained loyal to our father. Instead, most of us went into hiding. Those who openly defied Drakonias were eventually killed. I managed to elude Drakonias by leaving behind everyone I knew and loved and going into hiding, here, on this island.

In an effort to leave no trace of my presence, I forsook the comforts of a permanent dwelling and, for several years, lived amongst the other animals. That's how I met Kyla—the mountain lion who was with me when you found me. I befriended her.

Then, one day I was exploring the slopes of this mountain and discovered the entrance to a cave. At first, I approached the cave timidly, not comfortable with the idea of cutting myself off from the reach of the sun. I had dragon bones, but I was afraid of venturing too deep. However, as I began to familiarize myself with the cave, I gradually became more comfortable being inside the mountain and slowly explored more deeply into its depths.

My dragon-bone bracelets provided me with a source of light, and as I grew more familiar with the sprawling fingers tunneling deep into the mountain, I learned to be smarter with the Energy stored in them. I memorized the various tunnels to the point that I could navigate my way through them with no light at all. I saved the Energy in my bracelets until I reached a new area. As time passed, I was able to explore deeper and deeper into the caves. I proceeded in this fashion, gradually penetrating to the very depths of the mountain.

Then, one day, everything changed.

I was deep in the mountain, exploring a previously unexplored finger of the vast network of tunnels hiding below the great peak, when the finger opened into an enormous cavern. I flared the tiny flame hovering above me to illuminate the cavern and saw just how big it was. It was awe-inspiring— nothing like what I had yet encountered. Gigantic stalactites and stalagmites stretched toward each other, some of them bigger than the emperor's palace. Several of them had successfully met and formed giant columns. Entire cities could have easily fit inside the cavern.

As I entered the cavern, leaving the finger behind, I heard something. A deep rumbling—different from any of the subterranean sounds I had grown accustomed to—rattled me to my core. The rumbling reverberated off the cavern walls, amplifying the sound. I froze in place and extinguished the light. In my time on the island, I'd discovered that it was home to all sorts of exotic creatures, but I had yet to encounter any of them in these caves—let alone something that could have made a noise like that.

I waited tensely to see if the noise would sound again, but as I crouched in the dark, all I heard was the trickling of water. It was impossible to measure the passing of time inside the mountain, so I don't really know how long I crouched there, but eventually, not hearing the sound repeat itself, I decided to continue. I once again drew Energy from one of my bracelets and created a flame over my head. The moment light once again illuminated the cavern, the rumbling returned.

I looked around but couldn't see the source. So I walked cautiously around in search of what might be causing it. As I approached the center of the great cavern, I rounded one of the enormous columns and came face to face with a beast I had thought extinct.

Instinctively, I turned to flee back to the finger that had led me to the cavern, but I stopped when the deep growls emitting from the beast stopped, and it spoke.

"If you flee, you will die," it said, slow and deliberately, in a deep, rumbling snarl.

I slowly turned around to face the dragon. It crouched low with its legs drawn in. Its head hovered close to the ground. I knew this position well. It was a coiled spring, ready to launch in my direction. It didn't move, so neither did I.

I'd almost forgotten how enormous the beasts were. Its head was the size of a horse and its mouth hung slightly open, revealing the sharp teeth hiding within. Its serpentine eyes were gray, matching the color of its scales. The girth of its long neck was as thick as a mature pine. Four reptilian legs, ending in claws that rivaled the fierceness of its teeth, supported its massive body. It had a long tail that brought its length to that of twenty horses. Shimmering scales covered its entire body—the same scales we wore as armor—and giant wings folded along its length.

"How is it that you Synthesize so far from Solarian?" the dragon said.

I hesitantly looked down at the bracelets adorning my arms.

"If you wish to live, Daughter of the Betrayer, you will answer." Each time it spoke, its voice rumbled in my chest like someone pounding on an enormous drum right next to me.

I had no option but to reply. "D-dragon b-bones," I stammered.

The dragon snarled and a bit of fire shot from its nostrils. "Give. Them. To. Me."

I looked at the dragon and hesitated, afraid. If I surrendered them, I would surrender myself to the dark.

"Now!" it roared.

I shied back in fear while at the same time I slid the bracelets off my wrists. I gently laid them on the ground. When I let go of them the cavern went dark. In the blackness, I could hear the dragon moving toward me, its claws scraping on the rock floor. I retreated slowly backward, trying not to give the impression I was attempting to flee. The sound of its movement ceased, so I stopped and waited. The only thing I heard was its rumbling breathing and then, the sound of sniffing. Soon its breathing changed to an odd guttural sound. The sound continued for a while then changed back to its normal rhythmic breathing.

"Why have you come here?" it said.

I stood frozen in the dark, not knowing what to say.

"Tell me why I shouldn't kill you right now!"

Another burst of fire emitted from its nostrils as it snarled, momentarily illuminating its head and mouth full of razor-sharp teeth.

I fell back onto my haunches, avoiding the flames that shot dangerously close to me. "I-I-I fled to this island to escape my brother's tyranny," I stammered. "After he so ruthlessly killed our father, I couldn't—"

"You speak to me about ruthlessness?"

"I-I—"

"Your father betrayed us, destroyed us, then wore us like your shiny skins!"

"H-he-he did only what he had to. My brother was the first to—"

The dragon snarled, stopping my speech.

I listened to the dragon breathe slowly in the dark for an immeasurable amount of time and wondered if I would ever see the light of day again. Finally, I broke the silence and said, "What do you want from me?"

Light once again illuminated the cavern—not by my doing; I had no source of Energy—and I saw the dragon crouched with its head hovering over the bracelets.

"Do you recognize me, Daughter of the Betrayer?"

I shook my head. "Should I?"

"Did the Betrayer never speak of me?"

I scoured my memory for anything my father might have said about dragons. Unable to bring anything to mind I said, "Not that I can recall." We faced each other quietly. When the dragon did not speak or move, the feeling of my imminent death abated. I didn't yet feel as if I would see the sun again, but I also didn't feel that the dragon would kill me immediately. Instead, it seemed to be prodding me for information. I took the opportunity to ask questions of my own. "Why do you refer to my father as 'the Betrayer'?"

"He betrayed his oath."

"What oath?"

"Never to use the gift I gave him for ill."

"*You* gave him?"

"I see he did not betray his entire oath…"

"Please, dragon. Speak plainly."

"Do you not know the source of your power?"

"The sun," I said.

"Yes, but where did your ability to Synthesize come from?"

"The Great Dragon blessed my father."

The dragon snorted. Smoke jetted from its nose. "*Draego?*"

"Yes," I said, hesitantly. In that moment, I began doubting everything I thought I knew about our family's gift.

"Draego did not revere humans as he did dragons."

I had lived my entire life believing that Draego had blessed my family with our wonderful ability and selected us to rule over all of Dradonia's inhabitants. I gazed curiously at the dragon that stared at me, its giant, reptilian eyes boring into me. Then I realized. "It was you," I whispered.

The dragon nodded its head.

CHAPTER 47

So Draego had nothing to do with us being who we are?" Yolken said, stopping.

The others stopped with Yolken before Deanna turned to face them. "No. He did not."

Yolken imagined the others were just as shocked to hear this as he was. The priests in the Dragon Shrines taught that the Great Dragon had selected Draeko to bring peace to Dradonia. "But our entire culture is predicated on that fact," Yolken said.

"Because that's what our father taught us," Deanna said. "What they teach in the shrines is just a skewed version." She turned to resume her progress through the forest and said, "Now, permit me to continue."

* * *

I sat before the dragon and considered this revelation. The dragon waited patiently for me to process what it had said. As I sat, allowing this incredible revelation to percolate in my mind, I continued to study the dragon. Never before had I seen a dragon that looked like this one. Its appearance seemed off. Its movements were slow and rigid, not smooth and lithe as I remembered them to be.

"You seem different than the dragons I remember," I said.

The dragon slowly rose into a sitting position. It moved like I did when I'd let my body age. It stretched its long neck up and towered over me. Slowly, its giant leathery wings—translucent enough that the bones and muscles were distinguishable beneath the skin—unfolded and, like a vulture warding off another scavenger coming too close to its meal, the dragon stretched its wings out to either side, greatly increasing its appearance of dominance. It refolded its wings along its body.

"We were created to be the supreme species. Draego gave us Regeneration so we could govern the generations. However, the Assembly chose to live apart from the world, shirking their responsibility. As a result, your species grew in prominence. You bent the land and its inhabitants to your will. Moreover, you did not live in peace as we did—with the land or with each other."

The dragon paused in its speech and slowly lowered itself back to the ground.

"We stood by as you bent the beasts to your will and used them to fight your wars. We stood by as you fashioned shiny skin and made iron teeth to cut each other apart. We watched as you destroyed your cities by hurling boulders and fire, killing your mates and your hatchlings.

"Your wars grew wearisome. We held councils, but the Assembly refused to intervene. Your wars continued to the point where I could no longer watch you destroy yourselves. So I selected a human and made him a child of the dragons."

"My father."

"I renamed him to remind him that he was one of us now."

"You gave him Synthesis?"

"Yes."

"How?"

"All life has the gift, but it lies dormant in most. I simply ignited the flame within him."

"Why did you do it?"

"I believed it would end the wars. But that turned out to be the first of my mistakes."

"But it did end the wars! How could that have been a mistake? You could not have known that my brother would betray our father."

"No. I should have known that humans could not be trusted with such power. The Assembly was right; I should not have intervened in human affairs."

I remember pondering what the dragon had said for several minutes before asking, "You said it was the first of your mistakes."

"Yes. My other was teaching the Betrayer Regeneration."

"Why did you give it to him?"

"For him to bring peace to Dradonia, he needed time to grow in his power. Your lives are short. The Assembly disapproved of my actions, but they agreed to give him the chance. When he succeeded, we left him alone to rule over those he had conquered. However, in the end, the hearts of humans remained the same. And when you betrayed us, we were ill prepared to defend ourselves against the weapons you made to kill us." The dragon paused. "I watched you destroy my species."

Still I sat and looked at the dragon. During the war with my brother, I had done what we had to do—I had killed dragons in the interest of self-preservation. I didn't feel remorseful for what I'd done. But in that moment, as I looked at the creature lying before me, I could sense its anguish.

"I watched one of your flying talons pierce my mate. I watched her fall helplessly to the ground. My life ended with hers."

"You're growing old," I said, realizing why it moved the way it did.

"Without her I have no reason to live."

"So you're punishing yourself for what happened to your mate?"

"Her... my entire species. After her death, I fled. I hid

myself away in sorrow and shame. These caverns were our home. We lived together here, hatched our young here, so I resigned myself to die here. Alone."

I sat in silence with the dragon for a long time. I had so much to process. "Why have you told me all this?" I finally said. "Knowing who I was, you could have simply killed me."

"You deserve to die. But your presence has evoked in me something I have not felt in ages. Death does not come quickly to me," the dragon continued. "Time has caused my sorrow to abate. And, without my mate, I have grown lonesome. I desire… companionship… as I continue to await death."

This development gave me pause. Moments ago, I had thought that my past crimes to this majestic species had caught up to me. I didn't think I would make it out of the mountain alive. And now…

"Are you asking me to be your friend?"

The dragon didn't answer my question. Instead, it said, "After I fled here, what became of the dragons?"

"As far as we knew, all of the dragons…" I needed to choose my words carefully. I couldn't very well say that we had annihilated the entire species and then turned them into weapons or wore them as armor and not expect it to destroy me. I hesitated only briefly before I chose what I thought would be the least offensive thing to say. "They died."

Steam emitted from the dragon's nostrils. "I knew long before my mate fell from the sky that we were doomed," the dragon said, again pausing in its speech. "Friends, no. But since you have chosen to occupy this mountain, perhaps we could await death together."

"I came here to avoid death, actually."

"And what kind of life did you hope to live here? Loneliness is not life. Life exists only in relationship. My life was my mate. Without that, there is only death."

"So you want… a relationship with me?"

The dragon chortled. "No. I desire only to await death together."

"But I do not await death as you do."

"If you do not wish to accompany me, then I will permit you to leave. But never return."

I took a few minutes to think about what the dragon was offering. Never before, not even with my father, had any human been given such an opportunity. Dragons kept themselves apart from humans. Our paths rarely crossed. I couldn't leave here and give up that opportunity—an opportunity to learn from the dragon. But I also wasn't ready to die. "I'm sorry, I will not bother you again."

I turned toward the tunnel that had brought me into the cavern, leaving my bracelets on the ground before the dragon. I could find my way out of these caves without them, and I had more bones back with my belongings.

"Wait," the dragon boomed.

CHAPTER 48

The group had been walking for the better part of the morning while they listened to Deanna's story. The walk had transitioned to a steep incline as they made their way farther up the mountain. They pushed between thick shrubbery just as Deanna finished her story. She stopped and turned to face them. Behind her, the mountain continued up, rocky and devoid of any more foliage. It hid the sun from view.

"Let's rest here and eat before Yolken and I enter the cave," Deanna said.

Yolken and Kaylan found a flat rock to sit on. Deborah removed dried meats and fresh bread from her satchel and passed them around.

"When we proceed into the cave," Deanna said, addressing Yolken, "you must leave behind any dragon bones you have on you."

Yolken stood and began to unbuckle the Harachin sword from around his waist.

"Wait just one minute," Jax said. Yolken paused. "You want Yolken to face a dragon defenseless?"

"Weren't you listening?" Deanna said. "If he goes in there carrying dragon bones, he will stand less chance of surviving this encounter. With or without dragon bones, there will be risk. Why unnecessarily exacerbate the situation? I've developed a limited relationship with the dragon over the centuries, but that doesn't mean he'll give a free pass to another human simply because they're with me—especially if that human shows up with dragon bones. He has strictly forbidden them in his presence."

"So you expect Yolken to just go marching into its lair defenseless?"

"Yes."

Jax pointed toward Yolken and said, "I'm not sure I'm willing to risk the lad for aid we don't even know for sure we'll get."

"Then what are we doing here, Jax?" Deanna said tersely. "Are you so audacious that you come to my home seeking my help and then question me when I offer it? I may be amenable to the Order's cause, but do not forget for one second who I am!"

"How could we *possibly* have known you would march him into the lair of a dragon?" Jax retorted.

"Ahem," Yolken said, clearing his throat. "I'm the one who wants to rescue my brother, so shouldn't I be the one to determine what risks I'm willing to take?"

"This isn't about your brother, Yolken," Jax said, his voice now as terse as Deanna's.

"It's not about me at all, is it?" Yolken said, watching Jax look over at Deanna. As they stared at each other intently, pieces began to fall into place. Jax's evasiveness, the way he'd sidestepped Yolken's questions—things said between him and the Council, or him and Deborah… it all started to make sense.

"Yolken, tragic as it is that your brother is a prisoner"—Yolken glared at Jax—"the Order is trying to deal with a much bigger problem."

Yolken finally understood what had been happening.

"You're using me," he said, staring directly at Jax. "All this time… you've been dragging me around and leading me to believe that you were helping me rescue my brother. But you had no intention of helping, did you?"

Deborah placed her hand on his arm and said, "Yolken…"

Yolken jerked his arm away and shouted, "No! You're just as guilty as Jax!" He looked from Jax to Deanna. "You needed me, didn't you?" He pointed at Deanna. "The Council needed me to get to her. This has all been about her!"

"Yolken," Deanna said calmingly, "believe me when I say that if we can rescue Javen from my brother's clutches, we will. But the reality is that Dradonia is facing a grave danger that is much bigger than any one person."

"You knew this all along," Yolken said, staring intently at Deanna. "And have kept me in the dark about it. Why?"

"No, I haven't known all along. I didn't understand what was happening until you all arrived," Deanna said. "It wasn't until I tested you that I understood the true danger Dradonia faces. This is no longer about Drakonias. I finally know the real work of the Order."

"Which is what?" Yolken said, cooling off a little.

"Come with me," Deanna said, gesturing for Yolken to follow her. They walked along the side of the mountain until the craggy peak no longer hid the sun. The rest of the group held back. She pointed up to the sun and said, "Tell me what you see."

Yolken looked up, exasperated. "What am I supposed to be looking at?"

"The sun."

"What about it?"

"Describe it."

Yolken hesitated, struck for words, not knowing what she wanted. "What do you want me to say? It's the sun."

"Exactly. You're too young to see it. Even if you lived to an old age you might never notice—nobody does, even the regents are too self-absorbed to notice—but it's changing, Yolken," Deanna said. Yolken stared at her blankly. "The changes have been very subtle, almost imperceptible. But to one such as myself, isolated, with plenty of time to take notice, it's there. As I hid myself away all these years, avoiding further confrontation with my brother, I've watched the sun slowly change. I never knew why. I even spoke to the dragon about it, but he didn't know and didn't care.

"Thanks to Jax and Deborah, I now understand. The sun is dying, Yolken," Deanna continued.

Yolken's eyes widened, remembering old Relan's ominous words the morning Dorlan visited Lonely Oak. "It's dying, you know," he'd said. When Yolken asked him what was, he'd said, "The sun." Then, even more ominously, he'd added, "Just a matter of time." Yolken had thought old Relan was just talking his nonsense—he'd been blabbering about the scales sniffing around his place as well—but somehow, he knew. And Jax lied when he'd asked him about it. He'd called the idea foolishness and outlandish.

"And it's our fault—my brother's, my father's, mine. If nothing is done about it, it will destroy Dradonia."

Yolken stared at Deanna in disbelief. What she was saying was impossible.

"What do you mean it's your fault?" Yolken said.

"The war between my father and my brother brought this about," Deanna said. "Somehow, our war did something to the sun. We're not sure what, but we now know the path the sun is headed down."

Yolken saw the others approaching from the corner of his eye. He turned to face Jax. "You knew."

"Yes," Jax said.

"This… you *definitely* lied about. I specifically asked you if the sun was dying and you said no."

"I'm sorry, Yolken. I couldn't tell you."

He looked at Deborah. "Did you know too?"

"I did," Deborah added, "But not Kaylan."

Kaylan crossed to Yolken and wrapped her arms around him, hugging him tightly.

"The true mission of the Order is not simply to overthrow Drakonias—though that was its original intent," Jax said. "Our primary purpose now is to find a way to undo the damage we did to the sun. The emperor, on the other hand, has sought only to suppress it. Which is why you knew nothing about it. We—myself, Deborah, and Selena—were obligated not to tell you until you were ready."

"Is that why things are getting so bad in the south?" Yolken said.

"Yes. The sun's changes are already affecting Dradonia. It's what's causing the droughts, fires, even the cyclones in the East Sea," Jax said. "And Drakonias is keeping the Regency in the dark. They honestly don't know what's happening. The deteriorating conditions in the south are what sent Dorlan to Kyinth—he's searching for answers as much as we are. Except we know what's happening and are *actually* trying to do something about it."

"And I think our best chance of coming up with a solution is by conferring with the dragon," Deanna said.

"But what does that have to do with me?" Yolken said.

"I do not believe your coming here is a coincidence, Yolken," Deanna said. "You're stronger than you should be, and Synthesis doesn't work that way. My hope is that the dragon will be able to explain why. He gave us Synthesis, so maybe he can explain what's happening. I'm also hopeful that meeting you will prod him into action. By ourselves, I don't believe we can reverse what we've done to the sun, but with the dragon's help, perhaps there's a way."

"I don't know," Yolken said. He stared at his feet, trying to keep up with the emotions that flooded him. They'd been lying to him—for his entire life. None of them were who they said they were, except Kaylan. Feeling her arms around him calmed him. They'd been lying to him, but now he was all the way on top of a mountain on the island of Kvorga. Did he really have a choice but to trust them?

He needed to rescue Javen. That hadn't changed.

He squeezed Kaylan around the shoulders and looked up at Deanna. "I'll do it."

Deanna looked over at Jax.

Jax looked at Yolken and furrowed his brow. "The oath I made to your father demands I say no, but we didn't come all this way to leave empty-handed." He looked back at Deanna. "If there's a chance the dragon can help, then… fine, he can go."

"Then it is decided," Deanna said.

CHAPTER 49

Deanna led the way back to where they had stopped to rest. Jax and Deborah walked alongside her and discussed the plan, and Yolken trailed behind with Kaylan.

"What do you think of all this?" Kaylan said, her arm interlocked with Yolken's.

"I don't know. It's a lot to take in," Yolken said. "And kind of hard to believe."

"You had no clue about any of it?"

"I'm only just realizing how evasive Jax has been to many of my questions. There were times that he flat out changed the subject. I remember so many instances he said something, or intentionally avoided saying something, and it all makes sense now. Like the sword," Yolken said. "Jax told me it belonged to my father and that he was a descendant of Drae."

"Wasn't that the truth, though?"

"Yes, technically. But he wasn't just a 'descendant' of Drae; he was Drae's *son*. Why wouldn't he just tell me that?"

"I don't know. I'm sure he had his reasons."

"I suppose."

"I can't imagine how you must be feeling," Kaylan said, trying to be comforting. "I still can't believe I'm related to the

Dragon King as well."

"And that stuff about the sun dying?" Yolken said. "What are we supposed to do with that? I mean, all this time I've been worried about trying to rescue my brother—they never told us that it didn't matter because we're all probably going to die anyway! And what exactly do *I* have to do with it? I mean, wouldn't you think that Deanna should be the one to fix this? She's been Synthesizing for well over a thousand years. She has infinitely more experience; I only started Synthesizing a couple of months ago."

"Maybe there *is* something different about you," Kaylan said. "I'm sure we'll figure it out."

"We?"

"All of us. You, me, Jax, Mammy. And Deanna."

Yolken only nodded in return. He had a lot to try to process. He was unable to think very clearly about any of it because he was about to meet a dragon—a creature that, just a few hours ago, he had thought was extinct.

"Come, son of Danavin," Deanna said when they arrived.

Yolken removed the Harachin sword and handed it to Jax, hugged Kaylan tightly, then followed Deanna.

"Be careful!" Kaylan called after them.

"Do you have any dragon bones with you?" Deanna said as they began ascending the rocky mountainside.

"No," Yolken said.

"Are you absolutely sure? Because you will cause all of Jax's worry to come to fruition if you're foolish enough to enter the dragon's home carrying remnants of his species."

"I'm sure. The only bone I had was the sword."

"Good."

"What's its name, anyway?"

"What?" Deanna said, stopping.

"The dragon. Does it have a name?"

"He, actually," Deanna said. "And it's Dethoicrinth."

"Deth-oi-crinth," Yolken said, trying the odd-sounding name. Deanna resumed walking as Yolken repeated the name a few times. "Deth," he finally said.

"What did you say?" Deanna said.

"It's just sort of a mouthful," Yolken said.

"Yes, well, what did you expect?"

He repeated the name in his head a few more times. *Deth*, he thought. *Deth of the dragons. Death of the sun.*

Their progress slowed as the gradient steepened. As they climbed higher, the sun moved to the west and came into view. Yolken struggled, grasping the rocks before him, climbing almost vertically now. Deanna offered her hand and helped pull him up onto the rock outcropping on which she stood. He collapsed in exhaustion. The mountain still towered over them.

"We're here," Deanna said. "When you catch your breath, we'll proceed."

"How did you ever find this place?" Yolken said when he could breathe without gasping.

"I had plenty of time."

Yolken looked around. Before him was just more rock, ledges that continued to climb higher. Behind him, he looked down at the forest. The view was majestic. In the distance he could just barely see the straight that separated the island from the mainland. If he hadn't been about to throw himself helplessly into the lair of a dragon, he might have enjoyed it.

Yolken took a few more minutes to rest, then indicated to Deanna that he was ready to proceed. She offered him her hand and helped him to his feet. They rounded the large outcropping before them and the entrance to the cave came into view.

"You will need to hold onto my arm," Deanna said.

Yolken hesitated.

"Don't worry, I know these caves like you know ale."

"You know about...?"

"I'm looking forward to the day I get to taste it myself."

Feeling more confident, Yolken took Deanna by the arm.

Deanna led him into the mountain. Darkness quickly enveloped them. Within moments, Yolken had completely lost his sense of direction. He hoped his eyes would adjust to the dark so he could make out the rough outline of the cave, but the darkness was so complete he couldn't even see Deanna walking next to him. He held his hand up in front of his face but couldn't see it either.

Deanna's arm became his world.

Yolken was completely at Deanna's mercy. If he lost contact with her, he knew he would end up wandering in the pitch black for a very long time. He doubted he could ever find his way out, as Deanna's course changed often. He tried not to think about it.

After walking for what felt like hours, Yolken nervously said, "Deanna?"

"Just a little bit farther."

They walked for a few more minutes, then Deanna stopped. "Sit down and wait here."

"What?" Yolken said, his voice betraying his fear.

"We're almost at the dragon's lair. I need to go ahead and see if he will see you. Just sit here—and *don't* move."

"Deanna, no."

"If you show up unannounced, you might as well have brought that sword of yours. Sit."

Deanna guided Yolken as he groped for the ground.

"Lean back against the wall," she instructed.

Yolken leaned back blindly until he felt the cool rock against his back.

"We're in a small finger that leads into the dragon's lair. If things should go poorly, you'll be safe."

Yolken's heart raced as he began to panic. There was no way he could find his way back to the surface. "How am I supposed to get out of here?"

"Don't worry. I'll be right back."

Yolken heard Deanna walk away. He sat in silence and darkness, alone. He couldn't believe he had put himself at the mercy of a woman he barely knew and followed her into the depths of a mountain. Jax would be furious if he found out about this. If she didn't return, it didn't matter, though, even *if* he followed the cave he was in until it ended. Cut off from Energy from the sun, he couldn't make a fire to help him find his way back to the surface, so he was as good as dead.

A deep rumbling, almost like thunder, reverberated off the walls.

"What… was… that?" Yolken said aloud. *Was it the dragon?* He listened intently, but silence again overtook the cave.

The rumbling sounded a second time.

And then a third.

Yolken waited anxiously. His heart was pounding as though he had spent the evening dancing with Kaylan then spontaneously asked her to marry him.

A jagged sliver of light appeared to his right, forcing him to hold up his arm to shield his eyes. He squinted and waited for his eyes to adjust. After he could look without feeling as though he were staring directly at the sun, he saw that the light illuminated the wall of the small cave he was in. A silhouetted figure appeared around a bend and walked up to him.

"Dethoicrinth has agreed to meet with you," Deanna said.

She held her hand out and Yolken took it, welcoming her assistance in getting to his feet.

Deanna led Yolken toward the light, and as they rounded the bend, he saw the jagged end of the cave, only about a pace and a half wide. They passed through it, Deanna leading him by the hand and walking ahead of him so they fit through the narrow space. They stepped into a huge cavern.

Its enormity was breathtaking. It silenced the sense of awe that Yolken had experienced when he'd first witnessed the grandness of Croff or the beauty of Onta. None of it compared to the magnificence before him now. With wonder, he looked at the many stalagmites, stalactites, and giant columns.

Deanna led him deeper into the cavern. The grandeur of everything he saw evaporated when they rounded an enormous column and he saw the dragon crouched on the other side.

Yolken was without words. The dragon's gray scales shimmered in the light, demanding from him reverence and awe.

"You must be special," Deth said, his voice that of slow, rumbling thunder.

Yolken looked at the dragon, questioningly, then at Deanna. She gestured in the direction of the dragon.

"I…"

"Deanna has not looked as pleasing as she does today since she first began pestering me centuries ago. I thought perhaps she had decided to join me in death. But it turned out to be nothing but deception."

Yolken turned to Deanna for guidance, but received only a smile from her.

"You are her nephew?"

Yolken nodded.

"Speak. I will not harm you."

"Y-yes," Yolken said. "G-great-nephew, actually."

As soon as he realized the dragon was not going to harm him, he went from fearing for his life to being filled with questions. He forgot why he was here and only wanted to know more about the fabled creature.

"How did you get here? How long have you been here? What do you eat? Can you really eat a cow whole? What's it like to fly? How can you Synthesize without the sun?"

"Yolken," Deanna said tersely.

Deth rumbled oddly, almost as if he was laughing. "Leave him be, Deanna. After all, the hatchling has just seen a dragon. You ask valid questions, hatchling," the dragon said to Yolken, "but it is I who needs an answer."

Yolken looked at the dragon, wondering what he wanted to know.

"Is this true what Deanna says? That you are strong in Synthesis?"

"So she says."

"You know not for yourself?"

"I've only recently began to learn about my abilities."

"He is quite strong," Deanna affirmed. "As I said, he's stronger than me."

Deth lifted his head. "This should not be so."

"And yet it is," Deanna said.

Deth snorted and smoke emitted from his nostrils.

Yolken felt a comforting warmth fill his body. It melted away his fatigue and lasted for just the briefest of moments.

Deth breathed deeply, then slowly pushed himself into a sitting position. Yolken looked up at the dragon now towering over them. Awe and wonder filled him, but not fear. Whatever fear he'd felt had melted away with his fatigue. Deth lowered his head, touching his jaw to the ground in front of Yolken. He remained in this position for several seconds then returned to his previous position of lying on the ground.

Yolken looked over at Deanna. She was staring at him in shock.

"You have spoken accurately, Deanna. This hatchling's strength exceeds your own. He is stronger even than the Betrayer."

"How is this possible?" Deanna said, looking from Deth to Yolken.

"It is not."

"How, then?"

Deth stared at Yolken, the rumbling of his rhythmic breathing the only sound in the cavern. Finally, Deth said, "Blessed, Deanna has told me of the great evil you have brought to Solarian."

"Blessed?" Yolken heard Deanna whisper.

"*Me?* How can I possibly be held responsible for something that happened before I was born?" Yolken said. A surge of boldness flooded into him. "Besides, weren't you the one who gave Draeko Synthesis in the first place?"

"Yolken…" Deanna said.

"So is it not *you* who is ultimately at fault?" Yolken continued.

"Yolken!"

"And how have you taken responsibility? By hiding in this cave?"

"Draego has punished me far more greatly than you can know," Deth said.

"I'm truly sorry about what was done to the dragons, but if you have the ability to somehow right this wrong, then you would be atoning for your errors… and ours. I came to Kvorga naïve. I thought I needed Deanna's help to rescue my brother, but now I know I'm a part of something much bigger. Can you help us fix whatever it is that we did to the sun?"

Deth lay silently before them.

"*Please*," Yolken implored.

The dragon continued to lay motionless for a long while before speaking.

"Blessed, I too was naïve. I thought humans could exist in harmony with each other—as the dragons did. However, for some reason Draego did not instill in you that ability. And my naïveté caused the annihilation of my species. I have suffered for my actions."

"If you don't help us," Yolken said, "we're all going to die. Even you."

"I have been awaiting death since the day my mate fell from the sky."

Yolken looked at Deanna, not sure what else to say. She still looked like she was in shock.

"I truly am sorry for what my family did," Yolken said, turning back to the dragon. "I'm sorry that my family fell short of your hope for us. I'm sorry that we killed millions of people over a stupid feud. I'm sorry we betrayed the dragons. And I'm sorry we killed your mate."

Deth continued to lay quiet. Finally, after a long silence, he spoke, "Blessed of the Dragon, I have nothing to offer you. You already possess what you need."

Both Yolken and Deanna stared at the dragon in confusion.

"Your humility is reminiscent of your father's. It is why I chose him when I decided to intervene in the humans' plight. I can see why Draego has seen fit to bless you."

"What?" Yolken said.

"The power I gave your father was a mere spark by comparison to that of the dragons. However, in you is power that rivals ours."

"That can't be," Deanna said.

"Draego has selected you to accomplish this task."

"But… what am I supposed to do?" Yolken said. "We don't even know what we did."

"Solarian's balance has been disrupted, so you must restore balance."

"What does that mean?" Yolken began.

"Please, help us," Deanna said.

"The time of the dragons has passed," Deth said. After taking a long, laborious breath, he continued, "If you do not want your time to pass as well, then you must restore balance." The dragon lowered his head back onto his tail and said, "Blessed, permit me to rest. I am weary."

Deanna hesitated a moment, then took Yolken by the hand and led him back to the passage they had emerged from. The dragon growled in his resonant language and darkness returned to the cavern.

They walked in silence, Yolken holding tightly to Deanna's arm. Unable to bear the silence, Yolken asked, "The dragon knew my father?"

"He was referring to my father, Draeko," Deanna said. "Dragons do not think of heritage in the same manner we do."

"What did he say to you as we left?" Yolken said.

"That if I brought anyone else into that cavern our agreement would be void."

"What was it doing when it put his head on the ground by me?"

"Bowing."

"*Bowing?*"

"Yes."

"Why?"

"Weren't you listening?"

"I was, I just don't understand."

"You are the Blessed of the Dragon, Yolken."

"Aren't we all Blessed?"

"No. The only *true* Blessed of the Dragon was Dimras, the king of the dragons. If the Great Dragon has blessed you, then you share the same status as Dimras."

"Which is what?"

"Dragon King."

CHAPTER 50

I thought your father was the Dragon King?" Yolken said.

"I've learned a lot since I met the dragon, Yolken," Deanna said. "I, too, believed my father was the Dragon King, just as you've been taught. However, it turns out that it was a title he bestowed upon himself. It meant nothing. The true Dragon King was Dimras, the yellow dragon my father killed and wore as armor. *That* dragon was the true Blessed—the only Blessed of the Dragon. If what Dethoicrinth said was true, and Draego indeed blessed you, then that makes *you* the Dragon King and the Blessed of the Dragon."

Yolken stared over at Deanna in shock, even though he couldn't see her. He didn't know how to begin processing what she was saying. *The Dragon King was a dragon? And now I'm the Dragon King?* It didn't make sense.

"What does this mean?" he said.

"Now is not the time. We must make haste. Night is not far away, and we don't want to get caught on the mountain when it gets dark," Deanna said.

Yolken kept a tight grip on Deanna's arm as she moved quickly through the dark. As he walked, thoughts swirled. *I am Blessed. The dragon sensed a power in me that rivals his own. The Great*

Dragon selected me to fix the sun.

None of it made sense.

Yolken breathed a sigh of relief and shielded his eyes at the first glimpse of light ahead. Before he knew it, he was squinting in the brightness of a late afternoon sun.

When they exited the caves, Deanna immediately started down the rocky mountainside.

Yolken stopped, relieved to once again feel the warmth of the sun on his skin. The anxiety of being in the cave melted away the moment he felt the presence of Energy. He drew Energy in as though he was taking a deep breath of air after remaining too long under water. He felt it warm him as it seeped from his Core into his body. He dispelled it into the rock and set off after Deanna.

They hastily made their way down. It was almost completely dark by the time they approached the tree line where they had left Jax, Deborah, and Kaylan. As they approached, Yolken saw two flames hovering in the air, making it easier to locate them.

The moment Yolken stepped into the light, Jax exclaimed, "So! What happened?"

Kaylan ran to Yolken and hugged him tightly around the neck. After breaking off the hug, she handed him the Harachin sword. When he wrapped his hand around the steel-twined hilt, he felt the push of Energy. He drew it in and created a flame of his own.

"Deanna?" Jax said.

Deanna collected her belongings and soon a flame appeared over her as well. "Let's be on our way," she said. She set off in the direction of her cottage.

Jax followed her closely. "Well?"

"I'm not exactly sure yet," Deanna said.

"What does that mean? Is the dragon going to help or not?"

"Not as we had hoped."

"What do you mean? What did he say?"

"Ask Yolken."

Jax looked over his shoulder at Yolken, who walked hand in hand with Kaylan. "What did the dragon say?"

Yolken felt embarrassed, knowing how strange what he was going to say would sound, but he said it anyways. "That I was the Blessed of the Dragon."

"What...? That doesn't make sense," Jax said.

"It does, actually," Deanna said. When Jax looked at her questioningly, she added, "I'll explain when we get back to my cottage."

They walked for the remainder of the trip in silence. Kaylan held tightly to Yolken's hand the entire way. By the time they arrived at the cottage, it was late into the night. They sat at the table and ate a hasty, cold meal. Jax continued to prod Deanna for information but she rebuffed him, saying they would talk more about what happened after a night's rest.

Jax reluctantly acquiesced.

As the others drifted off, Yolken lay in the corner, unable to sleep. His mind raced as he pondered the meaning of the dragon's words. But when sleep finally overcame him, he still didn't have any answers.

* * *

The smell of warm bread woke Yolken. He was the last to sit at the large wooden table in the center of the main room. Deborah placed a hot cup of tea and a hearty breakfast before him.

The moment he set his fork on his empty plate, Jax said, "Now, tell us what happened."

Yolken recounted the story of meeting the dragon, leaving out the part about walking through the mountain in complete darkness. He described the dragon's actions after it tested him.

"It bowed to you?" Jax said. He sounded a bit incredulous.

"Why would it do that?" Kaylan said.

"The dragon recognized the boy for who he is," Deanna said.

"Who?"

"The Dragon King."

"*Deth*," Jax said, testing the name on his tongue, "named you Dragon King?"

"Yes," Yolken said.

"What does it mean?" Deborah said.

"As I told Yolken yesterday, my father was Dragon King in name only," Deanna said.

"Meaning?" Jax said.

"No one bestowed the title upon him. After Deth gave him the name Draeko, my father took the title upon himself."

"So what? It's just a title."

"No, it's not," Deanna said. "The title had great significance to the dragons. When Draego made the dragons, he made them to rule over the rest of creation. In order to facilitate that end, Draego blessed the first dragon with the gift of Synthesis. That dragon was the true Blessed. The *only* Blessed. The Dragon King. The other dragons all recognized him as their leader, their ruler, and he passed the gift to them. He was the ultimate authority for the entire species."

"So," Jax said, thinking aloud about what Yolken said the previous night. "If the first dragon was the only true Blessed of the Dragon, and if Deth acknowledged Yolken as the Dragon King, then that means that Yolken has also been blessed by Draego?"

"Exactly," Deanna said. "Which explains why his strength surpasses anyone who has come before him."

"Wait, what?" Jax said.

"Deth said his strength surpassed even my father's."

"But your father was the first human with the gift!"

"You're right. And yet Yolken's strength is greater than his."

"Couldn't his strength just be an anomaly?" Jax said.

"There are no anomalies in Synthesis, Jax. The power comes directly from Draego. And just as it does with us, the dragons' power grows weaker with each generation. Draego made only two dragons: the yellow dragon and his mate," Deanna said. "As they bred, each successive generation grew weaker in Synthesis."

"Just like us," Jax said.

"Which explains the difference in the strength of dragon bones. It's why the Harachin sword is so strong; it's made from the bones of the—"

"Yellow dragon," Yolken said. Although dragon bones were black, they all had ribbons of color in them that shimmered in sunlight. Yolken remembered his lesson with Jax when they compared the color in different bones. The Harachin sword was made from the bones of the Dragon King. Dimras' bones.

"If strength in Synthesis is the measure of power," Deborah interjected, "then wouldn't that mean that Yolken was stronger than the dragon?"

"I didn't think of that," Deanna said. "I suppose you're right, though. The dragon *did* say he sensed a power in Yolken that rivaled their own."

"I… I'm stronger than *Deth*?" Yolken said.

"It's the only explanation for the dragon bowing to you."

Yolken stared at Deanna, dumbfounded.

When silence overtook the group, Deborah busied herself by taking the dirty dishes to the washbasin in the corner, next to the wood-burning stove.

"If Yolken's strength is so great," Kaylan said, "then couldn't we just confront the emperor directly and make him release Javen?"

"I wish it were that easy, child," Deanna said. Turning to Yolken she said, "Deth has named you Dragon King, which means you have within you great power. However, you must always remember that the dragons were defeated. Draego's blessing does not make you invincible. The dragons underestimated us, and it cost them their existence. Do not for a moment think that my brother would treat you any differently than any other rebel attempting to take his throne."

"But if the Great Dragon has blessed me, then doesn't that mean that his will is for us to succeed?" Yolken said.

"Was that true for the dragons?"

"Well, no. But then why bless me at all?"

"I don't know," Deanna said. "But for now, whatever we do, we must proceed with just as much caution as we would have had we never visited Deth."

"How does all this relate to our problem with the sun?" Jax said. "What did Deth say about it?"

"He said that the war disrupted the balance of the sun and that Yolken was chosen to restore it."

"What does that mean?"

"I don't know," Deanna said.

"He didn't tell Yolken what he needed to do?"

"Beyond needing to restore balance, no."

The cottage again fell into silence.

Finally, Yolken said, "So, what now?"

"Yes, we must discuss our options," added Deborah, her sleeves rolled up over her elbows and her arms covered in soap.

"Deanna," Jax said, "the Council sent us here to solicit your help. Even though we don't yet understand what has happened here, I know—speaking on behalf of the Council—that we desperately need you to join us. Return with us to Croff. Go with us to the Council and let us all decide how to proceed, together."

Deanna sat quietly in her chair and stared blankly.

"Please," Deborah said, drying her hands with a towel, "join us."

Deanna looked over at Deborah, then at Jax, and finally at Yolken. "I came to this island to hide." She paused for a moment, then added, "I hid because I wanted to put an end to the constant and unnecessary death. I will hide no more. I can't. It is time to face what is coming. Together, we must try to unite the Order of the Dragon with the Regency. The problem we face affects us all. We must at last put an end to the war."

Deborah joined them at the table. "Yes, but the emperor is openly hostile to the Order."

"Then we will have to change that."

"The emperor has known what's happening for centuries, and it has done nothing to convince him to work with us," Deborah said.

"I realize that," Deanna said. "However, we have now added two pieces to the puzzle that have never existed before: Yolken and myself."

"Do you think your brother will just welcome you back with open arms?" Deborah said. "Somehow I'm guessing not, else why have you remained in hiding all this time?"

"The Council sent you to find me. Is it not possible that they might be open to acting if I add myself to their ranks?"

"I don't think Drakonias will respond positively if the Order comes to Kyinth in force," Jax said. "He will not see it as a plea for peace, but rather an assault on the Regency—*especially* if you are among their ranks."

"What if we don't show up in force?" Yolken said.

"What are you suggesting?" Jax said.

Yolken shrugged his shoulders.

"Maybe," Deborah interjected, "if only a few went to Kyinth, Drakonias would be more inclined to see it as a peace offering than an attack."

"The Order has tried that before," Jax said.

"But never with Deanna," Deborah said.

"Who else would take part in this envoy?"

"No one," Deanna said.

"No one?" Jax said.

"Yolken and I would be threatening enough," Deanna said.

"You want to go before Drakonias, just you and Yolken?"

"Any more would tip the scales to the side of assault, don't you think?"

"I can't allow that!"

"He is not a child, Jax."

"No, but I made an oath to his father to protect him."

"Do you not think that perhaps he is beyond needing your protection?"

Jax stared silently at Deanna for several moments before saying, "Let us think on it. For now, if you have no objections, Deanna, I suggest we stay here until Urgil's ship arrives to retrieve us."

"When is that supposed to be?" Deanna said.

"A month from when we first arrived."

"Then we have some time."

Yolken stood and said, "I need to go for a walk." He offered his hand to Kaylan, who rose to her feet and took it.

"Don't go too far," Deborah said.

"We won't."

Yolken and Kaylan left the others, who were immersed in discussion once more before they reached the door. As they walked in silence, enjoying the sounds of the forest, Yolken thought about his conversation with the dragon. He pondered what it meant to be only the second living being who was *actually* Blessed of the Dragon. He thought about the first of the dragons, the Dragon King.

Then it hit him.

He stopped.

Kaylan took two more steps and stopped when Yolken's hand pulled hers back. She turned to face him and, seeing the look on his face, said, "What is it?"

Yolken looked at Kaylan, his face lit up by the sun, and smiled.

CHAPTER 51

"How can you be sure Urgil will return?" Deborah said.

Yolken was glad she had asked, because he was thinking the same thing. What happened if Urgil didn't return?

"Because I made him an offer he can't refuse," Jax said. "Even if he doesn't return, we'll figure something out."

"Such as what?"

"We still have the dinghy."

"You plan on rowing that thing all the way to Onta?"

"No, but if we *had* to, we could make it to Ronig."

"Let's hope it doesn't come to that," Deborah said.

"It won't."

They remained at Deanna's cottage to pass the days while they waited. Jax, Deborah, and Deanna spent their time deliberating about the path forward. Yolken tried to sit in on the conversations as much as he could, but every time he tried, the banality of the discussion quickly bored him. He had no interest in the political maneuverings of the Council or of the Regency. Even though the principle issue was what to do about the threat of the sun, the conversation always devolved into how to best leverage Yolken being the Dragon King.

"You will have to grow accustomed to it if you intend to be

a successful ruler," Deanna said.

Yolken looked at Deanna with shock. "What do you mean?"

"You *are* Draego's chosen ruler."

Yolken looked at her, dumbfounded.

"What did you think being the Dragon King meant?"

"I…" Yolken said. "What exactly am I supposed to be king *of?*"

"I don't know," Deanna said, "but I *do* know that my brother's rule must come to an end."

"What am I supposed to do? March up to the throne, declare that I'm the Dragon King, and demand that Drakonias hand the scepter and empire over to me?"

"Of course not, Yolken," Deanna said.

"What, then? Should I rally the Order behind me and declare war on the Regency?" Yolken said. "I am *not* going to be responsible for starting another war."

"Hmm," Deanna breathed.

"Nobody is starting any wars," Deborah said.

"How do you know that?" Jax said.

"I don't. But there must be a peaceful way to resolve things."

"I'm not so sure."

"Me either," Deanna added. "My brother has had all the time he needed to resolve things peacefully."

"I'm not starting a war!" Yolken exclaimed. "Besides, shouldn't we be figuring out how to fix the damage from the last war? Isn't that the *real* mission of the Order? Who cares about who rules or doesn't rule, or whether they are or aren't legitimate. I just want to get Javen back and figure out how to fix the sun— if that's even possible. Saying it out loud makes me realize how silly the very thought is. Then I want to go home. I have no interest in being the king of anything."

"It's not that simple, Yolken, and you know it," Deborah said.

Yolken felt himself growing angry. Resisting the urge to

scream at the top of his lungs, he stormed out of the cottage. Kaylan followed him and hugged him. She was all he wanted or needed.

Together, they walked into the woods. When they were out of earshot of the cottage he said, "I came here for help in rescuing my brother, not to find out I'm some sort of king who's supposed to bring down the empire, let alone do the impossible. *Fix the sun...*"

"This is all crazy," Kaylan said.

Yolken silently agreed. It *was* all crazy. Nothing about his life had been sane since the day he'd healed Issa. He wished he could brew some ale to help him feel like a normal person again. Brewing had a way of calming him, making him feel closer to his father, who he barely remembered. He'd done a lot of thinking over the years while he brewed, sorted out a lot of thoughts. But that wasn't possible here—unless Jax had secreted away brewing equipment here like he did at the safehouse in the Mindons. But Yolken knew he hadn't. So, instead, he walked. For the rest of the afternoon, they walked. Together. In the woods. Without speaking.

In the next few days both Yolken and Kaylan fell in love with the woods of Kvorga. They loved the opportunity to spend time together, but they also loved the many different plants and animals that lived on the island. Many of the animals exhibited characteristics similar to the cat they had seen the day they met Deanna. The animals moved faster and plants grew bigger than any they had ever seen before. Spending a lot of time up in the Mindons, it was weird for Yolken to see many of the same plants here, only much bigger. It was the same with the animals. The squirrels moved faster; the deer leaped farther as they pranced through the forest; the birds flew higher. And the trees... the trees were enormous.

It didn't take long for Yolken to notice that the animals were much warier of them here than they were in the Mindons. He thought back on his time at the cabin and how he had coaxed squirrels up onto his legs and stomach with nuts. It was not so here. Despite his best efforts, the squirrels kept their distance. They wouldn't take nuts from him unless he left them and moved on. If he remained anywhere near, they would stay away.

From time to time, he and Kaylan saw the mountain lion that had accompanied Deanna the day they'd met her. It seemed to lurk nearby as they ventured through the woods. It became a game for him to see how close he could get to it before it darted away. A few times he even gave chase, using Synthesis to run quicker, but it always succeeded in losing him.

"I wonder why they're so afraid of us?" Yolken said as they walked.

"I've noticed it, too," Kaylan said. "Could it just be the area?"

"I don't think that's it."

"Why not? People change from area to area, so why not the animals?"

"Our customs change, sure, but we're still basically the same."

"I don't know what to tell you."

"There's got to be a reason," Yolken said. "Especially as unpopulated and untraveled as the island is. There should be no reason for them to fear us. They don't have a reason to be scared."

For the remainder of the time they spent at Deanna's cottage, Yolken avoided Jax, Deborah, and Deanna as much as he could. Together with Kaylan, he wandered the woods and tried to find peace in the beauty of the forest.

He didn't know why, but he kept the recent discovery of his new skill when he was walking with Kaylan to himself. Kaylan promised not to say anything either. He thought a lot about it, though. He wondered how he hadn't known it was there until now. He figured it was simply because he'd never thought of it before. Jax taught him that knowledge was key to Synthesis;

when he'd first tried to grasp the air with Synthesis, he had failed because he didn't think of it properly. And Deth's words had prompted him to think differently.

Three days before Urgil's scheduled return, Jax declared that it was time to descend the mountain and return to the shore where they'd left the dinghy. They packed their belongings and stuffed their satchels with dried foods from Deanna's wares.

Deanna walked into her bedroom and returned a few moments later with a sheathed sword in her hand. Its hilt was also made of woven steel, but in thinner threads and woven more elegantly than the Harachin sword's. She pulled it out of the scabbard and looked it over. It was made of dragon bone. Yellow ribbons in the bone reflected the light of the cottage. The blade was thinner than Yolken's sword.

"The Aliza sword," Jax said.

"Yes," Deanna said, holding it up. "I haven't held it since I built this cottage. It's not quite as powerful as Drae's, but it'll do."

"Even so," Jax said, "it's more powerful than any bone the Order still has in their possession."

"Should we wrap it with the Harachin sword?" Yolken said. "We probably don't want to board Urgil's ship with it out on display."

"Good idea, Yolken," Deanna said.

Yolken unwrapped his cloak, exposing the sword hidden within. Deanna lay her sword next to the Harachin sword, and Yolken rolled the cloak back up and repositioned it on his back.

Then they started on their way. But before the cottage disappeared behind them, Deanna stopped. She turned around and looked upon the small structure that had been her home for centuries. The mountain lion that had greeted the group when they'd first arrived on the island slinked up to her and nuzzled its head in her hand. Without taking her eyes off the cottage, she massaged its ears. "I've sequestered myself here for four centuries," she said. "This island is as much a part of me now as I am of it." She turned from the cottage and kissed the mountain lion on the top of its head. She whispered something inaudible to it, and it disappeared as quickly as it had come. "It is not easy for me to leave it behind."

"It's only for a time," Jax said. "Once our work is done, you can always return if you wish."

"No," Deanna said. "My time of seclusion is over." She rejoined the group and, together, they started down the northern slope of the mountain.

As they walked, Deanna ran her hand gently on the trunks of trees and felt the leaves of plants with the tips of her fingers.

Noticing that any forest creature fled from the party when they approached prompted Yolken to ask, "Why are all the animals here so afraid?"

"The animals of Kvorga are not trusting of humans," Deanna said.

"Why?"

"Have you ever wondered why so many stories exist about the island?"

Yolken nodded.

"Have you noticed that many of them are true?"

"Yes. Kaylan and I have seen a lot of animals while we've been out walking, and we've noticed that they all exhibit the gift to one degree or another."

"And where does the gift come from?"

"Deth?"

"Yes. Dethoicrinth didn't give Synthesis to all the animals at once, but over time, he gave it to more and more of them. After we turned on the dragons, he began to instill in them a fear of humans."

"How did you get the cat to trust you, then?" Kaylan said.

"Time," Deanna said. "Lots of time."

When the group emerged from the forest at the beach where

Urgil had dropped them off, they saw a ship anchored several hundred paces offshore. The dread of being at sea again filled Yolken as he helped Jax push the dinghy into the water. Everyone climbed in and they rowed their way out to meet it.

Jax rowed the dinghy up to the side of the ship where four thick ropes with hooks on the ends dangled just above the water. As he maneuvered the little boat, Yolken and Deanna reached for the ropes. They slid the hooks into metal rings at each end of the boat and the boat soon began to lift out of the water.

"Who's this?" Urgil said when they were all on board.

"Her name is Breena," Jax said.

One of the many things they had discussed while they waited for Urgil to come pick them up was how much to say about who Deanna was. They didn't want rumors to begin circulating about her, so they came up with a story to explain her presence.

"Is she why you came here?" Urgil said.

"No," Jax said. "But she was stranded."

"I was sailing around the island with my lover and our boat capsized. Poor Han d-died," Deanna stammered, "but I managed to swim to shore. I was stranded on that cursed island for months when these blessed people came across my camp."

"I haven't heard of any missing boats from Onta," Urgil said.

"We're from Turnig," Deanna said.

"Isn't Turnig in revolt?" Urgil said.

"That's why we left. We didn't want to get caught in the middle of a revolt we wanted nothing to do with."

"I see," Urgil said. Turning to Jax, he said, "Did you find what you came for?"

"Unfortunately, no," Jax said.

"That's a shame," Urgil said. "You're still keeping your end of the bargain?"

Jax nodded. "When we arrive in Onta, seeds will be planted to ensure you are the next captain of the *Vineyard*."

Urgil turned from the group and began barking orders.

Tanned men raised the anchor and the sails unfurled.

As the ship turned north and the sails filled with wind, Yolken stood at the very back of the ship and watched the island slowly grow smaller. His eyes were fixed on the towering peak where he knew the dragon resided. He couldn't help but think that whatever it was they were going to do, it would be easier if they had the dragon by their side. He knew that humans had wiped out the dragons, but that was a long time ago. Most now didn't even believe dragons existed. Their legacy had devolved to mere creatures of legend. The dragon's reemergence into the world would be powerful—if not against the Regency directly, then through the impact it would have on those they ruled. If the Order could get the people on their side, they would become a formidable threat to the Regency.

But the dragon had refused to leave its cave, resolved to remain in solitude.

The trip back to Onta went much better for Yolken. Kaylan, however, became as sick as she was on the trip over. Deborah spent most of the time caring for her or keeping company with Deanna, who remained out of sight in Urgil's cabin, not wanting to be the subject of further scrutiny.

Jax spent much of his time fending off Urgil, who pestered him relentlessly about becoming captain of Devin's flagship, leaving Yolken with plenty of time alone on the three-day voyage back to Onta. He spent as much time as he could with Kaylan, but she mostly wanted to be left alone.

The others continued to be obsessed about the dragon having acknowledged him as the Dragon King, which made him uncomfortable. He didn't like discussing it, so he wandered the decks of the ship instead.

Yolken knew he couldn't ignore the issue, though. He spent every waking moment reflecting on the purpose of his meeting with the dragon. He couldn't get over the fact that, at least according to Deanna, the dragon had acknowledged him as the true Blessed of the Dragon. He had grown up thinking that the Drakes were the Blessed of the Dragon, and to find out that the only *true* Blessed was Dimras, the first dragon, was hard to comprehend. How was he supposed to process the idea that the Great Dragon had now blessed him? And how could he possibly undo the damage his predecessors had done to the sun? He didn't even know what that damage was, only that if he didn't somehow restore balance that the sun would destroy Dradonia. If it truly *was* up to him to restore balance to the sun, he had no idea how or what he was supposed to do. And neither did anyone else. The trip had been, in large part, a huge waste. He was no closer to rescuing Javen than he had been when he'd first stood before the Council in Croff.

Deanna finally emerged from the cabin when Yolken delivered the news that they were entering the bay of Onta. She followed Yolken up and stared wide-eyed as the ship passed the guard towers.

Seeing her fixation, Yolken said, "Is it much different than when you were here last?"

Deanna nodded, not taking her eyes from the gleaming white wall and the spire that rose behind it. "The city was a smoldering ruin when I passed through it on my way to Kvorga."

Yolken stood by her side as the ship pulled into port. As men began shouting back and forth from the ship and the dock, Kaylan came up on deck with Deborah, carrying their things. They met at the gangplank the dockworkers had quickly put in place, and immediately started down.

"Thank you for your services," Jax said to Urgil just before he stepped onto the gangplank. "Rest assured, you will be the next captain of the *Vineyard*."

Urgil nodded.

Jax offered him his hand and Urgil shook it.

"I still think we should hire a merchant wagon," Deborah

said as they walked up the dock toward the ramshackle buildings cluttering the space between the bay and the city wall.

"Maybe once we're out of the city," Jax said.

As they neared the base of the wall where the road turned left, Yolken eyed the empty square where he'd healed as many of the people as he could. Beggars again filled it. Just as before, many of them were laying on mats. His heart pulled him toward them, but he knew he couldn't help them. A few of them looked up in their direction as they passed, and the urge to go to them became so strong he had to look away.

"This city dates back to long before the war," Deanna said as they walked down the street lined with marble buildings, "but not in such opulence. The vanity of my family is sickening. It's much worse than when my father ruled."

When they arrived at the roundabout in front of the spire, Jax kept to the right and followed the curved road toward the eastern road. However, Deanna broke away from the group and walked toward the statue in the center. She circled around it, and stopped when she stood face to face with the emperor—her brother.

Jax went over to her and said, "Let's go. I don't want to spend any more time here than we have to."

Deanna turned around and looked at the palace. It sat enshrouded in shadow, but the setting sun still illuminated the top of the spire. "I have a mind to march in there and talk to Reago."

"Why?" Jax said. "He's the Chancellor of the Western Realm, remember?"

"I know, but if anyone would be sympathetic to our cause, it would be him."

"Let's go," Jax said. "We need to get out of the city before the gates close."

Deanna turned from the spire. They hurried as best they could down the busy street and entered the large square at the

East Gate just as the sun's rays disappeared from the spire.

Jax increased his step almost to a jog, knowing that was the signal for the gates to close. The others followed close behind. Wagons and carriages crowded the square trying to make it out. Before they came into view of the guards standing around the gates—which had yet to begin to close—Jax slowed his step. They crowded together and joined rank with the column of those exiting on foot, which moved much more quickly than the line of wagons attempting to do the same. Just as they passed between the giant towers, the mechanisms that closed the gates began to turn, and the two enormous metal doors began to very slowly close.

Once they had passed through the gate and begun to climb the bridge that crossed the Onta River, the flow of travelers increased. Only a handful of runners and a few riders on horseback moved toward the city, hoping to beat the gate. They hugged the left side of the road, leaving the remainder of it to the crowd leaving. All the many travelers took full advantage of this, spreading out over the entire width of the bridge.

As people on horseback began to pass, Yolken took Kaylan by the hand and pulled her a little farther from the wall to give them more room. He looked at a few of them as they passed, but then his attention went back to trying not to bump into Jax, who walked in front of them.

Suddenly his arm jerked out as Kaylan's hand was ripped from his own. He turned, thinking someone had bumped into her, but he saw a man on horseback pulling her up onto the saddle and laying her across his lap. He stared in horror, his ears thumping. The world slowed and he barely heard himself scream, "Kaylan!"

The man who had snatched Kaylan urged his horse into a gallop. Yolken watched as he rode toward the gate. He saw Kaylan scream, but heard only his own heartbeat.

Yolken took off running after her but was pulled up short

when the rolled-up cloak he wore as a pack yanked his shoulders back. He looked over his shoulder to see Jax holding onto the pack.

"Yolken, don't!" he barely heard Jax say. "It's a trap!"

"I can't leave her!" Yolken yelled. He shimmied the pack off and took off in a sprint. His satchel banged against his side as he ran, so he lifted it over his head and dropped it on the ground. He ran faster than should have been physically possible and made it through the gates before they slammed closed.

CHAPTER 52

Hadie walked straight across the empty lounge, through the beaded doorway, to the staircase at the end of the hall. She climbed the stairs up to the fourth floor and went to the door at the end of the hall. Sonja's room. She opened the window blinds to let light in, then went over to Sonja's desk. If her plan was going to work, she needed clients. The wastebasket Ursella had used to burn parchment in still sat in the same place it had been when she was here last, so she hoped Ursella had actually stopped burning the client lists when she'd told her it wasn't necessary. She pulled open the drawer and sighed in relief when she saw it was still full of parchment.

Hadie sat in Sonja's chair and pulled the stack out. Sitting back in the chair, she thumbed through the names and thought her idea through a little more carefully. As her plan slowly coalesced, she started recognizing some of the client names. Many of them were names of Hantlo Silks.

Hadie sat back up abruptly and sifted through the sheets until she got to the M's. She went through each parchment one by one, and stopped on a familiar last name: Morrigan. She pulled the sheet out and looked at the full name. Phenor Morrigan; her father. She stared at the name with a blank face.

Her eyes eventually began to drift down to what was written below, but then she shoved the parchment back into place, not wanting to know what her father's bedding peculiarities were.

She pushed the drawer closed and sat back in Sonja's plush chair. She stared vacantly for several minutes—thinking—then looked over at herself in the mirror. She crossed to it and inspected herself, trying to put on an air of confidence. She stood straight, turned to the side, took a deep breath, held it in, and assessed herself. *I could pull it off.*

However, she knew she needed more than confidence in herself to do what she was thinking of—namely, she needed Ursella.

Hadie left Sonja's room and went back downstairs. She left the brothel and walked down to Rita's. She coughed into a fist when she stepped into the lounge half the size as Sonja's; incense hung thick in the air.

A woman wearing typical indoor southern attire—a sheer off-white dress—rose and walked over to Hadie and said, "How might I service you?"

"I'm looking for Ylonna," Hadie said.

"She's presently with another client. Would you like to wait, or perhaps visit someone else?"

"I'll wait."

The woman nodded. "Have a seat," she said. "She shouldn't be much longer."

Hadie sat on a couch, thinking she could use a glass of wine. However, the woman returned to where she had been sitting when Hadie walked in, so she waited awkwardly on the couch as other clients came and went.

After a heavyset man walked out tucking his shirt into his pants, the woman—Rita, Hadie presumed—walked over to her and said, "Ylonna is available now."

"Thank you," Hadie said. She stood up and headed toward the hallway on the far side of the room.

"Ahem," Rita said.

Hadie stopped. "Yeah?"

"She's not free."

"I—"

"It's a drake if you want to bed her."

Hadie started to speak, then stopped herself. She reached into her satchel, pulled out a drake, and handed it to Rita.

"Second door on the right," Rita said as she returned to her chair.

Hadie walked down the hallway and opened the second door on the right without knocking. Ylonna sat on the bed with her back to the door, her legs crossed, naked. When Hadie shut the door, Ylonna turned around.

"Good after—" Ylonna started. "Hadie? What are you doing here?"

"I came to see if you knew where Ursella was."

"Rita let you back?"

"I… paid her," Hadie said.

"You paid her?"

Hadie nodded. "So, do you?"

"Yeah, sure," Ylonna said, looking a little confused. "She's working at a pub a couple blocks over. You paid Rita just to come in here and ask me where Ursella is?"

Hadie nodded. She couldn't help but notice Ylonna's breasts when she reached her arms up to cover them, the moment being a little awkward. Hadie figured she probably wasn't used to conversing with clients, at least not in a non-bedding manner. She was very beautiful, though. And exactly the type of woman she remembered Drenan preferring—the type he demanded, really. Her hair was a beautiful auburn that shimmered in the light of the lantern on the wall, her skin smooth and olive-colored, her breasts full and heavy above a slender waist.

"What do you want with her?"

"A pub, you say? She's not whoring anymore?"

Ylonna shook her head. "Wanted out."

"That's what I don't get," Hadie said. "Why would any of you continue whoring—and for only your share of a drake—when Sonja saw to it that you didn't have to anymore?"

"She didn't see to anything," Ylonna said. "The gold she gave us would have lasted a little while, but not forever. And when it ran out, what then? Ursella's no different. She just traded whoring for wenching."

Hadie's heart ached for them. She wanted to tell Ylonna that she was going to make it so they didn't have to do it anymore, but she decided to wait until she talked with Ursella. "Which pub?"

"Hob's."

"Thanks, Ylonna."

Hadie turned to open the door but stopped when Ylonna said, "Hold on."

"What?"

"You can't leave right now. It's too soon—even for a quick bedding. Don't want to make Rita suspicious of anything, do you?"

"No," Hadie said. She walked over and awkwardly sat on the bed.

"We still have time," Ylonna said.

"For what?"

"For a quick one. You paid for a bedding, didn't you?" Ylonna slid closer to Hadie.

"I… no thanks. You… you're very beautiful, Ylonna, but I'm not… I don't prefer—"

"Stop," Ylonna said. "Not everyone does." She rose from the bed and poured herself a glass of wine from a bottle sitting on a small table in the corner. "Want one?"

"Yes," Hadie said. A glass of wine was *exactly* what she needed right now.

Ylonna poured another glass and handed it to Hadie. "It's

not like it was with Sonja. The clients aren't what they were, and I don't make a fraction of what I used to. I sneak this wine in to help take the edge off what I do, and for my clients if they need it. At least I don't have to bed regents anymore, though."

"You didn't like bedding regents?"

Ylonna sat next to Hadie and shook her head. "The money was good, but I got tired of the beatings."

Hadie sipped her wine. Made perfect sense to her.

"I mean, just this last month Sonja sent me to Portstown to accompany Drenan when he returned to the south, and he beat me on three separate occasions."

"I'm so sorry," Hadie said. She reached out and tentatively patted Ylonna on the thigh. "What about here? Isn't there a chance the same thing could happen?"

Ylonna shook her head. "For one, regents don't come here. And Rita strictly prohibits clients from hurting us. If they do, they aren't permitted to return."

"That's good. So, how many of you are still whoring?" Hadie said. If her plan was going to work, she would need several of Sonja's whores.

"Most of us. I only know of a few that got out entirely—such as Ursella."

Hadie drank her wine to hide any sign of satisfaction she might betray at the news.

When Ylonna finished her glass she said, "Well, you should be good to go, if you're sure you don't want a quick bedding."

Hadie blushed as she upended her glass. "Thanks."

"See ya, Hadie," Ylonna said as Hadie opened the door and stepped out.

* * *

Hadie watched as Ursella tended to the patrons who sat at tables enclosed behind a small metal fence outside Hob's Pub. She wore a loose-fitting white blouse and a brown apron tied around her waist. Her blouse was damp and clung to her body. It gave ample suggestion, but by southern standards it was quite modest. Hadie tugged on her own damp blouse to let a little air circulate through. The prevalent heat and moisture were reason enough to leave the south, but now she knew she couldn't—not until she had accomplished what she'd set out to do.

Ursella set steins down at one table, then moved over to another and took orders. She disappeared through the front door of the pub then returned with more steins. She checked on a few other patrons, then gathered up steins left at an empty table, scooped up coins and dropped them into a pocket in her apron.

Hadie walked through the opening of the gate and, seeing that there were more steins than Ursella could carry in one trip, said, "Can I help you with those?"

Ursella looked up and said, "Hadie! What are you doing here?"

Hadie picked up the remaining steins. "I want to talk to you about something."

"All right, but I'm busy right now."

"That's fine," Hadie said. She followed Ursella into the pub. The heat inside was even more oppressive than outside.

"Just set them right there," Ursella said, gesturing to the end of the bar. She disappeared through a swinging door with her own armload of steins, then returned for the rest. "What do you want to talk about?"

"Not here," Hadie said. "When do you finish for the day?"

"Not until late."

"When you're done, let's talk."

"Where?" Ursella said.

"Sonja's."

"Sonja's?"

Hadie nodded. "See you later?"

"Yeah," Ursella said with a nod.

Hadie smiled as she walked out of the pub. The small breeze

was refreshing. It was no surprise the tables outside were full. Back inside Sonja's, she left the door open, then moved around the room lighting sconces. Then she went from room to room down the hallway, pulling the velvet drapes and opening the windows. A breeze began to circulate through the building, rattling the beads that divided the hallway from the lounge.

She repeated the process on the other floors, then sat in the chair in Sonja's room. She put her feet up on the desk and sank down to get comfortable. She tried to think about exactly what she wanted to say to Ursella, but her eyes grew heavy and she fell asleep.

Hadie woke with a start when someone shook her foot. She opened her eyes and saw Ursella sitting on the edge of the desk. "I… I must have nodded off."

"You were snoring."

"I don't snore."

"I heard you from downstairs. You're lucky nothing happened to you, leaving the door open like that."

"I didn't mean to fall asleep," Hadie said. She sat up and rubbed her eyes. "What time is it?"

"Late," Ursella said. "What did you want to talk about?"

Seeing no reason to ease into the conversation, Hadie said, "Have you ever heard of the blood river?"

Ursella nodded. "Sure, the river of blood that flows from the sun when it's setting over the Kvorgan Sea."

"Well, I was thinking about making it flow through Hantlo," Hadie said.

CHAPTER 53

W hat do you mean?" Ursella said.

"I want to make blood flow in Hantlo," Hadie said.

"What are you talking about?"

"You know I came to Sonja for two reasons: to get help finding the man I love and to kill Drenan. Well, I failed in both regards. And now…" Hadie stopped to fight back tears welling in her eyes. "Now I want to kill them all."

"Are you crazy?" Ursella exclaimed. She rose from the desk and took a step away.

"Maybe," Hadie said. She sat up in the chair. "But that doesn't change the fact that they all deserve to die."

"I went along with it and helped Sonja prepare you for Drenan, but the idea that you can go around killing them is insane. They're Blessed!"

"They aren't any more blessed by the Great Dragon than you or I."

"I disagree," Ursella protested. "They're immortal, for one."

"They die just as easily as you and me. True, they have a gift that makes them powerful, but that doesn't give them the right to enslave us."

"We aren't slaves."

"Yes, we are. We aren't free. The chancellor and regents are nothing more than slave masters. Sonja was Drenan's slave. She loathed him but was unable to stop serving him. Despite how much she hated sending her whores to him, she had no choice. You yourself wondered why she kept sending you to them."

"That doesn't mean we need to kill them."

"In the last two months, Drenan has killed four people that I know of. He killed Panny and Kitt, Ursella. He also killed a girl from the town where I met Javen. Her name was Astora. She was an innocent girl and Drenan brutally killed her. He killed Javen's aunt as well. Who knows how many others we never hear about? Ursella, the Blessed are monsters. Somebody has to stop them."

"I… I need some wine," Ursella said. She left the room and returned with a bottle and two glasses. She filled both glasses and handed one to Hadie, then pulled a chair from the corner by the mirror over to the desk. She took a big drink, refilled her glass, and said, "And you want to kill them?"

"*All* of them. Something has to be done. We can't continue living as slaves."

"If you don't want them to rule anymore, couldn't you incite a revolt or something?"

"You've heard the stories," Hadie said. "That never works. The Regency has never been shy about reporting that they've quelled another rebellion. Because of their gift, we're weak and stand no chance of a successful revolt."

"What are you suggesting, then?"

"What Sonja planned would have worked, had I not been interrupted. Drenan never suspected I was trying to kill him. I don't see why the same shouldn't be true on a larger scale. If they don't suspect that they're about to die, they're powerless to stop it."

Hadie spent the remainder of the bottle of wine explaining to Ursella what she wanted to do. In the end, Ursella was skeptical. "Think of Panny and Kit," Hadie said. "The blood river already flows. It flows around the whole realm—around the whole empire; we just don't see it. Think about it, Ursella: The realm is collapsing and they're powerless to stop it. Most of them are already in Hantlo. We just need to wait for the right moment."

"I don't know," Ursella said. "And what about after? If we actually manage to do this, what then?"

"I don't have it all figured out, but I know someone who might be able to help." Seeing that Ursella looked unsure, she said, "You don't have to decide right now. Go home and think about it. I'll be right here when you decide."

Ursella nodded.

"Good," Hadie said. "Now, I need some sleep." She rose from the chair and walked over to Sonja's bed, pulling her shirt over her head as she went. She sat on Sonja's bed as Ursella walked toward the door. "I'll see you tomorrow?"

Ursella nodded, then slipped through the door.

* * *

The sun inched over the windowsill, shining into Hadie's eyes. As it rose it slowly filled the window. Its light made the red velvet wallpaper look like blood. Hadie rolled to the edge of the bed and sat up. She thought about retrieving her pants, but decided that if she wanted to convince Ursella to help her, she needed to be the person she had told Ursella she would be.

She left her clothes lying on the floor and went over to the armoire. She selected a corset similar to the one she had worn the night she'd intended to kill Drenan—but this one fit her body as it was, not how Drenan would have wanted it to be. With unpracticed fingers, she clumsily cinched the front-laced corset around her bodice, then found the pleated dress she'd worn while she worked Sonja's lobby.

Hadie looked at herself in the mirror, pleased with what she saw. She went over to where her pants lay on the ground and slid her knife off the belt. She didn't have the bust Sonja had, so she couldn't conceal a blade between her breasts. Instead, she slid the sheath up underneath the corset on the left side of her navel. The corset was tight enough to keep the blade snugly in place. It wasn't an ideal solution, but if she managed to convince Ursella to help her she'd find a more permanent place for it.

She walked out of Sonja's room, deciding to wait for Ursella in the lobby. When she stepped off the stairs on the bottom floor, she heard voices. She walked hesitantly down the hallway and looked through the beads hanging in the doorway. The lobby was full of women. Ursella was talking to them.

Hadie slid her hand through the beads and lifted them, making an opening. One of the girls standing next to Ursella saw and pointed toward her. The din in the room quieted.

Hadie stepped through the beads into the lounge.

"I gathered as many as I could find," Ursella said.

"So you've decided to proceed?" Hadie said.

Ursella nodded. "After I left here, I knew what I wanted, so I started collecting them from the other brothels right away."

"What did you tell them?"

"Nothing. I thought you should be the one to tell them, Madam," Ursella said with a small curtsy.

Hadie smiled, then looked around the room at the girls. Most of them were young and probably knew no life apart from whoring. She thought about what Ylonna said about the money Sonja had left them—they could subsist on it until it was gone, but then they'd be right back in the same poverty that had likely caused them to start whoring in the first place. Under the rule of the Regency, their lives would never improve. She yearned to help them, to somehow usher in an era where more prospered than just the Blessed and a privileged few.

Without thinking, Hadie lifted a hand and brushed the tops of her breasts lightly with the tips of her fingers. The eyes of every girl in the room were on her.

"How many of you enjoy whoring?" she said.

The room was silent.

"And how many of you enjoy bedding regents?"

Still, no one said a thing.

"How many of you would be interested in never having to whore again?"

Hands went up around the room.

"The money Sonja gave you when she left won't last—you already know that. That's why most of you continued whoring after she left. And unless something changes, people like us will never have the opportunity to prosper; we'll spend the rest of our lives selling our bodies—for what? A fraction of a drake? Whatever is left when whichever madam you happen to work for takes the majority? At least under Sonja you made a decent living."

"What are you suggesting?" a woman said.

Hadie looked around the girls immediately in front of her to see who spoke. She smiled when she saw Ylonna standing near the door. "I'm suggesting we change things. I have a plan. It'll be dangerous, but if we succeed, we'll change the very fabric of the realm and possibly give ourselves the chance at a better life. Now, there are no guarantees my plan will succeed, or even improve things, but what I do know is this: If we do nothing, you will spend the rest of your lives whoring."

"What's your plan?" another woman said.

Delori, Hadie thought, remembering the petite dark-skinned girl's name.

She hesitated for a moment, knowing that what she was about to say could very well end up getting her killed if any of the women present told the wrong person. It was a chance she was willing to take, though.

"It is no secret that those of you whom Sonja sent to pleasure regents often returned beaten. Two of you—Panny and Kit—were recently murdered."

Gasps flowed across the room.

"We were wondering what happened to them," a curvaceous girl said.

Ashla, Hadie told herself. She waited a moment to allow her words to percolate.

"The only way things will ever improve for people like us, is if we make it so the Regency can no longer oppress us."

"And how are we supposed to do that?" Ylonna said.

"We kill them," Hadie said matter-of-factly.

"We k-kill them?" Ashla stammered.

"Yes," Hadie said. "All of them." She looked around the room. Many of the girls looked frightened, but none of them moved toward the door as she had expected many of them to do. So she continued, "Now, I'm fully aware that I'm taking a big risk telling you this, but my innermost being knows that what I am suggesting is the right thing to do. You might be wondering why I want to do this, so I'll tell you: It's because I've only recently realized how truly evil the Regency is. In just the last couple of months the Regent of Hantlo has murdered—in cold blood—four people. And that's just the ones I know about. Who knows how many others there might be? And what about the other regents? You've all heard the stories—people disappearing simply for having the wrong idea.

"With the exception of Ursella, Sonja didn't tell you why she left. Well, it was because she helped me try to kill Drenan." Eyes all around the room went wide. "I was in his room, ready to kill him, and if he hadn't been suddenly called away, I would have succeeded. Our plan would have *worked.*

"Ursella and I have yet to work out all the details, but our plan begins with all of you." Hadie looked around the room at the women staring at her in shock. "It begins with you coming back here and working for me, Madam Sheena." Murmurs took over the room. Hadie put her hands up to quiet them. "I promise it will be better than what you have now. It'll be better than what you had with Sonja. Unlike Sonja, I am not interested in becoming rich—and you made her very rich. I promise that if you come work for me until our plan is complete, any money you make, minus that needed to implement our plan, will be yours."

"I heard you've never whored a day in your life," a tall, thin woman said.

"You're right, Eranna," Hadie said, addressing the woman by name. "I haven't. But did you ever know Sonja to whore?"

"I… I never asked. I just assumed—"

"Maybe she did, maybe she didn't, but life is not about what you were—it's about what you are. I'm not a whore, but I am someone who can lead you to a better life—a better life not just for you, but for the entire Southern Realm. Now, if you wish to join me, then come forward and pledge yourself to me. If not, you are free to go." Giving them the choice to leave was risky, but Hadie needed to show that she trusted them.

No one moved initially. Then Ursella pushed her way through the crowd. She took Hadie by the hand and kissed the back of it. "Madam," Ursella said with a curtsy.

Hadie nodded at Ursella then looked at the others. They looked at her, many of them looking unsure, but then Ylonna moved forward, kissed her on the hand, and said, "Madam."

After Ylonna came Ashla, then the rest of them lined up. One by one, every girl in the room walked up to her and kissed her on the hand.

Hadie choked back the urge to cry, to release the emotion welling. "Now it's time for the blood river to flow."

CHAPTER 54

Javen sat nervously on the back seat of the carriage. The driver had the carriage positioned facing west on the side of the road just prior to where it merged with the square at the East Gate. They were supposed to be in the square, but after assessing the crowded square, the driver had strategically positioned the carriage to best carry out the mission.

Javen stared out the window, fidgeting with the black bone carved in Karina's likeness. He ignored the temptation to draw Energy into his Core—he always felt calm when he Synthesized. A runner had come to the carriage about half an hour ago and reported that Urgil's ship had arrived in port, so he knew his brother was in the city. He scanned each face as the crowds moved down the street. There were multiple ways they could go, and three gates to get out of the city, so it was entirely possible that they would not come down the east road—carriages were also in position near the North and West Gates.

Then his breath caught when he saw a face he recognized. Missus Browning. Kaylan's Uncle Jorgan walked alongside her. Another woman he didn't recognize kept pace with Jorgan. Behind them, Yolken and Kaylan walked hand in hand. He shied back into the carriage, hiding himself from view. His body shook from a mixture of nervousness and anger.

I can't believe they're married. He knew how I felt about her.

An eternity passed after they walked by, giving Javen ample time to reconsider what he was about to take part in. Sudden doubt came over him, along with the desire to abort the plan. But he knew it was too late. There was no way he could undo what was already in motion.

The carriage shifted as the driver climbed down from his seat. The door opened and a horse came to a stop beside the carriage. Javen peered out and saw the driver take hold of a flailing woman handed down to him by the man on the horse. The driver forcefully shoved the woman into the carriage, then slammed the door shut. He climbed back up to his seat and the carriage lurched into motion.

Javen sat transfixed, staring into Kaylan's frightened eyes.

* * *

Running through the square, Yolken was forced to slow as he maneuvered through the crowd of wagons and people who hadn't made it through the gate before it closed. Fear overwhelmed him as the rider who had abducted Kaylan disappeared around a building situated at the corner where the east road met the square.

Yolken pushed and shoved people out of his way as he progressed through the crowd. Just as he stepped onto the east road, a bearded man with a ragged cloak stepped in front of him. He stepped to the side to go around the man, but the man grabbed him tightly by the arm. He tried to yank his arm free, but the man held his grip.

"Let go!" Yolken shouted.

"You must flee," the man said.

Yolken stared the man in the eyes, jolted by familiarity, but yanked his arm free of the man's grip.

He ran down the street looking for the man on horseback. Despair filled him as he realized he'd lost them.

He continued to run down the street, trying not to bump into anyone in the failing light. An explosion behind him caused him to stumble. He turned around and saw the light of fire beyond the wall silhouetting the towers. Hoping the others were okay, he turned and resumed his search for Kaylan. As he ran down the road, he slowed at each crossroad to see if perhaps the rider had turned down one of them. However, he came up empty at each street he passed.

Yolken ran until he entered the roundabout in front of the palace, then he slowed to a walk and stopped. The despair he had felt when he lost sight of the rider turned to fear as he realized he was the only one standing in the roundabout—there were no wagons, carriages, or pedestrians in sight. However, men wearing gray armor lined the roads leading south and west. He turned to look behind him; soldiers had moved into place blocking the east road as well. He turned to his left and looked at the palace. At least a dozen men wearing blue armor, and a few women wearing violet, stood on the steps. One of them stepped away from the group and descended toward him.

* * *

Kaylan looked at the man sitting across from her in the carriage in disbelief.

"Javen?"

"H-hi," Javen said hesitantly.

"We've been trying to—"

"Kaylan, listen to me very carefully," Javen interrupted.

"Javen, what's going on? Yolken and I, and Mammy and Jax, have been going all over trying to get help rescuing you from—"

"Kaylan," Javen said tersely. "Listen. My brother is in danger—"

"What do you mean he's in danger? What's going on? Where are we going?"

"There's something I need to tell you about your mother and

uncle. They aren't the people you think they are."

"What do you mean?"

Javen hesitated then said, "They're mixed up with rebels. You were in great danger with them, so I got you away from them."

"I was *not* in danger. At least I wasn't until that man yanked me up onto his horse."

"Kaylan, I had that planned so—"

"That was because of you?" Kaylan exclaimed.

"Kaylan!" Javen shouted. "Your mother and uncle are members of the Order! And they got my brother mixed up with it as well. Devin is currently in the process of trying to separate him from—"

"Devin?"

"Yes. He's trying to get Yolken away from your mother and uncle."

"Why?" Kaylan said, exasperated.

"Because they're rebels!"

"Javen," Kaylan said, "I'm so excited to see you, but Mammy and Jax—um, Jorgan—are *not* dangerous. I think you have it all wrong. It's the Regency that's dangerous!"

"No!" Javen shouted. "They have *tricked* you into believing that!"

Javen reached out and gently placed his hand on Kaylan's knee and she shied away from him.

"Javen," she said softly, "we have been trying to find you since the day Yolken healed Issa. In fact, we just got back from Kvorga—"

"What were you doing on Kvorga?" Javen said.

"You'll never believe who we found there."

"Who?" Javen said hesitantly.

"Deanna… I mean… Anivera."

"Anivera?"

"You remember, from the stories my uncle used to tell us as

kids."

"What did you want with her?"

"Help finding you!" Kaylan exclaimed. "We have so much to talk about, Javen. But first, let's go find Yolken and the others."

"Yes, we have a lot to talk about," Javen agreed. "But that's not possible."

"What do you mean? Why not?"

"I told you; they're rebels. And because your mother and uncle are probably…"

"Probably what?"

Javen hesitated.

"Probably what?" Kaylan repeated, her voice shaky.

"They're probably already dead," Javen said.

Kaylan stared blankly at Javen.

The door opened and an armored guard took Kaylan roughly by the arm and dragged her out of the carriage.

* * *

Jax watched in shock as Yolken ran toward the closing gate at an unnatural speed. He held Yolken's rolled-up cloak in one hand and clenched the other into a fist. He hesitated, knowing he should run after him, but at the same time knowing what they were running into.

Finally, he made up his mind and reached into the end of the rolled-up cloak. First, he pulled out the Aliza sword and handed it to Deanna. Then he pulled out the Harachin sword, dropped the pack, and began to walk purposefully toward the closing gate. Deanna walked beside him.

Following close behind them, Deborah said, "Jax, hand me your dagger."

Jax reached into his coat and pulled the dagger from his belt. Without slowing or turning, he held the dagger behind him. Deborah snatched it from his hand. He judged the closure rate of the gates and started to jog. The throng of people still trying to cross the bridge edged over to give the jogging trio room, but he quickly determined that they were not going to make it, even if they'd had Yolken's speed. He stopped when the gates slammed closed.

Deanna stopped on his right side, Deborah on his left.

"They let him pass," Deborah said.

"Because it's a trap," Jax said. He surveyed the lines of armored men standing on the balconies and tops of the towers. In the fading light, he couldn't make out the color of their armor, but he knew there would be blue and violet mixed in the bunch. "Somehow they knew we were here," he thought aloud.

"Could they have seen me when we passed the palace?" Deanna said.

"Even if they did," Jax said, "that wouldn't have given them time to plan this. No, they expected us. They were ready for us."

"What about when we came through the first time?" Deborah said.

Jax thought back over their first trip through Onta, then shook his head. "Unless someone who knew us saw us, I don't see how."

"Urgil?" Deborah said.

Again, Jax thought about their first voyage on his ship. "How could he have known who we were?"

"The gold we paid for passage?"

"Sailors are greedy."

"But you had already paid him. He could have talked to someone."

"He wasn't paid in full. And, if he at all believed I could place him as the captain of the *Vineyard,* he wouldn't have betrayed us until *after* he had command of the ship."

"It doesn't matter," Deanna said. "What matters is what we're going to do."

"I hadn't planned on assaulting the city," Jax said. He flexed his hand on the hilt of the Harachin sword. Energy beckoned to him.

"We have to go after them," Deborah said.

"I know," Jax said, thinking about his promise to Orwyn. At this moment he didn't give a dragon's scale about his duty to the Order—only the thought of his oath to Orwyn drove him. "I know."

He assessed the closed iron gates. He looked around for something that might be of use to force them open, but standing on a bridge made of a solitary piece of rock did not present many options. He considered the line of merchant wagons passing on their left, but they were all made of wood and would simply crumble against the metal doors.

"The moment we Synthesize," Deborah said, "they'll hit us with everything they have."

"Which means we have to act quickly," Jax said.

"I have an idea," Deanna said. She turned to the right and climbed up onto the sidewall of the bridge. She looked over the side of the bridge, then looked down at Jax and Deborah. "Protect the people."

Jax waited, tensed. Before he saw any outward sign that Deanna was Synthesizing, balls of fire began raining down from the towers. He reacted quickly, gathering air from the sides and making it flow up and away. The flames hit the flowing air and followed the channels of air down to the river. The fire hissed as it hit the water.

Next to him, Deborah yelled with an amplified voice, "Run!"

Mayhem ensued as travelers looked up and saw the fire falling toward them. Those on foot pushed each other as they frantically tried to flee, and merchants attempted to urge the horses pulling their wagons into a gallop.

People were going to get hurt, Jax knew.

Deborah shouted again, "Run! Get off the bridge!"

A boulder lifted from the river's edge and floated toward them. As it drew near, it began to glow red. Deanna's free hand, the hand not gripping the Aliza sword, moved as if she were guiding the boulder. She flung her hand forward and the boulder hurled toward the gate. It crashed into the iron barrier and exploded.

The concussion reverberated in the night.

The people on the bridge screamed.

Jax saw the damage Deanna had caused and smiled. She appeared to reach out for another boulder, and soon held a second one above her head. It was glowing red, infused with Draego's Fire. However, another boulder rose from the base of the wall and hovered over the left tower. Instead of throwing her boulder, Deanna held onto it.

Jax's current mode of defense would be useless if the second boulder was hurled in their direction. As he feared, the boulder over the tower began to glow. When it flew toward them, Deanna hurled her glowing boulder at it. The two boulders exploded when they collided, sending burning pieces of rock flying in all directions.

Jax, Deborah, and Deanna held their ground as red-hot pieces of rock fell around them. Wagons to their left erupted in flames and people screamed as rocks fell among them.

Jax felt helpless. It was taking all his effort to stop the continuous river of fire from reaching the bridge. "Deborah!" he yelled.

Deborah moved to the edge of the bridge. Moments later a stream of water arced over the side and began raining down on the burning wagons.

Bodies lay scattered about on the surface of the bridge, the clothes of many of them burning.

"We can't continue this!" Deborah shouted.

Jax looked down at the bodies. Deanna did as well.

"Deanna!" Jax shouted when he saw another boulder rise from the river's edge.

The boulder began jerking back and forth. If he had Glasses, he'd be able to see that Deanna was trying to wrest the boulder from whomever was controlling it with Synthesis. It eventually jerked sharply then glided slowly toward them.

"I've got it," Deanna said.

But another boulder replaced it.

"We need to go!" Deborah shouted.

"I won't leave Yolken!" Jax shouted back.

"We have to!" Deanna shouted.

While Jax struggled with the idea of abandoning Yolken, the boulder Deanna held began to glow. The enemy let the second boulder fly and Deanna hurled her boulder toward it. They exploded together, closer to the wall this time. Less debris fell around them. Still, two wagons caught fire and horses collapsed when flaming rock smashed into them.

"We *must* go!" Deanna shouted.

Jax looked from the burning wagons to Deanna. "Draego's Fire!" he screamed.

For the first time since the death of his friend, Jax was powerless to keep the promise he had made.

* * *

Yolken stood in the fading light as an armored man descended the steps. He looked back at the road leading to the East Gate and thought about fleeing.

"If you run," the armored man said, "you will die."

Yolken returned his attention to the approaching man. He held up his hand and shouted, "Stop!"

The man stopped. "Permit me to introduce myself," he said. "My name is Devin, and I am the—"

"I know who you are," Yolken said.

Devin frowned. "Then you know better than to interrupt me." He took a few steps toward Yolken. "As I was saying, I am Devin, the Regent of Onta, and I just want to talk with you."

Another explosion sounded in the distance. Yolken looked warily around him. Two soldiers approached from the right. As they drew near, he began to back away from them.

"They are just going to search you for dragon bones. After that, they will return to their places."

Yolken stopped and let them approach. He didn't have any reason to resist because he had dropped his pack. Had he still had it, things might have been different—he didn't want his father's sword to fall into the Regency's hands again. The soldiers searched him and, finding no dragon bones, returned to their positions.

Several large flames flashed into existence, illuminating the roundabout and the steps leading up to the palace. Eerily lit by the flickering light, the spire rose ominously behind the regents standing on the steps. The light of the fires caused the buildings behind them to disappear into shadows.

"Where's Kaylan?" Yolken said.

"Safe," Devin said. "And will remain so as long as you do as I say."

"Which is what?"

"Join the Regency, as your brother has done."

"Javen would never—"

"But he has. And soon, we will go to Kyinth where he intends to bow before the emperor and pledge his allegiance," Devin said. "In fact, he's here, in Onta, right now."

"Javen's here?" Yolken said. He shifted uneasily. Since the day he'd fled from Lonely Oak he'd had but one goal—to rescue Javen. Had he finally found him? "Where?"

Devin pointed past Yolken, so he turned. A carriage pulled into the roundabout, circled past Yolken, and came to a stop behind Devin. The door opened and Javen stepped out.

"Javen!" Yolken said. He fought back tears.

Javen wasn't wearing armor like Devin and the rest of the regents on the steps of the palace. He wanted to run and hug his brother, but he didn't dare move. He didn't want to get any closer to Devin. He was beginning to think that Jax was right;

this whole thing was a trap.

"Yolken," Javen said. "I'm so glad it worked."

"What worked?"

"Kaylan—"

"Where is she, Javen?"

"She's safe. I *knew* it was you."

"What do you mean?" Yolken said.

"Those beggars. When I saw that they'd been healed, I knew it had to have been you."

"Why?"

"Because of Issa."

"It was you," Yolken said, starting to realize what had happened. "You decided to trap me, Javen? By using Kaylan?"

"I had to get you away from them."

"Who?"

"They're the enemy, Yolken."

A blast reverberated in the distance, making Yolken look off toward his right.

"It sounds as though your friends have decided to resist," Devin said.

Yolken looked back at his brother. "Javen," he said sternly. "Kaylan's *mother* is out there."

"She's a rebel," Javen said.

"And we kill rebels," Devin said.

Yolken stared at his brother, dumbfounded. "Javen... what have they done to you?"

"They haven't *done* anything to me. They've told me the truth."

"What truth?"

"The truth about Auntie... about our parents. Our whole lives have been a lie."

"No, Javen. You're wrong. The Regency is the lie," Yolken said. He saw a flicker of agitation flash across Devin's face. "Everything we were taught about the Regency and about

Drakonias' war was a lie."

"No!" Javen shouted. "This time you're the one who's wrong. Our whole lives it's always been about you. I was always the one who was wrong or who got blamed."

"Javen…"

"But not this time. Not when it *actually* matters."

"Can we just go? We can talk about it together."

"You're not going anywhere," Devin said.

"Javen…" Yolken said. He couldn't believe what was happening. "Ever since that night, all I've done is try to rescue you."

"Who said I needed rescuing?" Javen said.

"Javen—"

"You need to do what Devin says, Yolken."

"Yes, listen to your brother," Devin said.

Javen wasn't going to leave with him, Yolken realized. He looked from Javen to Devin and then past him at the regents on the steps. Every single one of them was armed with dragon bones, he knew. Every road from the roundabout was blocked with armored guards. He shifted his stance, doubting his own ability to escape.

"Your situation is quite precarious," Devin said.

"I don't want to fight," Yolken said. "I just want to leave with Kaylan and my brother."

"That's not going to happen," Devin said.

"I'm not leaving," Javen added.

"If you don't want to die like your friends presently are, come with me. We'll go inside and have a quiet discussion over fine wine."

Yolken took a step back and said, "I'm not so sure they're the ones dying."

Devin snorted. "Do you honestly think they can outmatch the Regent of Hantlo?"

"Maybe not alone," Yolken said. "But they fight with

Deanna on their side."

Devin's eyes widened.

"That's right. Deanna Aliza Drake fights outside those walls! If you want to stay, Javen, fine. But I'm leaving. Where's Kaylan?" When Devin didn't move, he shouted, "Give her to me!"

"Fool boy," Devin said. He held both his arms straight out to his sides and swept them in. The soldiers that surrounded the roundabout began to march inward, toward Yolken, drawing their blades. "This is your last chance to surrender."

Yolken's eyes darted from Javen to Devin to the soldiers approaching in his peripheral vision. "Javen," he said when he saw Javen take a few steps back. "Please."

"You're out of time," Devin said.

Yolken had to do something. He was not going to let himself become a prisoner to the Regency like Javen had become. Regardless of what Javen might be thinking right now, Yolken knew the truth: Javen was a prisoner. His time for convincing Javen to come with him was up. Not that it mattered. Devin wasn't going to let either of them leave. He closed his eyes and took a deep breath. At this point he could only hope that what he was about to do didn't hurt Javen.

Yolken opened his eyes. The soldiers were only half a dozen paces away. He stretched his arms straight up and reached out with vast amounts of Energy. He pulled down a huge column of air and compressed it around himself. The great increase in pressure that fell upon him forced him to a knee. He smiled as Devin's eyes went wide. The soldiers continued to close the gap separating them from him.

Just before they reached him, he pushed out with all the compressed air with such force that he sent the soldiers flying backward away from him. Javen and Devin flew backward as well, sliding to a stop at the base of the stairs.

Yolken stood back up and began to walk toward the palace.

Balls of fire erupted from the hands of every regent standing on the stairs and flew in his direction. Javen scrambled to his feet, turned his back on Yolken, and ran up the palace steps.

Yolken drew more air down from above and created a whirlwind around himself, just as Jax taught him to do. As the fire hit the whirlwind, it whirled around him, encasing him in a swirling inferno. Through the flames, he saw Devin push himself to his feet and add his strength to the stream of fire. The heat inside the inferno increased, so Yolken drew more air and increased the diameter of the whirlwind.

In his periphery, he saw the flames grow immensely brighter to his left. He looked and saw that the inferno swirled over the statue of Drakonias. The bronze statue began to melt. Yolken looked back at his attackers with a smile, but it quickly disappeared as he realized his supply of Energy would not last.

His whirlwind demanded huge amounts of Energy. He needed to do something quick, but he had no additional strength left to mount a counterassault. He considered his options: Should he wait to see who ran out of Energy first, or should he flee? As much as he hated the idea, he decided the prudent thing would be to get out of the city and regroup with the others.

He turned to his right, toward the now-open east road, but before he took two steps, a building on the south side of the road came crashing down and blocked the road. He turned around just as the same thing happened over at the west and south roads. Panic filled him as he realized he was trapped. The only way he could quickly clear the rubble was if he abandoned the whirlwind and used Energy to jump. However, the moment he let the whirlwind die, the raging inferno would consume him.

An explosion erupted halfway up the spire. Debris fell on the regents standing at the top of the stairs, and their fireballs faltered as they shifted to protect themselves. Yolken stared in amazement, wondering what had caused the explosion. His hesitation cost him the small window of opportunity he had to escape. The regents quickly regrouped, and the assault continued.

Yolken slowly backed away. Debris from the fallen building blocking the eastern road began flying toward the regents on the marble stairs. *Someone's helping me*, he thought. But it wasn't enough. His Energy supply was nearly depleted.

Yolken realized the foolishness of his actions; he knew he should have stopped when Jax grabbed his pack. He looked over at the flying debris, but saw Devin moving toward him. Panic took hold of him and the fringes of his vision began to go black. He took another step back and stumbled on a piece of marble. He fell onto his back, barely maintaining control of the streams of Energy controlling the whirlwind.

He scrambled backward frantically, then stopped when a deep and booming roar pierced the night. The advancing regent stopped. The fiery assault faltered as Devin and the other regents looked up at the sky. Yolken cut off his whirlwind, saving the last vestiges of Energy remaining within his bones, and followed Devin's gaze upward. An enormous beast circled overhead.

The dragon tucked its wings and dove toward the roundabout, sending Devin scrambling back toward the palace. Its wings opened again and beat vigorously, slowing its descent. Its right foot crashed into the ground a few paces away from Yolken, its thick leg muscles flexing. The claws of its left foot wrapped around Yolken and then, with its right leg, it launched itself back into the air.

The dragon beat its wings and climbed higher into the sky. It turned toward the East Gate, where fire still streamed down from the towers. The dragon roared again and dove toward the structures. It showered the tops of the towers in fire as it flew over them, melting the exposed flesh of the armored men standing atop them.

After gliding past the towers, the dragon beat its wings again and carried Yolken into the night.

INTERIM

Reago's hands rested on the cool marble of the balcony wall as he stared down at the melted statue in the center of the roundabout, and he puffed on his pipe. Soldiers were busy clearing the rubble from the destroyed buildings. He shook his head and stepped away, walking over to the western end of the balcony. He looked up at the thin line of light still visible on the horizon.

Footsteps approached from his right, but he didn't turn to look at the man who approached—he already knew who it was. The man stopped a few feet away and, out of the corner of his eye, Reago saw him place his hands on the wall.

"You did well," Reago said. "The boy survived."

"What you do is treasonous, you know," the man said.

"I know."

"I'm thankful," the man said. "But I still don't understand why you're willing to betray Drakonias."

Reago turned and looked up at the Great Dragon constellation, which was slowly climbing into the sky. "Tomorrow we will be taking a Train to Kyinth," he said. "If you're in the servants' quarters an hour after the rising of the sun, you will be selected to serve on the journey."

"Why are you going to Kyinth?"

"To do what needs to be done."

"Will Javen be on board?"

"Yes."

After a moment of silence, the man said, "Why do you help me?"

Reago stared at the Great Dragon. "The war was a mistake. My brother refuses to confront the evil that we have wrought upon Dradonia. In light of what happened tonight, I fear things will soon spiral out of his control. I'm going to meet with him, but I fear he will continue to concern himself with the rebels and ignore the greater ill."

"I hope you're not starting to think you somehow control me," the man said.

"I don't," Reago said. "I am only sharing information that I know is of value to you and your cause."

"I have no cause," the man said. "And should I choose to accept this offer of yours, what would you have me do once we arrive in Kyinth?"

"I have watched you for a long time. I will do what I deem appropriate, and trust that you will do the same."

The man stood by Reago in silence. Then, he turned and walked back the way he had come, leaving Reago alone.

Reago turned back to the horizon. The light was now gone; darkness once again ruled. He turned his back on the horizon and walked into his quarters. Passing straight through his bedroom and sitting room, he walked to the front door, which his servant hastily opened, and through it. When he approached the first door on the right, the men standing guard saluted him.

Ignoring them, he reached into his pocket and pulled out a small black key. He inserted the key into the door and turned it to the right. When he felt it click into place, he reached into another pocket with his other hand and grasped a small bone figurine made in his likeness. Pulling Energy from the bone, he transferred it into the key. Mechanisms inside the door came to life and the door unlocked.

Reago pushed the door open with no regard to the guards—they wouldn't move from their posts and wouldn't dare to look inside the room. At this point, even if they did, he no longer cared. He reached out with tendrils of Energy and lit the sconces around the dark room.

As light enveloped the room, Reago stared into the hollow eyes of an enormous bone skull for the first time in a century. Its sharp teeth shimmered.

THE END
of Book Two of
THE BLESSED OF THE DRAGON

DRAKE FAMILY TREE

Previous Era (PE): the era prior to the establishment of the Dragon Throne became known as the Previous Era

Dragon King Era (DKE): the Dragon King Era commenced when Draeko established the Dragon Throne.

United Era (UE): the United Era commenced when Drakonias sat upon the Dragon Throne and proclaimed himself emperor of Dradonia.

Note: Provided below is the first and second generations of the Blessed of the Dragon. A complete genealogy of those loyal to the emperor is maintained at the palace in Kyinth.

(L) indicates those that pledged their loyalty to Drakonias during Drakonias' war.

GENERATION 1

Draeko Dairion Drake (m) (b. unknown d. 1150 DKE)
   Married to:
      Aliza Varias (f) (b 61 PE d. 1148 DKE)
   Children:
      Drakonias Draeko Arvarin Drake (m) (b. 42 PE d.)
      Deanna Aliza Drake (f) (b. 41 PE d. 1150 DKE)
      Eagan Draeko Calavin Drake (m) (b. 39 PE d. 1150 DKE)
      Reago Draeko Yarin Drake (m) (b. 37 PE d.) (L)
      Anshar Draeko Olivar Drake (m) (b. 35 PE d. 1150 DKE)
      Drae Draeko Harachin Drake (m) (b. 34 PE d. 44 UE)
      Reega Aliza Drake (f) (b. 31 PE d. 1150 DKE)
      Orlan Draeko Dairion Drake (m) (b. 29 PE d. 289 UE) (L)
      Thena Aliza Drake (f) (b. 835 DKE d.) (L)
      Nera Aliza Drake (f) (b. 837 DKE d.) (L)
      Lio Draeko Mattath Drake (m) (b. 980 DKE d. 30 UE)
      Atter Draeko Eber Drake (m) (b. 983 DKE d. 1138 DKE) (L)
      Mattha Aliza Drake (f) (b. 984 DKE d. 1150 DKE)
      Sheal Draeko Kena Drake (m) (b. 986 DKE d.) (L)
      Akim Draeko Nash Drake (m) (b. 992 DKE d. 33 UE) (L)
      Bathsheth Aliza Drake (f) (b. 995 DKE d. 80 UE)
      Esli Draeko Elish Drake (m) (b. 1001 DKE d. 19 UE)

GENERATION 2

Drakonias Draeko Arvarin Drake (m) (b. 42 PE d.)
  Married to:
      Mariana Hargen (b. 20 PE d. 1120 DKE)
  Children:
      Drashon Drakonias Irigwin Drake (m) (b 14 DKE d. 295 UE)
      Dorlan Drakonias Irigwin Drake (m) (b 150 DKE d.)
      Devin Drakonias Metra Drake (m) (b. 820 DKE d.)
      Drenan Drakonias Loid Drake (m) (b. 954 DKE d.)
      Darsi Mariana Drake (f) (b. 960 DKE d. 1142 DKE)
      Donlin Drakonias Ronn Drake (m) (b. 980 DKE d. 1128 DKE)
      Dalia Mariana Drake (f) (b. 982 DKE d.)
  Married to:
      Ceena Realag (b. 1101 DKE d. 40 UE)
  Children:
      Darek Drakonias Proogan Drake (m)(b. 1 UE d.)
      Dreanna Ceena Drake (f)(b. 3 UE d.)
      Dunlor Drakonias Metra Drake (m) (b. 3 UE d.)

Please enjoy an excerpt from:
THE DRAGON KING
Book Three of
THE BLESSED OF THE DRAGON

BEFORE

389 United Era

Orwyn stood in the burning tavern, Harachin sword in hand. He anxiously watched the wall of flames inch closer. As he waited for Jax to return from the kitchen, he looked down at the two bodies clad in black leathers at his feet and considered his options. He couldn't check the exit in the kitchen himself, so he'd sent Jax. He needed to maintain mental acumen at this crucial moment, and he knew the sight of Elen would shatter his concentration.

I should have sent her away with the boys.

The moment the entire front wall of the tavern erupted in flames he knew they were in trouble. The true extent of their peril became apparent when the flames unnaturally began to creep across the floor.

Draego's Fire.

Jax returned from the kitchen gripping the tattered cuff of his cloak in his hand. "The door's jammed. A trap?"

Orwyn nodded. With one less option to consider, he watched the flames creep closer and made up his mind. "They have us boxed in."

"Then let's fight our way out!"

"Jax, you know as well as I that the Sodality is out there in force. And they do not underestimate those they're sent to eliminate. The moment we attempt to open that door…" Orwyn looked from the unnatural flames moving toward them to the kitchen door, "…they will attack us with everything they have. We wouldn't make it two steps out of this building, and you know it."

"What do you suggest, then? That we stay here and die?"

"Our only hope is that they don't know you're here as well."

"I'm not leaving you here, Orwyn."

"It's our only option, Jax. I'm getting you out of here."

"No!" Jax exclaimed.

"There's no other choice."

"We should've left when we had the chance."

"I know," Orwyn acknowledged. His decision cost him his wife. He didn't know if he could ever forgive himself. She didn't deserve this.

"Orwyn, no matter what, we're in this together. I'm not abandoning you here."

Orwyn forced himself to look away from the assassins. They'd killed his wife. He looked intently at his friend. "If you stay here, we're both dead. And I won't permit it."

"Then I'll stay," Jax said.

"No. You know they're here for me."

"Orwyn, if I would have brought you—"

"Jax!" Orwyn shouted. "This isn't about that! The Regency's wanted me dead since the war. Now… listen to me. *Please.* Go upstairs and position yourself by the window in my room. I'll create a distraction to draw them in. Wait until I strike. When you see them close in on the back door, flee out the window."

"Orwyn—"

"I'll catch up with you in the Mindons."

Jax hesitated. He stroked his beard and looked intently at Orwyn. Then, he put his hand on Orwyn's shoulder and squeezed it tightly. "See you in the Mindons."

Orwyn knew when he said it that it was a lie.

He walked calmly into the kitchen as Jax positioned himself upstairs. He looked down at his wife lying in a pool of blood. He knelt beside Elen and moved a strand of hair so he could see her face one last time. He tried to hold back the tears welling in his eyes but when he blinked, he set them free.

Orwyn took a deep, shuddering breath and stood. He drew deeply from the Harachin sword. With Synthesis, he forced the door open.

When the first black-clad soldier appeared through the opening, he acted.

The kitchen wall exploded and sent bodies flying.

ABOUT THE AUTHOR

Patrik grew up in the southwest and presently lives in Idaho. Earlier in life he almost exclusively read fantasy novels but has since broadened his horizon and enjoys many genres, both fiction and nonfiction. He has wanted to write a book for a long time but never really had any ideas. Then, one random day, when he least expected it, he had an inkling and started writing. In his spare time, he enjoys hanging out with his family and entertaining his exuberant dog Pearl (or the Black Pearl when she is naughty, and yes, she is black). He also enjoys a good beer. He occasionally brews it as well, but he's not nearly as good as Yolken.